New York Times bestselling [author ...]
over thirty novels published [...]
her seductive Dark Carpathi[...] ...ed numerous
honours throughout her career, including being a nominee for
the Romance Writers of America's RITA and receiving a Career
Achievement Award from *Romantic Times*, and has been
published in multiple languages and in many formats, including
audio book, ebook and large print.

Visit Christine Feehan online:

www.christinefeehan.com
www.facebook.com/christinefeehanauthor
https://twitter.com/AuthorCFeehan

Praise for Christine Feehan:

'After Bram Stoker, Anne Rice and Joss Whedon, Feehan is
the person most credited with popularizing the neck gripper'
Time magazine

'The queen of paranormal romance'
USA Today

'Feehan has a knack for bringing vampiric Carpathians to
vivid, virile life in her Dark Carpathian novels'
Publishers Weekly

'The amazingly prolific author's ability to create captivating
and adrenaline-raising worlds is unsurpassed'
Romantic Times

By Christine Feehan

CHRISTINE
FEEHAN
Fire Bound

piatkus

PIATKUS

First published in the US in 2016 by Jove,
An imprint of Penguin Random House LLC
First published in Great Britain in 2016 by Piatkus

1 3 5 7 9 10 8 6 4 2

A CIP catalogue record for this book
is available from the British Library.

ISBN 978-0-349-41032-6

Printed and bound in Great Britain by Clays Ltd, St Ives plc

Papers used by Piatkus are from well-managed forests
and other responsible sources.

MIX
Paper from
responsible sources
FSC® C104740

Piatkus
An imprint of
Little, Brown Book Group
Carmelite House
50 Victoria Embankment
London EC4Y 0DZ

An Hachette UK Company
www.hachette.co.uk

www.piatkus.co.uk

For Barbara King,
a woman I've always loved, admired and looked up to.
I can imagine you going from country to country
with assassination in mind!
We'd have a darn good time!

Be sure to go to christinefeehan.com/members/ to sign up for my PRIVATE book announcement list and download the FREE ebook of *Dark Desserts*. Join my community and get firsthand news, enter the book discussions, ask your questions and chat with me. Please feel free to email me at Christine@christinefeehan.com. I would love to hear from you.

ACKNOWLEDGMENTS

With any book there are many people to thank. In this case, the usual suspects: Domini, for her research and help; Christopher Walker, for researching and getting the information to me immediately; my power hour group, who always make certain I'm up at the crack of dawn working; and of course Brian Feehan, whom I can call anytime and brainstorm with so I don't lose a single hour. What other person would be willing to discuss assassinations endlessly and have a great time doing it?

1

THE sound of laughter echoed through the house. Women's voices rose and fell. Soft. Happy. Loving. Lissa Piner wandered over to the door, opened it and stood looking out into the darkness, carrying those sounds with her. She wanted everything about this evening to be imprinted on her brain for all time.

Her sisters of the heart, always in her heart. So cliché. So often used, but in this case, true. She couldn't love them any more if they'd been born of the same parents. She met them, of all places, in a therapy group for the survivors of family members violently murdered. They'd come together, six women, all lost, all broken, and discovered that together they were much stronger.

The wind tugged at her hair, and she turned her face up to the night sky, inhaling deeply. She loved storms. She loved the northern California coast where the six women had pooled their resources, bought a farm and, for the last five years, grown close and even prosperous together. Tonight though, the clouds roiled and churned, a dark ominous black, nearly blotting out the moon. Not enough that she couldn't see the bright red ring around the moon as it valiantly tried to shine behind the layer of clouds.

"A storm's coming," Blythe Daniels observed over her shoulder. She handed Lissa a cup of tea. She was tall and blond and towered over Lissa by quite a few inches. "Don't you love when the moon is full and has rings around it and the sky is so dark it almost looks purple?"

Lissa took a sip of her tea. There was something soothing about tea. She'd only just discovered the properties of tea when she'd come to live on the farm with the others. Tea seemed to be the go-to drink when things were difficult. "I do love purple in the clouds," she admitted, avoiding all discussion about the red rings and what they might mean. To her, they meant one thing—death. A violent death. Probably hers. She sighed softly and then forced a smile. She had to be so careful with these women. They all were very astute at reading one another.

"Come on, you two," Lexi called from across the room. She was the youngest sister, the one Lissa was the closest to and the most protective over.

Lexi had recently fallen in love, and Lissa still went from being grateful for the match to being a little worried. Gavriil Prakenskii was no ordinary man. He was rough, scarred, and very dangerous. He was also very protective of Lexi. That, Lissa really liked, especially now.

Blythe leaned in close to her. "Are you all right, Lissa? You're very quiet."

Lissa felt her stomach flutter. Her heart clenched, a curious and disturbing physical reaction to the certain knowledge that Blythe saw far more than anyone else. It had been Blythe's idea to band together and buy the farm. She'd been the driving force and she continued to be the one they all looked to.

"I'm always quiet," Lissa pointed out, with another small smile. One, she knew, that didn't reach her eyes. "Especially before a trip. This is a big one. I've got three hotels interested in my work. If I can get contracts with even one of them, let alone all three, we'll be sitting pretty for a long time." She turned away from the storm. Away from the night sky and the moon with its red rings that signaled danger and violence. "Who knew my chandeliers would take off across the world and I'd become famous for my art?"

She'd deliberately courted the European market. Still, she hadn't expected, in five years, to be so successful.

"You know, with the men adding money to the farm, we're not teetering every month on the brink of disaster. You don't have to work so hard, Lissa," Blythe said softly. "We all love you for it, but we're good now. We can all take a breath. Thanks to Lexi, the farm is doing better than ever. Rikki, Judith and Airiana make certain whatever the weather, our crops aren't adversely affected."

"Exactly," Lissa said, closing the door against the rising wind. "Rikki, Judith and Airiana ensure Lexi's crops thrive. You boost their power. That's the five of you working together to make the farm a success. What do I contribute? When I first started my business, you all helped me. You believed in me. This is my chance to give something back to the farm."

Blythe opened her mouth to protest, took one look at her face and closed it again. "We're all proud of you. The fact that three hotels are all vying for your chandeliers says you've made it."

"I haven't gotten the contracts yet," Lissa said, pouring enthusiasm into her voice. "I had to delay the trip by a couple of weeks and reschedule because two of the managers couldn't meet with me in the time I'd allotted for traveling. As it is, it will be tight."

"Still"—Blythe led the way back into the center of the living room—"it's exciting that you can visit so many countries in one trip and write it off legitimately."

"That's the best part," Airiana Prakenskii said. She had recently married Maxim Prakenskii and was in the process of adopting four children, siblings she and her husband had

rescued from a human trafficking ring. "Writing your trip off
on your taxes." She looked like a beautiful pixie with her
natural platinum hair, large eyes and fragile appearance. She
was anything but fragile. She was bound to air and worked
for the defense department.

"I *despise* doing taxes," Rikki Prakenskii admitted. "I
love to dive, and it's great getting paid for what I love doing,
but then filing taxes makes it all a nightmare. Thank heavens
for Lev. He totally understands all that."

Lissa smiled at Rikki as she sank into the chair opposite
her. "I love that you call him Lev now and that all of you
have agreed to take the last name Prakenskii."

Lexi shrugged. "Since Gavriil is living here and both he
and Ilya use the name, why shouldn't all of them?"

"Don't you think it's a little crazy that all of you married
Prakenskiis?" Lissa asked. She set her teacup carefully on
the end table and folded her hands together, threading her
fingers rather tightly.

"Absolutely crazy," Lexi agreed, "although, I'm not married."

"It's a matter of time," Lissa said. "Gavriil will put his ring
on your finger, just the way he put his mark on your palm.
Don't deny it. I've seen you rubbing your palm on your jeans.
All of you do that."

"Sometimes it itches," Lexi said before she thought to
deny it.

There was more laughter. Lissa loved the sound of her sisters laughing. There was genuine joy in them. They'd all
started out so lost, so broken, especially Lexi. Intellectually,
Lissa knew it was a combination of things that had changed
for everyone. The way they united as a family, their farm and
then the coming, one by one, of the Prakenskii brothers. "Why
do you suppose all of you have settled down and fallen madly
in love with Prakenskiis?" she asked.

"Hello," Judith emphasized. "Are you blind? They're just
plain yummy." Judith was married to Stefan Prakenskii. Ju-

dith was nearly as tall as Blythe, with long flowing black hair, a legacy from her Japanese mother. She was an artist and did restoration of paintings as well as creating unique and beautiful kaleidoscopes.

"They are that," Lissa admitted, "but they're also overprotective, dominant and arrogant as well as pains in the butt."

All the women nodded in complete agreement. "They are *so* all of those things," Airiana said. "We can't even argue who is the absolute worst . . ."

"Gavriil," a chorus of voices said all at the same time.

Lexi looked shocked. "He is not. He's so sweet. How can you think that?"

Laughter rose and this time Lissa joined in, a true, genuine laugh. Of course Lexi would never see the dangerous side of Gavriil. He loved her. She was not just the center of his world, she *was* his world.

"That's why all of us are going to have Black Russian Terriers to protect every household," she teased.

Lexi flashed her a grin and then immediately disagreed again. "It's Lev."

"I push Lev into the ocean as often as possible," Rikki said with a little sniff. "It cools him off when he gets out of hand. No way is it my man."

Blythe held up her hand. "I have to say, all of your men are the absolute worst. Only Lissa and I have any sense left."

Lissa took a deep breath before nodding. "Which is why I am very glad I'm heading off to Europe and leaving you, Blythe, to the tender mercies of whichever Prakenskii brother shows up next, because I'm fairly certain it will happen. Sea Haven seems to call to those of us who are elements or, like the Drake sisters, have psychic gifts. As all the Prakenskiis seem to be or have both, I'm putting my running shoes on."

At least she wasn't lying about that. Practically everything about her was a lie, when she'd been so determined to give her sisters the real person. She gave them what she could of herself, but there would be no acceptance if they knew the truth about her. Sometimes, she could barely look at herself in the mirror.

"What would be so wrong with finding a man?" Lexi asked. "I was certain I never would have that kind of . . . intimacy . . . with a man, not after everything that happened to me, but Gavriil came along, and I can't imagine my life without him. Don't you want to have a relationship, Lissa?"

Lissa wanted to hug Lexi to her. Sweet, wonderful Lexi. She was so accepting. Kidnapped, forced into a sham of a marriage with a pedophile, forced into child labor, her family murdered by the vicious cult that took her, she still had the sweet nature no one could ever take from her. Lissa felt very protective of her and loved her like the sister she never had. She would do anything to keep Lexi safe and happy. She had vowed she would make certain no one took that feeling of safety away again.

"What is it?" Lexi asked, suddenly moving right into her, perching on the arm of Lissa's chair. Close. Her eyes moving over Lissa, seeing too much. "You look sad. As if you're saying good-bye to us." There was trepidation in her voice. Fear on her face. Yet she kept her voice low, instinctively protecting Lissa from the others.

Lissa was grateful. All of her sisters could read one another easily now. Lissa had lived a lie with them for so long she felt guilty and ashamed. They showed her who they were, yet she had to hide who she really was. *What* she really was. She tried a smile. "Baby, you know I'm heading off for Europe any minute, right? I have to catch a plane. Isn't that what this gathering is about?" She tried to inject a teasing note into her voice, but in truth, she didn't believe she would be coming home.

Lexi shook her head. "You know what I mean. This is your home. Are you happy here?"

"I've been happier here than I've been since I was a very small child. This is home," Lissa said firmly, grateful she didn't have to lie. That was strictly the truth, and Lexi would hear it in her voice.

"Are you coming back?" Lexi persisted, her eyes showing anxiety.

"This is home," Lissa said. "It will always be home. I'll always come back." *If I can.* She would. She would never ever leave Sea Haven and the beauty and peace of the farm if she had a choice. She raised her voice a little so the others could hear. "If I get the contracts for the chandeliers throughout these hotels, all three of them, then we'll be sitting pretty for the next few years. It will give the farm a real chance to thrive."

"It's already thriving, Lissa," Lexi said. "You don't have to overwork anymore. I have Gavriil to help me now, and during harvest all of you help. With him around, I won't mind if we hire extra help when we need it. Before, I was always uncomfortable with strangers, but Gavriil makes me feel safe. Well, all the boys do."

Lissa burst out laughing. "Only you would refer to the Prakenskii brothers as boys. I love you, Lexi. *So* much. You taught me a great deal about letting go of anger. It's still there, but I'm working through it." She would never—ever— say how to her baby sister.

"I love you too, but seriously, Lissa, don't take on more work than you can comfortably do."

Lissa nodded. "One hotel in Italy, a castle in Germany that's been renovated into a luxury hotel and the last in Russia. I really get to travel, and for free. It's a tough life, but someone has to do it."

Airiana sighed and leaned back, sipping at her tea. "I thought I would never want to travel again after all my adventures on the yacht and then the cruise ship, but the children are wearing me out. Benito is a crazy boy. He's getting to be more like Max every day. I swear, without adoption, he's already a Prakenskii. I could use a vacation. The other night, when Max and I snuck off to the gazebo to have a little fun, we were going at it when all of a sudden, red lights began flashing all around us and an alarm went off. That horrid boy rigged our only safe place."

The women erupted into gales of laughter.

"Of course he did," Blythe said. "I was waiting for something like that. No way was he going to resist. I can just picture Benito and his sisters hanging out the window laughing their little heads off."

"Until Max caught up with them," Judith said, hardly able to get the words out around her laughter.

"He chased Benito all over the house. The girls and I couldn't help laughing hysterically," Airiana admitted. "I didn't tell Max, but I think Lucia may have been the mastermind behind the red lights. The little girls thought they came up with the idea of the sirens, and Benito graciously and in the face of Max's wrath allowed them to take credit for it. Clearly, all of them had discussed it and were just waiting for us to sneak out."

"Bet that didn't take long," Rikki said.

Another round of laughter erupted.

"We *have* to sneak out," Airiana defended. "Those little monsters sleep in our room. We're hoping when we get the puppy, they'll all take to sleeping in Lucia's room."

"Most likely the puppy will be sleeping in your room along with the children," Lissa said, keeping a straight face.

Airiana groaned and covered her eyes. "So true. Just remember that if any of you are thinking about having children. They are *exhausting*."

"Not me," Rikki said. "I'm going to be the favorite auntie."

"That's my job," Blythe objected. "I'll be the old spinster with five cats."

Judith snorted. "Like you have a chance of that happening." She paused. Took a breath. "I didn't think I'd want children, but Stefan is so wonderful and he's going to be one of those hands-on fathers that helps. I like having Benito hanging around the house doing art with me. Nicia and Siena are darling children. Even Lucia, although she rarely comes over, is sweet. Stefan and I decided to try."

There was a shocked silence.

"Really?" Blythe asked. "That's wonderful. I love the idea of children growing up happy here on the farm."

"That's a good thing," Judith said, "because Airiana is pregnant. I have no idea when she was going to confess, but I can clearly see that she is. Her aura gives her away."

Airiana looked shocked. "I am *not*." She sat up straight, put her teacup on the table and glared at Judith. "I have four children. That's plenty. I couldn't possibly have a baby, I'm too tired all time."

"That's why you're tired, silly," Judith pointed out. "Didn't you know? Really?"

Airiana scowled at her. "As long as I didn't take a test or say it out loud, I thought I could dodge the bullet. We weren't exactly careful in the beginning. And sometimes we aren't all that careful now."

"I wouldn't worry about it," Judith said. "The horse left the barn and there's no need to close the doors."

"That ship has sailed," Blythe said.

"I hate you all," Airiana said. "Stop laughing at me. Now, Gavriil has this puppy that I'll end up having to take care of right along with crazy Benito and the girls. I'm so not looking forward to the next few months. Puking and wishing I could sleep."

"Lucia will look after the puppy," Lexi said. "She's learning already to care for them and she's very good at it. She has a natural talent. I think it will be good for her, and you should tell her you're pregnant, she'll help you."

Airiana shook her head, sudden tears welling up. Instantly the laughter was gone from their circle.

Blythe reached out and took her hand. "What is it, honey? You're complaining, but you love the children, and you know Lucia needs the puppy. You don't object to that. Are you really ill?"

Airiana shook her head and then shrugged. "I have morning sickness, but it isn't bad. I just am careful what I eat in the morning. It's Lucia and the others. I want them to feel loved. To know they have a home. They've been through so much. Losing their parents in a car bombing. Their little sister murdered. That awful ship. The things that happened to them on it. They need to feel as if they have a secure home with Max. With me. That we're going to love them and be their parents."

"Of course they know that," Blythe assured gently. "There will be an adjustment, but they'll accept and want the baby too."

Airiana shook her head. "I don't want them to think for one moment that by having a baby, we'll push them aside. I want this baby. Max's child, but I love all four of those children as if they were mine. I know Lucia in particular has a difficult time. They need time. I haven't said anything because I think the longer they have with us without a new baby, the better it will be for them, but then I think if they get used to the idea, the better it will be that way." She threw her arms into the air. "I have no idea what to do."

"What does Max say?"

Airiana bit her lip.

Lissa gasped. "You didn't tell him? Are you *nuts*? Max will kill you for withholding that kind of information. What were you thinking?"

"That he'll get even more protective than he already is. He can make me crazy, Lissa. They all can make me crazy, and lately I haven't had the tolerance and the humor I need to deal with him turning into a macho protective nutcase. All I want to do is cry or throw things."

"Honey, you're pregnant," Blythe said. "That's to be expected."

"Your hormones are all over the place," Judith added gently. "Sweetheart, you need to tell him. You do. You can't keep something like this to yourself. Tell him and then talk over the best course of action to take with the children. You'll feel so much better."

Lissa nodded. "And then we need to put the whammy on Judith so she gets pregnant and the children can be best friends." She nudged Lexi. "What about you? Do you foresee that man of yours giving you a gaggle of children?"

Lexi laughed. "Not a gaggle exactly, but we've talked about it."

Lissa shook her head. "I'm so getting out of this madness. The next thing I know, I'll get pregnant by proxy." She stood up. "I'd better get on the road. It's four hours to the airport."

The women immediately stood and surrounded her. She could feel their warmth. Their love. She had to struggle not to cry. This was her family. She had come to love them more than she could ever have thought she would be able to. She had never shared who she was with them, nor had she introduced them to the one member of her family still alive, but they were her world. She didn't expect to come back to them, but she was going to ensure their safety because they were *everything* to her.

Each and every one of them had had their lives ripped apart by violence. They had lost the ability to ever live in the world without fear. A home was supposed to be a sanctuary, yet these women knew a home could be violated at any time. She hated that for them.

She would never have the chance to fall in love with a man, but that was her choice. She would never have children, but again, she was making that choice. She knew she was making that choice for these women, all so very precious to her. They held one another in their tight circle the way they did to show solidarity, sisterhood, to show strength and love. Lissa planned on carrying that feeling of love and support with her everywhere she went.

"We'll see you when you get back," Lexi said, breaking the circle to hold her close. She hugged Lissa hard. "I love you. I want you back."

"I love you too, little sister," Lissa replied, meaning it. Feeling it. Fighting emotion when she was usually so good at pushing it down. "Take care of one another. And listen to the Prakenskiis when it comes to your security. I mean it. I'll be upset with all of you if you don't."

She hugged each of them hard, turned and nearly ran from the room, out into the rising wind. The storm was closing in on Sea Haven, coming in off the ocean, and she felt that was an ominous portent of things to come in her future. Her bags were already in the car and she had to get on the road if she was going to catch her plane. She drove away from the farm, from her place of peace, and never once looked back. She didn't dare.

THE ocean raged, the relentless wind whipping the waves into a towering frenzy. Water swelled high, forming a series of walls, some a good thirty feet. The waves rushed toward shore, breaking in white foamy crests up high on the rocks and cliffs. The constant roar and boom added even more drama to the wild sprays as they shot into the sky, retreated and burst against the stacks again and again as if trying to destroy them.

"It's a good night for it," Lev Prakenskii informed his brothers with a quick grin as they trudged across the sand toward the relative shelter of a series of high boulders that looked as if they'd been flung onto the beach. The rocks looked out of place on the wide expanse of sand. "A perfect setting as well. Even if our women caught on, they wouldn't be able to overhear us."

Gavriil, the oldest brother present, nodded. "That would be why I made certain we didn't hold this meeting anywhere near the farm."

Overhead, clouds spun dark threads, churning and rolling continuously in rhythm with the crashing waves below. The wind shrieked and howled, tearing across the sand, flinging drops of salty water from the sea at them and kicking up the fine grains of sand to pepper the five men as they moved quickly toward the relative shelter of the boulders.

"Airiana was extremely suspicious," Maxim reported. "Lissa is leaving tonight, and apparently they've always gotten together before one of her trips. She brings in a tremendous amount of money with her glassblowing and welding business, and she's nabbed two major hotels and a castle being renovated into a hotel in Europe. The women do something to bring her better luck and safe travel. Airiana wanted me home tonight to watch the kids, but when I told her I had to go out, she moved the gathering to our house."

"You're in such trouble," Stefan pointed out with a smirk. "You get home tonight and she's going to grill you. Big-time. Airiana has a way of making you talk."

"And your woman doesn't?" Ilya, the youngest of the Prakenskii brothers, demanded. "If I remember right, Judith crooks her little finger and you run so fast you burn the soles of your shoes."

Laughter broke out at Stefan's expense, mostly because they knew it was true. Judith was his world, and he wasn't ashamed of admitting it. In any case, he knew each of his brothers had found the woman they were clearly devoted to. The one that had surprised him the most was Gavriil. His older brother had recently moved in with the youngest sister on the farm, Lexi, and was completely and utterly in love with her. Even to his brothers, Gavriil was a very scary man, yet around his fiancée he was gentle and even tender, two traits no one, not even his family, would ever have attributed to him.

The brothers continued toward the row of boulders. In the dark they were powerful, intimidating figures, walking across the sand with fluid grace. The wind howled around them, but they didn't break stride, moving like a pack of deadly predators. It was impossible not to notice the confidence. They were imposing men with wide shoulders and thick chests. Mostly it was easy to see they knew how to take care of themselves.

Across the sand, the flickering of a fire flung the wall of a jutting boulder into sharp relief. The red-orange glow illuminated the homeless man sitting comfortably, his back to the curve of the rock, one hand curled around a bottle, his coat tight around him and his scarf covering the lower half of his face. At least he looked warm with the flames of the fire dancing high. He'd chosen the center boulder for his camp, leaving a few boulders on either side of him for them to choose for their private gathering.

"Do you want to tell us why you called this meeting, Gavriil?" Lev asked, keeping to the shadows, staying a distance from the man and his fire. He kept an eye on the only other living soul out in the fury of the wind. He'd been at the farm the longest and his affection for all the women who resided there ran deep. He didn't like leaving them alone and unguarded, even for a few hours.

Lev looked out toward the crashing sea. He'd been caught in those dark waters once, the power of the waves rolling his helpless body, slamming him into a rock with such force, he'd had a concussion. Rikki Sitmore, an urchin diver and one of the amazing women residing on the farm, had saved his life. He'd fallen like a ton of bricks for her. He didn't like to be separated from her for any length of time, but he wasn't going to tell that to his brothers. He'd never hear the end of it, even if they were all just as bad.

Lev narrowed his gaze on the homeless man's fist, wrapped around a bottle of Scotch. "We should move our meeting," he suggested, his voice low. "We're not alone."

"You noticed the Scotch," Gavriil said.

Lev's eyebrow shot up. "How could I not? The man's drinking Glenmorangie eighteen-year-old extremely rare malt Scotch. That's not something a homeless man could afford."

Maxim nodded his agreement. "Everything else about

him fits, but that bottle has to cost at least a hundred dollars. No way can he afford that if he's homeless."

None of the Prakenskiis had turned their backs on the man. They were hunted. In Russia, they'd grown up in special schools, trained to be assets for their country, assassins sent to take down enemies of the state. Because they opposed his politics, their parents had been murdered by Kostya Sorbacov, a very powerful man who had been the power behind the presidency at the time.

The boys had been taken, separated and forced into the brutal training from the time they were very young. Now, years later, Sorbacov's son, Uri, had recently decided to vie for the presidency. He couldn't afford to have any scandal attached to his name, so all evidence of the extremely harsh atrocities associated with the schools had to be erased. That meant he was having those raised in the schools murdered. No matter that they had served their country faithfully, there was a hit out on all of them.

"Do you recognize him? Any of you?" Gavriil asked.

Stefan shook his head. "No, but he's one of us. He's good. Plays the part perfectly. Without the Glenmorangie, I would have bought his cover. I wouldn't have given him a chance at us, but I would have bought it."

"Look closer," Gavriil encouraged.

Lev glared at him. "You know him. You knew he was here."

Gavriil grinned. "I can't believe you don't recognize your own brother. I've invited Casimir here to have a little meeting with us, but he doesn't have much time. He has to catch a plane tonight."

The others looked from him to the man sitting in the sand, warming himself by the fire, taking a drink from the bottle.

"You asked him to look after Lissa," Stefan guessed. "I should have thought of that. I was worried about her running around Europe alone. If either of the Sorbacovs is paying attention, they'd already have the information that she's living on the farm here. They'd know she's family, and they might try to use her to get to us."

Gavriil nodded. "I don't want any of the women going anywhere without protection. We can't go, and Lissa would probably torch our homes if she knew we were sending someone to look after her, but this way, we'll have peace of mind and she can do her work safely. I contacted him as soon as I learned Lissa was going on her trip. Fortunately, she had to delay it by two weeks, thanks to the German castle, so that gave him a month to work on a cover in Europe."

Lev nodded his approval. "Good idea, Gavriil."

The brothers hurried quickly across the wide expanse of sand toward the fire. The "homeless" man rose, a smile on his face. He stepped around the burning logs so he could meet them out in the open. Gavriil pulled his brother close, thumped his back and then passed him around to each of them. They had to introduce themselves, as they hadn't seen Casimir since he was a child.

Once they settled around the fire and the bottle of Scotch had been passed around, Gavriil spoke. "I know you don't have much time and the rain is going to break soon, but since you were here in the States, I wanted to see you. I knew the others would as well."

Casimir nodded. "I felt the same way. It was a long way to come and not get the chance to see all of you together. I wish Viktor were here as well. Has anyone heard from him? I check the emergency drop all the time, but in the last five years, he's gone completely off the grid."

They all shook their heads.

"He's in deep cover," Gavriil said, infusing confidence in his voice. "We'd know if someone got to him. It would be such a victory, they'd crow about it."

"Viktor's hard to kill," Stefan agreed.

"I've heard rumors lately that several of the men who went to school with him have been off the grid as well," Maxim said.

"The toughest, the most feared, the legends of our schools, seem to have gone quiet."

"And that includes our esteemed brother," Ilya said.

They went silent, passed the bottle of Scotch around a second time, each saluting the red rings around the moon with it before they took a drink.

"Lissa is one of us, Casimir," Lev said, breaking the silence. "Important to our family. She's tough, and thinks she can take care of herself, but she has no idea what the Sorbacovs are capable of if they do, in fact, know she's considered family to us. Gavriil tells us you're willing to look after her."

"I said I would," Casimir agreed. He didn't sound like he'd enjoy the job.

"She's smart and definitely notices everything," Stefan pointed out. "You'll have to be careful if you don't want her to catch on." He looked around the circle at his brothers. "And we don't want her to catch on. She could make trouble for us. She'd get those women riled up, and we'd all be in trouble."

Casimir gave a derisive snort. "From just the little time I've had for observation, all of you are whipped." He kept the wistful note from his voice. He was going to do this one favor for his brothers—men he'd been separated from his entire life. Men he didn't know but felt extreme loyalty toward.

"I'm not going to lie to you," Maxim said. "My woman is my world. I think I speak for everyone here, their women are the same to them. Lissa is part of that. She's important, Casimir. We need her safe."

Casimir shrugged. "You've got my word." He leaned across the warmth of the fire, his gaze caught for a moment. His eyes were molten, a liquid silver, nearly the same color as Ilya's, the youngest brother. His hair was nearly pitch-black. Strange streaks of silver radiated through, indicating that at some point something sharp had sliced along his skull and left behind those five thin lines. He kept his hair cropped short and neat. He had a strong jaw, covered with stubble.

His features were cut with angles and planes. Three scars ran from his chin to the top of his skull, thin slices, as if whatever had managed to cut into his head had also found his face. The scars were barely there, but they kept his face from being model beautiful.

"Tell me about your lives. Everything. What you've been doing all these years and what you're doing now. I've got less than an hour before I have to go, and I may never see you again. Talk."

2

SOMETIMES life was pure irony. Casimir Prakenskii was an assassin. A premier, elite assassin. He'd been an assassin since his fifteenth birthday. He'd been in training practically from birth to be anyone—anyone at all—with the exception of Casimir Prakenskii. He didn't even know who Casimir was. He wouldn't recognize the man if he looked in the mirror.

The role he found himself in was unexpectedly more difficult than he had anticipated. Simple enough on the surface, he'd certainly played such roles before—enough that this one was second nature to him. A bodyguard on the estate of Luigi Abbracciabene. He usually could slide into any position easily, but Luigi kept only a very few men on the Abbracciabene estate.

The house and grounds weren't overly large, but the estate was guarded by two roving men, not a team. Still, he managed to be in the right place when one of the bodyguards "unexpectedly" came down with a "serious illness" and decided to take leave. He'd been briefed and knew his target was coming for a visit and fortunately, he had a couple of weeks to get his cover in place.

His quarry was beautiful. There was no other word for her. Beautiful. She didn't laugh often, but when she did, every head turned toward her. It wasn't difficult to keep an eye on her because she liked to be outside, and her hair gave her away. When the sun poured down on her, her hair looked like a living flame. Sheets of thick red hair framed her delicate oval face. Her eyes were startling blue. Not blue green, but a true deep sapphire blue framed by thick red-gold lashes she rarely bothered to darken with mascara.

She had noticed him immediately and made inquiries. She didn't live there. She hadn't been there in over a year, but she still noticed he wasn't a regular in the household. For some strange reason, he found that sexy—that she seemed to notice things other women wouldn't.

She had come right up to him to introduce herself. Close. Unafraid. He'd never been affected by a woman before, not even when he slept with one, but there was no denying the instant attraction. She felt it too. He saw it in her eyes just for the briefest of seconds. Her breathing changed. One inhale. Two. That was it, but he'd noted it. Remembered. Would always remember that moment because, for him, it was significant. He'd felt the pull of their chemistry, and so had she. She was covering it and ignoring it, just as he was.

For the first time in his life, staring down into those amazing blue eyes, he wished a woman could see Casimir Prakenskii and not the man he was portraying. He didn't want *this* woman affected by a fictional character, a bodyguard who would do his job and walk away never to be seen again. He wanted her to see him—whoever the hell that was.

Her voice was soft, pitched low and melodious. The notes sank right through his skin and branded her into his bones— not a good start for a man like him. He was a master of disguise and, along with that, he was a master of his emotions, but he found himself listening for the sound of her voice wherever he was, inside or outside the house. He didn't allow her— or anyone else—to see his reaction to her; he tucked it away to bring out later to savor. It was a gift. Feeling. Anything at all besides loneliness and despair. Feeling for a woman was a gift.

She'd been there a week. He'd accompanied her security detail into town when she went with her uncle Luigi, which was nearly every day. She liked to wander around town. He knew it wasn't her hometown. She'd been born in Ferrara, the only child of Marcello and Elisabeta Abbracciabene. Her name then had been Giacinta and she'd been a true Celtic throwback, just like her mother with her flaming red hair and her incredible blue eyes. His information had included pictures from her childhood along with her extraordinary history.

The child had supposedly died with her parents. Luigi had managed to keep her existence from the world, and he'd sent her away when she was eighteen. She'd returned as the artist Lissa Piner. Luigi introduced her as someone important to him, like a daughter—or a niece—and she was to be treated that way. All the men seemed to accept that Luigi and Lissa had a relationship and Luigi considered her family.

He never heard her coming, she was that soft on her feet when she moved around her uncle's home. But he *felt* her. He knew where she was at any given time in the house, that was how aware of her he was. He had time to drape himself casually against the wall, a pose he knew annoyed her because she always made a comment about how easy his job seemed to be. He noticed she didn't say much to the other bodyguards as they spent their time playing pool or video games in the recreation room. Just him. And he liked that it was just him. Even if she was reprimanding him.

She always smiled at him as she came into the room, her bow of a mouth, lips full and red without adornment, curving into a soft smile that didn't quite reach her blue eyes. He'd thought about her mouth far too much. The shape of it. The way her lips appeared satin soft, giving him one too many fantasies. Leaving him restless at night. He could sleep anywhere, any time. He'd learned it was necessary in his line of work, but nearly impossible with her haunting his dreams.

Small white teeth flashed at him, while her eyes studied him. Carefully. Taking in everything. He was tall, wide-shouldered, but lean. That was one of the many gifts he had. That leanness allowed him to gain weight overnight or shed it, depending on the role he played. His sinewy body was deceptive in that it hid the enormous strength he had. He carried not an ounce of fat on him and was athletic. He was all muscle, with long ropes of sinew below his skin.

He had scars. A lot of them. Not, strangely enough, from his profession. He wasn't a man to get caught—most of the time. Most of the scars were from his training. It had been brutal, there in the schools he attended. He had been difficult. Defiant. He took to the weapons and hand-to-hand combat training with ease. Excelling. He was very good at his seduction training. But schooling, languages, that bored the hell out of him. Still, he learned, because if one didn't, one died.

He had learned to torture and what it felt like to be tortured. He'd never forget the feel of knives slicing into his flesh. The burns. The electrical shocks. Sometimes, he woke in the night, sweat pouring from his body, his gun in his fist, the taste of blood in his mouth from biting down hard to keep from making a sound.

His parents had been murdered for their politics—they'd been too outspoken about the reforms that were needed in their country. His parents loved Russia and wanted to see the government work for its people. Instead, a hit squad had come calling. Casimir and his six brothers had been taken to the schools.

The man running the schools, Kostya Sorbacov, hadn't wanted to take a chance on them being loyal to one another so had separated them. He wanted their loyalty to him, to his orders. He was the power behind the throne.

The brutality and sheer cruelty of the training methods employed had ensured that many of the students, most like him—sons or daughters of those killed for their opposition—had died during training. Others—like him—learned not to feel. Never to show emotion. He became exactly what they wanted, because if he didn't, they would kill one of his brothers. He knew what kind of death that would be. Slow. Tortured. He'd seen—and learned—how to administer that kind of death.

Like their parents, each of the Prakenskii brothers had psychic gifts. Those gifts were strong and enabled them to survive and thrive in the brutal environment. He had survived, but sometimes, like now, he wondered at what cost. He had no home, no name, no past and no future. He moved through the world, slipping in and out of identities, and none of them were real. Not. A. Single. One.

He kept his gaze on his target while he went over the facts of his prey in his mind. The woman now called herself Lissa Piner. She'd been born Giacinta Abbracciabene and had fled Sicily nearly six years earlier and gone to the United States where she'd become Lissa Piner. She'd joined a therapy group for women who had lost a family member to murder and felt responsible for that murder. He didn't understand why she would feel responsible—she'd been a child when her parents were murdered—but in a way he was glad she had.

During those sessions she'd met five other women she'd become fast friends with. In fact, they'd developed a family and bought a farm together. Lissa was a loner. She hadn't allowed anyone into her life until she'd met those women. He liked that she had them. He knew what it was like to live completely alone, off the grid, living a lie. He would die that way, without friends or family. He was glad she wouldn't.

She was coming toward him. Into the room. His body recognized the fact that she was in the vicinity, long before he actually saw her. She radiated heat. Maybe it was the hair, all that glorious hair, or the passion inside her she kept bottled up and contained. He saw it. He felt it. She could hide it from everyone else but not from him.

Lissa Piner walked right up to him. Close. So close his lungs filled with her scent. The fragrance was elusive, barely there, just enough for a man to want to get even closer so he could pull more of her natural perfume deeper. He couldn't remember the name of the flower it reminded him of.

Her eyes, that vivid, vibrant blue, remained steady on his face. On his eyes. He wore contacts, of course, dark brown ones, to fit with his image of dark hair. She had to tilt her head up to look him in the eye. He kept the scars and his hair hidden from the world. Tomasso Dal Porto didn't have those scars or that silver-streaked hair.

"Good morning, Tomasso," Lissa said.

His gut tightened. He didn't like the little purr in her voice. She had acknowledged him every single time she saw him, just as she did every other worker on her uncle's estate, but somehow, the way she treated him was very different. The way she watched him. So closely, as if she knew he was something other than what he appeared.

He was wary of her now. He didn't let his unease show on his face. His cover was solid. His character was solid. His accent was perfect. He had a history, and even he believed he was Tomasso Dal Porto.

Casimir inclined his head, his dark gaze sweeping over her a little insolently. She didn't rise to the bait as she usually did. Her eyes would get even bluer and her mouth would set in a perfectly sensual line right before she delivered some reprimand, although he was fairly certain she wasn't aware of that. His alarms shrieked at him that he was in trouble in more ways than one. "Good morning, Signorina Piner."

She pressed her lips together. "How many times do I have to ask you to call me Lissa?"

He shrugged. "It isn't done." None of the other bodyguards would dare be that familiar with her. Her uncle wouldn't like it. He wasn't about to get singled out. He didn't like that she had begun, over the last two days, to insist he call her by her first name.

She leaned closer to him, her mouth near his ear. If she'd been taller, she could have touched him, but her head came up to the middle of his chest. "Coward," she murmured softly. So softly it would be impossible for anyone else to hear had they not been alone in the room.

He didn't reply. He kept his expression completely blank, giving nothing away. Damn, but up close she was even more potent. All that bottled-up passion in her wild, blue gaze. Her hair felt like silk where it brushed his arm. He didn't have physical reactions to women, yet he found himself having to fight his cock. Just with the warmth of her breath and her scent surrounding him, he was growing hard. Full. Without permission. Something he hadn't done since he was seventeen and had been lashed so many times, the lash tearing open his flesh until he learned total discipline and control over his body.

"I'd like to take a walk around the grounds, and I need you to accompany me."

There was a slightly imperious note in her voice. She wasn't asking. He raised an eyebrow and managed to stand straight with a fluid graceful movement that brought his body right up against hers deliberately. He felt her breath hitch. Her vivid blue eyes went wide and then deepened in color. He had the mad desire to see what happened when he thrust deep into her and made her come apart for him. He let that show. Just for a moment. A glimpse, no more.

"I like that you need me, Signorina Piner." He kept his voice low. Sensual. Pouring meaning into his choice of words. Deliberately baiting her by using her surname.

Faint color stole up her porcelain skin. Her skin was a work of art, yet he was certain no painter would ever do it justice. He held her gaze a long moment and then he smiled and indicated she precede him. Lissa stared up at his face a heartbeat longer and then she turned abruptly and headed for the door. He didn't walk beside her, but fell into step behind her, annoying her even more.

He liked to watch her walk. She was always silent. Graceful. He couldn't imagine her ever stumbling. She moved like a ballet dancer, fluid and poised. Confident. She was small and even slight, but he was observant and he could see the way her muscles moved beneath her amazing skin. She had a great ass, and he liked the way she swayed when she walked, the material from her long skirt shaping and falling suggestively. She was a very sensual woman. She turned heads everywhere she went, but he hadn't noticed her flirting with anyone. The closest she ever came was with him, and it wasn't flirting. Just that small reaction she couldn't always hide.

She led the way to the gardens and then stopped and waited for him. There was a definite challenge on her face. Her chin had gone up; the blue eyes narrowed. "Which one are you?" she demanded in English.

He raised an eyebrow. "I don't know what you're asking me," he answered in fluent Italian. Perfect accent. He looked like a native. He acted like one. His movements were flawless. He never stepped out of character. Never.

"Yes, you do," she hissed. "I'm not playing this game with you. Gavriil contacted you, didn't he? And don't you dare lie to me or I'll go to my uncle and have him throw you out so fast your head will spin."

Gavriil, of course, had initiated the contact with him and supplied him with all the information necessary to shadow Lissa Piner, but she couldn't possibly know that. None of his brothers would ever give him up to their women, no matter how enamored with them. They were used to protecting one another, and he was on assignment.

"It had to be Gavriil. He's so . . ." She broke off, paced away from him, all fluid energy. She turned again to face him and glared, her fingers closed into two tight fists. *"Over-bearing."* She spat the word at him. *"Arrogant. Dominant.* I refuse to have you watching over me. *Babysitting* me."

He looked confused. Brought his hand up to the nape of his neck, frowning. Massaging. "It is my job to look after you. Don Luigi has insisted you have a bodyguard at all times . . ."

"*Not* Don Luigi, you oaf. *Gavriil.* Your *brother.* He sent you. I know that he did. Probably every last one of them is in on it. You are definitely a Prakenskii," she accused. "I should have known he would do something like this."

One week and she'd discovered his identity. That wasn't good. He'd stayed alive by being a master of disguise. He rubbed at his neck muscles, shaking his head. Frowning. He could play poker with the best of them. "How many brothers do I have?" There was just the slightest hint of amusement in his voice. Amusement and confusion. It was a work of art, that tone. He could see the sudden wariness in her eyes, as if for just a moment she doubted herself.

She lifted her chin at him. The gesture was a clear challenge and it brought out something unexpected—and wicked—in him. The need to tame. To dominate. She was all fire. A living flame, so beautiful she took his breath away.

"You have six brothers, as if you didn't know."

He raised an eyebrow at her. Quirked his lips as if the superior male was hiding his laughter from the silly little female. "Six? I didn't think I had any siblings, but now that I have *six* I think I need to know where I fall into the mix. Am I the oldest? Youngest? Please give me more information on my family."

"You're in the middle, which makes you the most obnoxious."

He burst out laughing. "I see. If you wanted my attention, *cara*, all you had to do was say so. You didn't have to make up an elaborate scheme." He swept his hand down the length of her long red hair, shaping the back of her head, down her spine to the curve of her very sweet ass. He allowed his hand to linger there.

To her credit, she didn't move away, but she went very still. Something shifted inside him, warning him. She had been just that little bit uncertain. Off-balance. Defending herself and her idea that she might know who he was. Now she was acutely aware of him again. The man. The man he didn't see himself. The man he didn't know. Casimir Prakenskii. That man without a real identity. Or a home. Or a family. *Him*.

She saw too much. Far too much. Vision like that could get a person killed.

He remained silent, his gaze on her face. He shifted closer, subtly, aware they were alone. She had deliberately ensured no one was in sight or hearing of them. He wanted to scare her into backing off. She didn't seem to scare easily. She didn't step away. Didn't move a muscle. Her gaze drifted over his face and then jumped back to his eyes.

"Four of my sisters are married to Prakenskiis. Joley Drake is married to a fifth. That leaves two more. I know you're Gavriil's brother," she prompted, one hand between them as if she could ward him off.

He studied her face. The blue eyes and lifted chin. There was something there. Fear, but of what, he couldn't be certain. Of him? She had to know if Gavriil sent him, it was to watch over her, not harm her. She was family. His brothers claimed her as family, and that meant she was to be guarded at all times. They had enemies.

Kostya Sorbacov's son, Uri, was making his bid for the presidency. As Gavriil had pointed out, in order to do that smoothly, Sorbacov had to erase all evidence of those brutal schools and the men and women who had been forced to become assets for their country. There were hits out on every Prakenskii brother. All of them. Even Ilya, the youngest, who had mostly worked Interpol for them out in the open.

Lissa would be a pawn for Uri. He would know the Prakenskiis would do whatever it took to protect her. They had protected one another by cooperating with Sorbacov, allowing them to be trained and used as weapons.

"Are you going to talk to me, or do we go talk to my uncle?" she demanded.

"Why are you upset?" He stayed with Italian. Keeping to his role. "Explain this to me."

Her breath hissed out between her teeth. "Would you like it if someone put a babysitter on you?"

"Babysitter?" He'd never been called that before. He wasn't in the least gentle enough to ever be deemed a babysitter. "I don't know what you mean." Because she was bluffing. It was a good bluff. Maybe even a great bluff, but it was still a bluff. There was no way she could possibly know who he was.

She glared at him. Her eyes were even bluer, a glittering sapphire, pure and natural just like the rest of her. He could have sworn sparks flew around her hair. He half expected any moment for the silky strands to flame.

He stepped closer to her. So close her breasts brushed his ribs. "If you are looking for a man, *bella*, I am more than happy to oblige you." He made the offer a second time, nothing subtle about it.

Her lashes fluttered. She didn't look away from him. She had courage, he had to admit that much, and that made him admire and respect her all the more. "Fine. Be that way. But I know. I want to go into town. I'm meeting someone," she snapped. "You will *not* be coming with me."

He slid his fingers through her hair, his palm shaping her face. He told himself it was to throw her off-balance, but he knew it was because touching her was a compulsion he couldn't resist. "I will be coming with you, Lissa. I am assigned as your bodyguard. Where you go, I will go. Don't try to run off, because that will only make both your uncle and me angry."

There was no way she was slipping out from under his guard. No possible way. Especially if she had a date. Why the thought of her with another man angered him, he had no idea, but it did and she damn well wasn't going anywhere without him.

She froze when he touched her. He felt her tremble. The reaction so slight it was almost undetectable, but he was too tuned to her to miss it.

Lissa stared up into that handsome, masculine face with the too-old eyes. It was his eyes that captured her. Not his wide shoulders or the way he moved, so silent, like a predator. So fluid like a dangerous jungle cat. Not his narrow hips or the muscles rippling beneath the shirt that was stretched so tightly across his chest. Not the strong columns of his thighs either. It was definitely his eyes.

When he looked at her, he wholly focused on her, yet at the same time, she knew he was aware of everything and everyone around him. When she looked at him so closely, she knew he was wearing tinted contacts. Colored contacts. There was no way of knowing what color his eyes really were, but they weren't that deep brown. Still, his eyes captivated her.

His face was all angles and planes. Hard. Masculine. Strong jaw. His nose was almost aristocratic when one looked closely, and she was looking. *Dangerous.* There was an aura of danger surrounding him. It was in the stamp of his mouth. His jaw. Mostly, it was there in his stillness. And in his eyes.

Loneliness. He was so alone. She knew, because she was. She had to hide who she was. What she was. If, as she suspected, this man was a Prakenskii, he'd been born in Russia. He'd watched his parents die . . . For a moment her mind shut down to block memories from flooding in, from taking her someplace she couldn't go.

Tomasso, or Prakenskii, took her breath away, and no man had ever succeeded in doing that. Her entire body reacted when he was near. She'd never had that happen to her either. She hadn't lived a life conducive to inviting seduction with a man. Truthfully, she'd sacrificed that side of living willingly for her purpose. She hid on a farm, one that had unexpectedly become a home to her, surrounded by women and their men she'd eventually come to love. That had been a gift. Finding out she could respond to a man was a gift as well, but one not so welcome.

"I don't like to be touched." She whispered the words to him. Breathing him in. Lying, because maybe that assertion had been the truth, but it no longer was, not with him. Her heart pounded and butterflies took wing in her stomach.

Lissa didn't move away from him even as she whispered the admission. For one moment Casimir saw behind her incredible blue eyes to the woman she hid from the world. She was every bit as alone as he was. Every bit playing a role for others. And every bit as attracted to him, but trying to hide it.

The pad of his thumb slid along her jaw of its own volition. There was no stopping it because he didn't think about it. He needed to touch her in the way he needed to breathe. He didn't understand it, because he was a hunter. Others were his prey. He didn't touch them unless that got him close enough to kill. He used expert seduction to further his goals, or for relief, but it was never like this. Never a compulsion. Never a hunger. A need. This woman was under his protection. He shouldn't need this, but he did, and that need was stronger than any compulsion he'd ever experienced.

"Who is it you're going to meet in town? I'll arrange your protection. And I will be there, Lissa."

He stepped away from her because if he didn't, he would kiss her. The idea that he could come so close to making such a huge mistake appalled him. He should contact his brother and tell him the assignment was off, to send someone else, but he knew he wouldn't do that. He wouldn't trust her life to anyone else. Not now. Not ever.

His gaze drifted over her face. His palm itched. Really itched. He used his finger to scratch at the center in hopes of alleviating the annoyance, but it didn't work. He pressed his palm hard against his thigh. Rubbed it up and down against his jeans. Her gaze followed the motion of his hand as he rubbed, trying to make that itch go away. She inhaled sharply. Audibly. One hand flew to her throat in defense.

"Oh. My. God. You really are a Prakenskii. I was taking a guess, but you are. That's why we're . . ." She broke off and backed away from him. "It isn't going to happen. I mean it. Whatever your brothers have done to my sisters isn't going

to happen between us." She curled her fingers tightly into a
fist and held both hands tight against her thighs. "I have to
think." She kept backing away. "This *can't* happen to me. I
don't accept it. I won't ever let it happen."

"*Now* what are you going on about?" he demanded. But
he knew. He knew because all Prakenskiis had psychic gifts.
The one considered the most important gift of all was when
they found the right woman, the perfect mate, the one who
fit with them; they could seal that woman to them. He felt the
power rising in him. Felt it in his hand. Knew that power was
close and wanted to come pouring out of him. Because Lissa
Piner, or Giacinta Abbracciabene, was that one woman. *His*
woman. He kept his palm pressed tightly against his thigh,
refusing to give in to the compulsion.

The problem was simple. He had no idea how to have a
relationship. He wasn't looking for one. He refused to claim
a woman when he knew he didn't have long to live. He
wouldn't do that to her. What he would do was make certain
that while she was in Europe, she was safe and then he would
ensure she returned to her farm in Sea Haven, back where
Gavriil and the rest of his brothers could watch over her.

He didn't confirm or deny her accusation. She shook her
head again and turned away from him, heading back to the
house. She didn't look over her shoulder once to see if he was
there. Obviously, she didn't want to know if he was a Prakenskii anymore. That irritated him on a primal level. Why,
he didn't know, only that her complete dismissal of him was
unacceptable.

Her uncle stood in the doorway watching their return,
clearly waiting for her. Luigi's face didn't hold the customary
smile. His eyes weren't lit. He looked as expressionless as a
man like him could look. Again, Casimir watched her so
closely that he saw the little tell in her fingers when she
curled them into a fist in reaction to her uncle standing there.
Something was wrong and she knew it.

She hurried up the last few stairs to the house. Luigi stepped back to allow her inside, and they walked in the direction of her uncle's private study. Casimir hurried toward the room that was on the other side of that wall—Luigi's library. The man hadn't read a book in ages, probably not since he was in school, but he had a huge, well-stocked library that Lissa spent a lot of time in. Casimir did as well, going through the books that Lissa read.

Most were maps and books on architecture. Buildings. Cities. Guides to cities. While in the library, he had discovered one very important feature. There was a common vent between the two rooms. He had removed the grate, placed a small wireless amplifier inside the vent in order to allow him to hear the conversations taking place in the study. When he was finished, he always carefully removed the bug and replaced the grate. No one was ever the wiser. He locked the library door, although it wasn't strictly necessary. Since he'd been there, only Lissa and he had gone into the room. Not even the maid went regularly.

"You found him, Tio Luigi? You're certain it's really him?" Lissa sounded matter-of-fact, all business, but there was an underlying excitement in her tone. Excitement, but grim as well.

"Yes. It has taken a number of years and a lot of money, but it is Cosmos Agosto. There is no doubt. I have made absolutely certain that it is the same man. He took the money from the Porcelli *famiglia* to betray my brother. Your father." Luigi spat the names at her.

"There can be no mistake, Tio."

"I have never made a mistake. Not in all these years of hunting them. It has taken years because we are careful. Very, very careful. We are not murderers, spilling the blood of innocents. This man ate at the table *di mio fratello*. He broke bread with your beautiful mother. With you, Giacinta. He was given the status of *la famiglia*. He was treated as one of you for years. He was trusted. He betrayed all of you. This man is living in wealth. His big house. His wife so much younger. He has grown lazy, thinking his betrayal has been forgotten."

There was a small silence. "Do you see the value of waiting, Tio? When they die, no one suspects it is payment for a debt from so long ago."

"You were right, I can concede that. Your restraint and wisdom has kept us safe all these years."

"Thank you for finding him." Lissa's voice was soft. Loving.

"I wanted him more than any other," Luigi admitted.

"I need a favor, Tio," she continued. "I need to go into the village to meet someone. I do not wish to have a bodyguard accompany me. I'll slip out alone . . ."

"No." Luigi's voice was firm. "I will not have you go unescorted. We *think* the Porcellis have forgotten us, but we don't *know*. You are not safe here. That's why I had you relocate to the United States when you were just eighteen. That's why you have become Lissa Piner. Your wonderful chandeliers hang in several rooms, so we have become good friends to the outside world. You and your work are famous throughout Europe, and many estates and hotels vie for the chance to have one of your creations. As each is handblown, they are prized for their beauty and rarity."

Lissa laughed softly. "Tio, you should do all my marketing for me."

"It is the truth, yes?"

"Perhaps. But I doubt if I'm famous. Well, my chandeliers are becoming popular in hotels, and I've been written up in a few magazines. That's helped to get my name out there. I like that I can contribute to the farm. Everyone works hard to make it a success and the last couple of years, I've been able to help out."

"You can travel easily into any country with no suspicion," Luigi pointed out.

"It is a help." She sighed. "If your heart is set on making

me take a bodyguard, I will take Arturo. I've known him the longest."

Casimir knew Arturo had slowed down considerably. He'd been with Luigi for years and Luigi didn't have the heart to retire him. Arturo always accompanied Luigi when he went out, but Luigi always took two bodyguards.

"Giacinta . . ."

"Lissa," she insisted. "You have to call me Lissa, even when we're alone. You have to think of me as Lissa Piner. I can get away with calling you Tio, because of your age. It makes it more proper for me to spend time in your home, but you have to remember I am Lissa."

Luigi sighed. "I'll do better. I'm not so young anymore. Where are you going? Arturo has to be able to prepare."

"I'll be going to Salvadore's. Arturo doesn't have to do a thing. There is no danger to me if I go out tonight. No one knows of my plans. Arturo won't attract undue attention. You know if anyone else goes with me, someone will notice. I'm not going out as Lissa."

What the hell did that mean? Not Lissa? Then who? Casimir didn't wait to hear any more. He had to escape to his room. Lissa would think she'd won this round. She'd guess he was sulking. Deep inside, where no one could see, he grinned. There was a ring of truth in her voice when she'd told her uncle where she would be meeting her contact. Casimir simply had to ensure he was close to her table and could overhear everything she said. If possible, he would even be bold enough to plant a listening device.

All the better to hear, my living flame, he whispered to the empty room. He made his way to the vent where he had secured his suitcase filled with his tricks of the trade. He could be anyone. Anywhere. Any time. He was a master of disguise. She might have guessed he was a Prakenskii, but then, she was family. She was around five of his brothers all the time. Few people knew them, but she was observant and she

probably suspected Gavriil and the others would never allow
her to go to Europe where their mortal enemy resided without some kind of backup.

It took less than an hour to decide on his next role, receive
the word he was off duty for the evening and make a show of
retiring to his room early. It took much longer to become the
man he hoped Lissa wouldn't see through. This time there
would be no identifying marks of any kind and he would
be older. Nothing she might associate with Tomasso.

Casimir slipped out the window, made his way over the
roof to the other side of the house, away from the courtyard
and garage where the cars were stashed. He had a bicycle in
the potting shed. The shed was overgrown with vines and
had long since fallen into a state of disrepair.

The bike was a good one and he practically flew down the
narrow track that ran alongside the drive. The dirt pathway
was used by the gardeners to drag bags of weeds, cut grasses
and branches out of sight of the main house. He turned onto
the road and put on another burst of speed. It wouldn't do to
be caught by Lissa and Arturo anywhere near the estate. His
new role was rather distinctive and they wouldn't fail to remember him. Never a good thing when she was already so
suspicious.

He switched to the small car he had stashed in a garage
just a few miles from the estate. He paid a nominal fee to
house the vehicle, and no one had bothered it. Still, he was
careful as he approached, looking for signs of disturbance.
He never took chances. That had been drilled into him in the
schools he'd attended and now, when there was a hit out on
him, placed there by the very men he'd served faithfully for
years, those lessons had come in handy.

3

CASIMIR arranged to enter Salvadore's just as Arturo approached with a dark-haired woman pacing just behind him. Casimir continued walking as they neared him, but it was all he could do to keep his mouth closed tight when it wanted to drop open in pure shock. He would never have known the woman walking with Arturo was Lissa Piner. She was . . . plain. Pretty enough, but plain.

Lissa was so vibrant and alive. A living flame. There was no way to deny the passion in her. She drew the eye of men and women around her. It was impossible not to see her beauty and be drawn to it. She looked sexy, sensual, a woman made for long nights and pure sin. She moved with the flowing grace of a dancer. The dark-haired woman following Arturo into the cappuccino bar didn't come close to Lissa's beauty.

Just inside the door Casimir stopped to read the menu posted on the far wall. He kept an eye on the two of them. Arturo broke off and went to sit at one of the tables along the far wall where he could look into the mirror behind the counter and see everyone in the cappuccino bar as well as have the advantage of facing the door and wide windows over-looking the street.

The woman was the same height as Lissa, but not as curvy. In fact, she looked straight up and down. There was no sign of Lissa's generous breasts. Her hair was shoulder-length, a glossy black. Her eyebrows and lashes were dark as well as her eyes. There was a beauty mark on the right side of her lips. Still, there was no mistaking her mouth. Casimir had far too many fantasies about that mouth to fail to recog-nize her. Under that thin, stick of a disguise was his woman.

She went straight to a table in the far corner. Fortunately, it was in his path. Casimir pulled his book from his backpack and peered at the pages, reading as he walked up the aisle toward the area where the single tables were located, right where Arturo had chosen to sit. He bumped into a woman, bounced off her and banged into Lissa's table, apologizing in fluent Italian the entire time. He had to grab the table's edge to steady himself, deftly slipping the tiny bug beneath the table as he did so.

He didn't meet Lissa's eyes, in fact, barely glanced at her, but nearly prostrated himself in front of the other woman. He hunched over, shuffling his worn shoes. He wore horn-rimmed glasses over his light brown eyes. His jawline was quite different, filled out, and he was slightly bucktoothed. His mousy brown hair, streaked with gray, was thinning. His voice was nasally. Even the shape and color of his fingernails were different. He didn't have a single identifying mark on his face or hands.

His clothes were loose, covering the paunch around his belly. The trousers fit his buttocks tighter, but that was be-cause he had a very rounded butt. The woman he followed continually smiled and reassured him until he wiped beads of sweat from his forehead with a handkerchief and dropped into a chair as if he was exhausted from apologizing.

Casimir deliberately chose the table on the other side of Arturo, a good distance from Lissa. He opened his book with a huge relieved sigh, loud enough for everyone in the bar to hear, pulled out his earphones and slipped them on after ordering a cappuccino and pastrami pizza, the bar's signature dish.

Lissa's chair faced away from him, but she sat sideways, better to observe the room. She placed gloves carefully on the tabletop, precisely on the small clutch she'd brought with her. A signal that meant all clear. He'd used such signals himself many times. Had she just left the clutch without the gloves, he surmised she would have been warning whomever she was meeting to stay away.

Casimir took a cautious look around the bar without appearing to do so. He had great practice looking completely absorbed in his choice of reading material. His glasses were slightly tinted, partially hiding his eyes as his gaze moved around the room. Two tables down he spotted her contact and his gut seized. He knew the man. A total weasel for the Russian mob. What was Lissa doing meeting such a man? He couldn't be trusted. He was known for double-dealing, selling information, but informing the mob who wanted it and where the meet would take place. He cursed under his breath in four languages—eloquently.

The weasel, a man by the name of Ivan Belsky, sitting a few tables down from Casimir, rose and made his way to Lissa's table and sank into the chair opposite her. He wore a shapeless coat and a hat, and his beady eyes were restless, constantly moving. Sweat beaded on his forehead. That told Casimir he hadn't come alone and this meeting was a setup.

"Before we go any further," Belsky stated, "I need to know who you're buying this information for."

"That's none of your business." Even Lissa's voice was different. Two notes lower. Slightly husky. Still, it was authoritative and clipped.

"I can't just hand over information like this to anyone," he hissed. "I could be killed."

"You knew that when you agreed to make the deal," Lissa pointed out.

The two stared at each another for a long time. Lissa didn't look away or back down. Her features were set and her hand crept toward her gloves and clutch, as if she would pick up both and walk away.

"I don't have time to play around. If you don't have what I need, just say so. I was told you were someone who could be counted on."

Belsky's breath hissed out. "I got you the information you wanted. It was much more difficult than I thought it would be. The price has doubled." He leaned across the table. "Miss *Patrice Lungren*." He sat back, satisfied that just knowing her name, identifying her, would frighten her.

Lissa hesitated, her hand fluttering for a moment, as if being called by name had thrown her. She straightened her shoulders and allowed her hand to fall gracefully to the table. "Your difficulties are not my problem. We agreed on a price, Belsky."

Casimir didn't react, but he felt his heart jerk hard in his chest. He wasn't a man to feel fear. He could go into any situation with ice in his veins because he had nothing to lose. Now, there was Lissa Piner with her flaming red hair and her soft, appealing laughter. He wasn't going to lose her to a weasel like Ivan Belsky. He knew the man. A rat for the Russian mob operating out of Moscow. He wasn't in the least bit trustworthy or reliable. Not. At. All. He would sell Lissa down the river in a heartbeat. Whatever she offered him, he had gotten more playing both sides.

What was she doing even talking to a man like Belsky? He nearly groaned when she casually took an envelope from her clutch and laid it on the table. The white packet, clearly thick with cash, lay beneath her palm. Belsky stared at it. Realization that she wasn't going to budge had him sighing. He reached for the envelope, but she didn't move her hand, just continued to stare at him.

Casimir's gut tightened. He stood up, snapping his book closed as Belsky removed a thin package wrapped in a brown paper bag and tied with a string. A neat touch, Casimir acknowledged. The man slid it across the table to Lissa. She put her hand on it before releasing the packet of cash to the weasel. Casimir shuffled right on past them without looking at either of them.

The trick to a disguise wasn't always the features so much as the details. The walk, the hunch, the particulars of a character one took on. He never forgot those details, especially not when someone's life depended on it—and he was certain Lissa's life did. Inwardly he cursed in Russian, his native language, and he was inventive about it as he kept to the slow, lumbering pace of his role. He didn't look at Lissa, or Belsky. He knew what was waiting for her outside. He had to get there first.

He'd known the moment he investigated Lissa and found out her uncle was Luigi Abbracciabene, a name connected to what had once been a small mob family living in the town of Ferrara. It had been easy enough to find the newspaper articles on the massacre of the family and all of the soldiers and workers on the estate. The Abbracciabene family had run afoul of the Porcelli family, a very large, connected family, violent and given to bloody wars. They'd instigated the massacre. He'd found Giacinta's name and it was reported she had died as well. He knew she hadn't.

Luigi lived a good distance from his brother, and had no part in the family business, at least that had been what every paper said. The Porcelli family hadn't bothered with him. It was reported he was quite ill. Casimir suspected he'd been much more than a mere bystander. Every family had an enforcer. An assassin. A man just like him. One that lived in the shadows and slipped out only when needed. Luigi had been that man for his family. He'd rescued his niece, hidden her from the world and raised her. Trained her. Set her on a path of vengeance, or justice—however one looked at it.

Casimir turned over every possibility of where the second assassin would be. They would want to catch Lissa away from people but before she made it to her car. Belsky would crowd close behind her, stay within striking distance. He had to believe she could handle Belsky. He had to trust that she would never meet him without the knowledge that he might betray her. When Belsky had called her Patrice Lungren, she'd faltered—clearly an act. She knew. She had to know.

He forced his mind away from Lissa and Belsky. Ivan Belsky was treacherous, but he could be handled. He was a weasel, always looking for easy money. He had made an art out of "selling" information and then killing the recipient. He had a partner he worked with, and unfortunately that man was by far the more dangerous. Borya Polzin specialized in murder. He enjoyed killing. Man, woman or child, it didn't matter. What did matter was he had come out of the same school Casimir had.

They'd had very little contact. Casimir had excelled and had been pushed in every area of learning possible, from languages to the art of seduction. He had reason to excel. If he didn't, one of his brothers would pay the price. Borya had little to offer other than a psychopath's hunger to hurt others. Borya had certainly outshone his classmates in that regard. He failed to learn any languages other than English and his native Russian. He could barely read. His masters hadn't killed him as they had so many others who failed far less classes than he had. He liked to hurt others and he learned how to torture, how to keep his victim alive as long as possible and how to kill in hundreds of ways, most very inelegant.

Some years earlier, he had killed his only sibling, his sister, the one his handlers held over his head to keep him in line. He'd slipped his leash and gone where there was money for his particular line of work—the Russian mob.

Casimir paused just to the right of the door, fumbling for car keys, dropping his book and bending to pick it up. The brief interval allowed him to scan the street and buildings across from the cappuccino bar. His car was parked just down from the front of the building, but he couldn't see the vehicle Lissa had arrived in.

As Casimir straightened, book in hand, Arturo sauntered out. The bodyguard didn't look in the least worried. He was nearing his sixties, was in good shape, working out all the time, and he'd been employed by Luigi.

Arturo had been employed by Luigi Abbracciabene nearly all of his life. He'd gone to work for Luigi at the age of seventeen. He'd been without a home and hungry for one. Luigi had been smart enough to see his potential and had taken him in. There was no one more loyal to the Abbracciabene family than Arturo. Casimir realized the moment Arturo came outside that Lissa had sent him ahead to get him out of the way of any potential violence. Lissa Piner was just as loyal to Arturo as he was to her—and she was determined to protect him.

Swearing under his breath, knowing he had only a few moments to pinpoint Borya's location, Casimir tried to pull up all he could recall of the man. Borya would want to commit murder up close. The assassin couldn't get satisfaction from killing at a distance. He would have to see the light go out of his victim's eyes in order to get his release. The actual kill was very personal to him. He would be labeled a serial killer in any other country, but Sorbacov had made him a personal pet and protected him. Kostya Sorbacov was his own brand of killer, and it amused him to keep Borya as his personal hit man. In running the schools, Sorbacov had come across several of the type of men Borya was, and he kept all of them. He had to have been very upset when Borya slipped away.

Casimir glanced toward his left. The corner was stark and open. No cover. To his right there was another store. Tables and chairs were set up in front of both the cappuccino bar and the small bakery next door. Too much furniture in the way for a clean kill. So where would Borya make his try for Lissa?

Behind him, he felt her presence. Lissa. His heart jerked hard in his chest as he took in her scent. Not the fragrance that had surrounded him at her uncle's estate, but a new, just as potent one. This one was jasmine and lavender, but very subtle, barely there. Her undercover signature scent then—when she played the part of Patrice Lungren. Behind Patrice was Belsky.

Lissa stepped up beside Casimir, her features expressionless. She gave him a vague smile, as if she wasn't really seeing him, but he was very aware of her piercing intelligence as her gaze swept over him, in seconds rejecting the idea that he could be the second killer.

Belsky came up behind her fast, crowding her so that she was forced to step forward, out into the open, onto the cobblestone sidewalk, beneath the canopy. *Beneath the canopy.* Casimir dropped the book as he withdrew the knife he carried from its sheath just inside his ill-fitting coat. As he did, he took two steps and leapt into the air right beneath the sagging canopy. He aimed for the heart of the prone figure waiting so patiently to murder.

Simultaneously, Lissa turned to face Belsky, a smile on her face, as if she might say something to him. He was already in motion, the blade of his knife concealed against his wrist as he stepped toward her, his hand going up to slice across her throat. Lissa used the momentum of her forward motion to slam a block down on his arm, deflecting the blade from her ribs as she stepped to the side of Belsky. She stabbed the needle she had in her fist into his neck, depressing the plunger as she did so, and retracted the needle, all in one motion. She continued walking past him, back toward the door of the bar where she'd artfully dropped her clutch.

Crouching low, she picked up the clutch as well as the book Casimir had dropped. Spinning, she saw a knife blade tear through the canopy. A few drops of blood hit the sidewalk. The man who had been reading the book continued moving toward the street, away from the bar. Shuffling. Bent. His body awkward. Not looking back. She looked around, but no one else was close. Her gaze went back to the man that had been sitting in the bar earlier. Who else could have delivered that killing blow to the assassin lying in wait, stretched out on the canopy above their heads?

Belsky staggered away from her, nearly fell off the sidewalk and then walked right out into the narrow street. A car honked. Slammed on brakes. He reached up to touch his neck. Looked at her. Another car coming at a much greater speed slammed into the rear of the stopped vehicle, spun and slid right into the man. The body went up and over the hood to land on the windshield.

Several women witnessing the accident screamed. Loudly. Shrilly. The canopy drooped. Big drops of blood plopped onto the sidewalk almost right in front of Lissa. The sag in the canopy grew along with the slit made by the knife. The man who had leapt up to kill the second assassin was long gone. He'd disappeared as Belsky staggered into the street.

The rip went wider overhead, and the body dropped nearly at her feet. She screamed and fell back onto her butt, like any self-respecting woman would. Being a Good Samaritan, she crawled the couple of steps to him, one hand feeling for a pulse. She wasn't taking any chances with fingerprints, although, as usual when she went out, she wore liquid prints. Not her own. Never her own.

She had only seconds to try to identify him. The dead man wasn't wearing gloves and his fingertips were absolutely smooth. He had a knife in his fist and it was stuck there tight. He'd died within seconds of the attack on him, and that certain knowledge set her heart pounding. Whoever had killed him had done so blindly. He'd leapt up and hit his target in the heart with his knife. That wasn't luck. That was skill. The knife had gone in smoothly, and then turned as it came out for maximum damage. There had been no sound. The killer had landed silently and disappeared within moments.

"He's d-dead," she stuttered, horrified, looking up at the first man who knelt beside her. "I'm sure he's dead." She nearly collapsed in his arms, forcing the man to drag her away from the body while others helped. He put her in a chair at one of the outside tables and then rushed back to the body.

A crowd gathered. She slipped out into the street, joining the crush there. She crouched low beside Belsky's body, one hand feeling for his pulse while the other slipped inside his jacket and deftly removed the envelope of cash. "He's dead," she said, and stood up, looking dismayed. The crowd pressed closer, and she slipped back into it.

She spotted Arturo in their car several yards down. She gave one last casual glance around and made her way to the car, carrying her clutch and the book. She couldn't say she wasn't grateful to her savior for dispatching a man who had planned on killing her—and there was no doubt in her mind that he was lying in wait for her—but she didn't want, nor could she afford to have a guardian.

Halfway to the house, she swept off her very expensive and beautiful wig, shaking out her own hair. It was always a production to get her wig on because she had so much hair, but she didn't want to cut it. Her mother wore her hair long, and it was one of the few things that always made Lissa feel as if she still had a part of her.

"I'm changing," she announced.

"Get to it," Arturo said, completely unaffected by the fact that she was peeling off her shoes, socks and jeans to pull on a long skirt. The top and band she bound her breasts with came next, and she yanked a thin, silky top over her head to match the skirt. The tiny pearl buttons were already done up. Her heels matched the color of the top, a pale blue to match the thin stripes in the skirt. She added gold bangles to her

wrist, pulled out the earrings that were simple studs and replaced them with gold hoops.

Her work clothes and shoes were thrust into a bag along
with the earrings, clutch, syringe and envelope of money. She
set the bag on the seat beside her and quickly began to brush
out her hair. She'd changed in under four minutes. A record.
The adrenaline was rushing through her veins. Her heart
pounded. Her mouth was dry. She'd come to expect the symp-
toms after working, but this was different. This was about
what she was going to do when she reached her uncle's estate.

Absently she picked up the book. *Old Poisons, New Prob-
lems*. She frowned and tapped her finger on the cover. She'd
read the book. Luigi had a copy of it in the library along with
other reference books on poisons. She smoothed her finger
along the spine and turned the book over and over. The more
she stared down at the copy, the more she was certain it was
from their library.

"Gavriil Prakenskii. I know you sent a babysitter." She
whispered the words softly and pressed the button to bring
the window down.

"I didn't hear you," Arturo said. "My ears aren't what they
used to be."

"I was muttering to myself."

"You only do that if you're upset. You got the information.
Belsky may be a double-crossing rat but he always brings the
goods. It's a point of honor with him. Whatever you have
there is what you asked for." There was curiosity in his voice.

Ignoring his unspoken question, she closed her eyes and
stuck her head out the window, allowing the wind to blow
through her hair and over her face. Cooling her. She was
bound to fire. Inside, *deep*, where it mattered, at her very core,
there was nothing cool and collected about her. She burned
hot and passionate. Sometimes she felt as dead as her parents,
lost to the world, existing, not living. The farther away from
the farm and her sisters, the more that feeling persisted.

She had to be focused. Completely alert and absorbed, concentrating only on the job at hand. She'd stayed alive because she pushed her natural nature down. The need to bring justice to those who had so brutally murdered her family and those serving them had been overwhelming. The need to let them know *she*, Giacinta Abbracciabene, was the one bringing that justice down on their heads was equally as overwhelming. The intelligent, logical part of her had kept her calm and allowed her to formulate a long-term plan.

Now, Gavriil Prakenskii was threatening that plan. It made no sense to her. He *knew* her intention. He knew she planned to kill both father and son Sorbacov. Her sisters deserved happiness, and the Prakenskiis had served their country with honor. They also deserved to live out their lives in peace. She was doing this for them. Why would he make it more difficult? Because she was certain—*certain*—that the man calling himself Tomasso Dal Porto was in reality a Prakenskii.

She felt he was in her very bones. It was his eyes. She had been on the farm with her sisters of the heart, as they often called themselves, for a little over five years. In that time, Rikki, a sea urchin diver, had pulled a man from the sea. He had been a Prakenskii. Lev Prakenskii. She had married that man. They all learned to accept and love him, but he was a protective, overbearing man.

Then Judith had fallen. Judith, who had all kinds of sense until a man showed up to protect her from her past. Her man just happened to be a Prakenskii as well and she married him. Stefan Prakenskii owned an art gallery and was just as protective and overbearing as Lev.

Next it was Airiana. She'd been kidnapped—by a Prakenskii. Together they had shut down a ship of human traffickers and rescued four children. She was married to Maxim now and they were adopting the children. Max was worse than the other two when it came to being protective.

Little Lexi, their youngest and most vulnerable, had succumbed to the charms of Gavriil Prakenskii. He was the most arrogant and dangerous of all the brothers she'd met. Lissa liked him and especially liked him for her youngest sister, but adding him into the mix was just downright scary. There was way too much testosterone on the farm.

The brothers believed in safety first and they'd turned the farm into a heavily guarded sanctuary, but Lissa wasn't safe there. She had too many secrets, and her work wasn't finished. She couldn't afford to have anyone watching her every move. Gavriil had guessed at what her plans were and he'd even provided information she wouldn't have been able to get on her own, but she didn't want help. She didn't need it, and she refused to allow a Prakenskii male anywhere near her.

She wasn't stupid or blind. She saw the pattern. Each of her sisters was bound to an element. Rikki was bound to water. Judith to spirit. Airiana was bound to air. Lexi was bound to the earth. Lissa blew out her breath and yanked the brush through her hair. She was bound to fire. That meant that every minute of every day, she had to suppress her passionate nature. Her need for action.

Lissa didn't dare show the Prakenskii brothers her skills when she was practicing martial arts or using weapons with them. She had to allow them to best her at every turn. It wasn't always easy. When discussions arose, she had to be subdued and keep silent when she wanted to argue fiercely for her point. She desperately wanted to be herself. *Desperately*.

Coming back to Italy, being in her uncle's home, she still couldn't be who she was deep inside. They had planned together, long ago, when she was a child, how to bring justice to the Porcelli family. Lissa had been a hothead, but Luigi had forced her to slow down to learn the things she needed to learn in order to keep from being killed. That had taken years. In that time, she learned the wisdom of patience.

The Porcelli family had no idea they were under attack. The accidents came infrequently. Two, sometimes three in a year. There was no pattern that anyone could detect, and

Lissa always made certain the accidents were random. She didn't care about tipping off the Porcelli family that the Abbracciabene family was coming after them. She didn't care anything about the second generation either. Only those responsible for the deaths of her people and her family. Luigi was her only living blood relative, and she didn't want him compromised in any way. He appeared to live quietly, surrounded by those he trusted, an older man who enjoyed gardening.

She hadn't known a real family again until she lived on the farm with her chosen sisters. Of the six women who had banded together to start a new life, only Lissa and Blythe remained unmarried. Unclaimed. Well . . . Blythe was up in the air. She had her own secrets. But Prakenskiis were overrunning their farm and the small village of Sea Haven. Even the famous Jolie Drake was married to a Prakenskii, which put *five* of the seven brothers in her small town. She could count. That left two. One for her. One for Blythe. It wasn't happening. Not to her.

"We're nearly home, Lissa," Arturo announced. His eyes met hers in the rearview mirror. "Are you settled, or do you need me to miss the driveway?"

She loved Arturo. She did. She loved few people in the world. She didn't dare get close to them. Her sisters. Their husbands—and she was still trying to hold herself apart from them. Her uncle and Arturo. Those were the few people she had in her world. In truth, Gavriil telling his brother about her hurt. She had trusted him to keep his word to her, not to let anyone know that she planned to go after the Sorbacovs. He'd given his word, and it hurt more than she'd ever expected that he'd broken his promise to her.

"I'm good. Thank you for going with me, Arturo. I don't know if I tell you enough, but I appreciate the way you've always looked after Tio Luigi. I don't ever worry because you're with him."

His teeth flashed at her, his smile dazzling. She hadn't trusted, even as a child. She'd learned the hard way not to, but over the years, Arturo had become another uncle to her. Her hand shook as she put the brush back in her purse. Lifting her chin, she caught up the book and slipped from the car. Arturo drove the vehicle into the garage, leaving her at the side entrance.

She knew her uncle would be waiting for her, worried as always, but Arturo would tell him what happened. It was too late to beat Tomasso to his room, if the man with the book had in fact been Tomasso—a Prakenskii—so there was no need to try to catch him in the act of reverting back to the bodyguard role. In any case, if he actually was a Prakenskii, she knew she wouldn't surprise him in the act of assuming another role. He would be too good for that. The Prakenskiis' craft had been honed in a hard school. They wouldn't make mistakes. Which left her the book.

Why had he dropped the book and then not recovered it? Especially if the book was from Luigi's library? She used the back stairs and hurried into the room she had grown very familiar with as a child. She'd often taken refuge here when she was lonely. She'd been lonely a lot. Luigi wasn't a man who knew how to comfort a grieving child. He was a man of action. He'd devoted his life to his brother and the family business. It had been small but lucrative. Now, he found himself with an emotional child who went from storms of weeping to fiery rants on vengeance.

Luigi had learned, over the years, how to express his love for her in more concrete ways, but she'd spent so many of the earlier days right there in the library, crying her eyes out. She tried to be brave in front of him because she wanted him to teach her what he knew. Then she'd discovered his books. She'd learned everything from Luigi, from self-defense and dirty tricks to weapons and poisons. She was a walking encyclopedia on poisons.

She knew right where the reference books were kept, and she hurried across the room to the shelves. The book should have been right there. She'd read it, put it back and granted, it was a number of years ago, but still, no one else was going to have taken it off the shelf. She scanned for the title. There was a small space between *The Elements of Poison—A History of Murder* and *Basic Illustrated Poisonous and Psychoactive Plants*, a book she'd read repeatedly as a child. This book, dropped by the man who had probably saved her life, belonged in Luigi's library.

She took a deep breath, let it out and replaced the book between the other two titles. She was going to confront Mr. Prakenskii and have him leave *immediately*. She couldn't afford to have him looking over her shoulder. She had work to do. Luigi had found the man she had wanted more than any other, and she intended to take care of Cosmos Agosto, the dog handler who had betrayed her entire family, and then she was going to see to the problem facing her sisters. No Prakenskii was going macho on her and stopping her.

Lissa hurried up the back stairs leading to the second floor, to the wing where Arturo, Tomasso and three other bodyguards resided. She knew which room was Tomasso's and she stood in front of the door, there in the darkened hallway. No sound emerged from the other side. No light slipped under the door.

She turned the doorknob very slowly. It was locked. That didn't surprise her in the least. It wasn't that difficult to pick the lock and she did so quickly. She pushed the door open cautiously, slipped inside and closed the door silently.

She stood just to the right of the door, waiting for her eyes to adjust to the darkness. It was much darker in the room due to the fact that heavy drapes had been pulled across the windows. She heard her heart pounding. As a rule, she could overcome fear rather easily. It was a matter of discipline and resolve. But this was a different kind of fear. Completely different.

Lissa's life had been destroyed by the attack on her family. Her parents had been brutally murdered. She'd nearly been murdered as well, and she'd been a very young child. That day was forever stamped in her mind, burned deep into her memories, but she kept that door carefully closed. The moment it was opened, the nightmares started. Standing there in the dark, she felt those murders and the memory of them all too close because the very air around her was fraught with danger.

She stayed still, inhaling to calm her pounding heart. The air was spiced with a dark, masculine scent. Dangerous to her. She recognized that immediately as she pulled her breath deep into her lungs—pulled *him* deep into her lungs. Prakenskii. No one else had those eyes. It didn't matter what color they were or if he wore glasses or not. It was the eyes. Hawklike. Piercing. Seeing everything. Seeing into one's soul.

Then there was the blistering chemistry between them she couldn't deny. She didn't have chemistry with men. She didn't allow it. She wasn't finished with her work and it was too important to screw that up for a man.

He made no sound. No movement. But he was there, somewhere in the dark room. Close to her. Very close. Somehow he'd seen or heard or was alerted to the doorknob twisting, or her picking the lock. It was impossible, she hadn't made a sound, but she knew he wasn't in the bed. He was there, very, very close to her. She held her breath, listening for the sound of his breathing, but there was nothing at all to give him away. She had trapped herself in the room with a powerful predator.

Lissa acknowledged and tried to learn from every mistake she made. She didn't just keep going on a path if it wasn't the right one because of ego. Right now, she knew she was in over her head. Whoever this man was—Prakenskii or not—he was much better at cat and mouse than she was. She was used to being the cat. In this room, she definitely was the mouse. Very slowly she inched back toward the door, her hand moving toward the doorknob.

"Don't."

The single command was low. Soft. Close to her right ear. So close she felt his warm breath stir her hair, disturbing a few stray strands. The hair moved over her face, causing an electrical shock to chase across her entire body, bringing every nerve ending alive. Her breasts felt tight, swollen, aching. Her nipples tightened into two hard peaks. She shivered—a full-body shiver. *He hadn't touched her.* She drew in another breath, suddenly terrified that this man—this stranger—had more power over her than anything else in her life ever had.

He couldn't stop her from opening the door, yet she hesitated, her hand hovering over the doorknob indecisively when she was always decisive. Her hand trembled and then she dropped her palm onto the knob. It felt solid. Reassuring. His scent tilted her world and made her feel disoriented. Alarmed. *Hunted.*

His hand covered hers. Gently. So gently. Still. She couldn't move. His body caged her in, inched forward just enough that she retreated before she even realized she'd given ground. Her arm was trapped behind her, and, consequently, one of her weapons was tied up, fingers still curled around the doorknob. His palm no longer surrounded the back of her hand. Instead, it was loose. A worry. A very lethal weapon.

"I want to leave this room. If you force me to scream, the other bodyguards will come running. Just step away." She managed to get the order out without her voice shaking. The threat level was extremely high. Her body didn't feel at all like her own. He stood facing her, his front solid. Muscular. Presenting her with numerous targets, yet she couldn't take advantage. It was too easy, and she knew it was a trap. He was baiting her.

His hand came up—the one she'd known was going to be trouble—and cupped the side of her face, his thumb sweeping along her cheekbone. "But you won't scream. If you brought them all here, you would force me to defend myself. I would, and I like most of the boys working for Luigi. With the exception of Enzo, who is a snake waiting to strike. In any case, I would kill them all and then your uncle would come . . ." He trailed off and swept his thumb over her lips. "You know you don't want that."

4

LISSA'S heart pounded so hard she felt the beat of it pulsing in her slick, hot, feminine core. Pulsing. Pounding. Demanding. She was in *such* trouble. Tomasso's voice was pitched low. So low it was only the fact that his mouth was against her ear when he spoke that she could hear him. She felt his breath stirring tendrils of hair. His lips brushed her skin intimately. Teeth slid down the curve of her ear and then tugged on her lobe. A million butterflies took wing. There was a definite spasm in her sex. Very definite. Strong. Maybe a quake more than a spasm.

He'd issued the threat so casually. Matter-of-factly. That frightened her more than anything else. He wasn't making an empty threat. He was capable of killing every one of her uncle's bodyguards and even Luigi himself.

"You wouldn't do that." She needed air. Needed to breathe. Because she believed he would. She absolutely believed that this man was capable of killing them all in a fight, and more, she knew the Prakenskii brothers. Each and every one of them, when cornered, would be capable of killing and walking away without a backward glance.

"I wouldn't have a choice, and you know me. You know exactly what I am. Don't play games and get someone hurt because you're afraid. You know I won't hurt you. You came into my bedroom at night. In the dark. Alone. You forgot to change your perfume, but I'd know both scents anywhere."

She closed her eyes and allowed her head to fall back against the door. It was him. She'd been right all along. He had saved her life tonight. She owed him thanks, but the words just refused to come. He was too close, his body too hot. The air still pulsated with danger, and suddenly she wasn't altogether sure why she'd come to his room alone at night. She had told herself she wanted a confrontation, that she intended to lay down the law to him, but she didn't need to do that in his bedroom.

Lissa had suppressed her own passionate nature for so long she hardly recognized the well deep inside that was already waking. Coming back to life. There was no stopping it now. For so long she refused to operate on any level but calm and peaceful, with little or no emotion, and she'd almost convinced herself that that was who she was. Now, the real Lissa was back with a vengeance. One couldn't have hair the color of hers without having the passion to go with it.

"Tell me your name," she whispered.

His tongue touched the soft skin behind her ear. His lips followed. The touch was light. Barely there. But she was branded. That soft stroke sank deep into her bone, sent little darts of fire streaking through her bloodstream.

"Casimir Prakenskii."

"You left the book behind for me to find. You did that on purpose knowing I'd know exactly who you were. What changed? Why are you doing this?"

"Because you're mine. You belong to me, and I'm taking what's mine."

Her heart stuttered in her chest. Simultaneously her stomach flipped and her sex spasmed. Went damp. Wanted him. She tried to make herself smaller, shrinking back against the solid door without appearing to do so. She couldn't think clearly with him so close. And he was close. The more she pressed her body into the door, giving ground, the more ground he took.

"You didn't feel that way a few hours ago," she pointed out. Why in the world didn't she just knee him and run for her life instead of standing there like a ninny waiting for something huge to happen? Something irrevocable that she could never take back?

She hadn't allowed herself to come alive, to be a woman. Not once. Not ever. She didn't make mistakes like that. She didn't dare. Her life was one of playing a role, and that meant she couldn't ever get close to anyone. Her sisters—were different. Still, they didn't know who she was. They couldn't know. To protect them. To protect herself. So she could have them, have some semblance of a family. People to love her the way she could love them. Fierce. Loyal. Still, they didn't know her.

The temptation of his heat was unbearable. She was pure fire—bound to that element—and she responded to heat. To fire. She tried to suppress her nature, but it was already loose, already answering him. Her body, of its own accord, went soft and pliant. She felt the rush in her veins, like an addicting drug. Fiery passion burned at her deepest core, and now, with one touch of his tongue, the whisper of his lips against her skin and his body close, he'd opened the cage and allowed her true nature freedom.

"You met with Ivan Belsky. There would only be one reason for you to do that, Lissa. You're planning on killing Uri and Kostya Sorbacov. Don't bother to deny it. Gavriil made me suspicious, but I didn't really believe it. Not after I laid eyes on you. Not when I flew all those miles with you. I established my cover here and then traveled to Sea Haven to meet with my brothers."

She stiffened. Her free hand went to his chest with the idea that she'd move him back, away from her, but the moment she touched him, she knew it was a terrible mistake. He had no shirt on, his chest bare. His body was inflexible. No give whatsoever. All male. All muscle. Hot as hell. So hot her palm seemed to melt right into his chest. Her breath slammed out of her lungs, leaving her burning for air. Raw with need.

She couldn't see his chest, not really. But she could feel it, his skin so hot. So tough. Her hand could feel his muscles, defined and rippling subtly beneath his skin, like a tiger, still, but coiled and ready to leap on her and tear her to shreds. She could move her hand. It was madness to leave it there, because he was more than a tiger, or a jungle cat, he was at the very top of the food chain and he was hunting. She knew he'd set his sights on her—he'd admitted it. He'd set a trap with that book and she'd stupidly walked right into it.

Lissa moistened her lips and tried to stay on target. "You met with your brothers?" She knew he had six brothers. All trained in the same way he'd been trained. An assassin, a product of those brutal schools no one ever talked about. No one wanted to admit they had ever existed. So much so, that Sorbacov, both father and son, wanted to make certain the existence of those schools never saw the light of day. They had put out a hit on all their graduates, men and women who had served them and were now considered disposable.

It hurt that his brothers would hold a secret meeting about her, that Gavriil would betray a confidence. She considered them family, at least the ones who lived on the farm. Lev, Rikki's husband, in particular. He'd been there the longest, and she'd spent quite a lot of time in his company. They both had worked with her other sisters on self-defense. It had taken a lot of discipline to keep Lev from knowing she was far better than she let on. Still, she had developed genuine affection for him.

"Gavriil was worried, I could tell. The others just wanted you safe, they have no idea who you really are. I'm certain Gavriil knew, but he just told me that I was to stick with you, no matter where that led. He didn't come out and say you might go after the Sorbacovs, but he alluded to the fact that he was a little worried, that you were a fire element and unpredictable. He said you were very close to Lexi and now that he was there on the farm as a Prakenskii, you knew that Uri Sorbacov would send anyone he could after him and the others. He also was afraid Uri would use you to get at our family. He would know you meant something to us. We protected one another in the schools by allowing them to torture us to keep the others alive; of course he'd know we'd do the same for you."

She lifted her chin. "Essentially, he told you enough that you could figure out my past. You know that my parents were murdered." Her voice was barely above a whisper. Her chest felt tight, as if it was impossible to breathe. The burn behind her eyes surprised her, as did the sudden clogging in her throat. She hadn't allowed herself to think about her parents and that terrible day in a very long time and now, over and over, that door seemed to creak open.

Casimir's hand, anchored in her hair, slid lower. His palm curled around her throat as if feeling her pulse beating there. Warm. Bringing fire to her skin. To the nerve endings so her body couldn't settle—didn't have time to do anything but react to his touch.

"My parents were murdered as well. My family was torn apart," Casimir reminded, his gentleness disarming. "I know what it feels like to need to bring those who committed those crimes to justice. My brothers, Viktor and Gavriil, hunted down the men who had been there that night, the ones following Kostya Sorbacov's orders. It took them a long time, years, to find out which ones pulled the triggers, but in the end, they killed every one of them. Only Kostya remains. None of my brothers could get near him. They're too well known."

She knew then. There was no getting air. No getting her breath back. "You become different people. You were that horrible man on the plane, bugging me every time I turned around just for your own amusement."

Above her head, he nodded.

Her lungs burned. Felt raw. "You were Tomasso and then the man in the cappuccino bar and now you're someone else. You're planning on going after them both. To keep your brothers safe. That's why, when you had the chance, you didn't put your mark on me."

She knew all about that claiming mark. She'd seen her sisters rubbing their palms. She knew they each could press their thumb into that mark and call their man to them. They belonged. They were cherished. They were loved. She wanted that and yet . . . She didn't have the personality needed to be with a man that dominant. The Prakenskii brothers, each and every one of them, were extremely dominant men. Total alphas. How could they not be, trained in the schools to become essentially weapons?

She had secrets just as all of her sisters did, but hers were dark and ugly. "I need to breathe and I can't with you this close," she said, uncaring that she revealed too much to him. She didn't know what she was going to do, but if she didn't get air, she might faint, right there, at his feet.

His hand didn't loosen from around her throat. His thumb brushed her chin and then lifted it. Easily. She was very short in comparison to him. He tilted her head at an angle that forced her to look into his eyes. His eyes were startling mercury. Silver. The only other person she'd ever seen with eyes like that had been his youngest brother, Ilya. It was no wonder he wore tinted contacts all the time. Those eyes were memorable. Totally rare. Eyes that left a woman weak. He had scars on his face. Lines of silver in his hair where the scars continued. She sucked in her breath, wondering how those faint white lines got there.

He stared down at her for what seemed an eternity. He bent his head slightly toward hers. She found herself wanting to go up on her tiptoes, to cover those last few inches, but she locked the soles of her feet firmly to the ground. She wasn't going to get in any deeper.

"I really can't breathe," she whispered again. Hoping he'd let her go. She couldn't make that move herself, so he was going to have to come to her aid.

"I'll have to breathe for both of us," he said gently. Softly. His voice a stroke of velvet, caressing her skin.

His lips touched hers. Just touched. Rubbed. Softly. Barely there. Her bottom lip. Her top lip. His tongue outlined both. Traced the curve of her lips and then along the seam. "I had a lot of hours on that plane to stare at your lips. I memorized the shape of them. I dreamt of them. Fantasized about them."

When he whispered the words to her, his lips brushed against hers, sending a million darts of fire streaking through her body straight to the very feminine core of her. She felt each one strike, igniting more and more of that terrible need growing in her.

"Open for me."

"No." She whispered the denial. She needed to stay strong. If she didn't, if she opened her mouth to him, she'd be lost.

Casimir was so hot. His mouth would be hotter. The fire inside would break free and she wouldn't be able to rein it in ever again. Not with this man. He would own her. He would. She knew it just by standing there. He didn't have to touch her or kiss her. She felt him around her. In her. His passion called to hers. The wildness in him, buried deep, suppressed just as the fire in her was suppressed, called to her.

"Yes." His mouth moved over her face, lips tracing her jaw, her cheekbone, her eyes, moving back to her lips.

He was gentle. Patient. Persistent. He knew she was already lost. He knew. She saw the knowledge in his eyes. The possession there. The absolute resolve.

"I can't, Casimir." She didn't sound determined or sure, she sounded pleading. More, with her head tilted this way, she could see the hunger in his eyes—for her. No one had ever looked at her with precisely that look. She was melting for him, and that wasn't a good thing at all.

His tongue teased the seam of her lips, his lips, firm and hot and very, very tempting teased at hers. "Open for me, *malyshka*."

"Not I won't. I can't. There's a difference." She tried reason. Her brain screamed at her to push him away. This was self-preservation. Self-preservation was strong in her. She had duties. So many of them. She had taken a vow with her uncle when she was just a little girl. She'd kept that vow. It didn't include having a man or a family. It meant, ultimately, she would probably die. But until she did, she had to stick to her absolute purpose.

"Golubushka," he murmured against her mouth. "You can. You will. I have waited a very long time and I never thought I could have you. Now, even if it is for a brief moment before we both die trying to save those we love, you have to give yourself to me."

He couldn't have said anything else that would induce her to let him have her. He intimated they would be partners. That he understood her vow. That he would never try to stop her from carrying out her plans.

Just this once, just this moment, she could have him for herself. She could be a woman. Real. Allow her fire to burn with his. She could let down her guard and just be herself. She opened her mouth before she talked herself out of it.

His tongue swept in and swept her away. There was no way to think, only feel. He kissed like he did everything. Sure. Confident. Perfect. Hot. So hot she knew she was melting, and it didn't even matter. She wanted to melt into him. Skin to skin. She didn't care if she paid the price later on. Right then, his mouth was all that mattered to her. All she focused on.

Hot lava poured into her veins, and melted her insides. Her legs went weak. He angled her face, poured himself down her throat. Took her breath, gave her his own. He was sweet and gentle and then rough and demanding. Coaxing. Commanding. He kept her wanting more. Needing more. He allowed her to come up for air and then she didn't know if she initiated another kiss, or if he did. She only knew she was lost in him. In pure feeling. So good. So perfect. Better than anything she'd ever imagined or dreamt.

His hands slid down her back to her bottom, shaping, kneading, pulling her up and into him. She wanted to be closer. Wanted to be skin to skin. He had no shirt, but she was fully clothed. Would it be so wrong to take this night? Flames burned through her body, settled low and sinful. She didn't know him, yet she did. She recognized him. She *saw* him. Casimir Prakenskii. She probably saw him better than he saw himself.

She hoped he saw her. She was Lissa Piner now, and she thought of herself as Lissa, but she wanted him to see the woman she really was. Giacinta Abbracciabene. Passionate. Needy. Greedy even. For him. For his body. For recognition that that woman existed.

His hands moved on her, sliding up her spine, under her blouse, slipping the material up over her head, tossing it aside. "I have to touch you."

She knew what that felt like, having to touch him. She had her hand back now that he'd moved her closer to him, imprinting her body onto his. She was free to explore, to run her hands over his chest, to feel the heavy muscles, ropes of them on his arms and shoulders, yet his body was still lean enough to have that amazing definition that allowed him to assume any build he chose.

She wasn't surprised that he didn't have tattoos. Those marks would be identifiable and he couldn't afford to be identified. His fingers made short work of her bra, and he slid it from her body, tossing it aside with her blouse. His mouth took hers again, a little rougher, almost fierce. She could taste possession. She could taste the male in him demanding she surrender.

She could do that—surrender herself to him for this one night. Whatever happened after, she'd have this. She never expected to have it. Such a gift. He obviously knew what he was doing, and she was ready to follow wherever he led.

He tugged her lower lip between his teeth. Bit down gently, just enough that she felt the little bite of pain flashing through her, and then his tongue was there. Soft velvet fire, teasing and stroking. He nibbled his way down her chin to her jaw, using the edge of his teeth and then his tongue. She had never considered that anything like that would be hot, but it was. So hot, she knew in another minute he was going to have to hold her up.

His hands slid around her back to her sides, shaping her waist, then sliding up her rib cage to settle at the sides of her breasts as if memorizing the very shape of her. She had no idea she could be so sensitive, but she was aware of his every touch, like a fiery brand, burning into her skin. His mouth was even hotter as he kissed his way down to the upper swell of her breasts. His thumbs moved, brushing her nipples, and she nearly jumped out of her skin. Cried out.

Chaos reigned in her mind. Pleasure ruled. She reached up to cradle his head in her arms, loving the way his spiky hair felt against her skin. Keeping her eyes open to watch as his mouth moved over her breasts, sucking at her very sensitive skin, scraping with his teeth, soothing with his tongue. She could see small strawberries left behind in his wake, but her body was on fire. It was all she could do to watch such an erotic sight and not scream for more.

She heard her own panting lungs, the ragged breathing she couldn't control. Her body didn't feel like her own, it belonged to him. She couldn't take her eyes from the sight of him feasting on her breasts. Her nipples ached. Hurt. Needed. The hunger in her was so sharp, so terrible, she gripped his hair in her fist and thought to push him toward the straining twin peaks. She couldn't. She could only cling. Her pulse pounded in her clit. Slick heat gathered so that her panties went damp. Her heart hammered. She moistened her lips with her tongue. Waiting. She thought she might die with the wait. His mouth kept moving, following the path she wanted him to take, but slow, far too slow.

Then he was there. His tongue lapped at her nipple and fire streaked. Raged. Flames rushed through her blood-stream, hitting her core like a fireball. She gasped. Cried out. His mouth closed over her breast, drew her nipple into the scalding, moist cavern, flattening the hard peak against the roof of his mouth. He suckled. Her knees buckled. She was forced to hang on to him or fall.

"I can't stand up," she admitted, gasping the truth when she wanted to scream with pleasure.

Casimir spent a good deal of time being a lover. He was expert at it. He could be anyone and easily became whatever his mark was looking for. Whatever they needed. He had complete command of his body at all times. He was that disciplined. He'd learned that discipline in a very hard, bru-tal school, but that had served him well over the years. His body never spun out of control. His cock never went hard and hot and aching, so painful he thought he might burst, not like now. Never without consent. Until now.

He'd lost that control somewhere in the hours on that plane, somewhere over the Atlantic Ocean. He'd been into his role, deliberately, for his own amusement, annoying her, getting under her skin, and somehow, she'd gotten under his with her soft-spoken kindness. His body forgot those long hours of harsh lessons and spun out of control. By the time they'd reached Italy, he was a walking hard-on, something he hadn't experienced since he was a boy.

In his youth, before he realized there was no escaping the life monsters had chosen for him, he dreamt of a woman of his own. Fiery. Passionate. Oddly enough, a flaming redhead. Lissa was definitely everything he'd ever dreamt of. She'd been so calm on the plane with all of his taunting, but he'd seen the fire in her. Caught glimpses of it. She would catch fire fast, burn hotter than any volcano and come apart for him.

Her skin was softer than he thought possible. He'd managed twice on the plane to get into her space enough to feel the satin under his fingertips. Any more than twice and he would have totally creeped her out. She wasn't a woman to be trifled with. The heat in her eyes warned him so he'd resisted touching her. Now, he couldn't get enough of sliding his hands over her narrow rib cage to cup her breasts while he fed.

She was sensitive. Very sensitive. He took every advantage of that. His body might not be in his complete control, but he had enough experience to know when a woman liked something and when she loved it. Especially when something drove her out of her mind with pleasure.

He wanted her hands on him. His cock was so full he was afraid he'd burst with the urgent, demanding hunger roaring through him, but he couldn't rush this. Couldn't let his own need make him lose sight of what was most important. She had kissed him back, her kisses better than anything he'd ever experienced because she was kissing *him*, Casimir Prakenskii, not one of his many aliases. She knew who he was and she wanted him, not one of them. He might not know who he was, but everything he knew about himself was definitely hers. All of him. What there was left of him. It might be miniscule, but the real man was there somewhere, and that man belonged to this woman.

He hadn't realized just how far gone he was. A man could only live so long in the shadows without an identity before the darkness consumed him. He'd made up his mind to try his hand at killing the Sorbacovs, both father and son. He knew they would be expecting those from the school to come after them, and they would be waiting. Kostya Sorbacov knew each of those students and what they were capable of. He would be looking for the master of disguises and suspicious of every man coming near them. Casimir didn't expect to come out of the encounter alive, but he was fairly certain he could kill at least one, if not both of his targets.

Holding Lissa in his arms, his hands moving over her soft skin, his cock pressed tight against her body, his mouth on her breast, touched something deep in him, something he hadn't known existed. She was like the sun itself. Hot and bright, burning for him. Giving him that light when he needed it the most—when he was all but lost. Her breathy little moans filled his ears. Music. Beautiful. Filling his soul.

He wasn't a poetry kind of man. He'd skipped the lesson on hearts and flowers, but there it was. He needed her to see him. To want him. He needed her like he needed air just to breathe. All along he'd been swallowed by the shadows, but somehow, she found him and her bright light burst over him.

He kissed his way back up the slope of her breast, her throat, nibbled on her chin and took her mouth again, needing to catch one of those soft little moans and swallow it. Her mouth was like velvet, but so hot he thought he might burn there forever. Her nails bit into his shoulders, scored down his back, and she went a little wild against him. He loved that no one else had kissed her. He knew they hadn't the moment her tongue danced so shyly with his. She was only for him. Made for him. Her body's reaction was real. For him. He loved that. Needed it like a man starving.

She shuddered. Trembled. He deepened the kiss and slowly began to walk her backward toward his bed. He wanted to take her against the wall, right there, or the floor, anywhere at all, but this first time had to be the bed and he had to find it in him to be gentle. To keep the brutal need, so stark and raw, from swallowing them both alive.

"Unbutton my jeans," he ordered against her mouth. He didn't stop kissing her. He couldn't. He was fairly certain if someone were stupid enough to walk in on them and stop him, their life would be in danger. He needed. It felt good to need. The vicious ache in his cock felt good because it was *real*. More, even better, she wiped away the long years of emptiness, the dark, ugly memories of living day to day in other roles with the sole purpose of killing. She took all of that away and replaced that darkness with her fire. With her skin, and the hot pleasure of her mouth. The promise of paradise in her body. *Real* paradise. Not the unemotional detachment and discipline his body was forced to perform when touching a woman.

Her hands didn't just drop from his shoulders, she moved them down his body, branding him with her touch. Little flames seemed to dance over him. The room temperature went up along with the heat centering in his cock. His heavy erection pressed so tight against his jeans he was afraid the material would burst—or melt.

Her palms continued down his body, gliding over his skin, lingering until he wanted to take command, but at the same time, with her feeding his natural hunger, the craving and anticipation grew in him, and he loved that. Loved he could feel so intensely. Her hands dropped to the waistband of his jeans riding low on his hips. She didn't fumble, but she did tremble. Emotion burst through him. A desire to protect her. To hold her to him and keep her safe from everything and everyone—even him.

He took a deep, shuddering breath and dropped his hands over hers. "Giacinta."

She looked up at him with her incredible blue eyes. He tried not to fall. Not to drown in all that blue. "I'm Lissa now. My sisters don't know me as Giacinta. I haven't told them yet, but if I get back to them, I will."

He nodded. Understanding. "In this bedroom, I'm Casimir and you're Giacinta. We have to be real. And you have to know what I am. The things I've done. Not once, but many, many times."

She continued to look up at him for a very long moment.

An eternity while time stood still for him. His blood thundered in his ears. Need pulsed in his cock. His entire being centered on her. Her lips began a slow curve. She ducked her head. Shook it. Her hands, beneath his, began to work on the buttons of his jeans, slowly, one by one, with his hands covering hers, opening them.

"Do you know what I've done, Casimir? You were there today, with Belsky. You knew I was there playing my role of Patrice Lungren. Patrice is still me when she goes after targets."

His jeans were open and her hands went to the waistband. Inside. Palms against his bare skin, thumbs hooked in the band. Her head tipped back and she looked up at him. Shyness, yes. Fear, no. She began to slowly divest him of his jeans and underwear. Her hands slid over his hips, down his thighs. She crouched, taking them lower to his ankles. He dropped a hand on her shoulder and lifted one leg at a time until he was stark naked, and his cock was harder and fuller than it had ever been.

She stood up, slowly, her hands on either side of his thighs, burning a brand there while her eyes locked on his cock. She stared at the length and thickness of his erection. She was close enough that he felt her breasts skimming against him. Hard little points that beckoned. Soft, lush curves that he craved to get his mouth around. His tongue on. His teeth. She was short enough that when she bent her head, he felt the breath of her on his broad, velvet crown. Small droplets leaked out. Her tongue swept the full curve of her lower lip.

Instantly every fantasy he'd ever had about her mouth flooded his mind. His cock jerked. As if mesmerized, her hands moved up his thighs, gliding over the muscles there, claiming him before they moved inward, cupping his heavy sac. His breath left his lungs in a rush. His mind slipped further into chaos. Into need. Into a place he'd never experienced. A fire roared. Threatened to break free and run wild.

He didn't stop her. He couldn't do that. He didn't have that kind of strength, when he'd been so certain he was stronger than any man alive, other, perhaps, than his brothers. He'd been sure he was more disciplined, had more control. All that was swept away by her small, delicate hands and her touch that burned through skin, straight to bone.

"You have to know what you're doing, Lissa. We do this, you give yourself to me, there's no taking it back. Not once it's done. You have to understand that. I get this, you hand it to me, you can't just take it away."

Her hands moved over his balls, so gently, reverently, as if she were memorizing the shape and feel of them. He could only see the top of her head as she bent to examine that part of him.

"You know neither of us has much time, Casimir. If we were always meant to be together, and I've seen that bond between your brothers and my sisters, then we deserve this night and any other nights we manage to get in before we make our try."

The heat of her breath was on his cock. Fiery hot. Scorching him. Her fingers rolled and kneaded for a moment and then her breath was there—right the hell on his balls—and he felt the first tentative touch of her tongue. This time his breath exploded from his body. His entire world narrowed to his balls and cock. There was nothing else but that part of his anatomy.

She licked over him. Like an ice cream cone. Clearly tasting him. Very gently she sucked at the tender flesh of his balls and then rolled them again before her tongue took a leisurely foray up his shaft. One hand still cupped his balls, but the other went exploring right behind her tongue, her palm sliding up his length and teasing the underside of his flared crown.

He threw back his head, trying not to roar with need. His hand cupped the back of her head, desperate to push her head down, to feel the velvet heat of her mouth surrounding him, but he knew better. His control wasn't in shreds yet, although she was fast bringing him closer to that edge.

He was aware of the way she massaged his balls, sending streaks of fire racing through his groin while her tongue continued exploring. She licked the droplets off of him, one fist closing around his shaft at the base. He knew she wasn't experienced, but the intensity of her investigation coupled with her obvious enjoyment sent his senses reeling. She made him feel more than he'd ever felt before with any of the experienced women he had deliberately seduced.

Casimir drew his hand down the length of her silky hair, fingers weaving and sifting, trying to distract himself enough from the fire spreading through his groin, from the need to have her mouth take him deep. She didn't. She used her tongue to get to know his size and shape, but denied him that one thing he craved.

"Are you afraid, Lissa?" His voice wasn't his own. He sounded husky, almost hoarse. His cock raged at him. At her. With needs all its own. Needs he had never felt before, not like this. Not real. Not without him forcing his mind to go there, thinking to pleasure a woman to get the information he needed.

Lissa wasn't looking to be pleasured by him. She made it clear she was giving him pleasure. That she wanted to know every inch of him. His thighs. His balls. His cock. She'd showed attention to his chest, his back and shoulders. She was exploring, taking her time about it, trusting him to let her do what she was comfortable with. But she was killing him slowly.

"*Golubushka*, tell me if you're afraid of this."

"No. I want to get to know every inch of you. I want to claim you. I know once I'm on that bed with you, you'll take over, and that's a good thing. I want that. But I need to do this for me. I'm trying to tell you something about me. About us. About what is important to me, and this is the only way I know to do it."

She didn't lift her head, but her gaze met his and once again that pure blue drew him into her. She wasn't pleading. Lissa Piner didn't plead. She wanted. Him. She was making that clear. Staking her own claim in her own way. She was claiming every inch of him, making him hers, branding him. His woman might be shy about this, but she wasn't afraid and she had confidence in them together.

He caught one hand and drew it beneath his balls, pressing her finger against that soft spot between his balls and anus, the one that could bring a man a great deal of pleasure just by stroking. He showed her and then brought his own hand back to her bare skin. Stroking caresses as her finger and mouth drove him mad.

His palm itched, the burn in the center reminding him that she belonged to him. That once he marked her, nothing could come between them. His mark would create a pathway between their minds. The silk of her hair brushed against the mark, and he felt it as if her tongue had glided over him, leaving behind a trail of fire.

"Give me this, Casimir, and then we do everything your way. I truly want that, but I need this." She didn't stop stroking him. Learning what pleased him that fast.

Her breath was hot now, bathing the velvet crown of his cock in scorching flame. His hips moved convulsively, thrusting toward that heat, and to his shock, her lips parted and she took him in. Her mouth was scalding. Soft. Moist. Everything and more than he'd fantasized over. Fingernails raked down his thigh and then around to his buttocks. She cupped him, drew his hips toward her, her fist tightening around the base of his cock as her tongue swirled over the crown, catching every leaking drop.

He was large. He knew that. In some cases it was a good thing. When it came to being in that hot, sacred mouth, that paradise he'd unconsciously sought his entire life, maybe not so much. He wanted all the way in. *All* the way. He wanted to bury himself deep, feel his balls against her delicate chin, the head of him with her throat squeezing around him. He wanted it all. He stayed in control, but just barely, he was losing it fast. She shredded it with her mouth and fingers so easily.

She used her tongue and then sucked him deeper. An inch. Cautious. Still exploring.

"Lissa, I have to tell you the truth here. You're done with claiming. I'm branded. Yours. No one else. You alone. I'm not going to be able to take much more, so let's move this to the bed." He meant it. He was more than about done, he was already gone. His icy, rigid control had melted under the siege of her fiery mouth and he had to end this before he began thrusting deep and scared the hell out of her.

5

LISSA tilted her head back, but she didn't release Casimir's cock. The head was so soft, like velvet, broad and flared, and he tasted delicious. Salty, but unique. She couldn't quite figure out how when everything she'd read told her some women didn't like the taste. Maybe the taste varied from man to man, but whatever, she wasn't letting Casimir take over until she was done. And she wasn't done.

She looked up at him and drew him a little deeper. Suckled. Watched his eyes grow even darker with lust. He liked what she was doing. She might not know exactly what to do, but her instincts and all the books she'd read gave her a few clues. Lust mixed with emotions she couldn't name blazed in the shocking silver of his eyes. She loved that look. That passion she'd kept locked up for so long answered that look. She felt it rise in her even more.

She loved the taste and shape of him. The steel spike under all that soft skin. She loved to run her tongue along that throbbing vein and tease the underside of the head with her tongue so she could feel him pulse hotly in her mouth. She really loved the way his fingers curled in her hair, forming two tight fists while he held her head in position without forcing it down over him. She loved that his hips seemed to thrust without his consent. Shallow, but with enough insistence that she knew he could take over at any moment, but he chose not to.

Staring into his eyes, she sucked him deeper, sliding her mouth around him, getting used to his girth. It wasn't easy, but Lissa never backed down when she wanted something, and seeing the look in his eyes, feeling the nearly helpless movement of his hips, she wanted this more than she wanted most things. For herself. For him. Because neither one of them ever had anything real. For her, this was the real woman giving something to the real man. She wanted him to understand that. This was for Casimir Prakenskii and not one of the many roles he played.

The silver in his eyes went molten. His face darkened. The lust grew stronger, but so did those emotions. She'd touched the real man, not the fake ones, and she knew it. Reveled in it. He didn't pull away from her, but tightened his hold in her hair.

"Get the shaft very wet, *golubushka*, use your tongue and saliva. That will help." He removed one hand from her hair to wrap around her fist, showing her the movement. "Keep your mouth tight as you work my cock, but Lissa, I'm not coming in your mouth or on you, not this time, I want inside you, so when I say to stop, I want you to stop."

There was steel in his voice. His will was steel. She wanted to smile around the length and girth of him because he didn't yet know that there was steel in her. She gave in because she wanted to, never because someone forced her to. He'd been forged in the fires of hell, but in a way, so had she. They matched. She knew that. She hadn't wanted or expected to feel for him like she did. She hadn't known it was possible to forge a bond so strong so fast when she knew next to nothing about him. Still, it was there. And she was giving them both a gift. Making them both real people, not the fake roles they normally lived their lives in.

She followed his instructions, using her tongue, her saliva, to spread moisture up and down his hard shaft. Her fist followed and then she took him into her mouth again. She loved having him there. Owning him. She did own him like this. He gave himself up to her and she had all the power in those heady moments.

She suckled, hollowed her cheeks, and each time she slid her mouth down over him in time to the rhythm of her fist, she took him deeper. Her jaws became used to the width of him while her mouth loved the feel and taste of him. His hand left hers to resume the fist in her hair and suddenly everything changed.

His hands took control of her head, forcing her a little lower. She would have gone on her own, but he didn't wait that half second and the action surprised her. She nearly lost the rhythm, but he didn't push her down too far and she tightened her mouth, hearing him groan. The sound was amazing. Perfect. Real. The feel of him in her mouth was real.

He took over the pace, making it a little faster, going a little deeper, his hips taking control when he held her head there.

"Harder, Lissa. Suck harder." His eyes closed for a brief moment and then he had to see that beautiful, incredible sight. Her fantasy lips wrapped around his cock, her eyes caressing him as her mouth pleasured him. *"Chertovski krasivaya,"* he swore in Russian, his voice guttural. "That's it, *malyshka*, that's perfect."

She kept her gaze fixed on his. The look in his eyes sent red-hot streaks straight to her core. Her temperature soared along with her need. The more drops spilled into her mouth, the more she craved. Mostly, she craved that look. She knew she was giving him something he'd never had before. Women had most definitely sucked his cock for him, she wasn't his

78 Christine Feehan

first, but from the genuine look on his face, she knew this was the first real time. His reaction to her wasn't a practiced art. It was all real. As his hips thrust, she took him deeper, feeling the solid length of him, not coming close to all of him, but he touched the back of her throat and was gone. She didn't want him to go. She used her tongue, curling and dancing, flattening it to stroke hard and then sucking even harder, trying to relax enough to take him deeper.

Abruptly, his hands gripped her with a fierce determination and he forced her head up and off of him. She heard herself moan softly, not wanting to let go. "I wasn't finished," she pointed out. "You taste so good, Casimir. I think I'm already addicted."

Casimir walked her backward until her knees hit the bed. All the while she kept her fist wrapped tight around his cock, and the action nearly sent him over the edge. He had never been this close to the edge of his control.

"This is mine," she said, her chin going up in a challenge. "You're taking away something that belongs to me."

"Temporarily," he said. "I'm only taking it away temporarily." He could make his home there in her mouth. She was beautiful. Defiant. Challenging him. He loved a good challenge, and his woman was about to see what he was capable of. "I want to eat you up. Devour you. Like honey. Like candy. You had your fun and now it's my turn."

Lust consumed him. Emotions he hadn't known himself capable of. For the first time in his life, he knew exactly who he was. Casimir Prakenskii was a real man and he had his woman there with him, wiping out every ugly thing in his past. Making him whole again. Filling that emptiness in him with her gift.

His body burned for hers. His mouth watered for the taste of her. His palms itched—both of them, needing her soft skin under them. Even his fingertips pulsed with a terrible ache. His cock raged at him. *Raged*. Genuine and hungry. That need so elemental, so primitive he felt savage. He told himself to go slow, that this time had to be for her. An assault on her senses, building her need until it was every bit as brutal as his own. He wanted this time to be perfect for her, and he had the feeling that stretching her so he could fit would take a little finessing. Still, she was made for him or his mark wouldn't be there, ready to be branded deep into her cells.

His body shuddered with need. He caught at her small waist and tugged her to him, bending his head so he could take her mouth with his. He wasn't as gentle as he'd been the first time, kissing her over and over, making demands, giving himself up to her fire, allowing it to pour down his throat straight to his heart like red-hot magma.

He knew what he was doing taking her inside like that. Letting that slow, thick lava fill every hole, every gap, seal his emptiness with her. He did so willingly. Let her enslave him. Let her claim him. Because he had every intention of doing the same with her. She owned his cock. She also owned the rest of him. He didn't care how it happened; he was grateful it *could* happen. He had forgotten how to feel, and now emotions were there, genuine, overwhelming him.

He took her mouth gently this time, tender even. "I need to know if you're on birth control. If you're protected. I'm clean, I always make certain."

She swallowed hard, her fingers still claiming his heavy erection. She nodded to let him know she was safe.

He kissed her over and over and then let his mouth drift down her throat to the upper curves of her breasts. "You're going to have to give me back my cock while you take off your skirt, *golubushka*. I need your body."

He leaned into her, forcing her back to bend slightly so his hands held her up. At the same time, her breasts thrust upward invitingly. She had beautiful breasts, full and round, high above her narrow rib cage and small waist. Her hips flared out. She was toned, keeping herself in good shape, probably because of the work she did. Regardless, he reaped the benefits of her body.

"I don't think so."

He loved that she was reluctant to drop her hand away from him. Her thumb continued to make lazy circles on the broad crown while her fist pulled up and down in a long, leisurely slide that kept his erection rigid and aching with brutal need.

"You give me no choice but to tear it off you." He murmured the warning against her nipple. Licked. Felt her ragged breath. Kissed. Used his lips to brush back and forth. "I don't mind, honey, but if you love that skirt, I wouldn't want to mess it up for you. Don't forget the underwear if you want those as well." It was the only warning he would give her. His mouth settled over her breast, sucked hard, and he used the edge of his teeth for the first time to test her reaction to a bite of pain mixing with the pleasure.

She gasped. Cried out. Her blue eyes went hot with excitement. She pushed closer to him to thrust her breast more fully into his mouth. Offering him more. Yeah, his woman liked that.

She let loose of his shaft, one reluctant finger at a time to drop her hands to her skirt obediently. He moved between her breasts, feeding. Suckling. Using his tongue and teeth to drive her higher. The skirt pooled at her feet and she stepped out, kicking it aside. The moment she did, he took her down to the bed, flat on her back, coming down over top of her.

He didn't waste any time. He was more than hungry for her. He was starving. He *had* to have her. Taste her. Claim her the same way she'd claimed him. He kissed his way around her breasts, under them, testing her sensitivity there, leaving marks. Each time he did, he got the same response, that needy excitement at the wicked touch of his teeth.

His tongue traced her ribs and then the muscles in her

belly, dipped into her belly button and lingered there. He bit her flat stomach, held her down with one hand and used his tongue along the crease of her hip bone and then to the vee of fiery curls at the junction of her legs. She kept herself neatly trimmed, a small strip of curls, just enough for him to nuzzle between lapping at either side of that soft little mound.

Her breathing turned ragged and she squirmed, her hips bucking, her head thrashing, telling him her entire body was sensitive to his touch. Her skin was softer than anything he'd ever felt, but hot, like the inside of her mouth. He knew when he got his cock inside of her she'd burn him up. Still, as much as he wanted to get there, he had to get his mouth on her. He had to stake that claim.

His hands went to her thighs and pulled them apart. Her gaze jumped to his face as he shifted to slide his body between her legs. He was a big man, much larger than she was, and he took some room, forcing her legs wide apart. He kept commanding hands on her as he looked into her eyes, telling her without words what he intended to do. What he wouldn't tolerate. She was giving him this because he needed to make a point, just as she'd given him something, making her point.

"Make me real," she whispered. "Whatever you have to do, Casimir, make me real and make me yours."

His heart actually stuttered in his chest. His cock jerked hard, spilled drops onto the sheets. He smiled, knowing he looked like a hungry wolf. Knowing he was going to devour her, push her so high she would need his cock filling her in order to assuage the burn. He lowered his head, his tongue swiping along her entrance, tasting her, bringing her honey and spice into his mouth. The taste of her burst through his senses, heightening his need, stripping him raw of everything he'd ever been before. She writhed, cried out, her legs trying to wrap him up as her fingers curled into the sheets.

Casimir kept his word to her. He ate her. Devoured her. Licked and suckled and extracted every bit of creamy honeyed liquid he could possibly get from her. He was ruthless, uncaring that she was new to this. He let his control slip more. Held her tighter, not allowing her hips to move an inch, holding her in place for his feast.

It had been all about her, making her slick enough, hot enough so her body would accept his. His good intentions had fallen by the wayside. The more aroused she became, the more addicted he was to her spice. The more he craved the taste of her. Not just her taste, but the need growing in her, coiling hot and bright for him. Only him. There was no ulterior motive for her to be with him. Only that she saw him. Recognized him. Knew exactly who he was and that she belonged to him.

He wanted his tongue to brand her. His teeth. He wanted his cock buried in her, causing skid marks, burning his brand inside her. It was a terrible, selfish need that rose in him, but he didn't care. He pushed her higher until her head thrashed, her breath came in ragged gasps and she moaned his name. Until she was sobbing and pleading for him to be inside her. Until she was nearly insane with arousal, with her need of him.

He pushed a finger into her. So tight. Burning hot. His cock jerked hard, swelled more. Wanting that. Needing that. He tried a second finger and found that was a very tight fit. He bent his head a second time and resumed his feast. He needed her so close, spiraling out of control, that she couldn't do anything other than allow him entrance.

"Casimir. Please. Oh, God, I can't even think. Please. Please. Please. Do something. Anything."

Her sobbing voice told him she was nearly there. He found her clit. Suckled. She screamed and muffled her mouth with her own hand, her body flying apart, rippling with life. He felt the explosion around his tongue and fingers, in the muscles of her belly and down her thighs. Instantly he shifted, lifting her bottom higher, going up on his knees, pulling her legs around him so he could lodge the head of his cock in her slick, burning entrance.

She kept moving, driving him wild. He had to clench his teeth, keep his control, pushing slowly but steadily into her scalding hot, tight depths. Her inner muscles closed around the sensitive head of his cock, trying to push him out, yet squeezing around him, holding him tighter than any fist possibly could.

"Relax for me, Giacinta. You're so tight it feels like paradise, but it's going to take some work to get this right. I don't want to hurt you."

"You *have* to be inside me. I need you in me right now, Casimir."

She tried for him. He could see her make the effort. Taking a breath. Forcing it out. He pushed forward as she took another breath.

"That's it. Open your eyes, *golubushka*. Look at me. Keep your eyes on mine." He could help her if she let him.

Lissa swallowed hard and forced her eyes to open. His face was purely carnal. Wholly sensual. Every line cut deep. His eyes liquid silver. His gaze held hers, captured her, giving her courage, so that she melted into him, giving herself to him. Letting him brand her his, knowing this moment changed her forever.

She was on fire. Burning from the inside out. She'd never known a person could be so stimulated, feel so much pleasure while needing so much more. Everything he did added to that burning need. The craving. She felt almost insane with arousal. She was used to the feeling of fire. The way it burned. The way it could make her crave more. But she had never felt anything like this before. Never.

Red-hot flames rushed over her body, her breasts, between her thighs, roaring with a life of its own so that it felt as if a fireball careened through her bloodstream and lodged deep inside her core, to burn out of control. His invasion was slow and steady, stretching, burning, impaling her on a red-hot brand, so thick she was certain she was going to die before he made his way inside.

She lifted her hips, wanting more, but frightened that if he gave her more she would come apart and never be put back together. She felt every inch of him as he pushed deeper into her body, her tight muscles reluctantly giving way under his steady insistence. She gasped for air. Burned. Writhed. Tried to get away. Tried to impale herself deeper. The feeling was brutal. Magnificent. Terrifying. Everything she'd ever wanted.

"Giacinta." He hissed her name between his teeth. Gave a soft groan that she felt in her deepest core. "You're so hot. Scorching hot."

His tone was harsh, and she could only stare helplessly up at his glittering, hooded eyes. The stamp of sensuality on his face only fed her hunger for him. He leaned forward, over her, pushing deeper, another inch stretching and burning, her muscles clamping hard, massaging, dragging him in, pushing him out. Allowing the invasion while she thrashed under him.

"Hold still, *malyshka*," he whispered, his voice no more than a groan. "Be still. Just relax."

There was no way to relax. She couldn't get air. She tried to keep her hips from bucking off the bed, but it was impossible with the fire burning her from the inside out. The slow movement of his body as he bent over her; drawing up her knees, forcing her thighs wider, his cock driving deeper, slowly and then stopping abruptly drove her wild.

His tongue brushed over her right nipple and lightning forked straight to her sex so that the walls of her sheath convulsed around him, holding tight. His lips kissed, his teeth tugged and then his mouth was around her soft breast, drawing it deep, his tongue working her nipple so that the whip of lightning became pure fire until she was certain she couldn't take the need consuming her one more moment.

There was a burst of pain and then he was fully seated in her. All the way. Every inch. She could feel him deep. Bumping her womb. A steel spike invading, taking her over, branding her from the inside out with his own particular fire—one she recognized. He was fire as well. Bound to the same element. The flames ran deep along with the passion. He had buried his true nature just as she had. Her body recognized his. They melted together, sharing skin. Sharing one body.

He moved again and a lash of flames burst over her. She suppressed a cry at the pleasure swamping her, and her muscles clamped down like a vise around his thick cock. His breath hissed out and his eyes burned right through her, claiming her. The lust there, the emotions swamped her. She wasn't certain she could live through wanting him. Just like this. The bite of pain, the searing pleasure. The man branding her just as she'd branded him.

"I can't hold on if you move. I've never lost control, Giacinta, but it's slipped so far away from me and I don't know if I can . . ."

"*Don't.* I don't want your control, Casimir. I want the real you. Let go. Let go with me." Lissa wanted him on any terms. She wanted the real man. The real body. Not the one his handlers had forced him to become, but the one under all those masks.

"You're not ready to handle that," he denied, his lips traveling to her chin to sink his teeth there, biting, nibbling, his tongue soothing the sting. "Don't move, *golubushka*," he ordered, his voice so harsh she winced. His hips ground against her, then retracted and plunged again.

She writhed under him. Bucked her hips. Wrapped her legs around him, driving her body up to his, watching his face, the lines carved so deep, the molten eyes igniting. She was wild, and she wanted him the same way. She wanted him to lose all that discipline and control drilled into him. *She* wanted to be the one to do that.

With a harsh groan, he shifted his body again, his hands at her hips, holding her, pinning her so that he could pound into her, burying himself deep. She cried out, shocked at the pleasure streaking through her. Shocked at his sudden fury. Hungry for more. Desperate for more.

"Please," she whispered. "Please, Casimir. Make me yours."

His gaze drifted possessively over her face. Devouring her. The look took her last breath, sent shivers through her body. He looked . . . ruthless. Implacable. So sensual she thought he was the epitome of the word.

He bent his head and took her mouth, so gently it turned her heart over, made it stutter in her chest. A million butterflies took wing in her stomach. The action of his body shifted his cock inside her, caressing her inside as he'd kissed her mouth. When he lifted his head, his gaze burning over her, her mouth continued to grow hot, just as her feminine sheath did. Scalding. Scorching. Hotter and hotter. She gave a low keening moan. The sound seemed to be a catalyst.

Casimir gripped her hips hard and plunged into her hard and fast. She felt the burning stretch along with a bite of pain mixing with a million other sensations driving her up higher. His hips took on a rhythm, a driving force, slamming into her, jolting her body, jolting her senses until she writhed and cried out, pleading, but for what, she wasn't certain.

Deep inside, the tension coiled tighter and tighter, flames burning through her, white-hot now. All the while his cock slammed home, filling her, stretching her, the friction so strong she thought she might burst into flames. Still he didn't stop, just gripped her tight and continued the merciless rhythm.

The tension continued to build in her, winding so tight, a harsh, desperate burn that refused to release, refused to ease. She whispered his name, fighting the fear that threatened to consume her right along with the pleasure that bordered on pain. He'd been right, she wasn't ready for this. She had no idea it could even be this way. So desperate inside. The endless, terrible pressure coiling tighter and tighter with no end in sight.

Her head wouldn't still, thrashing back and forth on the pillow. Her body writhed, fought, strained against his. That steel spike seemed to have grown, never stopping, never letting her catch her breath, driving deep, streaking fire through her with every stroke, pounding, while her body bathed his cock in hot moisture, yet the erotic pressure refused to ease even the tiniest bit.

She arched into him, needing more, always more, yet at the same time, fear built along with the brutal pressure. "Casimir." She whispered his name, uncertain if she was pleading for more or if she wanted him to stop. There was no controlling her body, her hips lifting to meet those brutal, magnificent strokes, needing this. Needing him filling her. Stretching her. Building the flames until it was a wildfire raging out of control, consuming them both—and it would consume them. She had no doubt and fear gripped her, every bit as strong as the terrible, relentless hunger.

"Don't fight me, Giacinta. Let go. Let yourself go."

She hadn't known until that moment that she was. "I'm afraid."

"I've got you. Trust me. Give yourself to me. All of you. I've got you."

His voice was harsh. Husky. Thick with a sensuality that shocked her. His eyes glittered like molten silver, moving over her face, commanding her. Soothing her. Claiming her. He didn't stop moving. If anything, he increased the fury of the strokes, impaling her over and over, a harsh, pounding rhythm that drove her into a frenzy of need. Of lust. The sensations were so strong, the pressure building, tension coiling, so that tendrils of fear burned as intensely as passion raged.

Casimir rose above her, his face a mask of pure carnal sensuality. Lissa heard the sound of their bodies coming together in a furious symphony. Her ragged breathing and pleading gasps punctuated each savage stroke as he slammed home, again and again. She heard herself, her cries rising in direct proportion to the firestorm building until the conflagration began to consume her.

He moved his body, a subtle difference, but the hot stroke of his cock created a searing, bursting friction directly over her clit and the fire roared through her. Fast. Wild. Wave after wave. Out of control. Her sheath came alive, gripping and milking, the orgasm rushed through her, spreading like a forest fire up to her stomach, to her breasts, down to her thighs, until she had to jam her fist in her mouth to muffle her scream of sheer pleasure.

Casimir buried his face in her neck, his teeth on her shoulder as his body erupted into hot jets of seed, filling her. She was scorching hot, squeezing him like a vise, taking every drop from him until he saw lights dancing behind his eyes. Never, not ever, had his release been like this. So good. Ecstasy. She took him to a place he hadn't known existed, and now that he did, he wanted to stay there.

He blanketed her body, knowing he was too heavy for her, but he liked her under him as he struggled for air. The feel of her silky skin melting under his was something he wasn't quite ready to give up. He nuzzled her neck. Inhaled the combined scent of both of them. Licked the small spot behind her ear and then left a trail of kisses along her delicate jaw to the corner of her mouth.

"You're beautiful. And you're mine." He allowed his Russian accent to emphasize his declaration. He felt her little gasp and eased his weight partially off of her, reluctantly allowing his body to release hers. "Are you all right?" He went to his side, staying over her, keeping her from moving. His hand swept down her body, from the side of her breast down along her rib cage and waist to shape the curve of her hip.

She looked up at his face. "I'm not sure. I could have died and you're just an illusion." Her soft mouth curved into a smile. "I admit, it was a great way to go. I'm still feeling it."

He slid his hand around her thigh until his palm was

inside, up close to the sweet junction between her legs. Her muscles still rippled and pulsed. He bent his head and pressed a kiss along the top of her breast. "In a minute I'll get a washcloth and take care of you, but I'm a little worn out."

She raised her eyebrow. "A Prakenskii? Worn out? What an admission."

Casimir knew she was struggling to figure out what she was supposed to do. She'd never taken a lover before. She hadn't given herself to anyone. She didn't trust. She avoided all relationships out of necessity. He knew, because it was the same for him. No woman had ever spent the night with him. He didn't sleep with others because he would be vulnerable in his sleep. Vulnerable equaled death in his world and in hers.

She started to slip out from under him, but the hand between her legs clamped down on her thigh. Her gaze jumped to his.

"We decided to do this thing, Giacinta. I'm not in it alone. I told you what to expect when you gave yourself to me. It was your choice. You don't get to take that decision back, not after that." He couldn't keep the harshness from his voice. She wasn't leaving his room. She wasn't leaving him. He didn't care if she felt vulnerable. He felt the same and she could just deal with it.

For the first time he saw indecision warring on her face. "I don't know what to do, Casimir. I really don't. I thought you'd want me to go to my own room. After. You know. After. I can't imagine you let other women stay with you."

"You aren't other women." He moved his hand from the warmth of her thighs to wrap his fingers around her wrist and draw her hand to him. "Lift up your palm."

Her breath caught in her throat. She tensed, curled her fingers into a tight fist and tried to pull her hand away. "No. I know what you're going to do and you can't."

"I have to. You're mine. You know you're mine. There

isn't going to be another woman." He leaned over her. Close. His mouth inches from hers. His gaze holding her captive. "Can you still feel me inside of you?"

"Yes." The admission was low.

"I can still feel you wrapped around me. Tight and hot, Giacinta. You're in my bones now. Inside me. That isn't going away for either one of us. Open your fingers."

She narrowed her eyes at him. "You get that I'm not a submissive woman, right? I don't let anyone tell me what to do."

"You get that I'm a dominant man, right?" he countered. "Being dominant doesn't mean I'm an asshole. I don't tell my woman to do something she doesn't want to do, and you want this every bit as much as I do. More, we need it. You're going after the man who betrayed your family . . ."

Her breath hissed out. "How do you know that? No one knows that."

"No one but you, me and your uncle," he corrected. "Open your fingers, Giacinta. I'm told this hurts for a moment, but then it's over and we're connected psychically. If I'm close, you can call me just by pressing your thumb into the middle of your palm. More, we can speak telepathically, which will help when we go after the man you need to kill and the Sorbacovs."

"You're going to be *so* annoying." She stilled her hand and allowed her palm to face him. "Just so you know, I can be equally as annoying."

"I don't doubt that for one minute." His grin flashed at her there in the dark.

His palm came up and he pushed air toward her and with it the energy rising like a tidal wave from his deepest core. She felt the zap like an electrical shock hit her palm and she cried out with surprise, while little sparks danced in the air between their open hands. She saw the mark, two intertwined circles blazing in the middle of her palm, fiery red and then golden before beginning to fade. Her skin itched all over her palm as the images faded. She could see the marks burned deep into his hand as well.

"I told my sisters I wouldn't let a Prakenskii claim me and now I'm a liar," she said with a little sigh. She pressed her head back into the pillows and smiled up at him. "I hope you know what we're doing, because I don't have a clue."

"We're going to find a way to come out of this alive. I hadn't planned on that when I made up my mind to take out the Sorbacovs, but now that I've found you, I have to figure it out." He brought her palm to the warm of his mouth and pressed a kiss into the faded image. "I'm sorry. I know that hurt. And I should have been more careful of your first time. I lost complete control."

She smiled at him, looking more temptress than angel. "I loved that you lost control, and I hope it happens many more times." She pulled his hand to her and pressed her own kiss over the mark. "I didn't have an exit plan either, not really. I didn't hold out much hope of survival, but the Sorbacovs put out a hit on the men in my family. I lost one family, I won't lose another."

"I'm good at what I do, *malyshka*. I've been in the business full-time. I know you're used to working solo. I am as well, but if we do this together, I think we have a much better chance of survival."

Lissa nodded slowly, her gaze turning thoughtful. Clearly, she accepted him already. It would be difficult for her to allow him to take the lead on accomplishing their goals, just as it would be for him to let her take the lead. It would take a little practice, learning to work together before they were ready to take on her first priority.

"Do you have everything you need to go after the man who betrayed your family?" Casimir kept his voice gentle. She had a difficult time talking about her family. Her body went tense and she avoided his eyes whenever the subject was brought up. He ran his hand up and down the curve of her bare hip soothingly.

"His name is Cosmos Agosto. He was young, just nineteen when my father hired him. He was really good-looking, at least to a six-year-old. My father and mother took him under their wing and made him a part of the family. I liked to spend time with him. He was really funny. He ate nearly every meal with us, and my parents really cared about him. If I wanted to play outside, if I was with him, none of the other men came with me, and I liked that. To this day, I'm uncomfortable with bodyguards."

"This man betrayed your family?" There was no way for Casimir to keep the menace from his voice. Loyalty was bred in him, deep in his bones. He hadn't seen his brothers more than once or twice in all the years that had gone by since Sorbacov's men had murdered his parents and the boys had been taken to the schools to train. Never once, in all that time, did he ever think of betraying his brothers. Not once. No matter what happened to him. He would endure whatever he had to in order to ensure their safety, even if that meant never seeing them again.

"Yes, he betrayed us all," she said, closing her eyes tight.

Casimir wrapped his arm around her waist and pulled her body tight against his, needing to shelter her from the pain he heard in her voice. He knew about memories and how one had to lock them away to preserve sanity. "You don't have to tell me, *golubushka*." He bent his head to hers and brushed kisses along her temple.

"I do. You have to understand why I wanted to find him even more than I wanted to get to Aldo Porcelli."

"What exactly happened between your family and the Porcelli family?" He continued to soothe her with caresses along her hip. He knew it would be difficult for her to open up and share the information with anyone, after keeping silent for so many years.

"I was a child, but I remember a man coming on to my mother, trying to insist she go home with him. We were at a friend's house, and he came in with a lot of other men. I wasn't paying much attention until the room went really quiet. I could tell my mother was upset. She wanted to go and this man kept grabbing her arm and stopping her. No one said anything to him, not even when she told him he was hurting her. We left fast. She told my father, and right away, he told her to pack, that we had to leave immediately."

"It was Aldo Porcelli, not the acting boss, that made the pass at your mother? Because Aldo only recently came into power. His father died of a heart attack two years ago, and he stepped into his father's shoes."

"I was the heart attack," Lissa said quietly.

"What about your uncle? Why didn't he take out the Porcelli family in addition to the dog handler? Why put that on your shoulders?"

6

LISSA took a deep breath. She was uncomfortable discussing her family's history while lying naked in a bed with a man she'd just allowed to do all sorts of things to her. "If we're going to have this conversation, I need to get cleaned up."

"Your uncle very politely included a Jacuzzi in the bathroom. We can run hot water and soak with the jets on," he offered, sliding out of the bed immediately and extending his hand to her.

She took it reluctantly, felt his fingers close around hers and instantly felt safe. He seemed to be able to do that to her. Whenever she had conflicting emotions, if his hand was on her, she seemed to feel much calmer. She let him pull her from the bed and onto her feet. It wasn't as if she had tons of experience standing naked in front of men, but again, with his fingers tight around hers, she didn't feel as strange as she thought she might.

"It's essential my uncle doesn't know or even think that we're in a relationship of any kind, even if it's just having sex."

He stopped so fast that she bumped into him and he had

to steady her. "Giacinta, I've had a lifetime of just sex, and what we did wasn't that."

She winced a little at the low, fierce note in his voice.

His fingers caught her chin in a firm grip, forcing her to meet his eyes. "I gave myself to you. The real me. I wanted to be gentle and tender and give you what you deserved, but with you, I lost control and that fire inside me I have to keep hidden at all times got loose. That doesn't mean what we did didn't mean anything."

"I know," she agreed instantly, giving him that. "I feel a little awkward, Casimir, because I don't know what I'm supposed to do."

He bent his head and skimmed his lips over hers. The light touch sent heat curling in the pit of her stomach and made her heart flutter. When he lifted his head, it was only a scant inch or two, leaving his silver eyes to pierce right through her, seeing too much. Seeing how vulnerable she felt.

"I just wanted to get that straight with you, Lissa. We're in this together."

She nodded her head, still very uneasy. She didn't know how to make him understand. He took them through to the bathroom and immediately turned on the dual faucets to fill the Jacuzzi. She wrapped her arms around herself, grateful he didn't turn on the overhead light. He snapped on a single nightlight that was plugged into the electrical outlet at the other end of the room.

"My uncle can't find out about us," she reiterated. "He would be upset. I don't honestly know what he'd do, but I don't want to chance anything going wrong."

"He won't find out. You can go back to your room before everyone wakes up. We both know where the cameras are and we can avoid them."

That was true. She could move all over the house and never be seen.

"Why didn't your uncle take care of the problem?"

Casimir persisted. "And more to the point, why did the Porcelli family leave him alone? Your uncle had to have been the
one to teach you your skills."

She bought a little time by deftly braiding the long length
of her hair and tying the braid into a knot on top of her head.
"Yes. Tio Luigi taught me the necessary skills to bring justice to those who murdered my parents. The Porcelli family
was—and is—too powerful for the court justice system to
work. They own half the police and judges."

"That doesn't tell me why Luigi didn't go after them himself." Casimir took her hand and helped her step over the side
of the tub into the steaming water.

Lissa sank into the water, not realizing until that moment
that she was shivering. She wrapped her arms around her
middle and leaned back against the curved porcelain,
watching him carefully. He was a beautiful man. Gorgeous.
All rippling muscle. Very, very dangerous. She had known
who he was on some level ever since she'd been around him.
He had the same shape eyes and that watchful stillness and
the confidence and graceful movements of his brothers. She
hadn't caught it on the plane, and he'd been seated right next
to her, annoying her every moment. She was going to have
to get him back for that.

"Giacinta."

His voice was a gentle caress, playing over her skin and
sinking into her cells until she felt him inside her. His voice
was a weapon, just like everything else about him. She knew,
from hearing what her sisters had told her, that the schools
had including seduction and sexual training.

Casimir sank into the water and reached out a hand for
her, spreading his legs wide. "Come here, *malyshka*."

She was already in so deep with him. She'd *given* herself
to him. She'd trusted him, and by doing so, she'd put him in
danger. Not just him, but her uncle as well. Luigi would
never stand for this. Never. He wouldn't understand. He
wouldn't even try. She shook her head.

"This was my mistake, Casimir. I wanted you so much, I wanted to feel real and I knew, with you, I could." It was only fair to give him the truth. "I didn't expect to have all the emotions I'm feeling right now toward you, but because I do, I have to tell you, we can't see each other again as long as I'm under this roof."

"*Malyshka*, I need you to come here to me." His eyes stayed steady on her face. His voice remained as gentle as ever. Gentle, but there was steel in it. He was a man who always got his way.

Lissa sighed and scooted around in the hot water until her back was against Casimir's chest and she was settled firmly between his legs. He wrapped his arms around her ribs, just under her breasts.

"Trust me to do what I have to do to take care of this. To take care of you. I've been alone my entire life, Lissa. Since I was a child. After a while, I couldn't even dream of having a life with a woman. You've handed me the most precious gift in the world. Do you really think I would screw that up?"

Lissa didn't reply. He'd handed her something equally precious. He'd seen past the mask she wore to her. He was the only person in her life . . . well . . . maybe his brother Gavriil had seen the real Lissa as well.

She let herself relax against Casimir's chest, and the instant she did, he buried his face against her neck, his teeth scraping back and forth against her sensitive skin. She was so susceptible to him, just that small action sent little darts of fire streaking like bullets through her body, straight to her core.

Lissa put both hands over his and let herself melt against him, surrounded by the steaming hot water. He touched a button and the jets activated, whirling bubbles around so that they popped and fizzed against their skin. Her body felt like a thousand tongues were teasing her.

"Tell me why your uncle didn't go after the Porcelli family."

He whispered the question against her ear, his lips

brushing her lobe. Kissing the sensitive skin behind her ear. She felt his tongue stroke, tasting her, and she closed her eyes. He was a seducer, all right. She felt weak with wanting him—wanting to please him. "You wouldn't ever have to torture a woman for information. You could just hold her like this, in your strong arms, your mouth against her skin, and she'd blurt out every secret."

"I only want your secrets," he said, male amusement in his voice. "Tell me about Luigi. Your childhood. All of it."

She knew she was going to, she had known it all along. If she was going to become partners with this man, she had to tell him the truth about her family—even if that made her feel more vulnerable than ever. She didn't want to put her uncle in a bad light and she had a feeling Casimir Prakenskii wouldn't like what he'd done. The Prakenskii brothers were very protective men, especially around women and children. In some ways, in their characters, they were all very alike.

"Giacinta."

Just her name. Her *real* name. A warning. Then his teeth found her lobe and he bit gently. A million butterflies took wing and her sex actually spasmed in response.

"Fine. Just don't judge us harshly."

"*Malyshka*, you're talking to a Prakenskii. My brothers hunted down the men who killed our parents one by one. They did it over time, much like you're doing with those who murdered your parents. If anyone is going to understand you, it will be me."

"Luigi was the enforcer for the family. He told me our organization was very small, only a few soldiers. We had a small territory and my father stayed allies with the Porcelli family because they were very large and much more violent. Luigi, when I was five, was diagnosed with MS—multiple sclerosis. He could no longer strike fear into anyone's heart. Once he was gone, my father was in trouble."

"He doesn't appear sick at all."

She shook her head. "He has long periods of remission

and then without warning, the disease strikes and he can barely walk. My father insisted Tio Luigi retire for his safety. My uncle moved away from us because it was too difficult to be around my father without wanting to be a part of the business. He later told me he settled by the sea with the idea that he would find a way to get better. People forgot about him over the next two years."

"Then the Porcelli family hit yours."

"They killed everyone at home that day. All the soldiers. Everyone working for us." She took a breath, trying to drown out the screams. "The gardener, his family, the housekeeper and girls who worked in the house." Her heart pounded. She hadn't let that door open, not like this. Remembering. Not telling a story from long ago, but letting the memories take her.

She could barely breathe with fear. The sound of gunfire and the smell of blood. The dogs chasing them across the field, into the trees and cemetery. The hot breath on her leg and the feel of teeth tearing into her flesh. She moved her legs restlessly, the scars running up her leg and ankle throbbing with pain.

"I couldn't keep up with my parents and they came back for me. The dogs were on me and they fought them off. My father shoved me ahead of them, told me where to hide and to stay very still. They led the dogs and Cosmos away from me. I saw when the dogs dragged down my mother. My father went back for her." She drew up her knees and rested her cheek on top of them, rocking a little to comfort herself. She would never forget that sight as long as she lived. Most nights, when she tried to sleep, she would see the dogs ripping apart her mother and father and the ring of men standing around them laughing.

He reached down, under the water, his fingers stroking the scars. Soothing her with his touch. His arm tightened around her. He kissed the side of her neck and then behind her ear.

She hadn't forgotten their faces. Not a single one. She had

identified the men to her uncle, and one by one, over the years, she had retaliated.

"Tell me about Luigi's illness. When he's ill, what happens?"

"I've never actually witnessed it myself. He always stays in his wing of the house. He told me he couldn't bear for me to see him that way. He's a very proud man. Papa never saw him ill either. He wouldn't allow my father or mother to talk to his specialist, he was too embarrassed."

Casimir pressed hard against the back of the deep tub, alarm bells going off. Nothing Lissa said sounded right. None of it added up. His gut tightened into hard knots. The sixth sense deep inside that always warned him of trouble, that had kept him alive these years of maneuvering through minefields, told him there was far more to the story than Lissa was aware of. Even if her uncle did have multiple sclerosis, he had long periods of remission. Why wouldn't he go after those responsible rather than training a child for revenge?

"The Porcelli family couldn't have killed all those loyal to your family."

"No, those left rallied around Tio Luigi. He was able to get enough strong alliances that the Porcellis left us alone. That was part of the reason he couldn't go after those who killed our people. He had to agree to a treaty with them in order to protect everyone else. Of course, I didn't learn any of that until I was much older."

"Let's go back to when the dogs and soldiers killed your parents. Did they search for you? Why wouldn't the dogs have discovered your hiding place?"

She frowned. "I don't know. Cosmos put leashes on them and took them back to the kennels. I was there while they took the bodies away. I could hear them laughing and talking."

"Do you remember what they said?" Casimir hated the tremors that wracked her body in spite of the hot water. He even added more heat in order to try to help alleviate the continual shiver that ran through her. He knew it was the memory, not the actual temperature of the room. "Come here, *krasavitsa*. Let me hold you. I know this is difficult for you, but now, more than ever, it is important you tell me everything you can remember of that day." Because something wasn't right.

She let him turn her around so she straddled his lap, and he pulled her tight against his chest, one hand to the back of her head to force it against his shoulder. He wanted her to feel safe. She was safe as long as she was with him. He wasn't about to trust anyone else with her life now. He rubbed her back and then brought his hand up to the nape of her neck, fingers massaging to ease the tension out of her. He knew she was going to give him everything he wanted when her body began to melt into his.

"It was a long time ago and I think I tried to block it out," she admitted softly. "They said things that didn't make sense, but I was a child. Something about my father being too stupid to see what was right under his nose. The new king was cooperative and they could get back to business without interference."

"What business?"

"I don't know."

"Who was the new king?"

"I have no idea what they were talking about. Luigi took over the family, but there was little left and you wouldn't call him a king. He retired to the sea, hours from our family home, and did gardening. With his illness, he wasn't active at all."

Casimir pressed his lips to the top of her hair to keep from speaking. She took everything her uncle said at face value. Clearly she'd never questioned him, but then, why would she? He'd raised her. He'd trained her. He sent her out after those who had killed her parents, giving her all the information on those responsible.

"Why do you think he'd be upset with you for having a relationship with me? He's your uncle. Surely he wants you to be happy." He tested the waters, striving for innocence when the question was anything but.

"He dedicated his entire life to making certain we tracked down those responsible for the massacre. No family, no wife, no one to love him. He has only me. I had only him until I went to the States and found the women I chose to call my family. He said he took a vow to bring them to justice and had me do the same. Neither of us would marry or have children until it was done."

Above her head he closed his eyes. Betrayal was a bad taste in his mouth. He took a breath. Had to tell her. Had to be the one to break her heart. "He has a family, Giacinta. A wife. Three sons. They live on a very large estate in the city. Only he comes here. And he only comes here when you are in Italy." He told her, knowing it would be a blow. Knowing he was going to break her heart. He cursed her uncle for being such a treacherous bastard.

Lissa pulled away from him, sitting up straight, her eyes meeting his. Searching his. She held herself very still. "That can't be." She didn't sound sure.

"It is. I thought you knew, but then little things you said told me you didn't. I wasn't certain why Luigi would keep the truth from you."

"A wife? Three sons? I don't understand."

She didn't want to understand. He understood that. He reached around her, turned off the jets and twisted the plug to allow the water to drain out. "Let's get you out of here and back in bed. You're shivering."

"I'm not cold," she protested. "I need to understand what this means. If he has a family, why wouldn't he tell me? Why pretend all these years? How long has he been married?"

"His wife is named Angeline."

She stiffened. Looked shattered. Breathed deliberately in and out. Took his hand and allowed him to pull her to her feet. He wrapped her in a large towel. "What is it, Giacinta? Tell me."

"I know that name. My mother had taken me to her friend's house. There was something going on, a party of some kind. I remember my mother getting upset with her friend. The friend was teasing my mother about Luigi dating someone named Angeline. My mother rarely got angry, but she seemed angry and said my uncle would never date Angeline. Then that awful man, Aldo Porcelli, dragged Mama off the chair and tried to kiss her. He said he wanted her to go home with him. But I remember the name Angeline because Mama was so adamant about Luigi not dating her."

Casimir remained silent. The look on her face, so lost, so vulnerable, tugged at his heartstrings. He wanted to go into Luigi's room and cut his throat.

"I know just about everything there is to know about the Porcelli family. Of course, Luigi did most of the research for me. I know that Aldo has one sister. Luigi didn't bother to name her because he said she was of no consequence, that the Porcelli family didn't allow their women to have any part of the business. I think I need to find out the name of Aldo's sister."

He took the towel from her hands and began drying the beads of water from her body. "*Malyshka*, come to bed. This is all too much to take in. We need a lot more research before we go any further." He didn't need to do more research to know Luigi Abbracciabene had betrayed his brother and sister-in-law for power and money.

"Why would Tio Luigi have me kill the men who murdered our family if he's in bed with them? That doesn't make sense."

Luigi's logic didn't make sense to her, but it did to him. Casimir knew Luigi had the perfect weapon in Lissa. He'd trained her himself. He'd taken her into his home and shaped her into being what in Russia would be referred to as a torpedo or a *kryshas*, an enforcer. The Porcelli family didn't know about her. They had no idea that child still lived. Her existence had been kept a secret. Casimir knew her existence would always have to remain a secret, and that meant only one thing . . .

When Luigi had wanted to visit his family, he became conveniently ill and "retired" to his wing of the house where she was strictly forbidden to go. Casimir would have bet his last dollar that Arturo, Luigi's most trusted man, had stayed behind with Lissa while her uncle had snuck out. Arturo had made certain she didn't try to go visit her sick uncle in his wing.

"We need more information," he hedged.

Her gaze jumped to his face. She went very still. "Don't. I'm hanging on by a thread, Casimir. If my uncle helped orchestrate the hit on my parents and deliberately deceived me all these years, I don't have very much to hold on to."

He dragged her into his arms. "You have me. Put your thumb into the center of your palm and feel that. My heartbeat. Your calling card. I'm there. Inside you. I can't lie to you, *malyshka*. I can't turn on you. That mark means we're sharing something so deep there is no deception between us that would ever work. When your world is turning upside down, hang on to me."

"He's my family."

Casimir shook his head. "*I'm* your family. My brothers. All of them. Why do you think they contacted me in the first place? They love you, and they were worried for your safety. Your sisters on that farm love you. This man, if he has done the things we are beginning to suspect he's done, then he is not family."

She lifted her chin. "You tell me why he would train me to kill and point me to the Porcelli family if he doesn't want justice. Tell me what you really think."

"What I think and what I know are two different things." He didn't want to be the one to take away her entire world. He'd already given her far too much truth, and he couldn't bear the shattered look on her face. He wrapped his arm around her waist and gently coaxed her back toward the dark of the bedroom.

"Why don't you want to tell me?" she persisted, sounding accusatory.

He sighed. "I've felt more for you than I have for any human being since I was taken from my family. I didn't expect to have the kind of emotions for you I have so fast. Do you think I want to be the one to cause you hurt?" He jerked back the covers, his anger seeping to the surface in spite of his determination to stay in control.

The temperature in the room had gone up several degrees, telling him he was close to an explosion. He was extremely gentle with her as he handed her into the bed. She didn't lie down, but scooted to the front of the bed, sitting with her back to the headboard, holding a pillow in front of her so tightly her knuckles turned white. He could see the slash of color in the darkness.

"Don't you think I've been deceived long enough? It would hurt more to think you suspected something and didn't share it with me. I'm not so silly that I would lose my mind and confront my uncle."

Casimir slid in beside her, sitting close, his thigh against hers as he drew her beneath his shoulder. He kept his voice very low. Matter-of-fact. Gentle. "He raised you to be his weapon. If he married Angeline Porcelli and Angeline's father and the son are dead, accidents a few years apart, what other heirs are there to the throne? The Porcelli family is already merged with the Abbracciabene family. Luigi has *all* the power and money for himself. He's been patient and appeared to be a good friend and ally. The old guard is dead. Everyone who would have been loyal to the father and son. You killed them off, one by one. You'd be his only loose end, and it would be easy enough to get rid of you."

She was silent for a very long time, staring straight ahead into the darkness. She didn't cry. She simply sat still. It made sense. Casimir hated that it made sense. He was more than certain he had it right. If the Porcelli family had decided to murder the Abbracciabene family, they would have started with Luigi, multiple sclerosis or not. He was the biggest danger to them. No way would they have allowed him to live.

"I have always trusted the information Tio Luigi gives me. I don't have very many other resources. I found Belsky myself because I didn't want to involve Tio Luigi in my hunt for the Sorbacovs just in case I missed. That's why I took a chance on such a lowlife double-dealing weasel like Belsky. I was protecting Luigi." She tapped her fingers on her thigh, her body very still, as if she held herself that way to keep from flying apart.

Casimir couldn't imagine what she was feeling. Her only blood relative, the man she'd trusted all those years, had betrayed her parents and used her to get what he wanted. "Tell me what you want to do, Giacinta," he said. "Whatever that is, I'm with you."

She drew her legs up slowly until she could trace the horrendous scars crawling down her calf, shin and ankle where the dogs had ripped chunks of her flesh away. He covered her hand with his own, feeling her fingers brush lightly over the deep scars.

"We need information before we make a move. If you're right about him, he won't make his try for me until after I've dealt with Aldo. He'll give me Aldo's information and where best to hit him after I've taken out Cosmos. He'll give me a story about how it's now or never to get to him. Aldo would be the final hit."

"What about Arturo? He had to have known. He's been with your uncle for years. All the other guards talk about him like he's the biggest deal to ever hit Italy."

"He would have known," she agreed. "But he's totally loyal to Tio Luigi. He'd defend him with his life. If anything, because I trust him, he'd be the one to kill me, unless my uncle wanted to make certain I was really dead and planned to do it himself. Both of them would know he would only get one try at me."

For the first time he realized that she might just be sitting beside him very, very still, but beneath the surface, a volcano was shimmering. It was there in the room with them, the heat rising so that he actually felt little beads of sweat forming on his body. A shimmer of light danced along the floor leading toward the door. He circled her ankle with his hand, keeping his eyes on the flame.

"You can't set the house on fire."

"Of course I can."

He took a breath, willed her to breathe with him. "Not yet. We've got to make certain this isn't all conjecture. No matter what Luigi did, Cosmos and Aldo were involved, and they need to go down. I can question Cosmos before he meets with his accident. He'll talk."

She shook her head. "Not if he's loyal to Luigi and Aldo."

"Never forget who and what I am, *malyshka*," Casimir cautioned. "He'll talk."

She turned her head and looked at him, her eyes searching his. He didn't know what he expected. Weeping. Anger. Shock. Anything but the determination he saw there. She was more like he was than he had first realized. She prized loyalty, and if her uncle had done such a horrendous thing as to have entered into a conspiracy with the Porcelli family and order the hits on her family, she was more than determined to see him pay.

"We have to be certain," she said softly. "Angeline is a common enough name. We have to find out the name of Aldo's sister and then find out if it's the same woman my uncle is married to."

"I can do that. I have many sources. We'll find out the information fast." His hands went to the messy topknot in her hair. She didn't protest when he took it down and slowly slid his fingers through the thick weave of her braid until her hair spilled free. "I brought your brush in." He picked it up off the nightstand. "Sit in front of me."

"I can brush my hair." It was a halfhearted protest.

"I know you can, but I want to do it. I wanted to do it from the first moment I saw you boarding the plane. You looked so proper, your hair all up on top of your head, twisted into that perfect style. I knew then I wanted to see you all messy, your hair spilling across my pillow and your lips swollen from my kisses. That want grew into a need, and now I've got you with me and I intend to indulge in every little fantasy, no matter how small or seemingly insignificant."

She turned her head to look at him, her eyes meeting his. He felt the impact all the way to his groin.

"I don't think any fantasy is insignificant." Her voice had dropped an octave or two, just enough that she sounded sultry.

Casimir wrapped his hand around her neck and leaned down to kiss her gently. Almost reverently. She didn't know it, but right there, in that moment, she was very fragile. Very vulnerable. Her world had shifted out from under her. The blow had to be terrible and, he knew, her mind would be racing, putting together all the little things from her childhood that hadn't added up. That she'd dismissed and refused to think about.

He settled her between his legs and began to draw the brush through the long silky strands, hoping the simple act of brushing her hair would help to soothe her. No betrayal came at a good time and certainly not one that had been going on since childhood.

"How could he do this?"

Her voice was low. Shaking. He wasn't certain whether the shaking was from anger or shock. He stayed quiet, knowing there was no answer to such treachery.

"His own brother. He ordered the hit on his own brother. On my mother. They loved him. *I* loved him." A shudder went through her body. She turned her head to look over her shoulder at him.

His heart nearly stopped. Her eyes were wet. Liquid. As blue as the deepest sea. The tips of her lashes were wet. Spiky. He didn't think tears could affect him, but his gut knotted and his heart stuttered at the sight of her liquid blue eyes. He wanted to go into her uncle's room and cut his lying, deceitful throat.

"Do you have any idea how many times I worried about his health? I was just a child and terrified I'd lose him. He'd tell me he had to go into his rooms and be alone. He wouldn't call the doctor, no matter how much I begged him to. He would be there for two weeks or more at a time. Once it was a month. I cried every night, afraid he would die, my only living relative. Arturo would be here with me . . ." Her voice trailed off. She turned her head back. "Arturo." She whispered the name.

He was a man of action. He'd always been a man of patience, but her pain was so deep he wanted to strike out. He couldn't take out her uncle, not yet, but Arturo was an altogether different proposition. His hands were steady as he pulled the brush through her hair, one arm around her waist, holding her to him.

"I love him too," she said. "Tio Luigi and Arturo. I love them both. I thought they loved me. I don't have . . ." She broke off abruptly.

"You do, Giacinta," Casimir said. "You have your sisters. They aren't blood relations, but they may as well be. They love you. My brothers, on that farm, they love you. They would never have taken the chance of sending for me if they didn't want you protected at all times. If you weren't family to them."

She shook her head. "They don't know me. None of them know what I am. What Tio Luigi shaped me into. I'm a killer. If my sisters knew . . ."

"They would still love you, *golubushka*. You're the

same person who threw in with them. You went to the counseling sessions with them and built a home with them. They would understand and help you through this. Look what their men are."

She shook her head. He kept brushing her hair, searching his mind for the right words, hoping to find something—anything—to comfort her.

"Think about each of them. Who they are. What they've gone through. Then you can tell me they wouldn't understand."

She took a deep breath. He knew she was trying to stop the tears from falling. He didn't want that. She needed to cry, to share that with him. He put the brush down and turned her in his arms. She was reluctant, her body stiff, but he was strong and she wasn't in any shape to put up a fight. He drew her onto his lap and held her close until she dropped her head on his shoulder in defeat.

"You're right," she said. A small shudder went through her body. Her voice was strangling on tears. "They'd accept me."

"And love you. That won't ever change," he confirmed. "Not ever. Those women are your true family, Giacinta. And my brothers love you, and more than anyone else in the world, they would understand and accept you. How could they not? The same thing that happened to you, happened to us. The others might suspect, but Gavriil knows. No one ever fools Gavriil. He's the one who used the emergency drop to let me know you would be coming to Europe and he wanted protection for you."

Hot tears fell on his neck and bare shoulders. He tightened his arms. The last thing he wanted was for Lissa to pull away from him or her family. Betrayal could do that. Isolate and eat away at a person until there was nothing left. He wasn't going to have that for her.

He knew Luigi would have to kill Lissa after she took

out the head of the Porcelli family. Aldo Porcelli would be the last target Luigi would give her and then he would have no other choice but to kill her. He had known all along, from the moment he had taken Lissa into his house when she was a small child, that he would have to kill her. The man was cold-blooded enough to kill his own brother and sister-in-law, take in their daughter and raise her to be a weapon for him, knowing all along he planned to get rid of her. He couldn't afford for her to put the pieces together because he knew if she did, she would come after him.

Casimir had been raised in a brutal school. No one had pretended to love him. There were no deceptions. He knew what was expected of him if he wanted to live and if he wanted to keep his brothers alive. Lissa had been raised in a home with people she thought loved her.

Casimir tightened his arms around her and dropped his head on the top of hers, wanting to surround her with comfort—with an emotion he didn't dare name. Emotions, for him, were deadly. It was never good to be vulnerable, and Lissa Piner made him very vulnerable. He understood his brothers now, their need to band together and protect their women. They'd found something to hold on to, and now he had that very thing in his arms.

She wept silently, and to him that was even more heart-breaking than if she'd screamed aloud. The tears were hot on his skin, and her body, in his arms, shook with the force of her grief, but she didn't make a sound. Not one single sound. He would have liked it better if she screamed out her pain at the depths of her uncle's betrayal. The soundless weeping was like an arrow piercing straight through his heart. Her heartbreak was too deep for anything but silent tears and made his resolve to make her uncle and Arturo pay all the more firm.

Lissa and Casimir had no safe place to go. They had no sanctuary. If they had even a small chance to get out of the mess they were in alive, they would have to trust each other implicitly. Rely on each other. Take each other's back. He had to convince Lissa that she could trust him.

He was practically a stranger to her. It would be human nature for her to pull away from him after her own flesh and blood betrayed her. He had to be very, very careful over the next few days to make certain she knew she could rely on him. Words wouldn't do it. He had to show her. She had to feel it. The only way he could guarantee her fidelity, absolute loyalty, was for her to see it for herself. There was only one real way.

They had a psychic connection. He'd established that through his mark on her. It would be uncomfortable and dangerous for her to see him. All of him. Know the terrible things he'd done. He would be taking a terrible risk, but if she could accept him with his bloody, vile past, she would know absolutely she belonged to him and he would aid her and guard her in anything she chose to do.

He took a deep breath, fear clawing at his gut. She lifted her tear-wet face, her eyes moving over him, seeing him. Seeing Casimir the man, not one of the many masks he wore. "What is it?"

7

CASIMIR studied Lissa's face. Not many women could weather a storm of silent weeping, have their heart ripped from their body, and still manage to look beautiful. She did. Her blue eyes remained steady on his, and he knew he had fallen hard and fast because of that look. She might be knocked down by the knowledge of the extent of her uncle's treachery, but she got back up. She would always stand back up and she would hold firm.

"What is it, Casimir?" she repeated.

He took a breath, knowing he was risking everything. "You need to know you can count on someone, *malyshka*. We're going to do this together. Beat them. All of them. Your enemies. My enemies. To do that you have to trust me."

She hesitated and then nodded. "I do."

Casimir shook his head. "You want to trust me, Giacinta, but how can you when you've known nothing but betrayal? You have to have doubts whether you want to have them or not. I can put your doubts to rest but in doing so, you will see Casimir. The real man. The killer."

She shook her head. "That isn't the real man."

"It is. I am what they made me. I can't separate the two. I lied to myself for a lot of years telling myself that it was the role I played—*those* men were killers—not me. But all of those roles, they were still me." He shackled her wrist with gentle fingers and turned her hand over, palm up. "Through this mark, you can see into my mind. Everything. I won't be able to hide from you. You will see that you will never have to have a single doubt about my loyalty to you. I can give you that. But you'll also see all of me, and I'm afraid that will terrify you. Repulse you even. I'm not a good man."

Her gaze searched his and he didn't flinch. Didn't look away from her. He was willing to strip himself bare for her. For this one woman, he would be whatever she needed. Do whatever she needed. There would never be another in his world. He waited for the verdict. His mouth had gone dry and blood thundered in his ears. He had faced death a million times and it had never felt like this.

"You'd do that for me?"

It was her tone more than her question that gave away the fact that she realized the enormity of what he offered. Holding her gaze, he nodded slowly. "I think it's necessary, Giacinta, for both of us. Do I want you to see inside of me? Hell no. *Hell* no. But you have to know, not think, that you can count on me. We have to be closer than any two people have ever been. I'm willing to risk everything for a chance at keeping you. A few days of you thinking about what your uncle did and your trust factor is going to hit zero. I don't want to be a casualty of the inevitable."

"There's a part of me that wants to pack up and run home to hide on the farm," Lissa admitted. She leaned into him and rubbed her forehead against his shoulder. "But I can't do that. I don't have the kind of personality that would ever allow me not to know the truth and then do something about it. I can't leave the Sorbacovs' threat hanging over us either, not when I know I have the best chance of anyone of getting close to them. As for my uncle and Arturo, if they really were part of the murders of my parents and all the people who worked for us, then I would never be able to live with myself if I didn't do something about that as well."

"*Malyshka*, you have to think hard about that. I'm willing to take them out, but if circumstances dictate otherwise, could you do it? You have to know that before you put yourself in harm's way."

She didn't answer right away. She kept her head down, pressed against his shoulder so he could no longer look into her eyes. He ran his hands down her back, along her spine, down to the curve of her waist and the indentation at the small of her back. The longer he spent in her company, the stronger he felt the bond between them.

"I've been going over my childhood, so many things that didn't make sense that add up now." She lifted her head and met his gaze.

His belly knotted. His arms tightened, trying to surround her with his strength. He wanted to shelter her next to his heart, the feeling of tenderness nearly overwhelming him. Simultaneously, he wanted to rip out her uncle's heart and feed it to him. He wouldn't mind spending a few hours making the man's life unbearable until he begged for death. The two emotions warred with each other, and he worried that she would see that in him as well.

"He doesn't have multiple sclerosis. That's why he wouldn't allow my father to talk to his doctor, or for me to ever see him ill. He went into his wing of the house and left to go to his family. I had to study night and day. Languages, reading maps, everything that could possibly help me along with my regular studies. Every type of weapons training and styles of martial arts, boxing and street fighting. I didn't play with dolls or watch television, not unless it was a training exercise. All the while, he ranted about going after those responsible and how no law would ever bring them to justice.

All along I thought I was the patient one, insisting we go slow and make everything look like an accident, but looking back at the conversations, he led me in that direction."

Casimir nodded. He was certain her uncle had the patience to carry out a long-term plan to reach his ultimate goal, which was to be the sole power of both families. Luigi wouldn't have been able to take over both families immediately. If Aldo Porcelli and his father had been killed right away, even his wife would have suspected him. By slowly reducing the old guard, and then going after the men in charge, Luigi had positioned himself, over time, to be the natural choice for head of the family. He would have had to plant the necessary lies in his niece's mind in order to make her think it was all her own idea.

"He sometimes sent me to boarding schools. Not for very long, but he said it was to gain an insight into other people. It never made sense to me. I was with other children. Gaining insights to how a child's mind worked didn't seem as if it was going to help me later down the road. Of course he was with his family during those times. It was his idea that I go to the States. Again, he needed me out of the way."

"You're intelligent, Giacinta. He couldn't take the chance that you might see or hear something he didn't want you to. You trusted him implicitly, but he still didn't dare chance it."

She took a deep breath and her gaze dropped to his throat. "Maybe you should get clear of all of this, Casimir. I have to see it through. I started something a long time ago, and I'm going to finish it."

He shook his head, his hand sliding up her back, beneath her long hair to curl around the nape of her neck. "Look at me, *golubushka*." He waited until she lifted her gaze back to his. "I'm not going anywhere. We're in this together. You may not want me right now, or trust me, but you need me. You're mine, and I'm going to protect you and help you through this. The best way to do that is to show you who and what I am. You'll see into my mind. I won't be able to hide

from you. Not anything. You have to be able to count on at
least one person right now. Your sisters are a long way away,
so you've got me. Only me. And, Giacinta, I'm more than up
for whatever has to be done."

He was looking forward to it. No job had ever been personal for him. This was. Still, he was a man of control. He
was fire inside. He always had been, but he could twist those
flames to be whatever he needed. He'd learned restraint
from the many lessons of his youth. He was able to use the
fire to his advantage, keeping it smoldering and under control all these years. The first loss of control he'd experienced
since the days of his boyhood had been this night with Lissa
in his bed.

Once more he took her wrist and turned her palm up to
him, laying it over his bare thigh. He didn't wait for consent.
He didn't want her to struggle with her decision. She was
trying to protect him, and he didn't need that from her. He
needed trust. He turned up his own palm and took her other
hand and pressed her thumb hard into the exact center, then
repeated the action with his own thumb on her upturned
palm.

At once the connection arced through both of them, much
like an electrical current. The sizzle started in their palms
and forked outward, spreading along pathways, nerve endings, straight toward their brains. He felt her in his mind and
deliberately, he forced himself to open to her, to allow her
access to his memories, to everything he was, both good and
bad. He wanted her always. He didn't hide that from her. He
wanted a home and a family with her. He wanted *everything*
with her, and he was ruthless enough to take it. To protect it.
He didn't try to keep that from her either.

His past flooded her mind. Memories of his mother and
father. He'd been so young, but he'd been traumatized, just
as she'd been, by their ugly deaths. He'd been ripped from
his brothers, so frightened, just a young boy, beaten and
threatened, humiliated and tortured to keep him off-balance

and afraid of those who held power over him. Unashamed, he left himself open for her to see everything.

Casimir Prakenskii, like his brothers, had been forged in the fires of hell. Lissa wanted to weep for the young boy—for all of them. She'd suffered trauma when her parents and those she loved had been murdered, but her torment had been swift and then over. Casimir's hadn't ended for years. He'd been caned, whipped, had electrical shock applied. He'd even been water-boarded.

Training sexually should have been at least pleasurable, but it was all about performance and control. If he failed to control his arousal, he was beaten severely. If the woman failed to arouse him, she was beaten. Sickened, Lissa nearly pulled her thumb away, but then his memories of work were there. Years of being alone. Lissa had never really felt completely alone, not like he did.

She saw the many roles he'd played in order to get close to his targets. He'd hunted with great efficiency and patience. He'd refined his skills over the years, relentless in his pursuit and yet never hurrying or making a mistake. Consequently, he had a perfect record. He was sent out and didn't stop until the job was done. She couldn't help but admire his skills.

Still, along the way, with as many hits as he'd made, things had been bound to go wrong. He bore those scars. The worst were on his face and scalp and had come from a fellow student targeted because the man had switched sides. He'd begun working for the Russian mob, using his skills for monetary gain. The elder Sorbacov hadn't liked that.

Lissa held her breath as that particular memory unfolded and she saw the weapon the target had used to try to take Casimir's head off. The man had forged the blades, curving them to fit over a skull and face like a mask. He wielded it as a sword, slamming the cage of sharpened steel onto his victims in order to hold them in place for the kill. The more they struggled, the deeper the blades penetrated.

Casimir hadn't struggled. He'd allowed the assassin to

pull him close and he'd struck with his own blade. It had taken longer to remove the mask of blades from his face and skull than it had to kill his opponent. Who had that kind of discipline? What would it take to be that man who could have his face and skull slashed to pieces, blood running everywhere, and calmly kill his attacker and remove the horrible device?

Then she was seeing past the roles, into Casimir, where he hid that last little piece of himself. He was loyal to a fault. He'd chosen her. His angel. He thought of her that way. His angel of justice. A sword honed for a good cause. He considered himself the darkest devil, a demon forged in the fires of hell. He had that fire burning in him, never to be put out. She shook her head at the way he looked at both of them.

Still, for all that, he wanted no other woman. There was only the real woman—Giacinta Abbracciabene—in his mind. In his soul. Somehow, she had crawled in where no one else had ever been. She'd slipped past his guard and was firmly entrenched. She was his choice. He gave her his heart completely. Utterly. Absolutely. His loyalty to his brothers ran deep, a choice he'd made long ago, but his loyalty to her was all encompassing. There was no way to deny it. He couldn't fake that.

Lissa didn't understand the connection between them. Why he would want her. Why she would be his choice so completely. How he knew and accepted the fact. But she couldn't deny the connection, nor could she deny the way she felt about him. Maybe it all happened too fast, but she didn't care. She'd wanted him before the mess she was in, now she wanted him even more. Someone in her life had to be real. He saw her. He thought her extraordinary. He accepted the real Giacinta.

He'd made himself completely vulnerable to her so she refused to do less. She gave him—her. Everything she was. He was her choice. She had made that decision when she gave him her body. This was different. This was more. She made the choice to give him her heart and soul. Her loyalty. All of it. No matter how little time they had, or how much, she wouldn't take that back.

She let him see her childhood. Luigi had been cold at first, unable to even kiss her or comfort her, but she'd put that down to the awkwardness of a man who didn't have children or a family. His affection came over time, slow and distant, occasional hugs, with Lissa always initiating contact. She had thought she was teaching him how to show affection.

She gave him everything. The terrible loneliness. The guilt that she couldn't find all those who had participated in killing her family. The love she had for her chosen sisters. The fear when Luigi sent her away to the United States. The careful planning of each target and her reaction after. Casimir walked away coolly, the job done. She spent hours throwing up in the bathroom. Still, her determination to bring the killers to justice was every bit as strong as his resolve to do his job to the best of his ability—and stay alive.

She gave him how she felt about him. The chemistry. The exhilaration of feeling such an attraction to him. Of having him recognize and see her. The emotions burning inside of her, fiery hot, passionate, blazing with hunger for him. Just him. Fear that it wasn't real. Fear that like everyone else in her life, he would disappear. Fear that her sisters would find out who she was and think her a monster.

Casimir closed his eyes and let himself relax for the first time since he'd realized her uncle had to be behind the killing of her family. Lissa accepted him as he was. The real Casimir Prakenskii with his unredeemable sins. She saw into him and still had that fiery craving for him. His woman. She would take the bad with the good.

He lifted her palm to his mouth and kissed the faded mark very gently. He was a man forged in hell. There shouldn't have been gentleness or tenderness. The fire in him alone should have precluded those emotions, yet with Lissa, they were his first emotions. He was already an addict when it came to her. The craving for getting as close to her as possible, for her taste, for her body. It was all there, but wrapped up in his deeper emotions.

She leaned into him, still holding his palm, her thumb pressed there. Her long lashes fluttered. He loved her lashes. Thick. Red gold. Feathery and turned up, surrounding deep blue, very vibrant eyes. Her hair fell around her like a curtain of fire. "Thank you for being here. I would never have suspected him and in the end, he would have killed me. You saved me." *In more ways than one.*

He heard the echo of her thought just as if she'd spoken aloud to him. He was very aware of the legacy in his family, the ability to talk to each other telepathically once they were connected by that psychic thread. He hadn't realized just how intimate that would be, her voice whispering in his mind, touching him inside, driving away every vestige of loneliness.

That soft whisper brought his body to life, his cock stirring hungrily. He lifted her off his lap and tucked her under the covers. She was exhausted mentally, emotionally and physically. "You need sleep, *golubushka*."

She shook her head, not lifting it from the pillow. "I can't sleep here. He can't know about us. He'd come after you, Casimir. You know I'm right."

"I know I have to keep you safe. I want you with me, so there's no chance he tries to arrange an accident early. I'll watch over you, let you sleep a couple of hours, and then I want you again. After that, you can slip back into your room and we'll get ready for the day. You'll have to insist on Tomasso being with you, not Arturo. Find a reason."

Casimir slid down in the bed, curling his body around hers, hooking her around the waist and pulling her into him until she was partially under him. He waited for her to relax, to melt into him in the way she did when she accepted him. It took a little longer than he expected and he found himself smiling. Lissa wasn't a woman to blindly obey. She would think out every decision for herself. He knew he was a controlling man, but he liked that she wasn't a woman to be controlled. It would make for fireworks, occasionally, but he could live with that.

She fell asleep fast, drifting off with a small sigh, leaving him wrapped around her, indulging himself by letting his fingers caress her skin just below her breasts, occasionally brushing the undersides just because they were so soft and he could. Her hair smelled wonderful, a faint, almost elusive scent he knew he would never grow tired of.

First, before any of the others, they had to get to the dog handler. He had a few questions for the man. He wanted absolute confirmation before they proceeded with any plans. He was positive he was right and Luigi Abbracciabene was a treacherous snake of the worst kind, but he wanted proof for Lissa. He would get that proof for her—for both of them. If they were correct and Luigi was guilty, then while she reported her successful removing of Cosmos Agosto, he was going to take care of Arturo. He didn't want to be nice about it either. With Luigi being Lissa's alibi when Arturo died, her uncle wouldn't suspect her of making a move against him.

Lissa moved, her body pulling in on itself, knees curling, drawing up so that she was in the fetal position. He tightened his hold possessively. She made a soft sound of distress in her sleep.

"Shh, *lyubov moya*, you're safe. I've got you. You're safe with me." He stroked caresses down the back of her head in an effort to soothe her.

Another small sound escaped and with a sinking heart, he realized she was weeping in her sleep. That tore him up. He lay there in the dark, holding her close, whispering to her in Russian, tempted to sing her a Russian lullaby, and all the while he planned out Luigi's death. If he'd ever once thought to prolong a death, or torture someone, it would have been Luigi.

"You're breaking my heart, Giacinta," he whispered

against her ear. "You have to stop." He was growing desperate. He wasn't a man who felt desperate, and yet, there it was, she was turning him inside out.

He cupped her breast, his thumb sliding gently over her nipple while he nudged the thick mass of hair from the nape of her neck so he could kiss his way across that tempting strip of skin. The soft weeping continued, but she turned from her side to her back so he could make out the distress on her face. The deep sense of betrayal. Grief for her lost family. She'd accepted the fact that her uncle had been the man behind the murders of her family. She knew Luigi had spared her in order to shape her into a weapon to use to further his cause. She also knew he had no choice but to kill her when the last obstacle in his path to become head of both families was removed.

Casimir wanted to weep along with her. That kind of treachery was beyond measure—beyond comprehension. He found it took all of his discipline, every bit of his control, not to stalk downstairs and put a bullet in the man's head. Instead he bent his head and brushed his lips across hers. Her face was tear-wet.

"Giacinta. *Lyubov moya*, open your eyes for me."

The terrible emptiness swallowing her whole receded just a little, pushed aside by the velvet caressing voice breaking into her endless loop of a nightmare. Lissa wanted to reach for the voice, but she couldn't seem to move, couldn't break free, not when she was so broken, pieces of her scattered on the ground all around her. Luigi had done that. Her beloved uncle.

She had worried about him for so long. Every time she came to see him, he had to spend time alone in the wing of his house suffering with his bout of multiple sclerosis. Now she knew: while she worried, he spent time with his wife and family so he would have an alibi when she took down another member of the Porcelli family. He'd left her with nothing at all.

"Come on, *malyshka*, look at me. I'm right here. Nothing can get to you. They'll have to walk through me to do it. Open your eyes. Come back to me."

That voice. Mesmerizing. Hypnotic. Impossible to ignore. Rough and sexy. Pitched low so that the sound sank through skin to her bones, branding her. Forcing out the nightmare— only it wasn't a terrible dream. Betrayal and treachery were realities in her life. If she opened her eyes, even for him, for Casimir, she would have to face those things. She would have to admit defeat, that her uncle had won. He'd broken her when not even the deaths of her parents had done that.

"Giacinta." The voice changed tone. Commanding. No longer coaxing. "You have to look at me."

She didn't want to obey. He would see she was an empty shell, that Luigi had managed to destroy her. Still, there was no way to ignore that tone. Lissa lifted her lashes, her heart so heavy she feared it was a stone in her chest. She felt him there. Casimir Prakenskii. Her rock when the world had shifted out from under her so hard and fast. A deep chasm had opened under her feet, threatening to drag her under, drowning her, and there he was.

She stared up at his face. Strong. Masculine. Cut beautifully, like a Greek sculpture, every line perfect. Strong jaw. That hint of a dark shadow. Long lashes. Glittering eyes so mercurial they stole her breath. His mouth drew her attention, his lips sinful, a wicked promise of pleasure she knew he was more than capable of keeping. Mostly, she saw strength in him.

He was beautiful. Gorgeous. He smiled at her, a gentle smile, a flash of his white teeth, his eyes drifting possessively over her face, taking in everything, assessing her emotions. Watchful. Caring.

"*Golubushka*. Little dove." He whispered the endearment softly.

Her heart turned over. A sound escaped, a low, keening whisper of loss. She reached up to touch him. To find him solid, not a dream. She needed reality in a sea of uncertainty, and he was there. His bare chest was pure, defined muscle. His arms rippled with muscles. So strong, not just physically, but in every way.

"I'm lost, Casimir," she whispered. Telling him the truth. Giving him her greatest vulnerability. She'd never felt so lost in her life.

She kept her gaze fixed on him. Casimir, the man who would see her through this terrible blow. The loss of her last living blood relation, a man she'd loved most of her life. She'd clung to him, believed in him, and deep inside, she felt shattered.

"You can't be lost, Giacinta, not as long as you're with me. I'll always find our way. Just hold on to me. We'll get through this together."

She didn't think that was true. She had always considered herself strong. She'd worked hard to make herself that way. She'd never felt like this. Not even when she'd been a grief-stricken child. She'd had a purpose then. She knew who she was. She was proud of that person. Now, she didn't know anything.

"He shattered me, Casimir," she confessed. "I'm so broken. Into a million pieces. I can't think what to do." To her horror, she heard the tears in her voice. She wasn't weak. Yet now, when she needed to be strong more than any other time, when it was necessary to be decisive and take charge, two of her greatest strengths, she was falling apart.

"You aren't, *malyshka*, you aren't broken. Luigi Abbracciabene could never break you. Never. He knocked you down. Hard. It was a hit, Giacinta, a blow that put you down, but you're going to get back up. That's what you do—what you've always done—and it's what you'll do this time."

She drew in her breath as Casimir bent his head and brushed his mouth over each eye, taking the burn away. He left a trail of kisses along her high cheekbones, sipping at the wet streaks, replacing the tears with tiny darts of fire. That fire seemed to find its way into her veins, warming her when she was so cold.

"I still feel so lost and alone, Casimir. He did that to me. Took everything, the foundation of my life, right out from under me. He made me afraid. I haven't been afraid since that horrible day when the dogs took us down."

Casimir's heart turned over. Her eyes, so vivid, as blue as the deepest sea, looked up at him with trepidation, with that lost, forlorn look he could barely stand to see in her. So vulnerable. So alone when she wasn't. She needed to see him standing beside her. He'd hold her up, support her in any way he could because she would always be his choice. "You aren't alone now, *lyubov moya*. You're safe here. It's okay to feel broken. Even if you were in a million pieces, I'd find every one and put you back together again."

He was so beautiful. A rock. She felt steadier just looking at him. His voice was pitched low, but he spoke with absolute conviction and she found herself believing him. Believing that she wasn't as broken as she felt inside. Luigi had knocked her down, but she wasn't out. She would never be out. "He did this thing. I know that he did."

He nodded his head slowly. She didn't flinch away from the truth this time. A part of her had held out hope when they were talking earlier, but she'd thought about everything, every little detail of childhood, growing up in Luigi's home. Pieces of the puzzle she hadn't ever known were missing fell into place. She knew, as she was falling to sleep, that Luigi had committed treachery far beyond what she could ever have conceived of. She would get proof before she made her move, but she knew, beyond all doubt, that he was guilty.

She reached up with an unsteady hand to rub her palm along Casimir's stubborn jaw, feeling the dark shadow bristling against his mark on her. The spikes rasped over her body, along her skin. There was compassion in his eyes. Tenderness. Heat. But he knew the truth too. He wasn't going to lie to her. He knew Luigi had orchestrated the hit on his brother and family.

"Kiss me, Casimir," she whispered. "I need you to kiss me."

He didn't hesitate. His hand framed her face and his mouth took hers. Gentle. Coaxing. She parted her lips, allowing his tongue to sweep inside and tangle with hers. His mouth was pure fire. She wanted to stay there. Burn there. Let the flames sweep through her, consuming every ugly detail of her life.

She tasted love for the first time in her life. She didn't know if he knew it or not, but it was there, mixed with hunger. With lust. With need. Love tasted different. Tender. Beautiful. She needed that now more than any other time in her life.

She had to blink away tears all over again. She had never thought to taste that emotion. Certainly not now in her darkest moment. She kissed him back, melting, feeling the fire in her grow, losing herself in his mouth so she wouldn't have to think anymore. She didn't want to think, only feel. Still, having him was terrifying. What if he left her too? What if she had him—like this—and then he took himself away? She wouldn't recover. Lissa pressed back into the pillows, her heart beating wildly, fear shaking her.

Casimir lifted his head a scant couple of inches, his gaze drifting possessively over her face. For the first time he saw how young she was. She was self-possessed. Disciplined. She had never felt young to him, but now, with her world upside down, he saw her so clearly. She had every reason to be terrified—and yet none at all. He wasn't going anywhere. Not. Ever.

He brushed a kiss over her lips, those beautiful, soft, full lips, more tempting than anything he'd known in his life. He blazed a trail of fire down to the pulse beating in her throat. That sweet spot allowed him to know she was breathing. She was alive. No one had taken her from him. He kissed that pulse-point, feeling her heart pounding beneath his mouth. His tongue. Her skin tasted like paradise.

He kissed his way along her collarbone. She was a woman of steel, her spine as tough and even stronger than most men's, but right then he could feel how delicate she was, how fragile her bones were. He took his time, finding his way over the lush curve of her breasts to the valley between them. He buried his face there, inhaling. Tasting. His shadow rasped against her soft breasts. He felt her answering shiver.

Lissa's hands went to his shoulders as if she might push him away. There was tension in her as she trembled beneath him.

"What are you doing?" she whispered.

"Memorizing you. Loving you," he answered against her tight little bud of a nipple. His tongue swiped gently. "With every breath I take, Giacinta, I'm loving you." She deserved gentle. Tender. She *needed* gentle and tender. She was afraid of it, afraid of trusting it, but she needed it now more than the fire burning through both of them.

He wrapped his arm around her waist and pulled her closer under him as he took the lush mound deep into his mouth, flattening her nipple onto the roof of his mouth with his tongue. Her breath hissed out of her and her legs moved restlessly.

His shadowed jaw rubbing roughly against her sensitive skin enhanced the stimulation of his mouth and tongue. He added his teeth—gently. Just a small nip but she reacted, gasping, her hips bucking.

"Easy, *malyshka*, you need gentle tonight. I'm going to make absolutely certain you know you're loved." He murmured the vow against her breasts, nipping again and then slowly beginning his journey down her body. He wanted to claim every inch of her. To love every inch. She didn't know how much she needed gentle, but he did, and she was going to get it.

He memorized her body with his palms, sliding over her

silky skin. The lush curves, the sides of her breasts, under them, all along her narrow rib cage, and then sweeping down to her waist. He followed his hands with his mouth, using his lips to kiss her, his tongue to stroke velvet caresses and his teeth to nip and show her how nerve endings fired under a slow assault.

His blood roared in his ears, rushed through his veins straight to his groin until he was so full and hard he thought he might burst. Just touching her did that to him. Looking at her. Feeling the silk of her hair against his body. The satin of her skin sliding under his palm. She was so beautiful, a woman he never believed he could ever have. His own.

He kissed her belly button, nuzzled her flat stomach and allowed his hands to drift lower, over her hips, tracing the bones there, lower still to her thighs. He felt her muscles shift and ripple, dance with arousal. His mouth moved lower, his hands parting her thighs, giving him access to her heat. His tongue swiped a slow, easy taste, languid and lazy, taking his time.

The breath slammed out of her and her hips bucked. She cried out his name, her fingernails digging into his shoulder. He tightened his grip on her hips, pinning her down so he could continue his exploration uninterrupted. She was pure liquid fire. She tasted like heaven, and he indulged himself. This was for her . . . but he couldn't resist.

He'd forgotten. The taste of her was in his mouth when he woke in the early morning hour, but still, he'd forgotten just how good it really was. The first few minutes were purely selfish. Her nails bit deeper and her breath came in ragged gasps as his mouth and tongue took her up so that the tension coiled tight and fiery deep inside her. He added a finger, pressing deep through her tight muscles.

"Casimir." Her breath exploded out of her lungs.

"Let go," he commanded softly. "Just let go, *lyubov moya*, let it take you." He kept up his assault on her senses, his mouth greedy, but still as gentle as he could be when he wasn't a gentle man. "Nothing is hotter to me than watching you come apart for me." He meant that. He loved looking into her eyes. Giving her that gift. The sound of her voice, breathy, ragged, gasping his name. It was music. Beautiful. A paradise he never thought he could ever have.

Her eyes on his, she did exactly what he commanded, her channel, scorching hot, clamped down on his finger, and his cock jerked hungrily. She shuddered, her hips writhing, pushing deeper against his finger, her hands moving over his shoulders and down his arms to his wrists.

"Please, honey, I need you."

He wasn't going to make her beg. Not this time. This time he wanted her to know in every single cell in her body that she was thoroughly loved. He wanted her to feel him, branded inside her, deep, where she would never get him out. He pushed her knees up and apart and moved over her.

"Wrap me up, *malyshka*," he ordered softly. "Lock your heels around my hips. I want to feel every inch of you against me."

He circled his cock with his fist and pushed the crown into her hot, slick entrance. The feeling was excruciatingly beautiful. Tight. Hot. Scalding. He waited while she obeyed him, while she circled him with her arms as well as her legs, until every inch of her front was melted into his.

Fire was there. Her fire. His. He felt it in his belly, a roaring he couldn't quite control. He felt it in his cock as he pushed through her fiery sheath, forcing her to give way for his invasion. So tight. So perfect. He didn't power through. He forced himself to keep to the gentle, leisurely pace that he knew was killing both of them.

One slow inch at a time. He watched himself disappear into her body. So beautiful. He could feel the slow assault, his thick cock forcing her muscles to give way, to stretch to accommodate his size. It felt as if a fiery fist clamped down around him, her muscles like a vise, stroking and caressing with velvet flames. Slowly, relentlessly, he forced his way, inch by slow inch, into her until he was seated deep, holding her still, letting her body adjust to the burning, stretched feeling. Letting his adjust to the fire.

Her mouth rounded, her lips forming his name, but only a soft groan escaped. Her lashes fluttered and her hips pressed deeper into him, urging him without words to move. She needed movement. Wanted it. *Demanded* it. She was so beautiful under him, her body swaying with every movement of his. Her breasts jolted invitingly, nipples hard little pebbles against his chest, the feeling unbelievably erotic to him. Her hips bucked harder, trying to drive down on him, to force him into compliance.

"You can't move, *malyshka*," he cautioned, clenching his teeth against the pleasure radiating out from his cock to the rest of his body. She gripped him so tight, the fire so hot, it bordered on pain, yet he didn't want it to ever end. "I'm not going to last five minutes if you don't hold still. You've taken away my control." He'd worked hard for that control. It had been beaten into him and now, when he needed it most, when it had never failed him before, he was in danger of losing it completely.

"I don't think I can stop moving," she confessed, panting, biting her lip, trying to still her body at the command in his voice.

He loved that about her. She tried to do what he asked, no matter how difficult, and staying still was difficult. He smoothed his hand over her bottom, those luscious curves he found so intriguing, taking a breath, wanting to live right where he was. He moved then. Slow. Withdrawing. All the way, almost losing contact. Her eyes widened and her ankles locked tighter, as if she could hold him to her.

He surged forward with a hard, fast stroke, driving through her tight folds so that the friction was nearly unbearable. Fire streaked through his body. She cried out, clutching at him, sliding her hands down to his hips to grasp him, to try to urge him to keep going. He withdrew again, even slower this time and, eyes on her face, he began a slow, steady assault on her nerve endings. Driving in slow, retreating even slower, allowing her fire to surround him, to grip and milk.

"Casimir." She wailed his name.

He kept the slow, steady buildup, keeping the friction right over her sweet little button, just enough to drive her wild, not send her careening over the edge. It cost him. Sweat beaded on his body. His blood thundered in his ears and roared through his veins. All the while he moved in her, loving her, he felt the assault on his own body, the power gathering like the force of a volcano rumbling, waiting, holding off for the bigger explosion. Arousal was so intense it was painful, arcing through his thighs, boiling in his balls, jackhammers drilling into his skull, and yet all of that only added to the pleasure burning through him.

Her breath caught in her throat. Her eyes widened. Fingernails bit deep. She went over the edge hard and fast, so unexpected, with such force, she swept him along in the wildfire. He plunged into her, several hard strokes while the flames burned over them, consuming both of them, and her cries reverberated in his mind.

He collapsed over top of her, pinning her small body beneath his, letting her take his full weight while he buried his face in her neck, his heart pounding wildly, his lungs raw and aching, his entire body sated. Aftershocks shook them both, her body still alive, rippling around his.

He lay there for far longer than he should have, letting his heart pound, absorbing the feel of her under him. Savoring it. She didn't protest or attempt to push him off. She kissed his temple and rubbed her hands along his back.

"*Ya lyublyu tebya,*" he whispered, meaning it. He shifted his weight off of her, but stayed buried in her, his hands framing her face. "Do you understand, Giacinta? Did you hear what my body said to yours?"

She traced his lower lip with the pad of her finger. "I

heard you, Casimir. I feel the same way. Thank you. I needed you tonight and I should have known you'd be here for me."

He rolled, taking her with him so that she sprawled over top of him. Grasping the covers, he pulled them over both of them. "Go back to sleep, *golubushka*. I'll wake you before you have to get back to your own room."

She laid her head over his heart, her hands moving up and down his shoulder and biceps as she drifted off to sleep, knowing he would watch over her.

8

PATRICE Lungren sat on the hard seat of the old bus and smiled at the little boy across from her. His mother gave her a quick grin in return. Patrice knew exactly what the woman saw, she'd assumed her role perfectly.

Patrice was short and very slender, almost a stick. She wore flattering trousers and a silk blouse with a short, flared jacket, very classy. Her black hair was glossy and hung just to her shoulders in a very sophisticated cut. Her eyebrows were dark and when she removed her very expensive dark glasses, her eyes and lashes were as well. She had a beauty mark just to the right of her lips. Her boots were expensive, soft leather, the color matching the dark red of her jacket.

"He's beautiful," Patrice said. When the woman shook her head, she repeated the observation in halting Italian.

The woman beamed at her. "*Grazie*. Thank you." She tried her own English. Clearly she spoke it but had been afraid to try it out with an American. She indicated Patrice's camera. "Pictures?"

Patrice nodded. "Shops. Homes. The ocean and country-side. Everything." She smiled wide. "I love it here. I come as often as I can to visit. I took a cooking class in the village just a few miles away and it was wonderful." Patrice Lungren, had, in fact, taken that cooking class.

"You like to travel?" The young mother now seemed determined to practice her English.

"I love it," Patrice admitted. "Fortunately, I'm in a position to indulge my love of traveling and I do it often. Italy is my favorite, but I travel all over. I just find myself coming back here over and over. Someday, I'd like to live here permanently."

"By the sea?" The bus traveled along the coastline, so it was a good guess.

Patrice smiled and nodded. "I'm taking pictures of homes. I want as many examples of places I could live as possible. I was in a cappuccino bar a few days ago and someone told me about the homes along this section of coast. Supposedly the homes are quite beautiful."

The young mother nodded. *"Costoso."* She floundered for a moment.

"Expensive?" Patrice guessed.

The young mother nodded vigorously. "Very expensive, but beautiful."

The bus pulled to the side of the road, and Patrice flashed another smile. "Nice talking to you. This is my stop." She waved at the little boy and, clutching her camera, hurried to get off. It was her experience that bus drivers started up just as fast as they pulled over.

As she snapped several pictures of the nearest home, she glanced at her watch. Luigi's information was very detailed, as usual. Now she knew how he got that information—he was friends with those he targeted. He walked right into their homes, inserted himself into their daily lives. He knew their routines just as well as he knew his own.

Luigi had become ill a few days earlier while she was out doing recon of Cosmos Agosto's home. Feigning embarrassment because he was walking unsteadily, Luigi had retreated, as he always did, into his wing of the house. That damned him in her eyes more than anything else. Thinking back, she realized *every* time she had gone after a target, he had retreated on the pretense of being ill. Before, she had accepted his chronic illness; after all, she'd known even before her parents had been killed that he was ill. Now, knowing it was a ruse, she was infuriated.

Lissa was grateful for the discipline she'd developed over the years, the practice of tamping down the fire always burning deep inside. For the first time in her life, she was glad Luigi had retreated into his wing, although she was tempted to come up with an excuse to have to crash into his empty apartment to see for herself that he was truly gone.

Patrice snapped more pictures. In fifteen minutes, Cosmos's beautiful young wife, Carlotta, would go to her weekly beauty appointment. She was a former up-and-coming model, and Cosmos apparently dictated that she work out, stay a certain weight and always look gorgeous. She complied. According to Luigi's information, Cosmos didn't want children and had also insisted that his wife—not him—permanently make certain a pregnancy didn't happen. She was young, but she had, again, complied.

Patrice continued her natural progression along the street. The manicured estates were large and set well back from the road. She took pictures of gardens, going so far as to balance on a fence to get a close-up shot of a certain flower in bloom. She took her time, out in the open, making certain she wasn't followed, the way she always did. She didn't deviate in the least from her norm.

Arturo remained behind in the house, supposedly to take care of Luigi. He slipped in and out of the wing, the only one permitted. She knew it was to help preserve her uncle's subterfuge. That hurt as well. She'd come to love Arturo. She worried about him almost as much as she did her uncle. He was part of the entire betrayal. He'd been with Luigi long before the death of her parents. She'd known him all of her life.

He had never followed her on a job, but always, just in case, she made certain she was entirely alone. Luigi had taught her that. He had said to make certain there were no witnesses, not even someone she trusted. Arturo hadn't followed her. None of Luigi's men had.

She moved farther down the street, ambling slowly, snapping pictures as she went. There was little activity in the quiet neighborhood—few cars and no foot traffic, exactly the way she liked it. Since most of the larger homes were set back so far, she doubted if too many people witnessed her camera-happy persona, but if they did, it was Patrice they saw, no one else.

The Agosto estate was one of the largest along that particular road. The grounds were covered with flowers and shrubs. Wrought-iron gates stood at the entrance to the long, winding drive, a drive that snaked through the property to come up on the three-story mansion, swung around to the guest home and then farther back, to the cliffs lining the property above the sea.

The estate was the crowning jewel of the area. A low wrought-iron fence surrounded the gardens on three sides. There was no fence along the cliffs, and the ornamental fencing was just that—for looks. It was known that Cosmos Agosto kept dogs and guns. No one entered his property without permission, not even children—and he spread it far and wide that he didn't like children. His reasoning for no fence along the cliffs was that he wanted an unobstructed view and he had no children to protect.

The gates opened while Patrice snapped several pictures of the gardens on the adjoining estate. A chauffeur-driven town car swept by, Cosmos's wife in the backseat. The woman stared straight ahead, not even glancing Patrice's way as she diligently took pictures of the flowers close to the wrought-iron fence at the corner of the Agosto property.

Patrice continued to ramble along the road, now peering into the beautifully kept gardens with their marble fountains as she trailed her hand along the black wrought iron. She always was careful to have liquid fingerprints, prints that would match Patrice Lungren's passport and identification papers.

A car moved slowly up the street, passed Patrice and the double gates to pull to the side of the road several yards ahead of her. The car was an older model and dusty, the windows clouded. A tall, well-built man got out. He wore a casual T-shirt under a sports jacket, dark trousers and nice shoes. His hair was silver, as was the stubble on his jaw.

The man looked around slowly and then reached into the car to pull a camera bag off the seat. He fiddled with the strap for a moment before closing the door and finally looking at Patrice. She sent him a friendly, sunny smile and a small wave, holding up her camera to indicate they were fellow travelers and quickening her steps to hurry to get to his side.

"Hi, I'm Patrice," she greeted with her happiest smile and an outstretched hand. "I'm from the United States, here on vacation."

The man hesitated a moment, leaning back against his car, his gaze drifting over her appraisingly. It took a moment for him to smile back and take her outstretched hand. "Friedrich Bauer. From Germany. Also on vacation."

The moment "Friedrich's" fingers touched her skin, an electrical charge skipped over Lissa's skin. Patrice might not be affected by just that skin-to-skin contact, but to her, it was almost as intimate as when he touched her in the bedroom. A little shiver went through her entire body.

It was important to stay in character at all times. This was the first time she'd ever worked with anyone on a job and just that was foreign to her, but Casimir had insisted. He didn't look at all like her Casimir, but she would recognize his touch anywhere.

When he let go of her hand after a firm shake, the pads of his fingers brushed gently along her inner wrist. She hadn't known she could be so sensitive, but that barely there touch felt like four firebrands sinking deep.

"All clear," she said softly. She glanced toward the house and then her watch. "He should be on the move any minute. Apparently he really enjoys walking to the cliffs when he's alone and staring out over the sea."

"I wonder why." Casimir's voice was strictly neutral.

His gaze did a long, slow sweep of the surrounding terrain, taking in the street as well as the vast estate across from the Agosto property. There was no one around, no one working on either of the grounds—something rarely done on a weekday. Both had suspected Cosmos wanted it that way. He liked a day to himself to do whatever he wanted away from prying eyes.

Luigi's report had been so thorough he had even had the information that Cosmos forced his wife to go to the beauty parlor for her facials and manicures even when she was ill. Never once had Lissa questioned Luigi's reports, but when Casimir pointed the remark out as odd, she just looked at him, understanding in her gaze. She knew Luigi had personal knowledge of what Cosmos did or didn't do with his wife.

Casimir reached out and, for just one moment, allowed himself the luxury of touching her again. Reassuring her. He couldn't take this away from her, she wouldn't let him, but he could let her know he was always at her back. He brushed his fingers along the side of her neck, trailing slowly until he reached the edge of her perfect little suit shirt.

"Pervert. I just met you." But she smiled. It was brief, and it didn't light her eyes, but he saw what he wanted in her eyes. She was clear. Ready. "Let's do this," Lissa said. She didn't ask him if he'd brought everything. It was in his camera case. She'd packed that herself.

*　*　*

COSMOS Agosto was in the prime of his life. At thirty-six he was one of the youngest men in the Porcelli family to be as wealthy as he was without all the hassle of being a soldier. He had a beautiful wife, a former model. Carlotta did whatever he told her to do and she did it immediately. It hadn't taken him very long to train her. He had two mistresses, one who lived close and another one town over. His life was fairly easy.

He went to work, training others to handle the dogs. He enjoyed the power of that, being in a position to snap orders at others and belittle them until they were nearly at the breaking point. He was a master at it. He practiced enough on his wife. Every once in a while he had to show his loyalty to Luigi Abbracciabene by doing some dirty job for him, but the pay was well worth it.

Luigi's wife, Angeline, didn't have a brain in her head. When they came over for dinner, Cosmos wanted to shoot himself just listening to her. He couldn't understand why Luigi, an intelligent man, had tied himself to such a moron. Of course, Luigi fucked everything that walked in skirts in a two-hundred-mile radius. He'd even bragged to Cosmos that he often brought a woman into his study, fucked her right there or had her blow him while Angeline knocked on the door. Luigi took great pleasure in roaring at his wife to leave him alone, and she would slink away in tears.

Cosmos wasn't a man to allow another to one-up him, so he'd done the same, but found the pleasure was even greater when he forced his wife to watch—or participate. Life was good. So good. When he was in a bad mood, he could take out his frustration on his beautiful trophy, reveling in her tears and her promises of doing better. When he was happy, he could do whatever the hell he wanted when he wanted—and that was often.

Luigi paid him well and always would. He would have that money coming in for the rest of Luigi's life. That had been the deal, and Cosmos wasn't a trusting man. If Luigi

ever thought to get rid of him to save that money, he had in-
surance to prevent that. Recordings. Times. Dates. Even at
nineteen he'd been smart. All that, along with recordings,
was locked up tight in his safe. When he died, his lawyer
would find the information. He often taunted Luigi with the
fact that he'd better not die of some illness.

Luigi had picked him up off the street and groomed him
for the position of his brother's dog handler. Cosmos had
taken that job knowing he would eventually betray them all.
Honestly, that had thrilled him. Every time he sat down at
the table with the Abbracciabenes he had secretly laughed
inside.

Luigi had to put up with a moron with the face of a horse
while he had a young model, her face and body beautiful. He
knew someday Luigi would kill his wife, and he wanted to
be there when it was done. Cosmos figured his own wife had
a few good years left until her looks went. He'd replace her
then. Until that day, he forced her to please him in every way
possible. He had to admit, he missed the exhilaration of
knowing death was coming to those close to him and sometimes, he couldn't help himself, he had to repeat that experience. He would know who was going to die, but they
wouldn't. It made him feel a little like a god.

Cosmos sauntered out of his house, the three-story mansion with glittering chandeliers and gleaming wood, another sign of success he didn't give a damn about, like his
trophy wife, but enjoyed showing off to others. He liked the
status. He especially liked to lord it over those who had said
he wouldn't amount to anything. His scum parents he sometimes saw just to remind himself of what his life could have
been like. Someday, he'd set fire to their little box of a
house and burn their alcoholic asses along with the dump
they lived in.

He walked to the cliff overlooking the ocean. It was one
of his favorite spots. This was where he disposed of anything
or anyone who got in his way. A teenage boy who had tried

to steal his car and had begged for food when caught, begged even to be turned over to the authorities. Cosmos detested him, that reminder of what he'd been. So pathetic. He brought him home on the pretense of feeding him and giving him a job. It had been so satisfactory throwing his ass off the cliff—a symbol of getting rid of his old self. Feeling the power. Knowing who he was now.

Another death had been that of a woman he'd spent hours with, taking her in every way possible, forcing her to service his friends and later Luigi. She'd been so accommodating until his friends had arrived. She had the audacity to threaten him. He was very happy to prolong her death, holding her over the edge, listening to her beg before he dropped her worthless ass into the sea.

Two dogs, ungrateful for his care, one biting him and the other cowering in the back of the kennel, both reactions after he'd disciplined them. Both every bit as worthless as the little bitch threatening him. He expected his dogs to obey him instantly. He kept them hungry and grateful for the least little bit of attention. The two hadn't been worth anything, turning on him like that.

The biggest thrill was the whining, sniveling, snot-nosed six-year-old son of his gardeners—a husband-and-wife team. The couple always brought him along and he was continually screaming and crying, running to his mother when his father told him to stop. She babied him endlessly, heaping insults on her husband when he tried to discipline the boy. Cosmos had complained several times of the noise, but she only glared at him while her son had looked smug. He'd arranged for an accident, the poor little brat falling over the edge on his mother's watch. Stupid cow. Now her husband had something to hold over her head for eternity.

He laughed softly, peering down into the crashing waves. He could do anything. He had that right. Here, in the world he'd created through his hard work, he was god of his domain. He loved reliving those moments of absolute power.

He could stand there and think about how it would feel to throw Luigi's wife right off the cliff. He fantasized about it often when she sat across from him at his dinner table talking endlessly about shopping with his wife.

A sound behind him had him whirling around. He felt a sting, as if a bee had landed on his neck and stung him. He slapped his hand over the wound and staggered a little as his legs turned rubbery. A hand caught his arm. Rough. In a vise. It hurt. He turned his head, finding it difficult to do that. His neck hurt and his motor movements were sluggish.

A man's face swam into view. Cosmos opened his mouth to speak, to demand what was going on, but his shock was so great that for a moment, he couldn't find his voice. He could only stare at the stranger, stunned that anyone would dare come onto his property uninvited and look at him the way that man was—as if he were scum. No one looked at him that way and lived. He'd grown powerful. Wealthy. He ruled his own little empire. *No one* looked at him that way, he wouldn't stand for it.

He found himself sitting right there on the very edge of the cliff. For the first time he didn't like being so close to the edge. He wasn't in control of his movements. His body shuddered, breaking out into a sweat. He swayed and tried to hold himself rigid. Tried to make out the face—no faces—in front of him. The man was still there. A woman had joined him. The man was older, with silver hair. The man slipped on a pair of mirrored glasses covering his eyes—the eyes that held so much contempt. He was exceptionally strong for his age. The woman had glossy black hair, beautiful features, but was far too skinny for his liking.

"Do you know who you're fucking with?" he asked, surprised his voice worked. He recognized a fast-acting drug rushing through his system. It hurt. Shredded his nerves. More, they hit him again with another needle. This one contained a dark liquid.

"You should have known Luigi would send someone after

you. You killed his brother, murdered him. He wasn't going to let you live."

The woman spoke, her voice soft, even musical. She might be skinny, but her voice was all kinds of sexy. Cosmos recognized that even thinking about whether she was attractive or not under the circumstances was fucked up and he started laughing.

"He can't have me killed. He knows I have proof he put me in his brother's house so we could kill him. He had to cement his relationship with Angeline and her family first and then when it was done, when she agreed to marry him, I could let the dogs loose."

He laughed hysterically again. Deep inside, Cosmos tried to stop talking, stop the flow of his consciousness from spilling every secret, but his nerve endings were on fire, and worse, he was beginning to feel as if he were drunk. He *was* drunk. He knew he was. His body swayed and he laughed again.

"Luigi and Aldo Porcelli are friends?"

"Luigi is tight with all the Porcellis. He's like a shark swimming in a tank with a bunch of bottom-feeders. They think they know him. I can't wait for him to take over—and he will. He says no, but I know he will and then he'll kill that fucking moron of a wife. She's so useless. She can't even give the man a decent blow job, too busy making sure her lipstick is perfect. I want to be there when he does it."

"I don't think you're going to be there," the woman said softly. "You're drunk and you're very close to the edge of the cliff."

He felt a hand on his arm. The man again. He found himself standing, facing them, the wind coming off the ocean blowing cold air across his neck and back.

"Do you know who I am, Cosmos?" the woman asked.

He shook his head. The action made the world spin. He recovered, holding himself rigidly upright.

"I'm Giacinta Abbracciabene. That little girl who followed you around and sat next to you at the table night after night when my parents invited you in for dinner so you wouldn't be alone."

His eyes widened. That child had flaming red hair like her mother. This woman couldn't possibly be her. She was dead, wasn't she? He didn't know what happened to her. He couldn't remember, his mind working very sluggishly. He shook his head. The action sent the ground under his expensive Italian shoes rolling. She stepped closer and he stepped back—into air. Empty space. The space where other bodies had gone before his.

He felt himself falling and knew it was too late to save himself. He didn't understand what happened, but when he hit the jagged rocks below, he felt his body breaking into pieces, the bones smashed. He opened his mouth to scream in pain, but the waves smashed into him, driving salty water down his throat and into his lungs.

Casimir indicated for Lissa to step onto the path out of the softer dirt. Meticulously, taking his time, he erased all evidence of the two of them being at the edge with Cosmos. He took Lissa's hand and they walked through the riot of cheerful flowers, staying on the stamped path so as not to leave any shoeprints behind. No one was around. It was the gardener's day off, just as Luigi's intelligence had reported. He had been thorough. Cosmos's wife was out of the house with her friends, getting her weekly pedicure and facial. There was no one around to see Cosmos Agosto drunkenly fall over the edge of the cliff he loved so much.

Just out of sight of the street, Casimir stopped, pulling Lissa to a halt as well. He had to know she was all right. They had the confirmation they needed. Cosmos had told them everything they needed to know, the alcohol rushing through his veins loosening his tongue. Had he not gone over the cliff, he would have died from alcohol poisoning before he was discovered, but this way, no sharp-eyed medical examiner could discover the pinpricks on his skin.

"*Golubushka*, look at me." She had to be hurting. She had expected the confirmation, had already accepted that Luigi was guilty, but it was human nature to hold out hope. Just a tiny sliver of hope, but still, it would hurt when that was ripped away.

"I'm okay," she whispered. "Let's get home and finish this."

"Look at me," he repeated, standing directly in front of her. A rock wall she couldn't move or get around. His voice was gentle, but there was command in it.

She tilted her chin. Lifted her lashes. Met his eyes. His gut tightened. He leaned down, framing her face with both hands. "I'm with you every step of the way. Your real family is waiting for you back in the States. This is just another job we have to do. A job, *malyshka*, something to be done. Don't feel one way or the other."

Her lashes fluttered. He loved Lissa's red-gold tips, not Patrice's black ones. He brushed his mouth over hers because there was no changing Lissa's mouth—and just for one heart-stopping moment her lips had trembled.

"Do you understand what I'm saying to you, Giacinta? That's how you're going to get through this. Hang on to me. To your sisters. To my brothers. We're real. We're solid. We won't ever let you down. If you called right now, they would all be on the next plane. You know that. I'm not going anywhere. You have to put distance between yourself and this man who was supposed to be your uncle. He's nothing but an illusion, and now he's a mark. He made himself that. You didn't put his ass there, he did. Do you get this?"

Her gaze moved over his face, studying every line there. She slowly nodded. "I do, Casimir. I'll put him where he belongs now. I have to sit down with him. Tell him it's done. He'll hand me my next assignment, Aldo Porcelli. Aldo supposedly was the one that got his father to order the hit on my family. He probably did. He believes Luigi is his friend. Luigi married his sister. Of course he would believe that. Aldo won't suspect, and he's the last obstacle before Luigi is head of both families. The Porcelli territory is large, much larger than the Abbracciabene territory ever was."

"I hope Luigi enjoys thinking about being the all-powerful head of both families, because he won't have time to enjoy it," Casimir said. "Are you going to be all right by yourself getting home?"

She nodded. "It will be good for me, taking the time on the bus. You go be Tomasso, the faithful bodyguard. Keep an eye on Arturo."

He smirked. He couldn't help it. He'd keep his eye on Arturo, all right. Especially when she was sequestered with her uncle in his study and she had an alibi—when there was no possible way Luigi would ever suspect his niece. Arturo was going to die. It was that simple. Arturo was every bit as guilty as Luigi. He had to know Luigi didn't have multiple sclerosis. He knew Luigi was married and had a full life in another town. He also knew that Luigi planned to dispose of his niece the moment she finished taking out the key figures in the Porcelli family to leave the opening for Luigi. Arturo was living on borrowed time. He just didn't know it.

"What are you planning?" she asked.

He smiled down at her. "Go, Lissa. Go now." He glanced at his watch. "You have a bus to catch. I'll shadow the bus until you get to your stop. If you have trouble, you know the signal. You'll be on your own once you get to that stop. I've got to take the car back to the rental place and get my own transportation."

She nodded. "I've done this countless times on my own, Casimir. I'll be fine. I won't pretend I wasn't holding out a little hope, but I knew. I was trained as a professional. *He* trained me. I learned a lot more on my own. He's very old-school. He got lazy. Once I was working and he trusted that I knew what I was doing, he lost interest. I kept educating myself. He's a very arrogant man and that can kill a man very easily."

He found himself smiling. Even his gut settled. His hand came up from the nape of her neck to sift through the strands of the very expensive wig she wore. He gave a little tug. "I get what you're saying. I won't let arrogance be my downfall."

"Have no worries, Casimir," she said. "If you do, I'll be right there to remind you."

Lissa left him, walking away from him as Patrice Lungren. She took the picture of his beautiful, masculine face with her as she rounded the corner of the garden and emerged from between two tall elegantly rounded bushes to step through a low, unlocked gate back onto the sidewalk. She ambled down the street, looking around her in the way an awed tourist would, occasionally stopping to snap another picture before moving at a little more brisk pace toward the bus stop.

She stood at the little stop, trying not to feel restless. Patrice wouldn't be restless. She was always calm and cool. Friendly. Easygoing. Lissa didn't want to have time to think about having to face her uncle. She would do it, because she had to, but it wouldn't be easy. She also didn't want to dwell too much on the look on Casimir's face. She had to walk a very fine line. If she allowed herself to be too upset and he knew it, he would definitely not wait to kill Luigi and Arturo.

Casimir had learned to push down the fire roaring in him, just as she had done. But it was there, smoldering just beneath the surface, and it would come blazing to life if she did anything at all to fan those embers. She knew, with absolute certainty, that she was the only one who could make Casimir lose control. He wouldn't wait to rid the world of Luigi and Arturo if he thought it would make her feel better.

Life didn't work that way. She had avenged her parents' death going through the Porcelli soldiers who had carried out the attack. They'd died, one by one, over the years. Their dying hadn't lessened her grief even a little.

The bus arrived and she climbed aboard, flashing Patrice's friendly smile to everyone as she sank into a seat. She made a show of looking at all the pictures on her camera before putting it away and turning to make small talk with the older woman sitting in the seat next to her.

She walked the three blocks to retrieve her car, changing directions several times to ensure she didn't have a tail. She saw the moment Casimir believed she was safe and he turned down a narrow street to return the rental car and get back to being Tomasso. She kept walking until she came to the small storage facility. Patrice Lungren put in her code, stepped inside and immediately became Lissa Piner.

Lissa was thorough, scrubbing off Patrice's makeup and carefully applying Lissa's. Everything Patrice went into a duffel bag with her papers, ID, passport, cell phone and charger. Lissa braided her own hair and donned a long skirt and elegant blouse. Her boots were soft leather and matched her wide belt. Her jacket was short and fit snugly, emphasizing her lush curves.

Lissa tossed her purse onto the passenger seat of the little car Luigi always had available to her and drove out of the private storage garage. Luigi owned the facility, so there were no cameras set up anywhere near the building reserved for her. She even had her own private entrance, kept for Luigi or someone from his estate.

She drove all the way to the road leading to the Abbracciabene property and then she had to pull over, fighting for air. It wasn't a panic attack, but her chest hurt so much she thought her heart would shatter.

She dragged her cell phone out of her purse and dialed a familiar number before she could stop herself.

"Lissa!"

Lexi's delighted voice nearly brought her to tears. She hadn't considered that she would turn into an emotional storm. The burning in her eyes and the lump in her throat were evidence that she shouldn't have reached out. Not now. Not when she needed to be strong. She was going to face

Luigi, and she couldn't go with red eyes and a face swollen from crying.

"Hey, girl."

There was an instant silence. Then Lexi's voice came again. Soft. Loving. So Lexi. "What's wrong? Do you need me? I can get a flight out tonight."

There it was. Exactly what Casimir had told her not even an hour earlier. She had family. They were chosen, not blood, but they were family all the same. She heard the love in Lexi's voice and knew it was genuine. For her. For a moment she had to bite down hard on her lower lip to keep from bursting into tears.

"No. No, I'm all right. I just needed to hear your voice."

"Gavriil wants to talk to you." Lexi sounded dismayed, as if she didn't believe Lissa.

"Come home." Gavriil issued the two words as a command. "You don't have to do what you're doing for this family, Lissa. We'd much rather you be home with us and safe. Come home."

She knew he didn't want her going after Kostya and Uri Sorbacov. He had no idea about her uncle and his betrayal. Still, it was nice to hear a badass like Gavriil wanted her to come home. He was totally wrapped up in Lexi, not so much in the rest of those living on the farm. He hadn't been there long and hadn't developed his relationship with the others yet. Lissa did feel a connection with him. He saw her when no one else had, and that had meant something to her. She had trusted him with her past, and that meant something to him.

"Not yet, but don't worry about me. I'm well taken care of." That was to assure him his brother was looking out for her.

"Lissa . . ." Gavriil began.

"I have to do this. I *have* to. I'll explain things when I come home."

"Just see that you do. Come home, that is. If you need me

for any reason, I'll be on a plane. Give me the word and I'll come."

She closed her eyes again and pressed the phone tight against her ear as if she could hold Lexi and Gavriil close to her. Gavriil would be risking his life getting on a plane and coming to help her, but he still offered and she knew he would do it if she asked. "Thank you. I needed to hear you say that, Gavriil. I have to go. Just take care of Lexi for me. I have to know all of you are safe and when I get home, you'll all be there."

"We'll be safe," Gavriil said gruffly. "You'd better be the same."

She hung up quickly before Lexi could get back on. She knew if she heard Lexi's voice again she'd break down and cry and nothing would stop her little sister from getting on a plane and coming to her. Probably all of her sisters would come. And then all the Prakenskii brothers would come. She found herself laughing instead of crying, because that was what true family did, they made life so much better, no matter how bad the problem was.

Lissa set the car in motion. Chances were, Luigi wouldn't be home yet. He wouldn't come back until he knew for certain she'd done the job. He would pretend he was still ill in his wing of the house, and that gave her a little respite and time to decide just how she would face him.

9

LUIGI'S cell phone rang as he sat down to dinner. Angeline scowled at him. "Don't answer, honey, we haven't seen you for weeks and this is our time together."

"Shut the fuck up, Angeline," he snapped. "Business doesn't wait while you sulk. You like spending money and living in a fancy house." He glared around the table at his sons. "I work all the time for her. She spends money and goes to her fancy-ass places and still she gives me shit."

The boys glared at their mother, and she ducked her head, picked up her fork and pushed the food around on her thousand-dollar plate. With another curse, Luigi flung himself out of the chair, sending it crashing to the floor, snapped open his cell and with long, angry strides, left the dining room.

"This better be important," he growled. "I'm eating my fucking dinner." But he'd seen the caller ID and he knew *exactly* who it was and why she was calling. He knew, and elation swept through him. His niece had struck again—successfully. She was a torpedo: once unleashed, unstoppable.

"Luigi. Luigi."

Hysterical sobbing. Luigi held the phone away from his ear, his smile widening. Yeah. His niece was a damn fine tool. He wished he could figure out a way to keep her alive. She was a better asset than any he had, but she was intelligent, unlike the idiot moron sitting at his dining table. He would kill one slowly and with extreme happiness. The other would be quick and with reluctance.

"Luigi. You have to come. Right now. He's dead. My Cosmos is dead and I don't know what to do. You *have* to come."

Of course he had to go see the new widow. His body stirred in anticipation. He rubbed his crotch. "You call anyone else?"

"No, no one else. I know to call only you."

Cosmos had trained the little bitch. She couldn't move without direction, but when directed, she did whatever she was told. Carlotta was beautiful, absolutely beautiful, and in his stable of women, she'd command a huge price every fucking time. His grin got even wider. He absolutely loved his niece.

"What happened?" he asked tersely.

More sobbing.

"Shut the fuck up and tell me what happened," he commanded.

"He fell over the cliff. He just fell. He was drinking wine. I found the bottle by the cliff. His body was on the rocks, but it went out to sea. I don't know if I can get him back to bury him . . ." She sobbed more.

"I'll be there as soon as I can make it." He snapped the cell shut. He didn't want to hear her crying, not when he wanted to dance around the room. He raised his voice. "Arturo. With me." When Giacinta was in town, he usually left Arturo behind, but he'd forced him to come to his home because Angeline complained about him not having a bodyguard. And he knew the widow would call . . .

Arturo would be glad when it was over. He hated going

back and forth between the towns when Luigi had to play sick. He had an aversion to Angeline. Luigi smiled again. He was a master at manipulation. Angeline's sons regarded her as unimportant, an idiot they all put up with. They even felt sorry for their father for having to put up with her. Over the years he'd even managed to subtly turn her father and brother against her. They didn't realize, but they began to treat her as if she didn't have a brain too. She had retreated more and more into her world of shopping, which only gave him more ammunition. When she was gone, his boys would accept her passing quickly.

He stuck his head in the dining room. "This is important. I'll be gone for a couple of days. Look after your mother, boys." He sighed and raked his fingers through his hair. "Go get that diamond bracelet you wanted, Angeline."

She looked up, her face lighting up. A smile curved her mouth and her gaze clung to his. He was very, very good at push and pull. Push her away and pull her back. She fell for it every time.

"Do you mean it, Luigi? Are you certain?"

He softened his expression, nodding. "Yeah, baby. I'm sorry I have to be gone so much, but the boys look after you properly, don't they?"

She didn't dare say otherwise. She nodded her head vigorously. He blew her a kiss, already anticipating the evening. He would go see the lovely widow, take care of business, retreat to his wing of his other home, stay a day and then recover enough to see Lissa and give her the last and final assignment—the one that would make him boss of both families.

The elation was so strong he thought his heart might burst out of his chest. He'd begun planning when his brother ascended to the Abbracciabene throne. Marcello might have been older, but Luigi should have been the natural successor. He was very, very good at what he did. That was when the plan had come to him.

He stared out the window as the car sped toward the town Cosmos resided in. It was nearly an hour away. He had plenty of time to anticipate what the good widow would be doing for him and all the money he'd make off of her after. Seventeen years of waiting was coming to an end, and the nearly euphoric feeling was almost better than when he was finally told his brother and sister-in-law were dead.

He really wanted to go see Aldo before he sent his best weapon after him. Smug, little Aldo who ruled his empire and treated Luigi as a poor relation. Luigi shook his head, a small smirk playing around his mouth. He could see his reflection in the window now. He was young enough to rule both empires for a very long time. He would have it all. Power. Wealth. Women. He enjoyed playing chess with other people's lives. And he'd won. He'd nearly toppled the king. It was his own little pawn that was going to take that king down.

He burst out laughing. "We're so close, Arturo."

"You got that right, boss," Arturo said, elation in his voice as well. "She came through again, didn't she? She always does."

The smile faded from Luigi's face. It wasn't that he had affection for Lissa. He didn't feel emotions like affection, but he definitely regretted having to kill her. He'd sent her to the States to get her away from him. She was too damned intelligent to keep around on a daily basis. She would have figured the entire plan out by now had he allowed her to stay close.

Angeline had been with him seventeen years and she hadn't figured out a damn thing. Not. One. Damn. Thing. She believed he loved her. He gave a little snort of derision. He *despised* the bitch. She claimed to love him, but she didn't know the first thing about him and she sure as hell didn't do anything to show him. She hated him touching her. She found sex too messy. She lay under him, the only position she'd go for, completely unmoving while he rutted like an animal. It was never fun, and she always had a look of distaste on her face afterward.

He'd given up long ago trying to make something of his marriage. In the beginning, he thought to keep her alive, but after the first five years he'd changed his mind. Once he had sons he could mold into what he wanted—and needed—he left her alone. Well, unless he was seriously pissed at her. Then he got drunk enough to make sex last a long time and he forced her to do her duty, just because he enjoyed punishing her that way.

Arturo pulled the car onto the private drive leading up to the Agosto mansion. It was a mansion, nothing less. This would be his as well. He pushed all thoughts of his wife away and looked forward to what was to come.

Cosmos's wife, Carlotta, stood anxiously waiting in the doorway. She was seriously beautiful. Her face was perfection and the flow of wavy, black hair tumbling around her soft, delicate features only accented her classic bone structure. Her eyes were enormous, dark and surrounded by thick, long lashes. She'd been in countless magazines, famous for that face and body.

Cosmos had dictated that his wife keep her body through diet and exercise, and she had obeyed him. He'd managed to make her submissive in a way Luigi had failed with Angeline, but that was all right, Luigi was going to reap the benefits of Cosmos's training.

He walked right up to her and took her into his arms, holding her close while she wept. She wore a skirt and blouse. Cosmos didn't like her in pants or underwear. When they went out, he liked showing her off and her clothes bordered on scandalous. Even now, her blouse was low-cut and thin, the material see-through to show her black bra, the one that lovingly pushed her breasts up so that the shadow of her nipples showed.

Luigi patted her back, moving her into the house, Arturo right behind him, closing the door. "I'll take care of you,

Carlotta," he assured. "You saw the body?" He put her from him gently, smiling down at her.

She tipped her face up, nodding. "He fell just at the cliff. I didn't call the authorities. I didn't know what to do, so I called you. I knew you'd come, that I could rely on you."

"You did the right thing. First, I need you to show me where Cosmos kept his safe. He had important papers he wanted me to deal with in case of his death."

"He had the safe in the bedroom, built into the wall."

He took her hand, again, quite gently, turned up her wrist and kissed the soft skin there. "Show me, *bella*. You have the code to open the safe." He made that a statement.

She beamed when he called her beautiful, eagerly nodding her head. "He made me memorize it just in case something like this happened. He said the papers were important."

He nodded solemnly as he followed her into the bedroom. Arturo trailed behind. Carlotta didn't seem to notice. She pointed to a picture on the wall and stepped back.

"Cosmos had a lot of enemies," Luigi said, pouring concern into his voice. "Did he explain that to you? Enemies he worried would harm you."

She nodded, her hand going defensively to her throat. She was tall, nearly as tall as Luigi, but slender and delicate looking.

"He wanted me to look after you." Luigi spoke to her, as he swung the picture aside. It opened like a door. "Tell me the code."

She did and he pressed the numbers she gave him. Already, Arturo crowded close to her. He and Arturo had a way of having a very good time with women. It mattered little to them whether or not the woman had a good time.

"I want you to look after me, Luigi," Carlotta said. "I need you."

He glanced over his shoulder, his gaze sweeping over her body. He turned back to the contents of the safe, dismissing her. "I don't know, Carlotta. I have a big territory and a demanding wife. What do I need with you? What can you do for me in return for my protection?"

He glanced over his shoulder again and saw her twist her fingers together. She looked deliciously anxious. He pulled out the heavy stack of papers from the safe, quickly sifting through them, looking for the journal Cosmos had kept of their pact together. He found it, scanned it and slipped it inside his jacket pocket.

"Please, Luigi. I don't know what I can give you in return, but anything." She sounded close to tears.

"Come here, *bella*." Luigi's voice was gentle. Loving even. "Right now, Carlotta." He pushed a little command into his tone, just enough that her submissive nature would demand she obey. That and her fear of being abandoned. She already looked at him with hope.

When she approached cautiously, he reached out, caught the front of her blouse and gave it a vicious yank. The material parted and he threw the scraps aside. "You know what to do to please me. Cosmos said you were very good at showing him how grateful you were to him for giving you this home."

She stood there, looking shocked, afraid, and a little uncertain. Arturo grabbed her hair in his fist and yanked her head back so hard she nearly fell over.

"You heard him, bitch. Get rid of the clothes and crawl to him. Show him you're thankful for his protection." He kept his hold on her hair with one hand and with the other he produced a knife. "Don't move yet. Stay very still. Luigi doesn't like blood. I don't mind it, but he likes a woman's body without a blemish." He slid the blade of the knife flat along her cheek and then down to the swell of her breasts.

Carlotta kept her eyes on Luigi. He smiled and winked at her. "Arturo won't hurt you, not as long as you behave. And you will behave, won't you, *bella*? You'll do whatever I ask."

"Yes," she whispered. "Yes, Luigi, anything for you."

The knife cut the straps of the bra and then slid along the side to cut the material, freeing her breasts to their sight.

Arturo slipped the blade into the waistband of the skirt and shredded that as well. She wasn't wearing panties, and she stood completely naked between the two men.

Luigi went back to looking through the papers as if dismissing her again. Arturo applied pressure until she was kneeling, and then on all fours. "Crawl to him," he snapped. "Show him how grateful you are."

She did, and the closer she got the more Luigi moved back, forcing her to follow him. Arturo laughed. "She's a well-trained bitch already, Luigi. I don't think it will take much time to get her into shape."

Luigi smiled at Arturo. "I think she's very cooperative." He stopped moving so Carlotta could catch up to him. He made certain it was in the center of the room where they could have plenty of room to do whatever they wanted with the woman.

"Luigi, I'll do whatever you want," Carlotta said.

Arturo's belt landed hard on her naked butt. She screamed. "You don't call him Luigi. He is no longer your friend. He's your protector. Show some respect."

"Arturo," Luigi said softly. "She's trying. Don't cry, *bella*. He wants only to help you remember how to behave so you won't get into trouble. Arturo, make her feel better while she sucks my cock. Open my trousers, Carlotta, and do a good job. I want to fuck your face, shove my cock right down your throat, and you're going to swallow all that meat I'm offering you. And you'll be grateful while you do it. I want enthusiasm. If I don't get that, I can't be responsible for what Arturo will do. He has a bad temper, that one."

Arturo was already rubbing his hand over the vicious mark of his belt, his fingers wandering lower. He pushed her legs farther apart with his foot and plunged his fingers deep into her. His thumb slid into the crease of her cheeks. She gasped and squirmed, trying to dislodge his hand, but he kept working her.

She had a difficult time taking down the zipper to Luigi's

trousers while Arturo used his fingers to spread her wider and wider. Luigi grabbed her head, suddenly tired of waiting, and pushed her down over his waiting cock. She swallowed him whole. He found it more than entertaining watching Arturo first fist her and then take her brutally, slamming into her, driving her mouth over Luigi with every stroke. Of course he didn't stop there. He took her in every way possible while she screamed deliciously around Luigi's cock. Tears poured down her face while Arturo opened her so Luigi could easily sell her body again and again to the highest bidder, allowing them to use her any way possible. When they were done with her, he could sell her to Evan Shackler-Stavros for use on one of his snuff freighters.

He rubbed her cheek, smiling benevolently. "I will take such good care of you, *bella*, you'll be a treasure in my stable. Arturo will take you to a safe house. He'll look after you. I'll visit later tonight, after you get settled. You'll have papers to sign. You can't ever come back to this house. Cosmos's enemies will look for you here." He leaned down and brushed a kiss on top of her head. "Have no worries, I'll take very good care of you. You'll have a nice apartment and you'll only be required to entertain the best of men. You'll enjoy yourself. Arturo will see that you know exactly what to do."

He stroked her head again and then presented his hand to her. "Show your gratitude, Carlotta, and remember, I expect absolute loyalty and obedience. No questions. You understand?" Suddenly he gripped her hair hard and yanked her head back to stare down into her liquid-filled eyes.

She swallowed hard, her face blotching, her mascara running. He thought she looked even more beautiful that way. "*Si*, Don Abbracciabene." Eagerly, when he released her hair, she bent to kiss his hand. "Anything you say."

"I will leave you in Arturo's more than capable hands. Arturo will see to it that you are fully trained and know what to expect anytime I come to visit you or send someone I want you to please."

Carlotta nodded her head, started to make a move to rise, but halted when the belt lashed across her bottom again. She cried out and received another blow. Luigi winked at her and, taking the papers, sauntered out, whistling. Behind him, he heard blows raining down on the woman's bare bottom and thighs. Arturo enjoyed inflicting pain. He took great care that the women he trained learned to enjoy that pain so they were worth something to Luigi. Luigi had found the man invaluable. Women in the Abbracciabene stable were the most sought after of any other ring. He made certain they were clean, beautiful, well-trained and would do anything at all when told.

He would slip back into his retreat, the house Angeline knew nothing about, and hide in his private wing for another day or two before emerging sick and weak to listen to the details of Cosmos's death. He didn't want to go back home and face his disgusting wife. He would visit Carlotta again in the middle of the night. Arturo would have her hanging by her wrists from the ceiling, her body deliciously striped. She would need his loving care, a gentle hand to guide her into her new life. After Arturo's violence, his women always welcomed him and were more than happy to comply with his every wish.

He needed to look over the papers, have his lawyer prepare the ones needed for Carlotta to sign over the estate to him and give him power over her bank account. All that money he'd paid Cosmos, coming right back to him. He laughed softly as he drove, anticipating his next encounter with the grieving widow.

CASIMIR watched the car come up the long drive, park just outside of Luigi's private wing and Luigi emerge from the driver's side. He was alone, Arturo no longer with him. It was very unusual to see Luigi without Arturo and Casimir didn't like not knowing where the bodyguard was. Luigi went inside and clearly, there was nothing wrong with the man. He drove alone and he walked without help.

Almost at once, Tomasso's pager went off, a summons from Luigi into his private wing. That too was unexpected. Luigi had barely glanced at him since his arrival, a month before Lissa had shown up. Tomasso had been working nearly six weeks for Luigi, and most contact had been through Arturo. All orders had come from Luigi's main bodyguard.

He went around the house to enter through the back so that he could go to Luigi's private wing through the main part of the house. Lissa was back and she raised an eyebrow as he knocked on Luigi's door.

"Entrare." The voice sounded weak.

Lissa was there in heartbeat. "Tio Luigi, is everything all right? Should I call a doctor?"

Tomasso dropped his hand to the door and found it unlocked. He opened it just a crack, enough to allow Lissa to see in, yet make it look like he was protecting Luigi.

"Go, go away, Lissa," Luigi said. He coughed. Waved his hand at his niece, adamant that she obey him. "We will talk tomorrow or the next day. I need Tomasso right now."

Lissa nodded reluctantly and turned away, allowing Tomasso to slip into Luigi's private apartment. The wing was huge and very well appointed. Luigi didn't lack for luxury— or his ability to defend himself. The walls were thick, ensuring absolute privacy.

"Come in, Tomasso. It's time we got to know each other." Luigi waved him toward a chair and Casimir toed one around and straddled it, facing his "boss." "Arturo says good things about you. I've looked over your resume. Very impressive. You come highly recommended, although both my friends say the same thing about you. You prefer to shoot first and ask questions later."

Tomasso shrugged. "I prefer to keep my employer alive." He glanced around the room, noting the fireplace was going in spite of the fact that the night wasn't cold. Wisps of blackened, curled paper lay smoldering among the logs. Clearly Luigi was destroying whatever evidence Cosmos had against him.

"I see that you've done that, but you had to leave until things cooled down," Luigi pointed out. "That's not good for you, never giving you a real family. Arturo has been with me since I was a boy. Some of the men have worked for me or my family for over thirty years. It is far better to have a family than to be alone in this world."

Casimir kept his gaze on Luigi, wondering where this was going. He nodded, only because something was expected of him. That seemed enough for Luigi, who took it that any of the men he employed would agree with him.

"I received word tonight that a good friend of mine died in a tragic accident. I don't always believe in accidents. I have learned not to be the most trusting of men with good reason. My own brother and his wife were murdered by a family I believed to be my friends and allies." Luigi watched him closely for signs of reaction.

Casimir nodded again. "I heard of this tragedy."

"The point is, when my niece visits me, Arturo generally watches over her, but I've got him watching out for my friend's widow. I would trust no one else with her. That means, while I assess the danger to this family, I will need someone protecting my niece. She's very precious to me. She won't like it and she'll protest, but she isn't to leave this house without protection. While in it, I want you close to her."

"Of course. No harm will come to her."

"Until I give the order, I don't care how much she protests. Sleep outside her door if you have to. If she knows I've set you on her, she'll try to sneak away," Luigi warned.

He shrugged. "I've never lost a client yet. But, she despises me. I don't know if Arturo has told you, but she definitely has an aversion to me."

"I'm well aware of that. I'm hoping by giving you this job

and giving you whatever authority you need to make her be-have, you'll keep her distracted. I'm worried she'll end up in the line of fire. She has an important meeting coming up soon at a hotel, a very public hotel. I don't want her going anywhere else but to that meeting until I say the word. You don't leave her side while she's in that hotel no matter what she says."

"In that case, I am more than happy to take on this job for you."

"She is a treasure to me, but she is a handful," Luigi said. "I don't want anything to happen to her."

"I understand the trust you're placing in me, Don Luigi, and it is not misplaced. You have only to ask those I've worked with."

Luigi beamed at him. "Good. Good. Arturo said to place Lissa in your care. He thinks very highly of you. You do this for me and we can talk about a permanent home. I think you're just the right kind of soldier I need in the coming weeks."

Tomasso managed a smile as he slowly stood up. "Thank you, Don Luigi, I won't let you down."

He liked the assignment just fine, although he was more certain than ever that Luigi and Arturo were up to some-thing. Luigi didn't want his niece poking around or leaving the property because she was too intelligent to miss much. She was no longer a young, traumatized child, or teenager being indoctrinated. She was a grown woman with a moral code of her own. She would never accept her uncle's plan of absolute power. He couldn't afford to make a single mis-take around her. She was too sharp-eyed.

Tomasso sauntered out of the room, looking for all the world like an arrogant, important, Italian bodyguard. He knew he was good-looking. He made his way into the small study where Lissa liked to curl up on the couch with a book. He draped himself against the wall, a pose that always an-noyed her.

She kept her nose in the book for a few minutes and then with a little huff of annoyance glanced up. "What? What are you doing?"

"Looking at you."

"Well don't. Go away." She wiggled her fingers at him. "Don't you have another pool game to play? You're wasting my uncle's money just standing around. He doesn't seem to mind, but I do. Go stand somewhere else."

He faced the camera they both knew was in the room and smirked directly at her. "I have new orders, Lissa. I stick to you like glue. You don't go anywhere without me and if you try, I can use whatever means available to me to stop you." His smirk widened into a taunting grin.

She hissed at him through her teeth and tossed her book down on the couch. "We'll see about that."

"Your uncle has retired for the night. Do I have to remind you that he's ill?"

"You know very well he isn't my real uncle. I'm a grown woman and I can do whatever I want or *don't* want. I don't want a bodyguard."

She was good, Casimir had to admit. Throwing that bit about not being his niece to protect that cover as well. The men weren't supposed to know Giacinta Abbracciabene was alive. He gave her the most insolent look he could, one that he played straight to the camera. "Throwing a tantrum because you don't want a bodyguard is a little childish, isn't it?"

She stood up and paced across the room to him. "I don't need a bodyguard."

"Apparently, whatever is going on in your uncle's life, he believes that you do. So suck it up and give him his peace of mind instead of acting like a spoiled brat."

Her chin went up, eyes flashing dangerously. "How *dare* you talk to me like that."

"Are you going to go tell on me? Get me fired? Beaten up? Killed? Is that what you like to do when one of your uncle's men annoys the princess?"

She glared at him. "I don't need to go running to my uncle every time one of his men is rude to me."

His eyebrow shot up. "His men are rude to you?"

She stuck her nose in the air, tossing her red hair in disdain. "I'm going to my room." She swept past him.

He halted her haughty exit by simply straightening and falling into step behind her. She swung around, her fingers curling in two tight fists. "Now what are you doing?"

"Don Luigi wants you protected at all times, that means inside this house as well as outside. He told me not to leave you. I'll be sleeping on the floor just inside your door."

Her eyes widened with shock. "You will *not*."

"Actually, I will. You have an important meeting at a hotel soon. He asked me to accompany you there, but otherwise, you are not to leave the property and I'm not to leave your side."

Lissa stuck her chin in the air and continued stalking toward the stairs. "You aren't sleeping on the floor in my room."

"You offering your bed?"

She stopped so fast he ran into her and was forced to grab her arms to keep her from falling. She sent him a withering look over her shoulder. "Absolutely not."

He allowed his finger to slide over her bare arm and leaned down to put his mouth against her ear. "You might like it." He whispered the taunt, his lips brushing her earlobe. For one moment his teeth tugged and then he stepped away from her.

Lissa didn't say a word. She went up the stairs, ignoring the fact that he followed closely. She yanked open her bedroom door, but before she could close it, he caught the frame and held it so he could slip through. Like Luigi, she had her own apartment. It wasn't so large or ornate, but it was beautiful, with all the amenities.

Casimir whistled softly. "Nice. I thought my room with my personal bath and Jacuzzi was nice, but this definitely is a step or ten above." He closed the door. "You certain no cameras or recording devices are in here?"

She nodded and stepped into him, hands going to his chest, pushing him back against the door. "You are such a smart-ass. I can't believe you. Tomasso is going to get something broken over his head if he keeps it up."

"Luigi wants me to antagonize you. He thinks that will keep you distracted."

She tilted her face up to his, looking puzzled. "Why would he need me distracted? He went to visit his wife. You tailed him. By now, he has the news that Cosmos is dead. What is he planning?"

"He was burning papers, and I saw more on his desk, all in Cosmos Agosto's name. Deeds. Bank statements, that sort of thing. He must be doing a takeover of Agosto's estate."

"Where is Arturo?" she asked. "Arturo is always with him."

Casimir shook his head. "Not this time. Luigi drove in by himself, and I'm certain he's going back out again tonight. He wasn't planning to retire to his bedroom."

"We'll have to follow him."

Casimir bunched silken strands of red hair in his fist and tugged gently. "Not we, *golubushka*. Me. I'll follow him. You keep the home fires burning just in case he has someone else with eyes on you. Make sure you make an appearance every now and then by opening the door and telling me to get out."

His hand slid under the curtain of her hair to wrap around the nape of her neck. "I just want to see where he's going, Giacinta. I'm not making any move on him yet. I need to know where Arturo is and what they're up to. You won't be missing out on anything."

"He had dogs."

Casimir went still. His gut knotted. She suddenly looked vulnerable, her wide, blue eyes looking up at him. No tears. Just that quiet statement out of the blue. He didn't have to ask who she referred to. He knew. Cosmos Agosto could rot in hell. He couldn't imagine what kind of trauma a little girl suffered after watching a trusted man send his dogs after her. Worse, watching as the dogs killed her parents.

He pulled her into his arms, tight against his body, holding her close, trying to comfort her when there was little comfort to give. "He's dead, *malyshka*, and we're one step closer to getting home."

"I called Lexi," she admitted. "After. I had to hear her voice. Gavriil told me to come home."

Her voice was muffled against his chest, but he heard every word. He stroked caresses through her hair and stared over her head at the wall. "Maybe that would be the best, Giacinta. I could finish up here and then join you." He wanted her safe. Out of the mess, away from Luigi and clear of the Sorbacovs. At the same time, he didn't want to give her up. The selfish part of him that had been alone all his life didn't want to be more than arm's distance from her.

"Go keep a watch on Luigi," she murmured, not relinquishing her hold on him. She leaned into him, tilted her head so she was looking up. "But first, kiss me. I'm not going anywhere. I think we have a chance of staying alive if we go after the Sorbacovs together. Certainly I have a better chance of getting close to them than you do. I'm not about to leave you now that I've found you."

Casimir closed his eyes for a moment, savoring her words. *I'm not about to leave you now that I've found you.* In spite of every reason not to trust, Lissa trusted him. She trusted in them. She'd given herself to him, committing to him and that meant something to her—and everything to him.

"Kiss me, Casimir. I need to feel alive again. I'm cold inside."

He didn't wait. He took her mouth and poured love down her throat. The fire inside him burst through him and into her. The temperature in the room rose by several degrees but neither noticed. Her mouth was soft and perfect. So perfect. He could kiss her forever. Somehow she always took him to another realm, a place where brutal schools didn't exist and he wasn't a man without a soul.

He reluctantly took his mouth from hers and brushed kisses over her eyes, trailed more to her temple and then down to her chin. "Will you be all right without me? Luigi and Arturo can go to hell. We don't need to recon tonight."

"I'll wait for you. He'll make a move soon. Luigi has endless patience, but whenever a job is completed, he wants to discuss it. That's a given. Every single time he comes out of his wing of the house and insists we go over every detail. He won't wait long, which means whatever business he has, he'll want to conclude it."

"I thought you said Arturo is always with him."

She nodded slowly. "That's true. It's highly unusual for Arturo to leave Luigi without a bodyguard."

He kissed her again. Meaning it. Letting her know she was his and he would never change that. "I'm going then. I'll be back as soon as I know where they are."

She reached up with one hand and stroked his face with loving fingers. "I'll be here. Don't forget the cameras." Just the slightest hint of amusement crept into her voice.

She was teasing him. In the middle of the biggest mess she could be in, she still found a moment for humor. He let himself smile, when all he wanted to do was wrap her up in his arms and carry her off like a primitive caveman. He took her mouth one more time and then turned away to take care of business. Because that was what men like him did.

10

LUIGI came out of his wing in the late evening two days later, looking older and shaken. His tall frame was stooped and he walked hesitantly, as if his balance was a little off, but he refused help. Lissa followed him down the hall, staying close just in case he fell. Twice he had to stop and hold on to the wall, but he didn't speak.

He had never before waited two days to go over every detail when she had disposed of one of their primary targets. Not one single time, and Lissa couldn't help but wonder what he was up to. He disappeared each night, driving himself, without a bodyguard, sneaking away from the wing, and heading to a building on the outskirts of town. He didn't go to his wife and children, or to a meeting with the heads of other families. There was no war going on. He simply drove to the building, got out, unlocked the door and disappeared inside for hours.

Casimir followed Luigi two nights in a row, and her uncle always went to the same place. The doors were firmly locked and the windows blackened out with bars on them. He couldn't hear a sound and hadn't yet discovered a way in.

Once, Arturo had walked Luigi out to his car, so clearly the bodyguard was staying in that building. Their behavior made no sense to Lissa.

She couldn't find sleep until Casimir returned, sneaking back into her bedroom, stripping as he came to the bed, reaching for her the moment he was there, as if he couldn't stand being away from her. As if he couldn't wait one more second to make love to her. Every time he touched her, it felt that way, as if he was making love. Sometimes he was gentle, other times rough and crazy, but she always knew he touched her with love.

Luigi, moving ahead of her toward his study, stumbled and grabbed at the wall. She reached out to him automatically, but couldn't make herself touch him. Bile rose and she had to force it down, force herself to breathe through the repugnance she felt being so close to him—the man who had raised her. The man she had loved and clung to. The man who had had his own brother murdered so he could have power.

"Tio Luigi, do you need help. I can call . . ."

"No!" He spat the word, glaring at her over his shoulder.

She ducked her head as she normally did when he reprimanded her. Her hair spilled around her face, covering her expression.

"I'm fine, Lissa." He softened his voice. "This disease is . . . humiliating. I don't like you seeing me this way. I thought I was better and we needed to talk so I came out before I was really ready, but the medicine is working. Soon I will be fine again."

"I'm upset that Arturo isn't with you, Tio. He has never been away from you, and now, when you need him most . . ." She trailed off, but her tone was very accusing.

Luigi held the door for her and she preceded him into the study. The nape of her neck tingled warily and she felt as if she had a giant target painted on her back. She kept her back to him, a study in discipline, as she walked to the most comfortable chair, the one where she always sat when they talked. Luigi liked to sit behind his desk. She realized it made him think he had an advantage. He looked in charge. A man of authority, and until she had discovered the truth about him, she'd always accepted that image he projected. Now she wanted to pull out one of the many knives hidden on her body and cut his lying throat.

Luigi took his time rounding the desk to sit in his extremely expensive office chair. He steepled his fingers and leaned back, looking at her. "What is it, Lissa? You look . . . upset. Did something go wrong?"

With everyone else she stayed in character. This was going to be much more difficult than she imagined. She shook her head. Leaned forward. "That man," she hissed. "The bodyguard. Tomasso. Really, Tio Luigi, was it necessary to assign me that arrogant, *bossy* man?"

His mouth twitched in amusement. "Yes, it was. There is trouble right now. My enemies are circling. I will not lose you, Lissa, so you must give me this need to protect you. Tomasso is good at his job."

"*Too* good," she snapped, waving her hand dismissively. "I'm used to Arturo. Where is he?"

"He only takes a few days off a year. He was scheduled for the time off and of course I gave it to him. He couldn't know I would have a relapse or that trouble would come."

Lissa shook her head and huffed out her breath in exasperation. "You don't know how truly irritating Tomasso is, Tio. You coming out of your apartment is the first reprieve I've gotten." She rolled her eyes. "He left to go check out the hotel. I've got an appointment tomorrow and he wanted to go talk to their security. If he loses me that sale, I'll kill him myself."

"Now, now, *cara*, he is only doing what I asked of him," Luigi soothed, his voice indicating he was well pleased with himself. "His job is to make certain you're safe at all times. Arturo will be back soon, but in the meantime, let Tomasso do whatever he deems necessary in order to protect you."

She glared at her uncle. "Do you really think, after all the years of training, that I can't take care of myself?" It was necessary to stay in character, and Lissa would never want a full-time bodyguard, especially one as bossy as Tomasso. She also needed to distract her uncle and make him believe Tomasso was the reason for her being upset.

"I know that you can, Lissa, but I'm not going to apologize to you for wanting to make certain you're protected. I lost my entire family once. You're all I've got now."

Lying bastard. Her fingers inched toward the knife hidden inside the form-fitting jacket she wore over her bright blouse.

"You will put up with Tomasso for a few more days. Especially at the hotel." Luigi made it a decree, as he did quite a lot of things.

He liked control, Lissa realized. He craved it. Issuing orders made him feel very powerful. She made herself sigh and then shrug. "Fine, but I don't have to like it."

"Tomasso is a good man, Lissa. Treat him with respect. He'll be of great use to me."

"I said I would put up with him. I've never treated any of your men with less than my full respect."

He nodded and let it go. Lissa rarely had an edge to her voice when she spoke with him, and he couldn't help but hear it. She could only hope that with the fuss she'd made, he'd put it down to her dislike of her bodyguard. She knew her protests would only cement Tomasso's position with Luigi. Luigi would believe that the new man was one he could count on and bring deeper into his organization.

"I know you succeeded because Cosmos's widow called me, frantic. She said he slipped over the cliff to the sea and rocks below. By the time the authorities came, his body was out to sea. I know they were trying to find it; if they do, what will they find?" Luigi rubbed his hands together, looking gleeful.

"Clearly he had too much to drink and accidentally fell. It will be ruled an accident. If anyone in the Porcelli family investigates, they will come up with the same conclusion," Lissa said with absolute confidence.

"I wanted this one, Lissa," Luigi confided, dropping his voice and looking straight into her eyes. "Your father treated him like a son. A boy like that off the streets, and Marcello and Elizabeta treated him like *famiglia*. He betrayed them in such a vile way."

Lissa nearly choked on bile. Her uncle was evil personified. She couldn't sit across from him and look at his face, listen to his rant and keep her face from showing she wanted to kill him. She stood up and paced across the room.

"I told him. Who I was. I told him before he went over. I've never done that before." She made the confession when she had never considered telling him, but he would think she was moody and edgy because of that.

She never deviated from her set scripts. Patrice Lungren killed, not Lissa. Not Giacinta. Patrice didn't feel personal toward her targets, she brought justice to them when the justice system had failed. It had to be that way. Patrice never talked to the targets. She arranged an accident and made certain it happened.

Lissa went to the tall cabinet with the display of ornate shot glasses. She touched one, traced the etching and turned toward her uncle once she knew she was composed enough to face him. "I couldn't help myself. I wanted him to know."

"Good, good, Lissa. He needed to know. I hope he died hard on those rocks, the *bastardo*." Luigi pounded his fist on the desktop. "There is only one left, just one. We have gotten every single one of those responsible for that dark day. You should feel proud of yourself."

"Not until it is over," Lissa said. "Not until the last man responsible for the deaths of my parents and all those who served them are gone. Then it will be over."

"Aldo Porcelli. He is now head of the Porcelli family. He won't be easy to get to. I've studied him and he has no set routines. He changes appointments at the last minute. This weekend he will be very vulnerable, but only this weekend. I believe it will be your best chance to take him."

She frowned and once more crossed the room to drop into the chair across from him at the desk. "No. No, we can't do that. It's too soon. We never do two jobs so close together. If his family puts it together, they'll come after you. Not me. No one knows about me, but they remember you, Tio Luigi. We can't take that chance."

"Sometimes, *cara*, we have to take chances if we want to win. Aldo is difficult. He is surrounded by protection at all times. He is never alone. I've spent the last few years studying him, collecting as much information as possible, and believe me when I tell you, if you don't get to him this weekend, it could be a full year before we have another chance like this one."

"I don't like it," Lissa said. "We've taken our time. That's what has kept you safe. Deviating from that rule is dangerous. We've waited this long, what's another year?" Let him have to convince her. She wasn't just going to hand a victory to him, he was going to have to earn it.

Luigi sighed and studied her face. "You can be stubborn."

"I have to be. It's just as important to me to keep you safe as it is for you to keep me that way."

She smiled at him. He smiled back. All teeth. Cat and canary. Her uncle planned on killing her. Lissa knew he couldn't afford to keep her alive. Not after he succeeded in taking out the heads of both families. They'd played chess for years together. Luigi always won. Unbeknownst to him, she'd been letting him win since she was sixteen. They were still playing chess, only the stakes were much higher.

"Lissa, I understand what you're saying, but I want this over with. I'm willing to take the chance. You go to your hotel meeting and sell your beautiful chandeliers. They'll want them, of course. Then you come home, take care of Aldo Porcelli and go on with your plans. Go to Germany. Stay in the castle. Go see the hotel in St. Petersburg. I will

have an alibi like I always do just in case. No one will suspect an old man getting his revenge after seventeen years. No
one. The idea is ludicrous."

She sighed, letting him see she was on the verge of ca-
pitulation. "I don't like it, Tio Luigi."

"No one knows about you, Lissa. And if they did, they
would never suspect a young woman, especially a woman
who lives in the United States and blows beautiful glass
chandeliers she sells worldwide. This is our moment to
strike." He closed his fist, hit his desktop again. "Smash him.
Crush Aldo Porcelli. It will be the end. We'll both be free of
this thing we've vowed. You will have your life back. You
can marry. Have babies. Bring them to see your Tio Luigi. I
have never been to the States. I would like to see this place
where you live. This farm. I could meet the women you love
as *famiglia*."

"I would like that," she murmured, and pushed at her hair,
hoping the gesture covered the expression on her face. He
was an excellent actor. He'd fooled her father and mother.
They'd both loved him with everything in them. He'd fooled
her. She'd loved him. She could almost believe it wasn't true,
that he was passionate about bringing those responsible for
his brother's death to justice.

"It isn't too late for you to find someone, Tio," she ven-
tured, wondering what he would say. "You aren't so old that
you couldn't marry, have children of your own. I always
wondered why you didn't."

"No. No. Not with this disease. So terrible. I would not
want to put this on any woman. No. I will stay alone, and you
will give me babies to dote on in my old age. I will be their
favorite *tio*."

Lissa pressed a hand tight against her churning stomach.
She couldn't take the game they were playing much longer.
"Why this weekend?"

She watched the tension drain out of him. She hadn't realized just how tense he'd gotten until he relaxed. She twisted

her fingers into a fist and massaged the hard knot at the nape of her neck threatening to destroy her composure.

"Aldo has a mistress." Luigi leaned forward, hissing the accusation. "He cannot even be faithful to his wife."

He delivered the condemnation in a voice of utter contempt. Evidently, now that she appeared to capitulate, he was back in his element. She was fairly certain if he'd taken to the entertainment industry, he would have gotten far.

"He sees her regularly, but never at the same time or day. He doesn't like routine and neither does his protection squad. He always has four bodyguards with him. They're good and very thorough. You'll have to find a way past them."

She nodded. Waiting. Making him give her the details without encouraging him in the least. She wanted to yawn. Luigi was so predictable.

"This Saturday is the anniversary of his finding his mistress. He never misses it. Never. She's been his mistress for the last eight years. When he isn't banging his wife, he's with her. All the time."

She couldn't resist. "So he's faithful to his wife and mistress. It's just the two women?"

Luigi made a sound, a snort of derision, and crossed himself. "I wouldn't call it faithful to break the holy vows of matrimony, Lissa. Aldo cheats on his wife, and she is very devoted to him. This is your chance. He will go to his mistress this Saturday."

She shook her head. "You know it's risky trying to plan something so quickly, especially when he has experienced bodyguards with him."

"He doesn't ever allow them into her apartment. I have gathered all the details you'll need to plan this. Aldo might not stick to a routine, but his bodyguards do. I have provided each of their locations when their boss visits his woman." He leaned even farther across his desk. "You can do this, Lissa. For your father and mother. My beloved Marcello and

Elizabeta. You have an opportunity to end this thing once and for all. He is the last and the guiltiest."

"Don't you think it strange that he killed an entire family because my mother refused to sleep with him, yet he's faithful to his wife and mistress?"

Her question was met with absolute silence. She knew immediately she'd made a terrible mistake. Luigi's face turned expressionless, his dark eyes searching her face for something she feared she couldn't hide. He looked sharp, piercing, very cunning. In the lines of his face she read evil. She knew she looked at the real man, not the mask.

That was the strangest thing of all. They all wore masks. Luigi had from the moment she'd entered his home. She did. When she went after those responsible for killing her parents. When she was on the farm with the women she loved as family. Casimir went through his entire life with a mask. No one saw them. They were hidden away, players on a stage—and she wanted off.

"What are you saying, Lissa? Do you not remember him being there? Directing the entire event? He *orchestrated* the murders. I showed you pictures and you pointed him out. *You* did that. I spent years making certain we had the right people."

"I know." She hung her head, covered her face with her hands for a moment, wishing for Casimir. Wishing for his arms to get her out of the study where evil permeated every bit of air. Evil smelled and it was sandalwood and spice, the cologne her uncle always wore. "I'm just so tired, Tio. I spoke to Cosmos. I broke a long-standing rule. I don't know if I can do this again so soon."

"You *will* do this," Luigi declared in his hard, authoritative, most commanding voice. "You will find a way into that house and you *will* kill this man who murdered your family."

She nodded. "I know. Of course I will. I'll start work tonight. I'll need to do recon. Will Arturo be back? When I'm scouting around, I usually take him with me, that way I can concentrate on what I need to do instead of constantly watching my back."

No one ever went with her when she did the job, but Arturo guarded her while she did the setup. Still, even with the setup, she was careful. Betrayed by a trusted family friend, watching Cosmos help to murder her parents, had taught her to be extremely cautious, even with those she loved. She always made certain Patrice Lungren did the reconnaissance, not Lissa Piner. No one went with her to the storage unit when she changed beforehand. She wanted no hidden cameras, no surprises later on. If she thought she was under surveillance by anyone, she aborted instantly.

"I doubt Arturo will be back so soon. You'll have to take Tomasso."

Her mouth dropped open. "You hardly know that man. Seriously, Tio, you have no idea if he's loyal or not. What are you thinking?" But she knew exactly what he was thinking. He didn't trust any of his men to keep their mouth shut with such an important mission. It was blackmail material. They would guess what she was up to. Luigi couldn't have that, not if he planned to take over the Porcelli family. There could be no witnesses. No one left alive who might know what Luigi had done.

All along he planned to kill Tomasso. That was why he'd been the bodyguard selected to watch over her while Luigi was feigning his illness. Luigi planned to dispose of him as well. She curled her fingers into a tighter fist. She should have seen that coming the moment Luigi assigned a new man as her personal bodyguard. He didn't want her to question his choice when he sent the man along with her on her recon of Aldo's mistress.

"He has already proven his loyalty. I think he's a good man and he'll watch your back while you put together your plan. So it is decided. You will get to work this week planning and then you will kill Aldo Porcelli and at last allow my brother to rest in peace." He sat back in his leather chair, looking very pleased. "Now tell me every detail of Cosmos's death. I want to know his every reaction, his expression, especially when he realized who you were."

CASIMIR drove quickly through the streets toward the building Luigi disappeared into each night. Arturo stayed there, he was certain of it. He didn't appear to leave, but stayed inside unless he walked Luigi out. The two men seemed very pleased with themselves, talking animatedly before Luigi got in his car to drive off. They laughed and slapped each other on the back or shoulder. Whatever they were up to made them both very jovial.

There were cameras set up around the building, but no one ever cleaned them off and spiderwebs covered the lenses. Casimir had to strike tonight, right now, while Luigi was Lissa's alibi. Arturo dying unexpectedly would set off alarm bells in Luigi unless they played this exactly right. He glanced at his watch. He would have only a short time to get this done before rushing to the hotel to make an appearance so when Luigi checked—and he would because he had a suspicious nature—the head of security would give him an alibi. He would make Arturo's death quick, something he didn't deserve, but there was no real time for anything else.

He used the shadows of the building to stay out of sight of the cameras as much as possible. With the amount of dirt and webs on them, even if they picked him up, they wouldn't see much. Still, he was going to make certain he removed the memory cards.

The door was locked, not coded. A big mistake, but one he wasn't surprised about. Luigi was old school. He didn't embrace technology. Even at his house, there were no real codes on anything. Luigi didn't want to memorize them.

Casimir made short work of the lock and then tested the door handle. He listened, but there was no sound at all. He'd noticed that before. Not a single sound escaped from inside.

He could only surmise that the building was soundproof, which meant Luigi probably brought men he wanted interrogated to the site. He'd been fairly certain all along that Arturo wasn't alone in that building.

He opened the door cautiously, inch by inch, listening for an alarm, a noise, anything that would tell him someone waited on the other side. In all the surveillance he'd done on the building, he hadn't seen anyone else come or go other than Luigi. That meant whoever was inside with Arturo was a prisoner. That man would present a problem if he saw Casimir. He wore his older gentleman persona, but still, he didn't want a witness. Arturo's death needed to look natural.

He found himself in an entryway, a large rectangular room with low-slung couches and a couple of overstuffed chairs. An empty fish tank took up an entire corner and there were several paintings on the wall, nude couples in various sexual positions, all depicting various types of bondage.

His heart sank. He knew what this was. Luigi was reputed to run a very brisk prostitution business, providing a particular service to men or women with "unique" preferences. The women commanded high prices for their services because they catered to a very sick lot. Luigi made certain that the circle of very sick patrons returned often and that the circle kept expanding. The women had to be trained somewhere. He'd just discovered Luigi's school.

The idea nauseated him. He'd been trained in the art of sex, every deviant and perverted act possible. Every type of seduction. The lessons had been brutal, and more than once a female partner had been killed for not performing up to the instructor's standards. He knew the type of sadistic person it took to train a man or woman in the kinds of sexual technique Luigi wanted from his girls.

He checked for cameras, but there were none in the waiting room. The main working area had to be behind the closed door. He shut down all emotion. That kept him sane, it always had kept him sane. There was no room for Casimir

Prakenskii. No room for fire or anger, or anything that re-
sembled emotion. He couldn't feel for the victims. He could
only exact justice as dispassionately as possible.

He stepped through the door into his own personal nightmare. The body of a once-beautiful woman, broken and
bloody, hung by her wrists from cuffs attached to chains dan-
gling from the ceiling. Blood spatter was on the wall behind
her as well as in a circle around the body on the floor. Casimir knew she was already dead, just from the way the body
hung. She was nude and there were hundreds of whip marks,
old and new, cut deep into her flesh.

"I don't know what the hell happened, Luigi," Arturo's
voice came from around the corner. "She just died. Her
fuckin' eyes rolled back in her head and the next thing I
know, she was dead. I don't know, maybe I took it too fast
for her. She just died. I'm going to have to get rid of the body.
I figured I'd take her back to her estate in a couple of hours
and then throw her over the cliff after Cosmos. You know,
widow jumps to her death after husband dies."

In spite of his resolve not to feel anything, the fire in his
belly began to burn through the ice he'd laid over top of it.
This woman was Cosmos's widow, Carlotta. Luigi and Arturo had taken her from her home and planned to force her
into prostitution. There was no remorse in Arturo's voice,
only disgust.

"Now? You want me to get rid of her now? I suppose it's
dark enough. Yeah, I'll take her out there now and I'll be
back in an hour or so. It won't take long. Yeah. I'll fucking
weigh her body down so no one finds it. Don't worry. This
won't be a problem."

Casimir backed out of the room and slipped back outside.
There was going to be another accident at the cliff. Arturo
was going to die there. He waited in his car until Luigi's bodyguard came out of the building with the body—wrapped in a
blanket—over his shoulder. He dumped it in the trunk of his
car, went back and locked the building before driving away.

Casimir didn't have to follow directly behind. He already knew where Arturo was going. Every mile made the fire burning in his gut grow hotter. He had training. Discipline. Control. He had it all, but he let it go. Rolling down the window, he drew the night air as deep into his lungs as possible. Lissa was facing her nightmare of an uncle, he had to face his past. The sight of that broken body and hearing Arturo talking on his phone to Luigi, clearly uncaring that he'd killed a woman, brought every memory he'd buried flooding back.

He was a trained killer. An assassin. He had taken out so many targets he'd lost track, yet he had more regard for life than Arturo, Luigi or any of his instructors ever had. He had found, over the years, that perhaps the law was in place for a reason, but some of the biggest monsters fell through the cracks. Men like him were necessary. Not good, but necessary.

He chose an alternate route to get to Cosmos's estate and parked his vehicle where he had before. Again, there were no cars on the street and no one was out walking their dog. It was always the unexpected that could sink a job faster than anything. That person that came home early or forgot something important and returned for it. He stayed in his car a few minutes, getting a feel for the neighborhood, learning the rhythm of it.

Making certain the dome light wasn't working, he stepped out of the car and moved with absolute confidence—as if he belonged—toward the back gardens where he'd entered the property before. He didn't hesitate once he was in the cover the foliage provided. He jogged toward the cliff. Coming around the shrubs, he spotted Arturo heaving the widow's body over the cliff.

Arturo turned and, without a glance around, snagged the bloody blanket and walked back to the house. Casimir had expected him to leave immediately. Instead the man clearly had something important to do in the house. He followed at a distance. Arturo left the door open. Casimir took that as an invitation, but just in case, he was even more cautious.

Arturo didn't consider that anyone might be watching him. He went straight for the study and the computer. Pulling on gloves, he turned the machine on and, while it was booting up, poured himself a drink of whiskey. He downed it quickly and poured himself a second. The death of the widow had rattled him more than he let on—that or Luigi wasn't happy she'd died.

Arturo kept his gaze fixed on the screen. Once the computer was running, he sank into a chair and began to type. Looking over his shoulder, Casimir could see it was a suicide note. The widow just couldn't live without her husband. Casimir moved in close like the phantom he was, coming out of the shadows to stand just behind the bodyguard.

"Arturo. I think we need to talk. Don't go for your gun. I'd have to shoot you, and right now, all I intend to do is talk. You make me pull the trigger and I'm aiming for your heart. In case you wonder, I don't miss."

Arturo leapt up so fast he knocked the chair over. Casimir hit him on the side of his head with the butt of his gun. Hard, uncaring if the blow killed him. Arturo crumpled like a sack of potatoes. Casimir pushed the body aside with a none-too-gentle kick from his expensive shoes and leaned in to add a few lines to the suicide note. He shut down the computer and hoisted the body to his shoulder, strode from the house and dumped the body in the trunk of his rented car.

He shouldn't do this. He should dump the bastard in the sea and let that kill him, but he couldn't stop himself. He used zip ties to bind Arturo's hands and ankles and then slapped a piece of duct tape over his mouth just in case he woke on their trip back to the building where Arturo and Luigi trained women for their prostitution ring.

Casimir knew better. He was making this personal, and one didn't make any job personal. Arturo represented every one of those instructors who had beaten him bloody, or beaten his partner in front of him. One always won and one always lost. Either the man had the discipline and control to withstand the sexual assault or the woman did. Either he could arouse the woman or she could arouse him. Whatever the demand, one of the partners was severely beaten or killed. More than one of his partners had been killed.

He closed his eyes for a brief moment, feeling bile rise, hating those memories. Hating that he'd caused such pain to the young women forced to partner him. Hating that he'd caused their deaths. Men like Arturo felt nothing for the men and women they tortured, used and discarded. He shook his head and drove back to the "school." Luigi had come to this place every evening. There was no doubt in Casimir's mind that Luigi had used the widow often and aided Arturo in her "training."

He cursed under his breath and slammed his palm against the steering wheel. He'd come here several nights in a row and sat outside. Waiting. Watching. All the while, inside, they had tortured the young woman. These men planned on killing Lissa. Her uncle would never try to keep her alive in his prostitution ring. She knew too much and she was far too dangerous.

Arturo was awake when Casimir raised the trunk lid. His eyes spat hatred and a promise of retaliation. Casimir smiled at him. "Hey. Don't look so surprised. You had to know it was coming. You're a loose end." He dragged Arturo from the trunk, not being in the least gentle, deliberately dropping him twice on the ground as if his dead weight was too much to lift.

Frown lines appeared in Arturo's forehead. He made all sorts of noises, shaking his head in denial.

"Seriously?" Casimir continued, shouldering the man. "You can't be that stupid. He's gotten rid of everyone else. That niece of his will do Aldo Porcelli, and he'll do her. You're the last thread leading back to him. With you dead, no one is going to know he murdered his own brother and the heads of the Porcelli family. He's next in line. Once he's accepted as the boss, Angeline disappears and he's the golden boy. He has it all."

He opened the door of the training hall, went through and kicked the door closed behind him. "If you're thinking, why wouldn't he kill me too? I do you and disappear. I come in for the hard jobs, and I've worked with Luigi in the past. He can't find me unless I want to be found. I like money, not women or boys or power. It's that simple. You've always been a risk because you can't resist hurting the women you get under your control. He told me all about you and after watching you with the little widow these past few days, I'd say he was right to get rid of you. You're blackmail waiting to happen."

Casimir dumped Arturo in the middle of the sticky blood where the young woman had died. Arturo tried to scoot out of the puddle, but Casimir caught his arms and yanked them up, securing the cuffs that had bound the widow to the chains. With a flick of his knife, he cut away the zip ties and pocketed them.

"It's just business to me. That's all. I get in and get out. Disappear." He yanked the tape from Arturo's mouth and replaced it with a ball gag before moving around him to the mechanism to lift the body from the floor and hang him by his wrists. "The clothes are going to have to go. You and your little friend were playing and she accidentally killed you before flinging herself off the cliffs. The cops will probably suspect her of murdering her husband, but she'll have to bear that little burden. Luigi will most likely be able to supply evidence that you and the widow were seeing each other and you both liked kink."

Arturo shook his head savagely, his body writhing, legs trying to kick out, but they were tied together at the ankles. Casimir smirked. "You don't think the cops will buy that? They will accept circumstantial evidence. It's been my experience that they accept what seems believable, and this scenario is close enough to the truth to make it look very believable."

He clamped his hands around Arturo's legs and removed

his shoes and stocks, stripped off his trousers, cutting them away with his knife, uncaring that every time Arturo fought to get free, the tip of the blade sliced open skin. "Whoa, looks like Carlotta liked knife play."

Arturo shook his head adamantly, making all kinds of noises around the ball gag. Saliva dripped from the corners of his mouth in a steady stream. Once he had cut the clothes away from Arturo, leaving him stark naked, Casimir locked the bodyguard's ankles into the tethers and again, removed the zip ties and pocketed them. He tossed the remnants of Arturo's clothes to one side.

"The widow's vehicle, the one you've been using, is at her home, but your prints are all over it. The suicide note tells how in love she was with you. How you loved to tie each other up and flog each other, but something went wrong and you died. She burned down the building and threw herself off the cliff where you both had thrown her husband over." He made little clucking noises and shook his head. "You certainly have a lot to answer for. Luigi will be properly ashamed when all this comes to light."

Casimir casually pulled plastic overalls and a jacket from his bag and donned both items over his immaculate clothing. He picked up the whip and held it up for Arturo to see. "To make this scene believable, we'll have to make it very authentic. Don't worry, I learned at the hands of masters, although it's been years since I practiced this particular art. I'm fairly certain I can do as much justice to this art form as you did on Carlotta."

A half an hour later, Casimir exited the building. If Arturo could have screamed around his ball gag, he would have. Flames were already licking at his feet and rushing up walls, responding to the direction of a true fire element.

11

LUIGI rubbed his hands together, more than pleased with the evening's event. His niece had done her job efficiently, the way she always did. He really regretted having to kill such a competent and resourceful tool, but he wasn't going to take any chances, not now when he was so close to his goals. He sauntered out to his car. He couldn't celebrate with the lovely widow. He didn't like that he'd lost her, but maybe this worked out better. He would see that the men he paid such good money to every week would be assigned to her tragic case. No one would ever suspect Cosmos had been killed on Luigi's order. No one. Not when the tragedy surrounding his widow would become the number one topic of gossip.

He needed a woman. He'd tried to call Arturo several times but the man hadn't picked up. Still, he'd left him a message to pick up one of the girls working for him. One that still wasn't as trained as they'd like. The fact that Arturo hadn't answered meant he had brought the girl to their little school and was working with her. By now, she would need his tender care. Arturo always commanded fear. When Luigi arrived, the girl would need gentle handling. Not gentle when it came to sex, but those little intimate gestures they misread into thinking he cared for them. Just a touch here and there, that was all it took after Arturo spent a little time with them.

He laughed aloud as he slid behind the wheel. He so enjoyed watching Arturo work, almost as much as Arturo enjoyed working. Still, he was going to have to find out exactly what happened, how the widow had died. He hated losing that income. Arturo was good at what he did, but sometimes he was a little too enthusiastic.

Luigi couldn't get too angry with his oldest friend, not when there were times when he was a little too enthusiastic himself. It was easy to forget the women brought them in money when they were having such a good time. Sometimes clients forgot that as well, but that was okay, because then they paid for that mistake over and over. If Arturo or Luigi killed the golden goose, they got nothing but that moment's pleasure from it.

He spent the rest of the drive fantasizing about giving Angeline to a couple of the men who were regular customers, men who had killed twice. They liked to make their purchase together. Of course Luigi charged them double, and since they'd killed twice, he made certain to give them the girl who brought in the least amount of money—just in case. Arturo had to clean up quite a mess both times.

It would be fun to film Angeline's slow, torturous death. He couldn't chance it, of course, but still, thinking about it was one of his favorite pastimes. Bringing anyone else in on Angeline's death would be a risk he couldn't afford to take. He planned the next best thing. He'd already discussed just how sweet Angeline would die with Arturo. His best friend had agreed to take her to the privacy of training school and spend a few hours with her before Luigi killed her.

Angeline had always been far too arrogant and haughty to ever talk to Arturo. She didn't like him in her house and made no bones about letting both Luigi and Arturo know.

Arturo would love to get her to himself in that training school. The instruments he had weren't toys. He knew how to cause a woman such pain she would beg for death. He was equally as good at humiliation. Arturo hated Angeline almost as much as Luigi did.

She always treated their soldiers with a kind of disdain and frowned on Luigi being friends with someone who never rose above personal bodyguard in the organization. She harped on the fact that her father would never have tolerated Arturo's familiarity with the boss. She was just the opposite of Lissa. Lissa threw her arms around Arturo, hugged him with genuine affection, joked with him, treated him like family and had, on more than one occasion, taken care of him when he was ill. If there was anyone Arturo cared anything for other than Luigi, it was Lissa. Still, like Luigi, Arturo knew Lissa had to die. It would be sad, but it was necessary.

Luigi turned the vehicle onto the long winding drive to the back part of the property. He'd scored with the building, snatching it up the moment it was on the market. In town, yet secluded, no one would ever have a clue what went on there. He loved being there with the women, and his enemies, all at his mercy inside the soundproof building, surrounded by the rest of the town. No one ever suspected.

As the car approached the last bend, nearly overgrown with foliage, he saw an orange-red glow. Frowning, he automatically accelerated and then slammed on the brakes as the building came into view. There were no flames on the outside, but windows were breaking, and through them he could see a vicious, hungry blaze leaping greedily at the walls and seeping under the doorway. The outside walls were black and blistered with the incredible heat.

Arturo must not have returned yet. He caught up his phone as he backed down the drive fast. Punching in Arturo's number, he swore as it went to voice mail. "The building's on fire. Inside. I can see the flames. Call me. Now."

Heart pounding, he drove fast away from the fire. He didn't want to be anywhere near the place when the fire department came. He had no idea how much of the inside of the building would be destroyed, but he knew the investigators often could read a lot in the ashes. He was going to have to spread money around to get the official report and either bury it, tweak it, or let it go at what they found. Thankfully, he knew Arturo had gotten the widow's body out of there.

What the hell happened? What had started the fire? Clearly it had started inside. Swearing again, he sent a text to Arturo. *Call me now.* An order. Where was the son of a bitch? What game was he playing? He should have disposed of the widow's body, picked up a woman for the two of them to play with and already be in the building. There was no car there. Unless . . .

Had he seen a vehicle? Parked down from the building under the trees? In the shadows? He rubbed at the frown lines in his forehead. Had there been a car? He slowed down and pulled over to park, trying to think. If he went back to look, would the fire department get there and catch him there? He didn't want questions. Arturo never parked that far away from the building, but maybe he had.

Swearing, he turned around and started back up the drive.

CASIMIR stood outside the inferno, feeding the flames, wishing, for the first time in his life, he could hear the screams of his mark. Arturo deserved death a hundred times over. He despised men like Arturo, men who enjoyed the pain of others. Men born, not shaped, into monsters.

What does that make you? The wind whispered the question in his ear. What did it make him? He wanted Arturo to suffer. He *needed* him to suffer. To do this terrible thing, allow it to be personal when his code was so rigid, unbending, when he swore to live by that code and yet he still didn't move.

The building was old and wooden with a flat roof. It had obviously been a small warehouse or storage building, but had been renovated more than once. The place had one bathroom, and the rest of the space, maybe a thousand square feet, had been divided into three rooms. The small reception area where Arturo and Luigi could watch television and take a respite from their work as well as a small bedroom where the women they brought there could sleep— when they were allowed sleep. The main room was the "classroom."

Casimir thought in those terms. He'd seen similar class-rooms before. Dungeons that held every type of contraption for bondage as well as the necessities for inflicting pain. He remembered every one of those items.

The skylight cracked and shattered as heat rose and there was nowhere for it to go. Instantly the oxygen pouring in fed the flames, so it wasn't as necessary for him to exert himself to keep the fire going. Still, he wanted the blaze hot, burning everything to the ground, destroying Arturo and Luigi's playground. Taking it all. Taking each room. The bedroom had fuel—the beds, mattresses and cheap dressers. Paper strewn around. Luigi and Arturo weren't neat and they didn't give the women much time to be neat and tidy either. Mostly though, it was the soundproofing they had padded the walls and ceiling with in order to keep the screams of the women from being heard that provided the best fuel. And that was pure irony.

The blackened windows began to crack. Spiderweb. The outside walls turned a color much like paper when a flame burned from the other side. They blackened slowly in an alligator-skin pattern and then here and there a flame broke through. Flames leapt out of the skylight, indicating inside the fire was towering, completely engulfing each room.

He kept feeding the flames, burning the building hot and wild, making certain that Arturo died by fire, not by smoke inhalation. He wished he could hear the man suffer each lick of flame, hear him scream for mercy the way his numerous victims had.

Shaking his head, he lifted his face to the sky as the outside walls continued to blacken and more windows shattered. Flames licked along the sills hungrily and danced toward the night. His chest hurt as he made his way back toward his rented vehicle. The car sat under the trees, deep in the shadows. He slipped inside and continued to watch the conflagration. He had to control the flames so there was no chance of them spreading. Fortunately the building was a distance from other buildings, but he didn't want to take chances. He had enough sins on his soul with what he'd just done.

He couldn't go back to Lissa this way. Not like this. He sat there, trying to feel remorse, but he just couldn't drum up any. Was it too late for him? Had he crossed a line he couldn't come back from? It didn't make sense that he'd finally found her and now, he'd let a mark get to him. He'd dealt with pedophiles, monsters involved in human trafficking rings, killers, a dozen other types of criminals and never once had he lost it, but this time—this was just the last straw. He'd had his fill.

Twin lights pierced the night, and he swung his gaze from the burning building to the back entrance road. It was mostly overgrown, but Luigi tended to use it. Fewer people would see his vehicle on that road than on the main one. He was a little surprised to see the man, since Luigi knew Arturo had killed Cosmos's wife.

Luigi halted his car the moment he saw the building in flames. He sat there staring and then abruptly backed down the road again. For one moment, Casimir wanted to chase him down and do the same thing to him, burn him alive, make him suffer for all the suffering he caused. Instead, he gripped the steering wheel hard and made himself breathe the need away.

He had to follow the plan. He knew better than to deviate. Casimir knew he didn't have a lot of time. He had to get to the hotel where Lissa Piner would be meeting with the owners the next day, hopefully tamper with the security tapes and meet with the head of security as Tomasso. He also needed to return the rental car. He drove without lights until he was back on the main street.

CASIMIR hadn't come to her. Lissa paced back and forth in her room, her belly tied in hard knots of fear and her chest hurting from the terrible pressure there. She knew he was back. He was safe. *He hadn't come to her.* She yanked her fingers through her hair in sheer agitation, unsure of herself. She wasn't a woman to be uncertain. She made split-second, life-or-death decisions with confidence—but this was different. She wished she could call one of her sisters and ask advice.

Why wouldn't he come to her? That was what she had to figure out and then she would know what to do. He could be injured. She paced more, rubbing her hand up and down her thigh. Her palm itched. Her heart hurt. She hated indecision. What if he was injured and *couldn't* come to her? She pressed her palm harder against her bare thigh. He would call her, using the mark on her palm. He had told her that was possible.

The need to go to him was strong. She blew out her breath and made up her mind. Whatever was wrong—and something was—she needed to be with him. To share whatever was wrong with him. Instinctively, she knew he would be there for her no matter what. Having made up her mind, she didn't hesitate. She yanked open her door and nearly ran right into her uncle. He was reaching for the doorknob.

"Tio Luigi, what is it?" she asked. She'd never seen him look the way he did in that moment. Visibly upset. Agitated. It was no act. He was pale beneath his olive skin, and there were lines carved deep into his face. He'd never looked older. She caught his arms and held on tight. "You look . . ." *Terrible. Rattled.*

"Come with me. The only man not accounted for is Tomasso."

"Tomasso?" she echoed. "Tell me what's wrong? Has that horrid man done something to you?" She turned toward the stairs. "I'll kill him myself."

"No, no, Giacinta," Luigi protested, catching her to him. His distress was very real. He actually clung to her. "I want to make certain he's in that room. Then I need to find out where he's been and what time he got back."

She *detested* him calling her Giacinta. Her real name. The name her father and mother had given her, but now wasn't the time to protest. She had to act out the charade perfectly, no matter what she felt inside.

"He went to the hotel this evening to check with their head of security and make arrangements for my arrival tomorrow. You gave him those instructions yourself. He told me he was going to go while I was in my meeting with you." She frowned at him. "We discussed it, remember? Tio, you need to tell me what's wrong. What happened to upset you this way?"

"I think Arturo's dead." He spat the words at her and then sagged, his weight nearly knocking her over.

She staggered, her arms going around his waist to help him sit on the bottom stair. She crouched down in front of him. "You *think?* But you don't know? Why do you think he might be dead? And what does Tomasso have to do with his death? Tomasso likes Arturo. Everyone likes Arturo. Tomasso talked about him all the time."

Luigi shook his head. "No. No, Gia." He lapsed into Italian, talking rapidly, rocking himself back and forth, telling her the police had come to tell him about the burned building. There was a body inside. A man. He'd burned to death. He'd been locked into cuffs, a sex game of some kind. The police believed it was a sex game gone wrong and the woman he'd been playing the game with had been Cosmos's widow.

"What?" Lissa widened her eyes in feigned shock. "Were

they having an affair? You know Arturo better than anyone. He's been on vacation. Did he run off with her? Was he into kinky sex games? Bondage? You have to tell me, Tio. I don't care what he was into. It won't make me think less of him. If I'm going to help you figure out what happened, you have to tell me the truth."

Luigi lifted his face to look at her. Then he nodded. "He was with her. She went to him after Cosmos died. They liked each other. Cosmos would have killed Arturo if she'd run off with him before that. No one could know. I've admitted this to the police. Cosmos is dead. There's nothing he can do now."

"Were there two bodies in the fire?"

He shook his head, looking older than ever. "Only one. Only a man's body. There was no car. The police found a suicide note at the Agosto estate from the widow. She said she accidentally killed Arturo, her one love, and she flung herself over the cliff after her husband."

Lissa sank back on her heels, her mouth open, one hand covering it in shock. "Oh, no. Tio. But if you know she accidentally killed him, then why do you think Tomasso has something to do with his death?"

He dug his fingers into her shoulder in a bruising grip. "You don't understand. I spoke to Arturo earlier. He had accidentally killed her in their sex games. She liked pain. She got off on pain. He always obliged her, but this time she had some kind of reaction, she couldn't breathe. He tried to save her. He called me sobbing. I told him to take her back to her house and dispose of her body there. He was alive. She was the dead one. He was alive. How did he get back to the building without a car? How did he get into the cuffs? How did the fire start? There had to be someone else there."

She was silent a moment. "You think that someone was Tomasso? Did he know Cosmos's wife as well?"

Luigi shook his head. "I don't know, but everyone else is accounted for."

"Then we'll go talk to him. Make certain he's home. But, Luigi, is it possible Arturo was so upset over the death of the woman he loved that he killed himself? Is there a way to put himself in the cuffs and rig a fire?"

"No. No. He would never do that. He would talk to me. No, Gia, someone did this terrible thing, and we have to find out who it was and punish them. Kill them. Make them suffer and then kill them."

For the first time in her life, Lissa had something genuine to compare with her uncle's acting. *This* was genuine grief. Instead of feeling compassion for him, she felt anger. Betrayal. When he'd come to her and taken her out of the hiding hole her father had told her to run to, this was not how he'd been. The grief back then had been acting. Totally.

She forced herself to put her arms around him. He was actually trembling. "I'll go to see if Tomasso is in his room, but really, as much as I dislike his arrogance, you know there is no reason for him to do such a thing. We have to look outside the family. Would Aldo come after you this way? If he suspected you had something to do with Cosmos's death? If he saw Arturo near the house, with Cosmos's widow, he might have drawn conclusions."

She patted his knee when he continued to sit there, shaking his head, his body so stunned she knew he was incapable of walking. "I'll be right back," she told him, and turned away.

Luigi caught her wrist so that she was forced to turn back to him and give him a small smile. "What is it, Tio?"

"You're a good girl, Giacinta. A good girl."

A girl he planned to kill. It was all she could do not to jerk her wrist away.

"Remember to call me Lissa, Tio. Even now, we can't make a mistake," she reminded gently.

She didn't want to think too much about Arturo's death herself. He'd been kind to her when she'd been a child. Kind when Luigi was distant. Hugging her when her uncle didn't.

When Luigi had been a stern taskmaster, teaching her the art of assassination, it had been Arturo who had been the one to dry her tears when her uncle was angry with her. He wasn't that man, but still, those were her memories of him.

"Go to your study, Tio. Call the hotel. Check to see if Tomasso was there tonight. You taught me well. I'll have a conversation with him and see if he knows anything. Trust me to get to the truth."

She had to help him stand, which necessitated touching him again. She felt repugnance at the closeness, at the way he leaned on her. Patted her shoulder. Acted like she mattered to him, when he was already plotting her death. Women meant nothing to him, not even his own flesh and blood. Evidently, his own brother hadn't either. But Arturo, Arturo had mattered.

She waited until he was back down the first flight of stairs and down the hall before she hurried up the stairs to the men's quarters. Knowing the security cameras were on, she knocked, when she wanted to rush right in.

Tomasso opened the door. He looked as if he'd been asleep, but she knew better. He was dressed in nothing but a pair of soft sweatpants and was pulling a T-shirt over his head with one hand. He stepped back to give her entrance and closed the door after her.

"Luigi wanted me to check to make certain you were here," she announced without preamble, watching him closely. Studying his face. Something was very wrong. His face was a mask, and his eyes didn't warm when they rested on her. "He's calling the hotel right now to make certain you were there."

Casimir turned away from her, turned his back. Paced. Didn't turn on the lights. "I was there. There are images of me walking through the hotel, checking everywhere a couple of hours before I met with the head of security. The recordings will pass inspection. I'm very good at what I do."

His voice was clipped. Abrupt. An undertone of anger and

something else she couldn't quite put her finger on. She moved toward him. He swung around and held up his hand as if he had eyes in the back of his head.

"Stay there."

She halted instantly. "What is it, what's wrong?" She had known all along something was wrong. She'd felt it. He hadn't come to her the way he would have. The knots in her stomach tightened to the point of pain.

Casimir didn't answer her. His mask didn't slip, not even for a moment. The knots in her stomach got tighter. "Luigi knows Arturo is dead. He said his body was found in cuffs, hanging from the ceiling by chains and he died in a fire." She kept her voice strictly neutral.

"Hell, yeah, he died in a fire," Casimir said.

His rage shook the room. She felt the floor shifting. The walls breathing in and out trying to contain the pressure.

She wrapped her arms around her middle. She knew Arturo had to die. "He used to hold me when Luigi would get angry with me because I wasn't fast enough or silent enough when I trained. He would sneak me chocolate bars and . . ."

"Don't." He snarled the command. Stepped close.

For the first time she saw the killer in him. She *saw* him. The man that was part of Casimir, maybe even the largest part. The man she'd so studiously avoided seeing when she homed in on the gentle soul he kept hidden from the world.

"Casimir, I can't help but remember his kindness to me when I was a child." She opened her mouth to continue, to tell him she understood that Arturo had to die, that he deserved it, but she couldn't help that small arrow of grief for the man she'd thought he was.

"Don't you even *think* about that fucker," Casimir snapped. He stared down at her, his face an unreadable mask, his eyes as piercing as they could possibly be even with the dark contacts—alive with something close to hatred. "That man played you. Don't you dare grieve for him. They had a little routine, your uncle and Arturo."

Her hand rose defensively to her throat. His voice betrayed him. The fire in him was roaring. Angry. No, it was raging. And it ran deep. "I don't understand, Casimir."

"They set up a little school there in that building and they brought unwilling women and trained them. Arturo was the one who tore the skin off a woman with his whips. He caned her. He gave her so much pain she would do anything to make it stop. While they hurt her, *tortured* and humiliated her, they manipulated her body so she eventually couldn't get off without pain."

Her throat closed. Her lungs seized. She couldn't breathe.

"Arturo, that man you want to grieve for, trained those women by hanging them from the ceiling or tying them to a wooden bench or cross or whatever the hell he wanted in the moment. He beat a woman until she was cooperative and would do whatever he said, whatever any man they gave her to ordered. Your uncle had to have been the good guy, the one who came in and soothed her, cared for her, gave her those little intimate moments that gave her hope that someone actually cared. Then he used her. Abused her. Sold her time to very ugly, perverted men who hurt her over and over. Then Luigi would come back and soothe her all over again. They just reversed the roles with you, Giacinta. Luigi was the assassin. He trained you—was the disciplinarian—while Arturo assumed the role of the man who gave you those little touches to make you think he cared."

"Stop. Stop it, Casimir. I was a child. I lost my parents, my family, everything. You're taking everything."

He glared down at her, implacable. "You never had it in the first place. It was an illusion they created for you, not something real. Arturo was as sick as they come. I hung that sick fuck in the bloody chains and the pool of blood where he'd killed Carlotta. They took her there. They tortured her for days, while I sat in a fucking car a few hundred yards away and let it happen." He spat the words at her.

She couldn't stop the tears from burning her eyes even

though she knew that would only fan the fire burning so hot in him. She should have known the moment she stepped in the room and found it so hot. He hadn't turned up his thermostat, he was fighting to keep from setting the house on fire with his rage.

She understood his rage. He blamed himself for not getting into the building, not discovering what was happening until it was too late. He hadn't saved the woman. That had to have brought flashbacks of the partners he'd been forced to have as a young teenager when they were teaching him control. The women who died because he'd had that control.

"*Don't* you fucking cry for him," he snarled.

He caught her face in one hand and she felt every fingerprint burning into her jaw. She didn't try to pull away or explain that the tears weren't for Arturo or Luigi. She wouldn't cry for either of them. The tears were for her lost childhood. For those women. Most of all they were for him. For Casimir to have to witness such a thing. To have to remember. To relive that nightmare. To let that terrible door crack open and memories spill out when the brutal tragedy happened all over again. He hadn't saved the woman. That was all he would see. All he would feel.

"Arturo tortured those women in his little sex school. I did the same to him and made certain he was alive when he burned. He didn't get to die easy. He felt every touch of the flames. And I was glad he felt them. I *needed* him to feel every one of those flames that crept up his body. He was the torch that started the building on fire. Arturo. Your little childhood buddy. Every lick of flame on his feet and legs, just like the whips he struck those women with. So precise. The maximum hurt with the least amount of actual damage to their bodies so they couldn't die and be free. I did that, to him, with whips and then with fire, Giacinta. I let that fucker and your bastard of an uncle turn me into a monster when all these years I've never allowed that. I gave that to them."

"Casimir." She said his name softly.

"Get the fuck out of here."

She remained where she was. She understood everything now. He detested himself for not saving the widow, but more, he believed he had become the thing Sorbacov tried to create—the monster he'd refused to be all those years of empty loneliness—of being everyone but Casimir Prakenskii.

She shook her head. "I'm not going to do that. I'm never going to do that. You're mine, Casimir. *Mine.* You aren't Sorbacov's. You don't belong to him. You never did. Luigi and Arturo can't turn you into a monster. You aren't capable of being a monster. Don't you dare ever put yourself in the same category."

"I burned that fucker alive."

"You found a woman dead, in a pool of blood, a woman he tortured and killed. We're fire elements. What did you think was going to happen? Had I come across a scene like that, do you think I could keep fire under control? You can blame yourself for Carlotta suffering those nights you were outside, but you and I both know, we can only make decisions based on what we know. We had a timetable. You couldn't risk getting caught just to satisfy curiosity. Had you broken into that building, you might have blown our covers. We didn't know what was in there."

He didn't respond, he just looked at her. There was pain in his eyes. Pain a monster would never feel.

"I need to come to you now, Casimir. I need to put my arms around you and hold you. Will you let me do that?"

He continued to stand there without speaking, his eyes drifting over her face. He was utterly still, as if holding himself together and if he moved he would shatter into a million pieces.

She didn't ask again. She crossed the space between them and slid her arms around him, pressed her body into him tightly. Laid her head over his heart. "If I haven't told you yet, I love you. I know it's too soon to say that. I know you're going to say I don't know you, but now, right now . . ." She tilted her face up so her eyes could meet his. "I saw all of you. The best and the worst. I saw what they tried to shape you into, and I know that's part of who you are. I also know they didn't succeed the way they wanted because of your character, because of who you were born to be. Because of your genetics and your parents and your brothers. You might not have been raised with them, but they were there for you. Inside you. Helping you hold out against the monsters. I see you, Casimir, and the man I see, the one you are, that's the man I love. Don't take him away from me. Don't let the Arturos, Luigis and Sorbacovs win."

Very slowly his arms came up to wrap tight around her. He didn't say anything at all, but he nearly broke her in half tightening his hold on her, locking her to him so hard he clearly wanted to share the same skin. They stood there, just holding each other, and then he finally dropped his head over hers, his lips in her hair.

He drew in a deep, shuddering breath. "You have to go to Luigi. Can you do it? Can you play out this charade? The cops will want to question him about Arturo. We can't kill him now. Not and have it look like an accident. Someone will be suspicious." He loosened his hold on her to catch her chin in his palm, lifting her face to his. "Can you do this, Giacinta? Because if you can't, we'll leave. We can disappear and come back in a few weeks or I will, and finish this."

"I'll finish it."

"It might be best if you go to the States and wait for me there."

She shook her head. "You can't get close to the Sorbacovs and you have no chance at all without me. With me, with both of us acting together, we can eliminate them and come out of this alive. I'm not about to let Luigi and his plan to rule Italy as head of two families ruin our chances to ensure your brothers and my sisters a peaceful, happy life."

His gaze moved over her face. Possessive. Still angry.

Still upset, but loving her. She felt that. Loving her. He didn't say it, but she felt it.

"Kiss me, Casimir. Right now. I need to carry your strength with me when I go down to him. It's going to be a long night. Tomorrow I have to be the real me and go to the hotel as if none of this has touched me. The world doesn't know me as Luigi's niece. I'm the woman who sold him chandeliers. Everyone thinks he gave me my big break here in Italy and that we remained friends."

He didn't hesitate. He framed her face with both hands and brought his mouth down on hers. Gently. Tenderly. A haunting, evocative kiss that would stay with her for a long, long time, as he meant it to.

"I'll be in your bed, *malyshka*," he whispered against her lips. He kissed her again. A little harder. A little longer. A lot more aggressively.

A slow somersault started in Lissa's stomach. Little darts of fire streaked through her bloodstream. It didn't seem to matter what the circumstances were, his kisses got to her. Claimed her. Took her out of whatever horrible world she was in and brought her into a much better one.

She stepped away from him because she had to. She wasn't going to cling. If she did, he was in no state to let her go. He'd walk calmly downstairs and put a bullet in Luigi's head and take her out of there. She was certain of it. She didn't need that connection between them to know what was in his mind and what he would do if she hesitated.

Lissa walked slowly down the stairs, dread in every step. She'd told Casimir she could do this—and she would—but it wasn't easy and she didn't want him to witness her struggle. That definitely would be a disaster. She stood in the doorway of her uncle's study. He was on the phone, his back to the door, swearing at someone. She caught the name "Angeline" and she closed her eyes and rested her forehead against the doorjamb. Of course he would have to call his wife and tell her Arturo was dead. She would find out sooner or later, and it was better coming from him. He would give her the tale he'd given to Lissa—that Arturo and the widow were lovers and into kinky games.

"Tio." She didn't want to eavesdrop on his conversation. He spun around, and she shook her head. "Sorry," she mouthed. "I didn't see you on the phone." She made as if to leave, but he waved her inside.

"I have to go," Luigi said decisively into the phone, and hung up. "He was up there of course, or you wouldn't have taken so long."

"Tomasso liked Arturo. I had to tell him something since I went into his bedroom."

He nodded. "I called the hotel. He was there and very thorough. He familiarized himself with the layout before he even spoke to the head of security. I had them pull the tapes to see what time he arrived. He couldn't possibly have had anything to do with Arturo's death."

"I know this sounds horrible, Tio, and I don't want to speak ill of the dead, but if the widow was having an affair with Arturo while Cosmos was alive, could she have been carrying on with someone else? Someone who might have been jealous?"

"I don't know. I didn't hear any rumors about anyone else. Cosmos was pretty demanding. To get information, I had to become friends with him. I even had dinner at his house occasionally. That's how Arturo met her. I needed to know the layout of the house and the routine his bodyguards had so I could give it to you. Maybe Aldo thought an Abbracciabene shouldn't be spending so much time with a Porcelli soldier and he arranged to have Arturo killed in order to send a message. Who else, Gia?"

"Tio." She gentled her voice. "You have to call me Lissa even when we're alone. No one can know who I am. That was your order."

He sighed heavily, nodding as he did so.

"And you can't go to see Aldo Porcelli. You can't. Even to

get more information. If he put out a hit on Arturo, then I have to take him out this weekend. In the meantime, you need to retire to your wing of the house and have the men you trust the most guarding this place. Don't get into your car, don't go anywhere. Don't allow even a cop to talk to you alone. Have your bodyguards in the room with you and have at least one standing behind anyone insisting on meeting with you at all times."

"Yes, yes, I'll do that," he agreed.

"I don't need a bodyguard. I'm nothing to Aldo. Keep Tomasso here with you. He's been loyal and now, with Arturo dead, you need someone good."

"Absolutely not." He stood up. "He'll go with you. Someone needs to watch over you. I'm not taking any chances with your life."

He was back to being Luigi, head of the Abbracciabene family. The man who had ordered the hit on his own brother. He wanted Aldo killed. He was too close to his goal to allow even the death of his oldest friend to delay his plans. He needed Lissa alive to take out his last obstacle.

Lissa nodded. "I'm exhausted, Tio Luigi. You must be too. You've been so sick and you don't want to have a relapse, so let's both go to bed." She didn't give him a chance to protest. She couldn't be in the same room with him, not for one more moment.

12

LUIGI had purchased his home in a small town far from Ferrara, supposedly to keep his niece safe. If Lissa hadn't taken everything her uncle told her at face value, she would have realized that the Porcelli family would have kept tabs on the new head of the Abbracciabene family, no matter where he was located. Italy wasn't so huge that he could hide.

Polignano a Mare was a very small coastal town rising out of the cliffs on the Adriatic Sea. The population varied at times, but it rarely reached more than four thousand. The town offered breathtaking views over the sea, was magnificent with its white-washed streets and variety of old churches, and boasted a beach with stunning, warm, turquoise waters, and cliffs rising on either side.

Lissa loved the town and the people who lived there. They were friendly, waving and chatting when she wandered around town or stopped at Salvadore's, the little cappuccino bar. The town was one of her favorite places in the entire world. She looked forward to visiting it often.

Casimir told her that Luigi's wife and sons were in his much larger estate in the city of Bari, only about forty-seven kilometers from Polignano a Mare, a short enough drive. Bari had an international airport, making it easy for Lissa to fly in from the States. That also made it easy for Luigi to travel back and forth in forty minutes or less using the main highway. He could retire to his apartment feigning illness, sneak out, and be home in record time.

The hotel was beautiful, family owned and an enchanted retreat for celebrities that heard about the gem on the staggeringly beautiful cliffs. Lissa had been there a few times just for drinks and dinner. The food was always amazing and the views spectacular.

Tomasso reached around her to open the door of the hotel for her, his body brushing against hers. A shiver of awareness went through her, the way it always did when he was close. She leaned back into him for a moment and turned her head to look at him over her shoulder.

Casimir would be gorgeous to her in any role he assumed, but she was particularly fond of his bodyguard persona. "I inherit Luigi's house here in the village if he dies. He showed me the papers many times over the years. I love it here."

He dipped his head, his mouth brushing her ear, sending more shivers arrowing straight to her core, igniting a fire.

"Is that your subtle way of telling me Luigi's home needs to stay intact with no fire damage?"

His body crowded hers, forcing her to step inside the beautiful lobby. She laughed softly, grateful Casimir could make an attempt at humor when he'd been so quiet the night before. He'd held her all night, his body tight against hers, one leg between hers, the other over her thigh. His arms had wrapped her up, locking her to him. She hadn't minded being close—she loved it—but she hated that he was so quiet.

They'd both drifted off to sleep that way, and when she woke, he was still close. Closer even. His mouth on her breast, his fingers gliding over her body, sliding down and in, until she was panting and pleading. He made love to her so gently and tenderly, almost reverent in his touch on her body. The memory brought tears to her eyes.

Casimir was wild in bed, and she caught fire every time with him. They burned together, hot and passionate and so out of control it was crazy—ecstasy, but crazy. This time had been different, his every touch slow and beautiful. He'd whispered to her in Russian. She spoke the language, and he'd said, *Ya lyublyu tyebya fsyem syertsem.* I love you with all my heart.

She cherished those whispered words. He'd said them like they were ripped from his soul as he buried his face in her neck, his body deep in hers, while she pulsed around him, the moment so beautiful she knew it would be forever etched in her mind.

"Something like that," she admitted with a quick, teasing grin.

Coming to the hotel gave her breathing room. Without Luigi close she felt alive again, happy. Relaxed even. She was Lissa Piner, a glassblower from California, enjoying a favorite area of Italy. She had business with the owners of the hotel, yes, but she could appreciate her surroundings and even the bodyguard who had been appointed to her for security.

"Miss Piner?" An older woman dressed in a streamlined skirt and jacket greeted her with an outstretched hand. She was flanked by the head of hotel security and her manager. "I'm Mariana Loria. Please call me Mariana."

"And I'm Lissa," Lissa said, taking the woman's hand.

Mariana had a firm handshake. Her nails were beautiful as was her skin. Her hair was streaked with gray, but it only added to her elegant beauty. "Welcome to my hotel, Lissa. We're so grateful you made the trip. We're very excited about the unique designs you've come up with for us." She gestured around the lobby. "As you can see, we strive to give our guests a very different experience here. We want them to never forget their visit. Private balconies with dramatic views of course are offered, and the rooms are utter luxury, but we want every appointment inside the hotel, everywhere a guest looks, to look and feel like luxury."

"This is one of the few hotels that isn't owned by a conglomerate," Lissa said. "I love that it's a family hotel and so welcoming and beautiful. I think you've managed to convey that as well."

Mariana inclined her head with a small smile of approval. "I like to think so. We're very proud of the fact that this hotel has been in the family for generations and each generation has improved it. We want it to be very modern, yet maintain the old-world feel of a glamorous past."

Lissa walked through each room Mariana wanted to add a chandelier in. Five in the lobby. Two in the ballroom. Three in the five-star restaurant. If she got such a large order, the farm would be in money for a long while, especially since Mariana wanted the hotel's chandeliers to be original designs no one else had. She had sketched ideas based on the hotel's history, in keeping with a days-gone-by, opulent era. The chandeliers she had in mind would drip long spiraling white buds and cascading white leaves that shimmered with light from every angle.

"You do understand that because I have to do each piece by hand, each will be slightly different."

Mariana nodded. "We looked over the crystal chandeliers every other hotel has. They're beautiful but not unique. We want beautiful and unique. We want each piece to shout luxury and glamour. Your work does that. It's innovative, creative, and each piece is a work of art."

She led the way into her office. Tomasso put his hand on Lissa's back, barely there, but she felt his touch and it warmed her. He moved into the room with her and stepped to one side to stand against the wall, his hands at his sides, appearing relaxed. He didn't give anyone the option to tell him to wait outside.

Mariana waved gracefully toward a high-backed chair,

and Lissa sank into its comfort. It had taken an hour to walk around the various rooms and allow Lissa to study each room's unique signatures.

"We would very much like three separate designs, but ones that look similar, so they go with our hotel and are unique to us."

Lissa caught that Mariana had used the term "unique" several times. Clearly it was important to her that the designs for the hotel were strictly theirs. A brand for them. Everything in the hotel was that way, from the silverware in the restaurant to the furniture and pictures on the walls.

Lissa nodded. "I can do that."

Without warning she felt the brush of a thumb across the nipple of her left breast. She had to suppress a gasp as little arrows of fire streaked straight to her sex. Instantly she was damp. She glanced over her shoulder at Casimir. He wasn't looking at her. His gaze was straight ahead, as if zoned out, but his thumb was pressed tightly into the center of his palm.

Clearly your thoughts are on something besides your job, she accused.

Casimir didn't reply or show in any way that he heard her.

"The family particularly loves this design." Mariana handed Lissa the sketch of the chandelier she'd loved the most and had hoped the hotel would go with. It was a little bit more difficult to create, but it was gorgeous. The piece spoke to her. Beautiful, like Italy, glamorous and even a little decadent.

"I do too," Lissa admitted. "It was my favorite." Another nipple brush. A hot mouth closed over her breast, drew it deep, tongue pushing her nipple hard against the roof of his mouth. His teeth scraped erotically. She gasped as flames rushed through her bloodstream to burn low and sinful between her legs. She felt the familiar dampness.

Two can play this game, Casimir, and I have a vivid imagination.

Not as vivid as mine. Pure male amusement. Pure arrogance.

She didn't want to start a war with him she couldn't win, but she was definitely going to retaliate.

"Using this design for the lobby, can you make a variation of it for the restaurant and another for the ballroom?" Mariana asked.

Lissa nodded, trying to keep the flush from creeping up her body to her face. "I've already been playing around with ideas because I loved it so much."

"It's elegant—exactly what we want, and it feels like it comes from this region. That it might have been here in times gone past, but yet is very sophisticated."

Casimir's tongue teased at the underside of Lissa's breast. Clearly his imagination wasn't nearly finished.

I'm conducting business here.

I'm just standing here passing the time while you close this deal.

Lissa had to concentrate on what Mariana was telling her. She clearly liked the design, but really, for the chandelier to come off the way they needed it, color was important. "The other thing I love about this piece is the color. It is a muted white like the cliffs in places. It says your hotel like nothing else," Lissa admitted. "This is one of my favorite places in the entire world, so it was a privilege to create something that made me feel it was part of a place I love."

They got down to business, discussing price. Fortunately, Casimir didn't continue his assault on her senses during the money discussion. Lissa had learned not to sell herself short. She knew the worth of her masterpieces, and these chandeliers would be masterpieces. Mariana didn't wince. They'd had a tentative discussion before. In the end, they came to agreement, one that made Lissa want to dance around the room, but she kept her business face on, smiling and allowing the talk to drift into personal avenues.

She found out that the Loria family expected their children and grandchildren to work in the hotel from the bottom up, learning every aspect of the care and maintenance of their family business. Their employees were treated with respect and many workers were generational. Clearly Mariana was proud of her hotel and family. Lissa liked her even more for that.

Wrap it up, malyshka. *I'm hungry for you all over again.*

You worked yourself up, she teased, although in truth, he'd worked her up. Still, she wanted to be somewhere she could practice a little payback.

"We would love to have you eat lunch here," Mariana said. "You're welcome to walk around the grounds. They're beautiful and very extensive."

"Thank you," Lissa said, rising with her hostess. "I'd love that. It's very relaxing here and I would enjoy exploring." She turned to Tomasso. "Are you hungry? Would you join me for lunch?" Better to ask him right in front of Mariana than to have any speculation afterward. She was from the United States and who knew what they did there, maybe everyone had meals with their bodyguards.

Tomasso raised an eyebrow, but inclined his head. "I would enjoy that, Miss Piner."

"Lissa," she corrected, sounding slightly annoyed, as if she'd corrected him a million times. If anyone was reporting back to Luigi, they would tell him his houseguest found her bodyguard a little irritating.

Mariana graciously hid her smile as she opened the door and waved them through. "If you need anything at all, let us know."

Lissa nodded, wanting to kick Tomasso in the shins when he deliberately crowded her. His body heat set her heart pounding. His masculine scent enveloped her, and the brush of his body against hers sent more damp heat spilling into her panties. "Thank you, Mariana. I'll get the contracts to you and get started on the chandeliers right away."

As they walked away she glared at Tomasso. "You are terrible. I should kick you."

"I prefer you kissing me."

They were given a secluded table on a balcony overlooking the Adriatic Sea. Each of the small balconies was designed so a couple could be totally private. Celebrities visited the hideaway often and they came to relax, enjoy themselves and not be bothered by fans or the paparazzi.

Casimir sat close to her, rather than across from her, both facing the turquoise sea. He threaded his fingers through hers, brought her hand to his mouth to kiss the back and then brought it beneath the table to his thigh, pressing her palm deep. "It's beautiful here, Lissa," he observed.

"I love the farm," she said. "It's become my home, but this place will always be my first love."

"In spite of the terrible things that have happened?"

She nodded. "Luigi doesn't represent these people. He's the anomaly. I'm Italian. I love being Italian, and I'm proud of my country."

"I understand," Casimir agreed. "I feel the same way about my homeland. When this is done, and we're free, I want to show you my country. It's beautiful as well. We can make our home on the farm, but we'll have Italy and Russia to visit often."

"I hope so." He'd just said *our* home. As in he'd be moving in with her. She knew that was the natural progression of things between a man and a woman when they loved each other, but she had always considered she wouldn't live long—people who did the things she did rarely saw old age.

He brought her hand up to his mouth again, this time scraping at the pads of her fingers with his teeth. "What is it, *golubushka*? You suddenly looked as if you might faint on me."

The waiter came, took their orders and smiled at them both. "This balcony is very private. When you prefer more privacy, you can close the doors and the privacy sign will be up. No one will disturb you."

Lissa burst out laughing when he left. "He thinks we're having an affair."

"Of course he does. He's very romantic and you're a beautiful, classy woman and I'm your bodyguard. That's the epitome of romance."

She laughed softly. "I'll have an affair with Tomasso, but I think Casimir might object."

"Not necessarily, as long as you don't fall in love with him. And you aren't going to get off that easy. Not that I would mind closing those doors and cutting us off from the rest of the world for a time, but we need to get a few things straight. What made you look a little faint?"

"Of course you aren't just going to let it go," she said with a little sigh. "This doesn't bode well for our relationship."

"Our relationship will be just fine," he corrected. His eyes pierced right through her, saw too much. "You're the one not quite ready to commit."

She scowled at him. "I've totally committed. *Totally*. I admitted I love you. That's a huge step, Tomasso."

"I was in the security room for a while and these balconies are private, no cameras or audio, so we're alone, and you call me Casimir when we're talking about our relationship. I want you to know just who you're talking to."

She ducked her head. "It was nothing."

"*Malyshka*, just tell me what's gotten you upset."

"Not upset, just a little thrown. You said we'd make our home on the farm. I hadn't thought beyond the here and now. I didn't think about you coming home with me and moving into my house."

A slow, sexy smile softened the hard edge to his mouth. "*Our* house. Prakenskii men claim it all. Woman. House. The contents. All of it. It belongs to us."

She couldn't help but laugh. "I can't say I haven't noticed that trait in your brothers. I don't know why I didn't think ahead. I'm not good at sharing space."

"You share just fine. I'm in your bed, you give me whatever I want."

She couldn't control the blush. He was talking about more

than space in her bed. He made certain she didn't require much in the way of space. At night he dragged her body tight against his, clamped his arm around her waist or ribs, pinned her with one thigh while the other slid between her legs. He liked to sleep that way. Her back to his front. Not a whisper between their bodies.

Lissa didn't think she'd ever go to sleep with another human being in her bed, but she found he wore her out in very good ways and she drifted off immediately, feeling safe, her body sated and her heart happy. She liked the way he kept her palm tight against his thigh, his long fingers occasionally stroking a caress along the back of her hand. He liked contact and he wasn't shy about demanding it.

"I guess I just hadn't thought beyond the Sorbacovs." She whispered the admission.

"*Malyshka*, I hadn't thought much beyond the Sorbacovs either, until I met you. Now, it's imperative we both survive—and we will. So that means . . . We share the same house. Our house. Our bed. Our world," he finished.

Lissa liked that he was so confident they'd both come out alive after going after the Sorbacovs. She wasn't going to back away from that goal, not even now that she'd found Casimir. The truth was, the Sorbacovs would continue to send killers after all of them. There were children to protect now. Her sisters. The men she was coming to love as brothers. She had a family now—a real one. They might not be of blood, but they certainly were in her heart. "I lost one family. I'm not about to lose another."

"You're as determined as I am," he said, his eyes on hers.

When he looked at her like that, completely focused on her, as if she was the only person in his entire world, she melted inside.

"I've always wanted to come here and explore the grounds," Lissa admitted, changing the subject again, wanting this time to be for them alone. "I've never had the chance, but we've got time today if you don't mind."

His smile was slow in coming. Sexy. "Giacinta, I would take the opportunity to spend the day with you anywhere, any way I can. I was alone my entire life. Now, I've got you. I'll never get enough of being with you."

She liked that. How could she not? She tried not to beam, but she was fairly certain the expression on her face could have lit up a dark night.

"Tell me about them. Your sisters. I'd like to know about the women who managed to tame my brothers, especially Gavriil. I didn't believe there was any hope for him. How did your sister—it's Lexi, right? How did she manage to get him to stay around long enough to convince him to remain there on the farm?"

Lissa knew her expression softened. She loved Lexi, truly loved her. "Lexi's special. They all are, but she's . . . fragile. Strong. Perfect. She wouldn't think so, but I think Gavriil saw all of that right away. She was kidnapped when she was just a little girl by a cult. She didn't escape until she was seventeen. She's an earth element and can grow anything just about anywhere, so the cult's farm thrived with her around. The man forcing her into marriage was a pedophile, so he wasn't enamored with her more adult body, and suffice it to say, her life was a nightmare. When she escaped, the cult murdered her family in retaliation."

He drew in his breath sharply. "I hope Gavriil got them."

She nodded. "They came after her again, and it was a big mistake. Gavriil isn't going to let anything happen to Lexi. He's different with her. Not yet with the rest of us, but he's getting more comfortable around us."

"You like him."

She nodded. "Very much. I didn't think I would. He's . . . alpha. I don't know any other word for it. No one is going to get around that man. Well, with the exception of Lexi. Not even his brothers. I could tell they were a little uneasy around him and that made me worried for my sister, but I didn't need to worry. I should have worried about the men coming after her."

Casimir suddenly released her hand, and she glanced up to see the waiter heading their way with their orders. He made a show of putting the artfully presented food in front of them and then disappeared back inside.

"It doesn't surprise me about Gavriil. My two oldest brothers had it the worst. There were several schools. They were taken to the two most brutal of those. Viktor's school had the worst reputation. About half of those going through that school died before their training was complete. I don't know much about Viktor, he's been undercover for years now. Deep undercover. He's got a target that so far he's been unable to get to, but he won't quit until he's taken him out. I'd never want that man coming after me."

"Are you saying that Viktor is even scarier than Gavriil?" Lissa was half joking. She couldn't imagine anyone being more frightening that Gavriil.

"That school was disbanded after Viktor and about seventeen others finished. Even Kostya Sorbacov realized it was too brutal. There are rumors that the seventeen disappeared along with Viktor. Sorbacov has put out hits on all of them, but they can't be found. I wouldn't be in the least surprised to find out that Viktor secretly organized them all in school and they've disappeared together. Even young he was a leader."

"If Viktor knows Sorbacov put a hit on him, wouldn't he just leave whatever job he's doing and go into hiding?"

Casimir burst out laughing. "Viktor isn't the kind of man to hide from anyone. He's going to go after Sorbacov, which is probably what he's planning on doing the moment he finishes off his mark. He's after someone big, Lissa, and he isn't going to stop because of a little thing like Sorbacov turning on him. He's always been in the most dangerous of situations. Always. He went after the most high value targets, the ones that were considered extremely dangerous."

"Isn't that what all of you do?" Lissa asked. She found the conversation fascinating. She wasn't alone in what she did, or in her conviction that the job was needed in certain circumstances—when the law couldn't touch the offender. "The seafood is delicious," she added, because it was.

"Mine too," he acknowledged. "And yes, we all go after targets, but Viktor and Gavriil's targets were men surrounded by heavy protection. One had to find a way to penetrate that protection and get inside the inner circle. They spent months, or even years, doing that and living that life day in and day out, never making a mistake. It's not easy."

She nodded. "You admire them."

"I know how difficult role-playing is. Each character I play is for a short period of time; they have to be that person for months or years. You can lose yourself in a role. Life gets confusing when you don't have anything to anchor you."

His gaze held hers. She knew what he meant. Her. She was his anchor. Gavriil had Lexi now. Viktor had no one. "Maybe he's not alone, Tomasso, maybe some of the men and women he went to that horrible school with are with him right now. Maybe they have one another's back."

"Maybe. I doubt it. They went off the grid, one by one. No one has found them. Or if they have and someone quietly killed them, no one has taken credit for it. I can't imagine Sorbacov not crowing about it to someone. He prides himself on being smarter than any of us."

"He isn't," Lissa said. "His arrogance is going to be his downfall. Uri never married. Is he gay?"

Casimir shook his head. "No. He likes women. I honestly think he got caught up in his political role and just didn't have time for a real relationship. He's had a couple of mistresses, but they didn't last long. I haven't heard he's into kink. He was close to his mother and reveres his father. Cleaning up his father's mess isn't just about his own political aspirations, it's also about keeping his father's reputation clean for the history books."

Lissa nodded. "That's good to know. Uri and Kostya Sorbacov are part owners of the very prestigious Krasnyy Drakon hotel in St. Petersburg."

Casimir frowned. Shook his head. "I know practically everything there is to know about that family. How would I not know that?"

"They bought into the hotel or acquired the shares through a dummy corporation. Renovations were done, mostly to make the hotel over for the Sorbacovs to have an underground tunnel system that doesn't just extend beneath the hotel, but under other buildings as well. They want the hotel to compete with St. Petersburg's finest. By staying silent partners, the extra renovations, the tunnels and hidden hallways, enable Uri and Kostya to have a public place to go where they have extra protection."

"You've been reading the file you got from Ivan Belsky."

She put another forkful of delicious shrimp pasta in her mouth and nodded as she chewed. "Yep," she admitted after she chewed and swallowed, trying not to moan, the food was so delicious. "Belsky has a reputation for delivering the real information. It was somewhat of a point of honor with him. You got what you paid for. Of course he often killed those he delivered to, but in his mind he earned his money because he actually came up with the information. Nuts, but I suppose in his mind, it worked for him. So, yes, I believe the information is reliable."

"Gavriil." Casimir nearly spat his brother's name. "He had to have supplied you with enough information to give you a direction. Damn him. He put you on the trail."

"I was already going there, *Tomasso*." She emphasized his name to remind him that he was there because his brother had sent for him to protect her. "He knew he couldn't stop me and apparently he kept his word to me and didn't tell anyone, not even you, what I had come here to do."

He ate quietly for a few minutes, obviously getting his temper under control. There was no way his temper didn't burn hot and ferocious, not when he was a fire element. Hers did. She'd learned to control it, just as he had, but she didn't fool herself into believing it wasn't there, smoldering just beneath the surface and ready to burst into flames at any moment.

"Did Gavriil give you Belsky's name and a way to contact him?"

"Casimir . . ."

Casimir leaned close, his eyes behind the dark contacts burning with fire. "Did he? It's not that hard to answer the fucking question, Lissa. A yes or no will work."

She sighed. "Yes. He warned me not to trust him. He also said the information would be reliable. He'd heard a rumor that the Sorbacovs had bought into the hotel."

"Gavriil always did have a good network."

"Why are you angry with him for helping me?" She put down her fork and rubbed his thigh with soothing strokes of her hand. "I was going to go after them whether Gavriil helped me or not. I wasn't going to tell anyone, least of all him. He came to visit me and he found my maps strewn all over the floor. He guessed, and there was no dissuading me. I should be the one upset with him because he called you in."

He didn't answer her question. "Once we get the job done here, we're going to sit down and plan out an attack. I take it you have an appointment with the owners or management of that hotel in St. Petersburg."

She nodded. "They said they read an article on me and were intrigued with my work. I sent them some of my designs and they loved them."

"*They* made the initial contact?"

She nodded. "I know what you're thinking. Of course they know of my association with Sea Haven. My hometown was in the article."

"This doesn't concern you?"

"I think that's what got me the foot in the door. But regardless, they're going to look at my work for their hotel. Uri Sorbacov is a control freak. He won't be able to resist being at the meeting. I don't know about his father, but he'll be there for certain. Everything I've read about Uri says anyone entering into any kind of business deal with him is doing so at their own risk. He's a shark. He isn't going to let someone else decorate his hotel. My guess is the other owners wanted the chandeliers dripping crystals. I sent other designs after they contacted me, blown glass with crystals dripping from twisted glass ropes. Very cool. Modern, beautiful and yet old-world enough to satisfy the more traditional hotel owners."

He sat back in his chair, his hand once again covering hers and pressing her palm deep into the heat of his thigh. "You plan on charming the socks right off of him."

She smiled. Faintly. Because there was something in his expression she didn't like. "Something like that."

"Well you can just forget it, Lissa. He *is* a shark, and you can't play him. He's intelligent and he knows his life is in danger as long as any of the products of those schools are still alive. He will have had you thoroughly investigated. *Thoroughly.* You may think Lissa Piner has a great history and won't be discovered, but he'll find out who you really are."

Lissa nodded. "Honey, I'm counting on that. I intend to tell him my entire history. Volunteer it myself. Luigi will be dead, my adoring uncle. Tio Luigi insisted on changing my name and sending me to the United States in order to protect me. It will work, Casimir. You know it will."

"And what of your connection to Sea Haven and the Prakenskiis? He knows Ilya is there. He has to know Gavriil is as well."

She smiled at him. "I'll admit that as well when he brings it up. He'll try to trap me, but by that time, I'll have maneuvered him just where we want him."

He sighed and shook his head. "You have a plan."

"The beginnings of one, but we'll get into that later, not today when I want to spend my time alone with you."

He brought her hand to his mouth, this time pressing a kiss into the exact center of her palm, his face soft and warm and so loving she wanted to cry.

"You're so beautiful, Giacinta. Do you have any idea what it means to a man like me to have you sitting here with me, out in the open, *seeing* me? To know that no matter what I look like, no matter what I act like, you see me—Casimir Prakenskii. It's a gift I never thought possible."

She opened her mouth, but nothing came out because his teeth teased the pads of her fingers and his gaze held hers.

"It's the truth, *malyshka*. You make me believe I can have something more than the life I was leading. Stuck in the shadows with no name or face. No one saw me until you came along. I felt dead inside."

Her breath stilled in her lungs. Burned. Casimir always seemed easy. Relaxed. Even when he smoldered with passion, there was a relaxed quality about him. Now she could see past the contacts to the focus in his eyes. His entire focus was on her. It had been almost since the moment he'd laid eyes on her, when he'd been playing the role of the obnoxious man on her flight to Italy. He'd escorted her the entire way. Looking out for her. Taking care of her even when she didn't know it.

She might have seen him, but he saw her first. He recognized they belonged before she did. More, when her world was falling apart, he had her back. Tears burned behind her eyes. He gave her more than she thought possible from any man. He laid himself out there for her, made himself vulnerable to tell her what she meant to him.

Casimir pressed her palm into his chest. "You made my heart beat again, Giacinta. I know that sounds ridiculous, but it's the truth. I had nothing left. I was going to find the Sorbacovs, but I didn't expect to come back. On some level I didn't even want to come back. I had nothing at all to come back to. I don't know my brothers. I love them and am loyal to them because I had to have something, some code, something to hold on to, but I haven't seen them or really talked to them since I was a very little boy. I didn't mind going out in a blaze of glory for them, but I didn't have it in me to live for them." He brought her hand back to his mouth, teeth teasing her fingers until she thought her heart would explode with such emotion there was nowhere for it to go.

"Then I saw you. The way you moved, like music on the wind. The way your face lit up when you laughed. No matter how annoying I was to you, you were kind to me on the plane. That touched me, Lissa. Your kindness. In my world, there isn't much of that. You're the most beautiful woman I've ever seen and, although you're that on the outside, I think it's what you are inside that makes you so beautiful to me."

"You're making me cry," she whispered.

Her voice wouldn't go above a whisper. In that moment, she knew she had fallen all the way. Love. It was strange to her that love would come to her now, when she was committed to making a life for the five women so entrenched in her heart, but there it was. Love. The real thing. The emotion overwhelmed her. *He* overwhelmed her with his declaration. Every word out of his mouth was honest. Raw. She might not have anything else, but she had him. Casimir Prakenskii would always be hers. How could she want anything else?

"There will never be another woman for me, Lissa. You're it. My shot at a life. If you give me that, I swear to you, I'll never let you down." He pressed a kiss into the center of her palm, his eyes on her face. "Will you do that, *malyshka*? Will you take me as I am and give me the one shot I've got? Will you take a chance on me?"

Her heart thudded in her chest. She stared up at his handsome face. This was more than a declaration. "What are you asking me, Casimir?" Because there was no way he was talking abstract, not when the air itself stilled.

13

⟋

"MARRY me. Before we do the rest of this. Marry me now, Giacinta. Be my wife."

Everything in her stilled. She could hear the sound of the sea below them. The birds in the trees and insects buzzing in the gardens. She was aware of everything about Casimir. His height, so much taller than she was. His chest, all defined muscle. His strong arms and tapered waist. His narrow hips and long, muscular legs. His hands were a man's hands. Beautiful.

Most of all she was acutely aware of Casimir beneath Tomasso's gorgeous Italian image. She would always see him. The real man, not the one everyone else saw. It would never matter what role he was playing, he would always be hers. She would always see the real man.

"Honey." She kept her tone gentle. "You know we can't do that. Lissa Piner is an American. You're whatever role you're playing. We can't possibly get permission to marry here in Italy."

"Giacinta and Casimir can get married. That's your legal name. That's mine. We can get married right away. The documents have been taken care of."

She shook her head. "That's impossible. A Russian citizen would have to appear in person at the Russian Embassy in order to get the necessary papers. I'd have to go with you and prove I'm an Italian citizen. You need a stamp of . . ."

"Marry me, Giacinta Abbracciabene. Come with me now. Let's do it. I've got a priest standing by. He'll marry us today." He reached inside his jacket and pulled out a small black velvet case.

Lissa swallowed hard. He wasn't joking. He meant every single word and she could tell this meant something to him. Not just something. *Everything.* She couldn't speak. She could only look at him. He'd planned this. After. After knowing about Luigi's betrayal. After knowing Arturo betrayed her. Knowing she had loved them both, at least the illusion of who they were. He had somehow managed to arrange this. He had to have had help. Still. He gave her his declaration of love.

"Are you going to give this to me?" he asked gently. "For me, Giacinta. For me."

It wasn't for him. He might think it was, but in reality, it was for her. To belong somewhere. Everyone needed to belong.

"You're certain, Casimir? Because this is a lifetime commitment. We might actually survive our encounter with the Sorbacovs, and then what? How are you going to get out of this if you marry me legally?"

"*Malyshka.* Baby. Do you really think I would ever want out? *Ever?* I haven't been to the farm, but my brothers seem to love it there. Lev told me he goes sea urchin diving with Rikki. Stefan owns an art gallery with Judith. Max heads up security for Airiana. And Gavriil . . ." A grin broke through, as if he couldn't quite believe what his older brother did. "Gavriil is working the farm with Lexi. I intend to learn the art of glassblowing with my wife. Welding as well. I want to work with you. Live with you. Share your home and your bed. Permanently. When we're eighty, I want to be sitting on the front porch with you in a rocking chair while our grand-children play where we can see and hear them."

She moistened her lips. "You want children?"

He nodded. "I want the family neither of us ever got to have. With you. I want that with you. And I want us married before we go to Russia."

"I didn't expect this." Her heart beat so fast and so hard she felt the ache spreading through her body.

"Do you love me?"

Her breath caught in her lungs. In her throat. The raw emotion on his face tore her up inside. "More than anything." It was true, truer than she'd even known. In that moment, everything was crystal clear to her.

"That's all that matters. We have today to be us. Casimir and Giacinta. Luigi is with his wife and children. Tomorrow we can deal with the underbelly of the world and the ugly people residing there. But we have this day for us. The documents are legal. The priest is as well. I just have to text him, and we'll go get clothes. A dress for you, a bridal gown. A suit for me. We'll get married and spend the night in a beautiful little villa overlooking the sea. Say yes, *golubushka*. Give me you."

"Tell me when you put this all together."

For the first time he hesitated. "Does it matter?"

She knew then. He'd done it when he'd discovered Luigi's treachery. When he knew and she didn't. When he knew he would have to tell her, to take something precious from her. He had set this day in motion then.

"Won't the Sorbacovs hear about a Casimir Prakenskii applying for permission to marry Giacinta Abbracciabene, an Italian citizen?"

"I told you, I have friends in high places. The priest will delay the paperwork getting to public records as well. The Sorbacovs will not have a clue that a Prakenskii has married and is the happiest man alive. When they are gone, whether we live or not, those papers will be made official to the world."

She moistened her lips. He was so beautiful, sitting there looking at her with his dark, tinted eyes and the spill of dark wavy hair. Still, she preferred the gorgeous Russian with his strange, silver eyes and short, spiked, black and silver hair.

His thumb slid along her inner wrist, a lazy, languid slide that sent a million butterflies winging their way south. Her heart thundered in her ears. Could it be that easy to take something for herself? She was giving up her life for everyone else. Could she really do this? Marry him? It didn't seem possible that he could have planned this down to the minutest detail, including making it actually legal, but who cared if it wasn't? She doubted if they would live through the Sorbacovs' security.

"*Malyshka*. Are you going to give this to me?"

The little breeze that had been flirting with her hair there on the balcony went still. The insects below in the gardens sounded more like music than an annoying drone. She nodded slowly, because she couldn't speak. She couldn't bring herself to ruin that perfect moment. She hadn't had a lot of perfect moments in her life and this was number one. The best.

His slow smile turned her heart over. Maybe that moment was even better. He kissed her wrist. So gently. A caress that she felt all the way to her toes.

"Do I get Casimir? Not Tomasso?"

"I'll change at the church."

"Church?" she echoed, because she couldn't imagine that they could walk into a church and get married. He'd said "priest" and that went with a church, but perhaps he was unaware that people were in them even during the day and they couldn't very well get married in a small village and not have the news leak out.

"Trust me. Our wedding will be beautiful. We need to find you a dress."

"This is Italy. One-of-a-kind wedding dresses. It isn't like we can walk into a store and find a gown hanging."

"You never know until you try, *golubushka*," he said.

They found the dress in the third shop they walked into:
Sophie Rigoli, a very famous Italian designer. Lissa hadn't
wanted to go into the shop because the gowns were beautiful
beyond description, terribly expensive and one of a kind.
Very original. It wasn't like they could walk in and have one
made in a day. She went because Casimir was so insistent
and there was something in her that compelled her to give
him whatever he wanted.

He'd planned their wedding. He bought her a ring. He
intended to go with her to get the Sorbacovs. Most impor-
tantly, he had her back when her uncle and Arturo had broken her heart and turned her world upside down.

The shop was small, and she stayed back, near the door,
while Casimir did the talking, explaining what they needed.
To Lissa's shock, the little Italian woman was practicing the
dying art of traditional bobbin lace. She found herself moving forward, fascinated by the way the woman's hands moved
swift and sure when she already had at least nine bobbins
hanging from the pattern she was creating, twisting the
thread in the labor intensive and beautiful way rarely seen.

The woman's eyes went to Lissa while Casimir talked,
assessing her figure. A smile broke out and she nodded. "We
had a dress made that couldn't be used. The bride ran off. A
big scandal. Her parents were embarrassed. Sophie's beautiful creation sits here, but the dress could have been made for
you. Would you like to see it?"

Lissa thought it was rather interesting that the bride had
fled before her wedding and Lissa and Casimir were marry-
ing in secret. She was absolutely certain the dress would be
perfect, and more, it would fit as if it had been made for her.
There was something beautiful and very right about finding
the dress.

The shopkeeper put down her bobbins and led her to a
small changing area in the back and brought out a dress.
Lissa's breath caught in her throat. Tears burned at the back
of her eyes. The exquisite ivory wedding dress was definitely

a Sophie Rigoli. The slip gown was heavily beaded with jewels. The neckline plunged low and the back was an illusion of jewels made of the traditional bobbin lace, with sheer fabric from neck to the waist. The natural waistline held more beadwork done with jewels. Silk organza ruffles accented the skirt and train.

Lissa stared at herself in the mirror. The dress clung to her every curve, emphasized her small waist and lush breasts. The shopkeeper brought out a veil with the same sheer material and illusion of jewels done in the bobbin lace. The veil went from her head to the floor, to add to the beauty of the train. She ran her hand down the dress, unable to believe she was actually standing there, looking at herself in the mirror in something so beautiful.

"I want this," she breathed. Still, it had to cost a fortune.

"Your gentleman said anything you wanted. Cost did not matter. I have the silk stockings and garter to go with it."

She also had ivory lace underwear and a pair of silver strappy heels. There was a beautiful silver necklace and drop earrings that looked perfect with the plunging neckline. Lissa didn't ask the price. She knew if she did, she would never allow Casimir to pay for it all. She told herself after she sold the chandeliers to the other hotels she would have the money to pay him back, but this was a once-in-a-lifetime event. Her day. Her only day. She just hoped Casimir thought the dress and veil would be worth the money as well when he saw them on her.

He didn't raise an eyebrow when he paid, laughing and talking with the shopkeeper, oozing charm in the way he did. With the dress inside a garment bag, they drove the forty minutes to the city and straight to a Russian Orthodox church. He seemed to know exactly where he was going. The church appeared deserted, and they went around the building, through a garden to a side entrance. Casimir knocked twice and waited. The heavy door was unlocked, and Casimir took her hand and drew her inside.

The small room where they stood was unlit, and a man in robes stood in the shadows. Lissa couldn't make out his face.

"We need a room to get ready," Casimir said.

The priest closed and locked the door and then gestured for them to follow him.

"Do you have the paperwork?" Casimir asked.

The priest nodded, paused by a door, opened it and indicated for Lissa to go in. She did, and Casimir followed her. The priest shut the door, leaving them alone.

"It's bad luck to see me before the wedding," she said.

He smiled at her. Happy. She loved his smile. "*This* is our wedding. Part of it. A ritual. The groom helping the bride into her dress. The bride helping the groom with his tie."

She nodded, shocked that his answer made her even happier.

He hung up the garment bags. "I'm going to get rid of Tomasso. We won't need him again until tomorrow. I'll get dressed and help you into your dress." His hands framed her face. "Thank you for this, Giacinta, it means the world to me that you'd trust me this much."

She found her eyes burning again. He had no idea how much she felt for him. The emotion nearly overwhelmed her. She knew she was living in the moment, but she also knew this might be all they ever had together and that made their decision all the more important.

While Casimir was in the small bathroom, she carefully did her hair in an artfully messy cascade that was pulled back from her face and twisted into a loose knot at the back of her head to allow her back to show in the dress. The drop earrings would show off the sheer fabric at her shoulders and the long necklace would accent the plunging neckline. She had on the stockings and heels and had stepped into her wedding gown when the door opened and Casimir emerged.

He looked . . . *gorgeous*. So handsome he took her breath away. He wore a black suit that fit him as if it had been made for him. She was certain it had been. His shoulders were wide and his body made for such a beautiful cut of jacket. His gaze jumped to her carefully made-up face, makeup with an edge toward drama but still muted, looking almost barely there.

Casimir looked at her as though he couldn't believe his eyes. Stark love was so raw on his face, stamped into his masculine features, every line, and his eyes, that incredible, slashing silver held the same intense desire—so much so that the absolute intensity brought on a flutter in the region of her heart. "Baby," she breathed, because that was all she could do. All she could say.

He swirled his finger, indicating for her to turn as she drew up the gown, the sheer lace fabric settling over her shoulders. He did up the long row of jeweled buttons up the center of her back, adding to the mystique the jeweled illusion back created.

He bent and kissed the side of her neck, his breath warm. *"Krasavisa."* He whispered the word against the skin behind her ear. *"Ya lyublyu tebya."*

She knew the first word was "beautiful" and the second phrase was "I love you." They both sounded amazing in his native language.

He turned her to face him, his hands gentle on her arms. When she was fully facing him, only a whisper away, he traced the plunging line of her gown in the long vee, over the curve of one breast, down to where the vee came together at her waist and back up over the curve of the other. "Perfect. You're perfect."

She found herself staring into his eyes. This man belonged to her. He was dangerous, yes, but he was also unexpectedly romantic. It meant something to him that she had agreed to dress in a wedding gown for him. She still couldn't believe that he had planned the entire event knowing there was a good chance she might not agree. She liked that he was romantic and that he'd showed that to her now. She needed it. She needed to know she was important to him.

Because she couldn't talk, couldn't tell him what he meant

to her, she reached up to knot his tie. Her hands trembled. Even in heels she was quite a bit shorter than he was and she had to reach to get his tie straight.

"Are you ready?"

She nodded. "Are you?"

He took her hand. "More than ready. I never thought I'd ever have you, Giacinta. Never. I couldn't even imagine a woman as perfect for me as you are."

She ducked her head and allowed him to secure the long, sheer veil in her hair. Heart pounding, she stepped out the door with him. The priest was patiently waiting. Hand in hand, they followed him into the small chapel. Just inside the entryway, the priest stopped and turned to them.

A man stood to one side of the priest. He was tall and broad-shouldered. His hair was long. Very long. He wore it pulled back in a very tidy tail down his back. His arms bulged under his suit jacket. Tattoos drifted up his neck. His eyes were a piercing green. Not silver, but green. Still, she recognized those eyes. Prakenskii eyes. Beside her, Lissa heard Casimir's swift intake of breath and knew he had recognized those eyes.

"Viktor." He barely breathed the name. Stunned. Shocked. His voice sounded choked.

Viktor was the most intimidating man she'd ever seen in her life. That was saying something when she knew six of the seven Prakenskii brothers. Even dressed in his suit, he looked more a dangerous, badass biker than a businessman. She doubted that he could ever have changed roles the way Casimir did. Even so, emotion played over his face for just a moment, the green in his eyes going dark. He hooked his younger brother around the nape of his neck and dragged him close, right into a deep hug—something she almost couldn't believe someone so scary-looking would do.

"How?" Casimir asked as he straightened, his hand still firmly clasped in his brother's as if they'd both forgotten they were also shaking hands.

Viktor jerked his head at the priest. "You needed a *koumbaros*, one to watch over the two of you for the rest of your lives. He sent for me." The smile faded from his face. "This is your woman?"

"Giacinta Abbracciabene, my brother, Viktor," Casimir introduced, reaching once again for Lissa's hand. He brought her fingertips to his mouth. "She's the one. My woman." He put her hand in Viktor's.

"Little sister," Viktor said. "It is good to meet you. Let's get this done and we'll have a few minutes to visit before I have to go. I have to be on a freighter in a couple of hours." He squeezed her hand, his eyes searching her face before he put her hand back in Casimir's.

Her heart pounded. She had the feeling that he could see into her soul and if she didn't measure up, he'd slit her throat right there on the spot. In front of Casimir. In front of the priest. Right there in the church. He'd do it without hesitation and walk away, never looking back.

"Your woman is beautiful, Casimir."

Casimir pulled Lissa closer to him. "She is," he agreed.

"I'll need the rings."

Casimir handed Viktor the wedding rings. "Your being here means the world to me, Viktor," he said. "I don't know how . . ."

"Means the world to me as well," Viktor said, cutting him off.

He sounded like he was stating the stark truth. Lissa felt her throat close, a huge lump there. Tears burned behind her eyes and she blinked rapidly, not wanting to mess up her makeup, but so grateful that Casimir had his brother there. His oldest brother, the one he—like all the others—worried about the most. None of them had heard from him for a very long time. He was operating deep undercover and hadn't surfaced in so long they were all afraid something had happened to him.

The priest began the ceremony, reciting Bible passages and blessings. He then made the sign of the cross while he held the rings in his palm, declaring the betrothal. Holding the rings in his hands, he pressed first Casimir's forehead three times and then followed suit doing the same to Lissa's forehead. Viktor took the rings from the priest and exchanged them three times between Casimir and Lissa, symbolizing that the weakness of one would be offset by the other.

Lissa's ring was slipped onto the third finger of her right hand. It was a beautiful, ornate band, matching the thicker band that was Casimir's. His ring was put onto his finger next. They stood for a moment, Lissa smiling up at Casimir, her heart in her eyes. She became aware of Viktor watching her closely. She couldn't blame him. He wanted to know that his brother was really going to be happy with the woman of his choice, but still, the direct dark green gaze was disconcerting.

Casimir held Lissa's right hand and the priest handed them both a lit candle to be held in their left hands. Casimir leaned down to whisper in her ear while the priest continued his blessings as they approached the altar. "We hold hands for the rest of the ceremony, *golubushka*, to show we are one."

Viktor leaned down from the other side. "The flames from the candles show you are both willing to receive God's blessings."

At the altar, with the priest holding his hand over their joined hands, Viktor presented them with crowns of orange blossoms and other beautiful flowers mixed with semi-precious stones. The garlands were joined together by a white ribbon. "These crowns stay with you for life," Viktor whispered to Lissa.

The priest took the crowns and placed one on Lissa's head and the other on Casimir's while the two of them faced the altar. Viktor switched the crowns three times between the couple in the age-old ritual symbolizing unity.

While the priest read more Bible passages to them, Lissa looked up at the man who was joining his life to hers. He was absolutely confident, following the priest's every word, his hand firmly in hers.

Wine was next, each drinking three times from a shared cup. "The cup represents life and symbolizes sorrow and joy that the two of you will always share from this day forward," Viktor explained. "As you drink from the cup, be reminded that you will divide your sorrows and your joys will be doubled."

Lissa liked that he explained the various ceremonies. She knew enough Russian to understand the priest, but she wasn't familiar with the wedding rituals and what they meant. The priest spoke rapidly in his native language, making it harder to follow, so the explanations were very welcome.

Viktor and the priest led Casimir and Lissa around the altar three times. She noted that both a Bible and a cross were prominent on the altar. Everything clearly was done in threes. Viktor sang three hymns softly, his voice rich and deep, as they took their first steps as man and wife together.

The priest said a few more prayers over them, ending with the traditional, ancient phrase "May you live."

He shook Viktor's hand and then Casimir's before he faded away, leaving the three together.

"I've got a villa for the night," Casimir said. "No one will be there but us. Do you have time to visit?"

"I'm sorry," Viktor said, shaking his head, his voice tinged with regret. "I took a chance coming. I have to be on the freighter before it sails. No one knows I'm in the country. Officially, of course, I'm not. I've got some friends taking me back, but they won't be able to cover for me for long. I don't dare miss my ride." He put his hand on his brother's shoulder as he leaned down to brush a kiss on Lissa's cheek.

"Lazzaro has a small room set aside where we can visit for a few minutes."

Casimir held tightly to Lissa's hand as they followed Viktor down a narrow hallway to a small room with four chairs and a coffee table. Other than those five pieces of furniture, the room was bare. Casimir helped Lissa to remove her crown and veil and sit in the most comfortable chair before he sank into the one beside her, taking off his crown as well.

"You haven't checked in with anyone, Viktor." Casimir knew it sounded like a reprimand—and it was. "All of us were worried. We weren't even certain you were alive."

Viktor shrugged. "It couldn't be helped. In the beginning, when I first joined the motorcycle club, I was watched all the time. I've managed to work my way up in rank and I'm trusted far more than I was, but my target is very paranoid. He used to ride with the club all the time, but now he's elusive. I've managed to slowly get my people in place and they have my back, so it isn't as dangerous as it was in the beginning when I was out there with no one, surrounded by a hundred enemies."

Casimir swore in Russian. "We would have come."

Viktor nodded. "Precisely why I didn't tell any of you what I was doing. Of course you would have come. I didn't want that for you, for any of you. You're the last one to find his woman. Tell me about the others."

"*You're* the last one to find his woman," Casimir corrected. He didn't want Viktor to give up his life because his brothers were settled.

Viktor shook his head. "I was the first," he said. He pressed his thumb into the middle of his palm. "When this is over, I'm going to stake my claim. She won't like it, me being gone so long, but . . ." He shrugged. His features were hard. Implacable.

Casimir didn't think that boded very well for his woman. "Does this woman know she's been claimed?"

"She'd better know it," Viktor said.

"Really?" Lissa asked, her voice innocent. Too innocent. The sheer arrogance of the man rubbed her the wrong way. "So you kept in touch with her for the past . . . how long have you been undercover? Five years?"

Viktor narrowed his gaze. "*Deep undercover* means no communicating with the outside world that might put someone you care about in jeopardy."

Lissa nodded. Casimir shifted closer to her, uncertain what exactly was taking place between his wife and his brother.

"So this woman of yours knew you were going undercover."

"*Wife.* My fucking *wife.*"

Lissa's eyebrows shot up and her fingers tightened around Casimir's. Glancing down at her, he realized she was angry. "Your *wife* then. You told her you were going *deep* undercover, right? There were ways you would let her know you weren't dead."

"She knows."

"Good. Otherwise she might be dating someone else, or maybe, if she didn't know she was already someone's wife, *married* to someone else."

Viktor went still. Scary still. The room shuddered. "That happens, *sister*, and her new husband won't have long for this world."

"Not a good idea to leave a woman alone for five years, *brother*," Lissa continued, "especially if she's smokin' hot. And a runner. She goes running down the highway and she's bound to stop traffic and then where are you going to be? Oh wait. I know. Somewhere *deep* undercover while she's all alone and lonely. Surrounded by men who think she's smokin' hot, because she is."

"What the hell, Giacinta?" Casimir demanded.

Beside him, Lissa moved restlessly, drawing Viktor's

sharp gaze. Lissa looked down at her wedding ring, the band that was tucked up tight against the diamond he'd given her earlier in the day.

"I just wouldn't want you to ever do that kind of thing to me, Casimir," Lissa said. "I wouldn't be in the least understanding, and I'm a little outraged on all my fellow sisters' behalf."

There was a small silence, Viktor staring down at her face for a long moment before he sighed and changed the subject. "Tell me about the farm. You live there, right? Where my brothers live?"

Her gaze jumped to his face. "They're happy." Her voice was strictly neutral. "Even Gavriil. He's still in a lot of pain, but Lexi is working with that and hopes to alleviate it, at least most of it. All of them are doing well."

Casimir waited, but Lissa didn't mention her other sisters. He took a breath and then let it out. The temperature in the room had gone up a couple of degrees. That wasn't his brother's temper. That was Lissa.

"Your brothers are going to want to know what your life is like."

"My life?" Viktor echoed. "Baby, my life is totally fucked, but I put myself there and I'm going to get the job done no matter what. Then I'll go claim my life." There was no bitterness in his voice, only a statement of fact.

Casimir knew that no matter how bad they might think Viktor's situation was it was probably a hundred times worse, or he would have at least contacted his brothers. "You know the Sorbacovs have a hit out on all of us, Ilya included."

"I heard. I know that you told Lazzaro that your woman planned to go with you to take them out for us."

Viktor didn't sound in the least approving. In fact, he sounded like a freaking male chauvinist. Just looking at him, seeing the hard, set lines in his face, she could see he was implacable. He'd be hell to live with. Difficult to understand.

And he wouldn't care. His woman would be expected to live life his way. On his terms.

Lissa's fingers tightened in Casimir's. "Actually, Casimir is going with *me*," she corrected, her chin going up. "We figured with him along the chances were better that we'd get them both and walk away alive."

"You do that, call Lazzaro. He'll be waiting for that call and he'll get the two of you out of the country fast if you need it. He's more than willing to help, and he's one of the few we can absolutely count on."

Casimir nodded, not bothering to correct his woman. He'd been planning all along to kill the Sorbacovs. He still wasn't certain he liked the idea of Lissa going with him and taking center stage, but he knew there was no dissuading her. She had a stubborn streak and she'd made up her mind, even more so now that she knew he had planned to get rid of them.

"These men backing you up, Viktor. You're sure of their loyalty?"

Viktor nodded. "They grew up with me. We're all that's left of the old school. Eighteen of us from one hundred and thirty. We stuck by one another in training and after. The strongest, all psychics, all men Kostya Sorbacov couldn't control. He was afraid of every one of us. One by one, the others slipped Kostya's leash and signed on with me. Our target was the president of the motorcycle club called Sword. The club started in the United States but now has chapters in Europe. He ran drugs, arms and was the number one suspect across Europe for human trafficking. He's originally from Greece. His mother took him and ran to the United States to get away from her husband. She ran with the club in the States, and he detested her man. Actually, her man's son. When I say detested him, I mean, he thinks about killing him every minute of every hour of every day. The target inherited a shitload of money from his brother and with that, the ships to help hide the worst of his trafficking, and that includes children."

Lissa pulled in a breath. "You're talking about Evan Shackler-Gratsos. Airiana and Max rescued four children from one of his ships. They say he's a ghost."

"He's no ghost. Word is, he wants to kill Jackson Deveau himself. He put the word out that no one else can touch him. He'll have to come out of the shadows to make his try and then we'll have him."

"You're telling us this because?" Casimir said. "Deep undercover is for your protection, Viktor, not just those you care about. You shouldn't have said a word of this to us, or anyone else."

"I don't get the fucker, you tell Gavriil and the others. They have to get him." His gaze lingered on Lissa's face. "You know enough to keep your mouth shut until there's no other way."

Lissa nodded slowly. Casimir could see that she was more inclined to feel favorably toward Viktor, although she still had a look in her eyes that indicated she wanted to rip into him and the temperature in the room hadn't gone down in the least.

"Viktor, these men you have with you, are you certain they'll stand with you? You take down the president of a club that size and you're vulnerable. The members know you. They know your face. You've ridden with them for five years. Say you manage it, what's to say they don't come after you a year from now, and you're hunted, just like the Sorbacovs are hunting us now."

"They'll stand with me. They've always stood with me." Something crossed his face. Something dark and sinister. In that moment, Viktor looked every inch of what he was— what he'd been shaped into. It was dark and it was ugly. "That school, Casimir . . ." He shook his head. "We had to hold on to something or we would have died like the rest of them. We had to trust one another. We've been doing that since we were boys. They're solid. They'll stand with me, before it's done. While we're getting it done and after. They'll be with me."

"After?" Casimir echoed.

"We'll get this last job done, and if you do manage to rid the world of the Sorbacovs, we'll finally be free."

"The club will send someone after you, Viktor," Casimir repeated.

Viktor shrugged, his face hard, eyes dead and flat. "Let them. Sea Haven isn't their territory. They can't just ride around openly with their colors and not get retaliation from the local clubs. We'll be together, and there isn't one of my brothers that isn't lethal. Most of us are too fucked up to try to live in society with society's rules, but we have a plan. We'll stick to it and we'll be all right, looking after one another."

"Do your *blood* brothers have any place in that plan of yours?" Casimir asked, trying not to be hurt. They'd all waited so long to be together. Casimir was risking his life to free them all, and it sounded as if Viktor didn't plan on hanging around.

"I'll be living right there on that sweet farm with you," Viktor said, his gaze suddenly sharp. Piercing. On Lissa.

Casimir glanced at his woman, saw her eyebrows shoot up again, and this time she dug her nails into his palm.

"How lovely." Her voice dripped sarcasm. "Gavriil's dog just had puppies. I'm certain there's room in the doghouse for you to stay."

Viktor's green eyes glittered with menace for a long moment and then he burst out laughing. "Your woman has a bad attitude, Casimir. You aware of all that sass *before* you married her?"

"Yes," Casimir admitted. "And that makes me either the smartest man in the world or the dumbest."

What in the hell is wrong with you? he demanded.

Her chin went up. He'd forgotten she could also be the most stubborn. *Someone ought to kick him very hard in the shins. And when I say hard, I mean hard enough so he carries a big fat bruise for a month. He needs to wake up.*

"I'll take the doghouse until I get things straightened out," Viktor said. "And trust me, little sister, when I decide to straighten things out, they get that way fast."

14

"WHAT was that?" Casimir asked as he opened the door to the villa overlooking the turquoise sea. He stepped back to allow her to precede him, his jaw set, eyes hard. Lissa lifted her gaze to his face. He could see the answering anger, the one smoldering in his belly, glittering in her eyes. That just brought that fire roaring to life. "Viktor is my brother. He came all this way to be with us. I can't believe you would talk with such open hostility to him."

"Your brother is a Neanderthal and he belongs in a cave somewhere."

She stalked past him into the wide-open room. He followed her. Close. The fire inside of him growing with every step he took. He hadn't seen Viktor since he was a little boy when the soldiers came and ripped his family apart. The tortures they'd all endured were indescribable. He'd never talk to her about his childhood, especially not when that door had been cracked open and he was close to losing control.

The villa was beautiful. One wall, on the far side, was all glass, the view spectacular. He forced himself to stare down into the sea, to try to calm the flames and shut the door on his memories.

"Your brother has the mentality of a biker. Clearly, to him women are nothing but second-class citizens."

He spun around to face her. "How the *hell* did you get that from our conversation?"

She stalked over to the long bank of windows, stopping beside him, looking beautiful in her dress, more beautiful than he'd ever seen her. The sun shone through the glass, turning her hair into a fiery mass of silk spilling down her back and around her head, like a crown of flames. Her skin appeared luminous, petal soft, inviting touch and that defiant, stubborn lift to her chin brought his body a sudden urgent ache.

"It's Blythe."

Her eyes met his, hers suddenly liquid, framed by long, thick lashes darkened into submission with mascara, but he knew beneath that color were fiery tips of red and gold to match the flame of her hair. Her voice had gone low, quivered even, and his body went still and the surge of intense lust immediately mixed with his need to protect her.

"Blythe?" he echoed, trying to understand.

"Yes, Blythe," she hissed. "*My* Blythe. My sister Blythe. She's the one he's talking about. He left her five years ago without a word. Not one single word. She doesn't know she's married to him. She would have told us. She's . . . *haunted*. She runs every day to escape demons. I've seen that look on her face and *he* put it there."

"Viktor somehow did something to your sister?" He struggled to understand. *"Malyshka."* He tried to soothe her. "Viktor has been in deep cover for five years. What could he have possibly done to your Blythe?"

She glared at him. *"Your* brother hurt my sister. He *devastated* her."

She paced across the floor in her wedding dress, needing the action. He could see the fire in her belly roaring to life, matching the burning in his. The room took on a golden glow. *She* glowed. His woman. Lissa. No, Giacinta. He had married Giacinta Abbracciabene, and she deserved to be her father's daughter. She shouldn't have to hide who she was any more than he should have to be anyone but Casimir Prakenskii.

His other brothers, with the exception of Viktor but— even Gavriil—had managed to leave their lives behind, to get out of the shadows. Giacinta and he deserved that as well. They'd paid their dues in that hellhole they'd been forced into. They'd nearly clawed their way out, and if they made it, neither of them was ever going back. His woman could finally be in the sun where she belonged.

"That whole thing about Evan Shackler-Gratsos, Viktor telling us who his target was, that wasn't about you and Gavriil and the others taking over if something happens to him. That was making certain I couldn't tell my sister about him. He's a *dick*."

She was beautiful in her anger. A fiery princess dressed in a jeweled silk and lace gown that he couldn't wait to take off of her.

"Woman, when you're pissed, you have a mouth on you." And he knew *exactly* where he wanted that mouth. His cock was harder than a rock and needed attention immediately.

He hooked her around her sweet little waist and pulled her into him, his front to her back. His fingers found the small jeweled buttons, sliding them from their loops. She tried to turn to face him, her anger radiating off of her. He didn't mind. He wanted to taste that fiery passion. Drink it down his throat. He tightened his hold on her, pinning her against him. Bending his head, he nuzzled her neck and then sank his teeth there.

Shocked, she stilled. He held her in place, his hands moving up from her waist to that alluring plunging vee of a neckline, the one revealing the full curve of her breasts. Every time she'd moved and more satin-soft skin had been revealed and then hidden, temptation had skittered through his body. A long trail of molten fire burned through every vein and artery, leading straight to his heart and then back to his cock. That force centered there, pooled until his balls became deep magma chambers and his erection was fiery hot and so hard with need that he knew he could explode any moment.

He slid his hands inside that jeweled bodice, claiming her lush mounds. Her hard little nipples poked into the palm of his hands. He cupped the sweet flesh for a moment, savoring the feel of her. He turned his head, his lips against her ear. "That wasn't a nice thing to do, *golubushka*, calling my brother names. Do you really think I'm going to let you get away with that?"

Her outraged breath hissed out of her, just like he knew it would. Her breasts rose and fell as she drew in air and exhaled. His fingers and thumb found her nipples and tugged and rolled, pinching and then brushing caressing strokes while his teeth went to her earlobe. She made a sound, a moan and involuntarily pushed her bottom against him.

"I'm going to fuck you until you can't walk, *malyshka*, and you're going to come for me over and over until *I* say enough. Do you understand?" He whispered the declaration in her ear. Thought about taking her, right over the couch by the window with the sun shining on the sea below and sending rays to turn her red hair into pure fire. "Say you understand." His hands kept moving, kneading and tugging, sending tiny pinpoints of pain to sharpen the pleasure sweeping through her.

"This is for me. Right now. Here. Then it will be all you, *golubushka*, I promise, but when you give your man a raging hard-on, then you take care of it."

He felt the shiver go through her body. Her nipples hardened even more and she squirmed, her hips pushing into him. Deep. Needy. Hungry. He used his tongue to ease the sting on her earlobe. "Right now," he whispered, his lips brushing against her sensitive ear, "in this beautiful gown, I want you to turn around and open my trousers, take out my cock and wrap your lips around it."

His heart pounded hard in his chest. The moment his anger had surfaced, the moment hers had risen to meet his, their passion colliding, he could barely think of anything else. Her, in that exquisite gown, looking like a princess, so beautiful she took his breath away, the hint of her breasts tempting him. Every movement of her body in that figure-hugging jeweled sheath fed the fire in him. The red of her full lips—*hell*, he *had* to see them wrapped around his cock. Feel her hot mouth surrounding him.

She turned to him, right there in front of the bank of windows, the turquoise sea surrounding them, tilting her face up to his. She was so beautiful his heart actually ached. Her tongue touched her lips and then she sank to her knees on the Persian rug right in front of him, her hands reaching for his zipper. Fingers brushed his cock so that he felt it jerk. Hard. So much anticipation. He took a breath. Let it out.

"Giacinta, first, push the material of that gown off your breasts. I want to see them while you suck me off." Deliberately he kept giving orders. Stark. Raw. Watching her face. Watching her hunger grow.

Her lashes fluttered. She swallowed. Her breasts heaved. Her hands left his trousers and settled on the bodice of her dress.

"Look at me, *malyshka*. I want to see your eyes while you take your breasts from where they're hiding from me. Ease them out."

She obeyed him, going slow, her small hands filled with her lush, soft, very white breasts. The sight of her breasts in her palms, her fingers curled around the mounds, sent more fire pounding through his cock. Her nipples were hard little pebbles and his mouth watered, wanted to feast. Still, there were other things he needed more.

"Now my zipper."

She let her breasts go and the material of her gown pushed

them closer, deepening the cleavage, her breasts jutting toward him, even more of an enticement. "You look so beautiful," he said, his voice going rough. "Gorgeous. That gown
open for me. Your breasts straining toward me. You're hungry, aren't you, *malyshka*?"

Her fingers fumbled with the zipper, but then she had the
trousers parted and she pushed open the slit in his silk underwear so that his heavy cock sprang free.

"Answer me, Giacinta. You're hungry for me, aren't you?"
He needed to know he wasn't alone in the fire raging through
his body. She looked flushed, her eyes dark with lust, her lips
glistening with moisture, making him want to groan and
thrust deep.

"So hungry, Casimir," she admitted. "I'm already damp
for you. My little lace panties are going to be wet."

He groaned aloud. "You're killing me." He needed his
balls free. They were aching and sore, pressed tight against
the material. He started to reach down but she was there
before him, taking care of her man, freeing him, her fingers
drifting over the heavy sac. Her touch sent streaks of fire
spearing straight up his groin to his pulsing cock and radiating outward like a burst of fireworks.

He stilled, watching her face. Her blue eyes. Her red lips.
That silken red head slowly, inch by inch bent toward him.
He felt her breath. Warm. Silky. Her hands cupped his
balls, fingers stroking caresses. He felt each touch searing
through skin to stir that seething mass of pure magma waiting to explode. Her lips parted. His breath caught in his
throat. Burned in his lungs.

Looking straight into his eyes, she caught at his hip with
one hand, the other still cupping his sac, and her tongue slid
up his shaft, from root to the underside of the crown. His
entire body shuddered. The muscles in his thighs tightened.
The fire in his belly burned hotter, sending more liquid
flames racing through his bloodstream. It wasn't just the exquisite feeling of her tongue and hands, it was the sight of

her, the dress, her hair, the look of hunger on her face as she parted her lips and drew the broad flat head of his cock into the heat of her mouth.

Once again his breath hissed out of him as her red lips stretched around his girth and she hollowed her cheeks and sucked. Hard. Tight. Hot. So hot. The sensation was beyond paradise. She sucked hard and then her tongue began a little foray over his shaft, teasing at the one spot that sent liquid drops spilling into her mouth. She caught them, swiping at them, hungry for more.

His enjoyment wasn't just about the way she looked, at his feet, her lips wrapped around his cock buried deep in her mouth, or the sensation now, it was the *way* she gave him this. Eager. Wanting to please him. That mattered to her. *He* mattered to her. His pleasure. She wanted that for him and she gave it to him. This was all for him. Every sweet stroke of her tongue, every hard suckle of her mouth—was for him.

He murmured encouragement to her. Love to her. Swore in his own language when the fire turned scorching and he knew he should end it before he exploded down her throat, but he couldn't force himself to pull away from her. His hips began moving of their own accord, little surges that pressed him deeper, that took him further into paradise. She didn't pull away or try to take back complete control. She gave him that. Her eyes lavished love on him. Burned with lust. Her breasts flushed even darker, her nipples so hard and beautiful he couldn't resist reaching down to feel that beauty—take what was his, what she gave him.

He tugged and rolled while her breath hitched around him, and then she moaned. The sound vibrated up his shaft and he dropped his hands to her hair. All that silky, wild, *fiery* hair. The knot was sexy, and messy enough that he could delve his fingers deep, curl them into two tight fists and hold her head still while he pushed his hips into that incredible inferno.

So close. He felt it in his balls as they drew tight. Boiling hot. Her fingers stroked. Caressed. Her mouth pulled and suckled hard. Milking. Drawing that hot, liquid magma right out of him. He felt the eruption start somewhere in his toes, move up his calves and rush through his thighs until his cock jerked and pulsed, pouring into her, down her throat, hot as hell.

She didn't pull away, didn't try to lift her head, but she took every drop of his release. Every drop that belonged only to her. He groaned with the pleasure burning through him. Watching her, unable to look away from the sight of those red lips stretched around him, her throat working, her eyes on his, giving him that gift.

She was so fucking beautiful, and what she gave him was even more so. She gentled her movements, ran her tongue up and over him, lapped at him with care, still watching him.

She'd drained him dry, but the sight of her kneeling there, her lips swollen, eyes on his, a pearl drop resting in the corner of her mouth to be caught by a swipe of her small tongue, stirred him to life.

"I'm so wet for you. I *loved* that. Watching your face, watching what that did to you. You're delicious, honey." Her purring voice was stark with honesty.

He caressed her face with the pads of his fingers, slid them into the silk of her hair and massaged her scalp gently. "I think you love my cock, not me."

Her tongue slid around her lips, both top and bottom and then she smiled at him slow. Sexy. "I have to admit, I'm a little addicted to your cock, so yeah, I love it, but I love you too, so don't be jealous."

"Take my shoes off, *malyshka*." His voice was husky.

She did as he asked, leaning down to untie his shoes and loosen the laces. He loosened his tie, took it off and shrugged out of his jacket. He steadied himself by putting a hand on her shoulder, allowing her to slip off his shoes and socks. He unbuttoned his shirt, his gaze still holding hers, and tossed it aside.

Immediately, without him having to direct her, she reached up to tug at the waistband of his trousers, removing them and his boxers at the same time. She leaned into him and pressed a kiss to the crown of his cock before taking his hand and coming to her feet. He bent his head and took her left breast in his mouth, suckling hard, using tongue and teeth to draw gasps. His other hand caressed and soothed her right breast while he worked her left one hard, creating warring sensations in her.

She cried out and cradled his head to her, stroking his hair, her body shuddering with pleasure. She was already ready for him, completely turned on just from sucking him off. He loved that. Loved that she admitted it to him without any embarrassment. She was fire, to match his, burning from the inside out. Going up in flames with him and getting off on it.

He took his time, bending her back so that her breasts thrust upward, an offering. Switching to the other breast with his mouth, he used his hand as a counterpoint to the searing heat and stinging bites. She moaned, her body nearly writhing against his. He savored the feel of her breasts, her hard nipples, the way she reacted, telling him everything he needed. Her breathy moans, the little gasping hitches. His woman liked it hot and rough. She went wild when he used the edge of his teeth. When he lapped with his tongue and then suckled hard.

He lifted his head when her hips began to push into him, seeking relief. "Turn around, *malyshka*." His hands were already guiding her. She was too dazed and needy to comply on her own. Her little cry of protest was not lost on him, so he pulled her against him briefly, reaching around her to give her one last tug and roll on her nipples, his mouth against her neck. "You like that, don't you?"

"Yes." She barely breathed the word.

"You like it rough." He licked over the sweet spot where her shoulder and neck connected.

"Yes." Her assent was a breathy whisper.

He bit down. Hard. Her back arched. She cried out. He suckled. His tongue lapped. "I'm going to leave my mark all over you. Every fucking inch of you, Giacinta. Inside your body. Outside. Every square inch of you is mine and I'm marking my territory." He sounded primitive because he *felt* primitive. "That's what you do to me. I turn into a caveman. You think my brother's one, but you've got your own and you love it. You love every fucking thing I do to you."

He slipped the buttons out of the loops, opening the back of her dress, his mouth against the nape of her neck. "Say, it, *golubushka*, I want the words. You'll give me anything I want, won't you?"

Very slowly, keeping her turned toward the window away from him, he slid the dress from her body, leaving her in her lacy panties, silk stockings and garters and the sexy silver heels. He ran his hand down her spine while she stepped out of the gown, all the way to the curve of her ass. He caressed the firm globes and then moved his hands up to cup her breasts, his body urging hers forward until she was at the couch, still facing the window.

"Kneel on the couch, Giacinta," he whispered against her nape. "Facing the back, knees spread wide."

She didn't hesitate, but placed first one knee and then the other up onto the cushions, her knees wide. She looked sexy in her ivory silk stockings, high heels and bare skin. He put a hand to her back and pressed her breasts against the cushioned back, so that the materials rubbed against her sensitive nipples. She gasped as his mouth slid down her spine, trailing kisses, occasionally nipping. His fingers trailed up the inside of her thigh. Barely there. Only a whisper of a touch.

Lissa bucked, pushed her face into the top of the couch, gasping for breath. He was making her come apart and he'd barely touched her. "Casimir." She said his name, her mind in chaos, unable to think clear enough to demand what she needed from him.

"Hush, baby, I'll take care of you. I'll always take care of you. Just feel." His fingers moved between her legs, again just a gentle touch, a wisp, and then he was gone. Her entire body shuddered. The action pushed her nipples against the back of the couch. That action in turn sent streaks of fire racing to her clit. She cried out at the sensation and pushed back, trying to find his fingers again.

He ran his knuckles over the curve of her buttocks and then his palm rubbed over her. Kneaded. Massaged. His teeth nipped. His tongue eased that sting. His fingers found her again, disappearing into the wet, sliding across her aching clit and then retreating. She cried out trying to follow.

"Do you feel how good that is, *malyshka*? So good, that burn. You willing to try anything with me? You don't like it you just say so, but I can make you burn hotter. Give that to you before I eat you like candy. Once I start, baby, not sure I'll be able to stop, so we've got to try this now. You want that burn?"

"Yes." She moaned the word, unable to articulate anything else.

"That's my girl. Give me anything I want. Love that, Giacinta. Love that you trust me with your body. With your heart." His hand smacked her ass. Not hard. Just enough to wake up every nerve ending. The burn lashed across her and then his finger pressed deep, so that her muscle grasped, her sex wept and she cried out, mindlessly rubbing her nipples against the material.

"More?" he asked, withdrawing his finger slowly and then pumping once, lingering against her clit before running his tongue across the red mark.

"Yes."

"Yes, what, baby? What do you need?"

"More. I need more." She panted the plea.

He loved every fucking second with her. Every one. Her body was responsive to his every touch. He gave her what she wanted, keeping it light, just enough to ensure the nerve endings flashed with fire, and then plunged his finger deep to feel her body's reaction, that slick, scorching liquid fire.

"Ride my fingers," he ordered.

She complied instantly, grinding down, her breath hitching again, her hips setting a rhythm that took her close, but he pulled out, denying her relief. She wailed her protest and bit down on the couch.

He caught her waist and tugged her back. "Want to play, *golubushka*, but I've got to eat you. You're dripping and all that fiery honey is mine. I want it. Lie down and spread for me. One leg over the back of the couch, the other foot on the floor."

Lust rose, sharp and brutal, taking him by surprise the moment she complied. She lay back, the top of her head against the armrest, her body laid out like a feast. Her garter extended to accommodate the stretch in the stockings along her legs. One high heel went up the back of the couch while the other rested on the floor.

He stood over her a moment, drinking in the sight of her, staring down at the junction between her legs. She kept herself trimmed so that there was a small patch of fiery curls beckoning him. Her lips were slick and wet with invitation. Her breasts swayed with every breath she took in.

"Giacinta, I have to tell you, there is no one more beautiful or sexier than you are. Bar none. I've never seen a more beautiful sight. I love that you give yourself to me."

Her hands cupped her breasts, her eyes on his. He watched her thumbs slide over her nipples, watched the reaction in her belly, the way her muscles rippled there and along her thighs. Her hands glided down her rib cage to her flat stomach, fingers teasing the top of her fiery red curls. "Hurry, honey, I'm on fire."

He knelt on the floor between her legs. "Slide your finger inside. Feel how hot and wet you are. Coat your fingers and feed me." His voice went hoarse. Rough. His cock was so fucking stiff he couldn't believe he'd come so hard just a bit before. His mouth already had her taste on his tongue. She'd said she was addicted, but he knew he truly was. He could never get enough of her, not in this lifetime, not even if he took her dozens of times a day.

She smiled. Slow. Sexy. Her eyes dark with lust. With hunger and need. He loved that look on her face. Watching him, she slid her fingers deep into her body, gasping as she did, her hips thrusting up, bucking, straining for release. He caught her wrist before she could give that to herself and pulled her hand to his mouth. Her lips formed a pout.

"*I* give that to you. Not you. You feed me." He pulled her fingers deep into his mouth and stroked his tongue around them, catching every last bit of honey coating her fingers. "I love how you taste."

Her eyes went even darker. Her lashes lowered to half-mast and her red lips parted. Sexy. Watching him as he drew her fingers deep, sucked hard and then pulled them free. He shoved both his hands under her ass, and lifted her to his mouth. With the first swipe of his tongue her entire body shuddered and a single sound escaped. Low. Moaning. Pure music.

He settled in, savoring her taste and the sounds she made when he drove her up fast, kept her there just to enjoy her pleas. He loved the way her nails dug into his shoulders and biceps. She turned into a little wildcat, grinding down, seeking release, and he finally gave it to her, pleased when she let out a keening cry as the orgasm swept over her hard and fast.

"More." He breathed the command against her thigh and started all over, using fingers and mouth to take her up again before the first one even had subsided. His woman. Perfect for him. She was spread out like a feast and he gave her his full attention, devouring her like a starving man.

Her head thrashed back and forth against the armrest, her hair spilling out from the messy knot. He liked that. All that fiery silk matching the scorching-hot liquid, the silken channel and that sensual flush on her breasts.

"Again," he demanded.

"I can't."

But she could. She did. Another long, wailing cry that sounded more like music than anything else. He gave her one last swipe of his tongue just to feel the shudder in her body again, rubbed his shadowed jaw along the insides of her thighs and then was over top of her, sliding in. Fast. Hard. Taking what was his. What she offered him. So beautiful. Perfection.

She was slick, but she was tight and he drove through that gripping channel, her wet, scorching-hot silk clamping down around him, dragging at him, the friction sending fire dancing through him. There was no going slow, not when she was so responsive, not when she chanted his name and begged for hard. For rough. For more. He gave her everything she asked for and more.

Her body shuddered around his twice more, clamping hard, squeezing like an exquisite vise of silk and velvet. So wet and hot. Nothing better. He buried his face in her neck and let the fire roar through him, erupting like a volcano. He kept his weight on her, feeling her soft breasts, her silky body melting under his, savoring the feel of her sex clamped down so hard around him, still rippling with aftershocks.

Lissa's arms were around him, holding on tight. She did that. She gave him that. Holding on to him, wrapping him up with legs and arms. Her high heels were locked around his back, the silk of her stockings rubbing sensuously over his ribs.

"This has been a perfect day," she whispered. "Thank you."

She'd just come hard for him four times and she was thanking him. Casimir was lost in her beauty for a moment, nuzzling her neck, kissing her jaw and then slowly easing his weight from her to kiss his way down the slope of one breast even as he glided gently in and out, prolonging the pleasure just a little longer for both of them.

"I love you, Giacinta Prakenskii. You gave me life. Purpose." He gave her the stark truth, because she deserved it. "Somewhere in all the roles I played, I lost myself. And then there you were on that airplane, so sweet and kind to that most annoying man seated next to you." He eased out of her, sliding to his knees beside the couch, looking at his woman. Savoring the sight of her. Committing it to memory. He never wanted to forget this moment. The picture of her sprawled out on the couch, so sexy, thoroughly taken, thoroughly loved.

"You were annoying. I did consider accidentally sticking a fork in you."

He laughed. Happy. Truly happy. He helped her to straighten her legs and put them on the floor so he could pull her into a standing position. "The bathroom is right over there." He indicated a door.

She stood in front of him, her hands framing his face while he looked up at her. "In case I didn't tell you, I'm madly in love with you." She brushed a kiss along his forehead. "I'm not certain where my clothes are. I can't get back into my wedding dress."

He laughed and stood up. He'd set a small bag just inside the door. "Grab one of my shirts. I brought a couple because if you said yes, I knew you'd need something to wear, not that I'd mind in the least if you wanted to walk around just as you are."

"I'm leaking everywhere."

"I like that. Me. In you. That works for me."

She laughed softly and walked to the bag in her silver heels and silk stockings. He watched her, unable to take his eyes from the woman who had changed his life just by seeing him. Recognizing he was real when he'd long ago given up on himself. She was so beautiful. All of her. Inside and out.

He marveled at that. She'd lost everything. Been betrayed by the two people she loved. She had to have had a difficult childhood, being trained as an assassin and set on a course of vengeance for her uncle. None of that had corrupted her. She was pure light to him, a fire that burned hot and bright, cleansing him.

He found the second bathroom and took a quick shower before pulling on a pair of jeans and nothing else. Dinner would be delivered soon. He'd chosen that carefully as well. To surprise her, he'd ordered a mini, traditional wedding cake. The cake he chose was that of *millifoglie,* layers of a kind of filo pastry, very, very thin, intermixed with light cream, chocolate and mascarpone, topped with fresh berries and a slight dusting of powdered sugar.

He'd left instructions for the champagne to be chilling. There should be strawberries and whipped cream in the refrigerator. He had plans for both items much later. Strawberries mixed with her honey and the cream sounded like a great combination to him. His mouth watered, just thinking about it as he hung up her wedding gown and his suit.

She emerged from the bathroom dressed in one of his tees, a dark navy that fit like a long dress on her. Barefoot, no makeup, her hair wild, cascading down her back in a fiery sheet of red. "They have everything, really good shampoo and a hair dryer. Toothpaste. Even toothbrushes in packages." She grinned at him. "No underwear though. I left my lace ones hanging on the shower curtain all nice and clean, but not dry enough to wear."

"You don't need panties," Casimir assured her. He had to kiss her because she was too tempting looking the way she did. She looked innocent yet, to him, she was a sexy temptress. "They have a pool. We can lie in the sun." He glanced at his watch. "We've got two hours before dinner will be delivered." He held out his hand.

She didn't hesitate, reaching for his hand, threading her fingers through his. He drew her to his side and wrapped his arm around her, holding her there. Pressing a kiss onto the top of her bright hair, he led her down the hallway, outside into the sun. The series of patios led to the long, endless pool.

The water looked as if it poured over the edge into the deep turquoise sea below. Loungers lined one side of the pool with a few unopened umbrellas scattered here and there just in case shade was desired. Outside was quiet and very tranquil with the sound of the water looping endlessly.

"Take the shirt off, *malyshka*, no one can see you but me. The villa is protected on all sides from prying eyes. The sun will feel good on your body."

"I'm a redhead, honey," she murmured, tipping her head up for another kiss. "I burn easily."

He obliged her, giving her what she wanted, taking her mouth and taking his sweet time about it. He loved kissing her. She was great at kissing. Perfection. She tasted of love and her addicting honey. When he lifted his head, he caught the shirt and pulled it over her head.

"Sunscreen." He showed her the bottle of lotion. He looked forward to covering every inch of her with it. His cock jerked again, just thinking about it.

She dragged her hair up onto her head, tying it into a messy, fancy knot, the action lifting her breasts. Unable to resist, he drew her breast into the heat of his mouth, suckling, teeth scraping just enough to have her come up on her toes, gasping, her hands gripping his hips hard.

When he let her go, he was more than satisfied to see he had left more marks on her, just as he'd promised he would. He indicated for her to lie down. She did immediately, stretching out on her belly like an offering to the sun. He crouched down beside the lounger and took his time, rubbing the sunscreen into her shoulders, back and arms, moving lower to massage it into her firm buttocks, paying special attention to every crease, crevice and dimple. He smiled when she began to squirm, unconsciously moving her hips restlessly. He was careful to get every inch of her legs.

"Turn over, Giacinta, let me get your front."

"If you do that, I'll be attacking you, Casimir," she informed him.

"Turn over, *malyshka*." His cock was already hard and erect and pulsing with need.

She did as he said, presenting her breasts and fiery curls to his hands. Again, he took his time, massaging the lotion into her skin, every little inch, paying extra attention to her breasts and nipples, then moving down to make certain her partially bare mound was properly coated before moving on to her legs. The moment he was done, she reached for the jeans riding low on his hips.

He took her slow, leisurely, there by the pool. They swam, made love again and then fell asleep. He woke her just before dinner arrived, grateful she got in a nap, because he had a very long night planned for both of them.

15

ALDO Porcelli had four bodyguards. Lissa had three days to study the layout of the building where Porcelli's mistress, Lydia Sartini, resided. Luigi had carefully marked the places the bodyguards always waited for him. One stayed by the car at all times. The car was out as a place of attack, not if they wanted Aldo's death to look like an accident.

One bodyguard always stayed at the top of the stairs leading to the second floor where his mistress's apartment was. One remained down the hall, a good distance from the apartment, near the window. His angle on the apartment wasn't the best. Lydia Sartini's apartment was set back, creating a small alcove effect, changing the angle of the hall so one couldn't see anything going on in the doorway. The apartments in the building were deliberately built for privacy. Porcelli wasn't the only man to keep his mistress there.

The fourth bodyguard acted as a roving sentry, prowling through the garage, up the stairs, through the hallway and down the flight of stairs at the far end of the second story. The lift was an open wrought-iron cage, rarely used by the residents' visitors. There were no security cameras for obvi-

ous reasons. The men wanted complete privacy and deni-
ability.

Luigi had stayed hidden away, supposedly in his wing of
the house, grieving for Arturo. In reality, he was home with
his wife and family, a great alibi when he knew Aldo, his
wife's brother, was going to die. There was no way anyone
could blame him, he was with Angeline and his boys. Casimir and Lissa actually drove by the house to confirm he was
there. Even with the knowledge that Luigi had betrayed her
father and lied to her for years, pretending to be alone, forsak-
ing a family of his own for her and their ultimate goal to bring
justice to those who had killed her parents, seeing him with
his wife and sons was a much bigger blow than she expected.

She glanced up from the blueprints spread across her lap,
to look at her husband. *Husband.* In her wildest dreams she
had never once imagined herself married, and certainly not
to a gorgeous, romantic man. Her wedding day and night had
been spectacular. Casimir had planned every minute, every
detail. They'd worshiped each other's bodies over and over
in so many ways—and her husband could get very creative.

"What is it, *golubushka*?" His voice was gentle.

He knew. He was like that with her. He knew when she
was melancholy, like now. She shouldn't be thinking of
Luigi; she needed to concentrate on the plan to take Aldo
without harming anyone else. Without getting caught. Without anyone suspecting his death was anything else but an
accident.

"Talk to me, Lissa."

It was back to Lissa and Tomasso. But now, she wasn't
even Lissa. She was Patrice with her glossy dark hair and
stick figure. He wasn't Tomasso, he was Steve Johnson from
Philadelphia, just in for a few days of sightseeing. Steve
looked much older, but distinguished with his graying hair
and cool shades.

"I was thinking about seeing Luigi with his family," she
admitted.

Although he was driving, he instantly reached for her hand, connecting them physically, pulling her palm to his thigh and holding it there. *"Malyshka."*

Her heart stuttered. She loved when he called her "baby," or more precisely, "little girl," in his own language. He had different inflections, depending on why he was using the endearment. This was sheer love. She heard it in his voice. Stark. Raw. Honest. Soft and so very sweet when she needed it most. He always seemed to know. He could read her that well.

"I watched him for a long time."

She didn't have to tell him that, he'd been there with her. They'd set up surveillance just across the street from his backyard. The house was a mansion. Angeline wanted status and Luigi gave it to her. Soldiers were in and out, moving through the grounds with dogs to ensure safety. Luigi wasn't taking any chance on any of the families in power hitting his family.

He was head of the Abbracciabene family, but his territory was small. Through his marriage to Angeline, he was allied with the Porcelli family. That territory was much bigger, and Aldo wielded a tremendous power in the underworld, so he was protected. That protection clearly wasn't enough for Luigi. He led a double life and had to be paranoid. Still, he spent a lot of time on the large patio, hiding from his wife.

"I know you did," Casimir replied softly, his hand squeezing hers. He rubbed the back of her hand and once more tightened his fingers, pressing her palm deep into the heat of his chest, right over his heart. "Talk to me," he repeated.

She moistened her lips, trying to think how to word what was preying on her mind. She didn't want Casimir to get upset. Like her, he was a fire element. He could burn hot with passion or be just as destructive as a roaring fire could be. He was intensely loyal. He hadn't known his blood brothers growing up, hadn't been around them as a man, yet he'd remained loyal to them, so much so that he was willing to die for them. He had planned to sacrifice himself for the sake of his brothers' happiness. He wouldn't understand someone like Luigi. He'd never tolerate such a betrayal as Luigi had committed, conspiring to kill his own brother and family in order to gain power. Raising a child as a weapon to continue his thirst for power.

"*Malyshka.*"

That "baby" was a clear warning. He expected her to tell him why she was upset.

She sighed. Pushed at the fall of black hair surrounding her face. "Luigi really is grieving for Arturo. I studied his face through the binoculars. He stared off into space forever. I guess I wanted to think he was wholly a monster, incapable of loving anyone."

Casimir glanced at her sharply. "He certainly doesn't love his wife. That was clear. It was a little shocking that she doesn't see it."

"I think she sees it, she just doesn't care. She has what she wants. She lives a certain way and has filled her life with friends and events. They appear to almost live apart. The three boys . . ." She trailed off. "Much more difficult to judge." She *detested* the wistful note in her voice. "I'm sorry, it's just that . . ." She left it. How could she possibly explain why she was so conflicted about Luigi?

"Don't you think I understand?" Casimir asked. "That man was your only family growing up. He wasn't just your uncle. He was your mother and father. He put a roof over your head, food in your mouth and clothes on your back. He taught you everything he knew about his business and he made certain you were good at it, good enough that you weren't going to get killed. It might have been harsh training, but in the end, you recognized that he was ensuring you stayed alive. That had to feel like caring."

"I remember when he first brought me home. He was stiff. He'd always been around when I was growing up, but he wasn't particularly affectionate. Over time, he became that way. Arturo started it, giving me hugs and wiping away tears when Luigi was upset with me, but then eventually, Luigi began to thaw. He laughed more. He took me more places himself. He ate dinner with me. I thought we were close. I thought he loved me." She finished the last in a small voice, staring unseeing down at the blueprints.

"Luigi is incapable of love."

She shook her head. "That's not true, Casimir. He loved Arturo. I could see it on his face. He still can hardly bear the loss."

Casimir inclined his head, his thumb sliding over her hand. Back and forth. She found the motion soothing.

"I'll give you that," he conceded. "But, *lyubov moya*, you know you can't save him. There's no way to do that."

"I know." She did know. It was just that, when she thought of him, she still thought of her uncle, not of the monster who ordered the hit on her family. She tried to remind herself that he had made certain anyone loyal to her father had been murdered. Even those working in the house—maids, the cook. The gardener and his entire family including children. Her uncle had done that. The thought made her sick. It made her feel worse that knowing all of those things, she still had a difficult time thinking he was that person.

"He'll have to kill you," Casimir reminded. "After this. He's going to ask to meet you somewhere, a place he can arrange an accident for you—one where you won't be identified as belonging to him. He can't have any blowback if he plans to take over the Porcelli family. The counsel won't like it, and they'll be scrutinizing his every move. That's why he wanted accidents, no more than a couple a year. That's why he stayed patient. He knew they would be looking at him and he had to appear absolutely clean."

She knew he was stating the truth, but she didn't have to like it. She wanted to believe that Luigi at least loved her the way he did Arturo—that all those years together meant something to him. It was true that he had to be planning her death, there was no other way he could be certain she wouldn't find out about Luigi's betrayal of her family and come after him. He'd lived on the edge of that sword for so long it would be a relief for him to get rid of her. He'd sent her to the United States once she had turned eighteen to make certain she didn't have a chance to stumble on the truth about his wife and children.

"I love you, Giacinta," he said softly, bringing her hand to his mouth. His teeth teased her fingertips, scraping back and forth gently. "I know this is difficult, but I can do it for you. There's no need . . ."

"It's my mess," she interrupted. "He killed my family. He's planning on killing me. I have to be the one . . ."

"No, you don't. *I'm* your family. Your husband. When he killed your family, *malyshka*, he killed mine. My father-in-law. My mother-in-law. They belonged to me as well. My parents were torn from me, just as yours were. Viktor and Gavriil hunted those responsible down one by one, over the years, just as you have done. You planned on taking care of the last of them—the Sorbacovs. For my brothers."

"And my sisters."

"So Luigi is my duty just as much as yours."

She nodded her assent. "Okay."

He took his eyes off the road long enough to glance at her. "Okay? You aren't going to argue some more?"

She narrowed her eyes at him. "I don't argue."

He smiled at her and returned her hand to his thigh. "You argued with me over Viktor. Still, I find all that fire sexy, so we're good."

"Why didn't Viktor and his seventeen assassins go after Sorbacov?"

"He was planning to do just that. *After* he brought down Shackler-Gratsos. All of us knew he would do it. We didn't know about the others, but we knew Viktor would make a try. He's always been about protecting us. He takes that job very seriously."

"Too bad he doesn't do the same with his wife. If she is his wife," Lissa said, trying hard to keep the biting sarcasm from her voice.

Viktor looked and acted like a biker, a one percenter, more, an outlaw biker. That didn't surprise her. He had come from a brutal background, learning a thousand ways to kill a man, torture him or just plain fuck him up. He would do so without mercy and with no remorse. If any of the Prakenskii brothers was truly a straight-up killer, Viktor was one. Gavriil maybe, but Viktor for certain.

He also had the mentality of a man who believed he could get away with telling his woman what to do and she'd do it without question. She knew Blythe Daniels. Had known her for five years. Blythe wasn't a jump-on-command woman. Lissa couldn't imagine elegant, beautiful Blythe with Viktor.

"That school, Giacinta, they took those little boys and flogged the skin off their backs for any infraction. They were forced to hurt one another. You can't imagine what it was like. Each of the schools was progressively worse. We all knew that if we were sent to the one Viktor was in, odds were, we weren't coming out of there alive. Those who lived through it were given the dirtiest, most dangerous jobs Sorbacov had."

"There are eighteen of them. They're all trained assassins. Are you telling me they couldn't get to Sorbacov?"

"All eighteen had someone they protected. Viktor had us. Each of the others no doubt had siblings as well. I'm not surprised Viktor managed to bring them together. If he trusts them, believe me, *malyshka*, those men are loyal to him and one another."

"They must be a terrifying bunch riding motorcycles down a highway. I'd think seasoned criminals would be afraid of your brother, let alone seventeen more just like him."

He glanced at her again. Worried. "He would never hurt you or your sisters. You're married to me. Your sisters are married to his brothers. That makes you all family. That means something to us. It also means something to the men he travels with. Viktor wouldn't be with them unless they have the same values he has."

Lissa sighed. Shook her head. "You don't see it, Casimir, because he's your brother, but he's absolutely terrifying. I can't imagine him with Blythe. I just can't. He's not going to be sweet to her like Gavriil is to Lexi. Gavriil's dangerous and scary to the rest of the world, but to her—and us—he's different. I can pretty much guarantee your Viktor has had a lifetime of telling everyone around him what to do and they jump to do it."

Casimir shook his head. "The men surrounding him, the ones taking his back, if they came out of that school, they're anything but 'yes' men. They'll be every bit as lethal as Viktor."

"I hope he doesn't expect them all to live on the farm. We'll have to add ten more properties, ones with hundreds of acres," she said, giving him a little sniff. And her chin.

"You give me that chin, *malyshka*, and I get this instant need to lean over and bite it. Don't tempt me when I'm driving."

Her gaze jumped to his face. She couldn't help the little surge of heat rushing through her veins the moment he talked to her in that low, sexy voice. *God.* He was beautiful. Now that she saw him, she would always see Casimir under Tomasso or Steve, or any of the other roles he assumed. "My Casimir," she murmured.

His face softened. His eyes were warm when he took them off the road long enough to glance at her. That meant something to him. She could see it on his face. He was like Gavriil, showing one thing to the rest of the world and giving her his best. She hoped his brother was the same, but she was a good judge of character, and sometimes, when one lived too long in a violent world, having to be part of it, fitting in and taking on those roles, there was no way to get out. Viktor had lived in that violent world from the time he was a boy. Still . . .

"I'll give him a chance," she promised.

"Thank you, Giacinta."

Again, his voice made her shiver. That meant something to him too, something big. "He's yours, Casimir," she replied. "That means he's mine as well." She meant that. She had no idea what any of them were going to do with Viktor and his seventeen motorcycle-riding badass assassins, but family was family and they would deal. Whether or not Viktor could have Blythe was another matter altogether.

"I don't like this plan," Casimir said, indicating the blueprints in her lap.

"I know, honey, you've mentioned that about, oh, I don't know, a *thousand* times." Lissa tried not to feel exasperated, but truthfully she was. Casimir was being overprotective. If he weren't with her, she wouldn't be getting an argument. "I've done this before." She tried to pull her hand out from under his.

He heard the irritation in her voice. How could he not? She tried to hide it, but he was so tuned to her, the slightest inflection would tip him off.

His fingers tightened over hers, preventing her from taking her hand back. He pressed her palm even tighter against his thigh. "You don't have physical contact with your target, not as a rule. You'll only have one shot at this. He's got two bodyguards in close proximity, and if you miss, you won't get a second chance."

"We've gone over this a hundred times, Casimir," she said. "There's no point in going over it again. I've already rigged the doorbell. Lydia always has a drink before Aldo gets there. *Always*. She's had that little glass of wine for years. I've researched her thoroughly myself. She's an innocent in this. She genuinely loves him. I'll have no trouble putting the sedative in her wine. She'll be asleep only a few minutes. It will give me enough time to do the job."

He swore in Russian. "Too many things can go wrong."

"I know that. Timing is everything, but it is with any job. This is our only shot at getting to Aldo. It's tight but doable. The fountain in Lydia's alcove has been prepared. You did that yourself. I dealt with the doorbell."

"You weigh a hundred pounds, Giacinta," he snapped. "Aldo is five foot ten and weighs in at two hundred pounds."

"I don't miss." She didn't blame him for being worried. How could she? It was a life-or-death situation. She'd be worried if the situations were reversed.

"You're everything to me, *golubushka*, everything. If something goes wrong, I can't get to you. Not in time. I can take out the bodyguards, but not him. I won't be able to get to him before he can kill you."

The raw pain in his voice was nearly her undoing. Usually she took out her targets from a distance, an accident, not a sniper rifle. No one had ever questioned the accidents she'd arranged. Never. Not once. She was careful. She didn't care if her target knew an Abbracciabene had exacted retribution for the crimes committed. That had never mattered to her until she'd spoken to Cosmos Agosto, and that had been only because she was there—close. She only really cared that justice was served in the end.

They could kill Aldo with a sniper rifle. Casimir was a crack shot. That would leave a trail. A faint one, but a trail nevertheless. She didn't want the Porcelli family coming after her or anyone she loved. That type of circle was endless. Her way, no one would ever suspect Aldo's death was anything but an accident. A tragic, senseless one, but still an accident.

She wanted to take away the worry etched so deep in Casimir's face, but she couldn't risk her sisters, or for that matter, his brothers. She leaned toward him. "Baby," she said softly. "I can do this. I swear to you, I can do this."

He was silent, slowing the vehicle as he turned into the parking garage. "I know you can, but I don't like you having to do it," he finally said.

She let her breath out on a note of relief. He wasn't going to keep at her. They'd covered every inch of the parking garage. Aldo didn't have his men park in the same spot when he came, but he always parked on the second floor, not wanting to deal with a flight of stairs.

Lissa took off her seat belt and leaned across the seat to kiss Casimir. The moment she did, his arms went around her, yanking her so hard she fell into him. One hand anchored at the nape of her neck and the other remained an iron bar across her back. His mouth moved on hers.

No one kissed like Casimir. She loved his kisses. Deep and hard. Gentle and sweet. A mixture of both. It didn't matter. Every single time his mouth was on hers, her heart stuttered, butterflies took wing in her stomach, little darts of fire went from her nipples straight to her clit and she went instantly damp, so ready for him she often wanted to yank down his trousers so she could sit on his lap and ride him. Just like now. Right there. In the car.

"I've got to go," she murmured against his mouth. So hot. So perfect. She loved that his lips could be soft and firm at the same time. She especially loved the way he generated heat.

"I know. Be safe, Giacinta. You make a mistake and I'm going to be angry with you. You won't like me angry."

She kissed the corner of his mouth and left a trail of kisses along his strong jaw. "I can do this," she reiterated. "Don't worry." She sat back in her seat and slid on the cap that would cover the very expensive black wig that held human hair, but would never identify the owner.

She wore a tight one-piece catsuit and soft, crepe-soled ballet slippers on her feet. As a precaution, they'd disabled the dome light in the rented car so when she opened the door and slipped out, no light came on. The parking garage was dimly lit, and she slid into the shadows immediately, making her way to the entry point—the small grate covering the ventilation shaft. Deftly, she dealt with the screws—Casimir had already loosened them on their last trip. Only two screws held the screen in place, and she had them out in less than a second. She slipped inside, pulling the grate closed after her. Casimir slid the screws in and continued on his way, up the stairs, to get into position just in case he needed to cover her escape.

The shaft was very small. There was no way Casimir could crawl through it, his shoulders were far too wide. As it was, she had to scoot on her belly, propelling herself forward by using her toes and hands, slithering like a snake. She inched her way, taking her time, careful not to make any noise. She knew the route, she'd done it physically twice, but a hundred other times in her head, following the blueprint.

It took time to make it to the second floor and then to Lydia's apartment. Lydia had her own ritual before Aldo came over. She'd told Aldo and once, when Aldo had been drinking, he'd told Luigi. He thought it was sweet that she always spent half an hour soaking in strawberry-scented water because he loved the fragrance on her and in her hair. She sipped her glass of wine and relaxed in the hot, steamy water, her gel mask covering her eyes and music playing. Aldo had even recorded a list of love songs and given them to her. She told him she played them over and over, and he believed her.

Lissa believed her as well. Lydia showed every sign of being in love with Aldo. She had pictures of the two of them framed and hung in every room. She dressed carefully for him, always made herself available, and she never threatened him, not once, according to Luigi. Luigi, having married Angeline, had managed to insert himself into Aldo's life and confidence.

Aldo had told Luigi time and again that Lydia was content to be his mistress as long as she got to see him and stay in his life. There was no evidence that Lydia had ever cheated on him. Aldo once had arranged for a friend to ask her out. A very handsome, wealthy friend. She had refused and later, told Aldo of the incident.

Lissa scooted down the shaft until she came to the grate covering the opening in the ceiling just over the toilet. At least the setup of the master bath was conducive to her entry. The door to the toilet area was kept closed, at least it had been the two times Lissa had made her dry run. It was now and Lissa could hear the occasional splash of water as Lydia moved in the bathtub.

Opening the grate carefully, she lowered herself to the toilet seat and then stepped off to the floor. Her crepe-soled slippers didn't make a sound as she crossed to the door and inched it open. Lydia lay in the deep tub, head back, mask covering her eyes, earbuds in her ears, one arm stretched out, fingers closed around the stem of a nearly full wineglass. One finger kept time to the music. Lydia sighed contentedly, lifted the glass to her lips without removing the mask and replaced it, unerringly. Clearly she'd done this ritual many, many times and didn't need sight to place her glass.

Lissa didn't hesitate, but moved across the floor to the edge of the tub as Lydia lifted the wineglass to her mouth and took a small sip. The moment she replaced it, Lissa dumped the small vial of liquid into the wine and was already back across the room and behind the door again before Lydia took another sip.

It was a little more difficult to get back up into the shaft than to get down out of it. Still, she made it on the first try. *Phase one complete,* she reported to Casimir as she replaced the grate. *I'm making my way to the bedroom to make certain she lies down. It should only be another ten minutes or so.*

So far, no sign of the target. I'm in place.

He shouldn't be here for another twenty minutes. I'll need that time to get to the alcove just outside her apartment. That was the number one thing they had no control over that

could mess up their plan. Aldo couldn't arrive early. Any
number of other factors could make the job difficult, but if
he came early, she wouldn't have a chance to get to him.
What mattered to her more than killing Aldo Porcelli was
making certain Lydia wasn't a witness to anything that might
get her harmed.

Lissa took several deep breaths and waited while the minutes ticked by. Sounds came from the bathroom, water drain-
ing from the tub, Lydia standing, walking across the floor,
the bedroom door opening. Lissa saw her then, wrapped in a
large, fluffy towel the color of peaches, her hair still up on
her head, mostly finished wine in her hand as she made her
way, yawning, to the bed. She drank the last gulp of wine, set
the glass on the stand and lay down.

"Just for a minute," she murmured softly to herself.

Lissa scooted back. There was no turning around, so she
had to carefully, without making a sound, ease herself back
down the shaft to the next branch that led to the alcove. *She's
lying down to rest. Should be out in another minute or so.
I'm on the move.*

All right, malyshka, *still no sign of him.*

She appreciated that Casimir's voice was confident and
matter-of-fact now that their plan—*her* plan—was under
way. He didn't like it, but once her mind was made up, he'd
stopped fighting her and instantly went into work mode. Taking her back. In all the years she'd worked with her uncle,
even when she was only fifteen and sixteen, Luigi had never
once taken her back. For that matter, neither had Arturo.
Luigi had pretended to be ill, disappearing into his wing of
the house. Arturo had needed to be seen in a public place.
She'd taken buses. That had been when Patrice was born.

They had removed the grate the day before and it was still
off. In the deepest shadow, it was impossible to notice unless
one was looking for it. The shaft was located above and came
in on the same side where the doorbell was. She glanced at
her watch.

The alcove was lit by the fountain. It was made of marble and stood right in the center, a freestanding rather beautiful fountain. Water burst from the spouts and rained down in a series of colors. It splashed down the layers, little mini waterfalls that eventually ended up in a circular narrow ring around the fountain itself. The colors of the fountain lit the alcove, and the water sounded peaceful and soothing. Aldo had bought the fountain for Lydia because she loved water so much.

Lissa liked it because the sound of the water would hopefully cover any sounds made when she revealed herself.

Target's vehicle just pulled in. Target is out and heading up the stairs, one bodyguard moving ahead of him fast, and another behind him.

Her heart jumped and then settled into a natural rhythm. She kept breathing, slow and even. The bodyguard came first, checking out the alcove, waving his boss forward while he proceeded down the hall. The second bodyguard had stopped just at the top of the stairs, guarding the door to the stairway. With a guard on either side of the hall, no one would get past them to cause their boss harm.

Aldo came next, a bouquet of flowers in one hand. He stepped into the recess of the alcove and instantly was out of sight of his bodyguards. Lissa took a deep breath. Held it. Timing was everything. Aldo jabbed his finger on the button to ring the bell. Instantly it shorted, shocking him, creating a blackened circle on the surface. He jumped back and as he did, Lissa exploded out of the shaft, slamming her head into his chest, driving him backward toward the fountain. Her hands caught his head and, using her weight and momentum, slammed his skull into the already broken and jagged fountain.

Flowers fell to the floor. Aldo's body slid down the marble slowly, a dead weight. She went with it, reaching to feel his pulse. The spike of rebar exposed by the earlier break had gone into the back of his neck and his head had hit hard on the marble, shattering his skull. He was dead before he slid to the floor.

Lissa was up instantly, turning and leaping for the shaft, dragging herself inside and refitting the grate. It took precious seconds to slide the screws in using a special tool she'd made just for such jobs, a tool that could reach through small holes and do the work quickly.

Target down. I'm on my way out.

The drop of the body had made noise. She knew that it would. The bodyguards might have heard it over the fountain, so she wanted to move quickly and get to the parking garage on the first floor and get out of there before his body was discovered. She especially wanted Casimir out of there. Even looking like Steve from Philadelphia, he would come under suspicion. The bodyguards would be suspicious of *anyone*, but especially a man.

Aldo Porcelli was the head of a very large crime organization. No one would rule out foul play until they absolutely had to. It was a bizarre accident, and that was what made it so believable. She scooted faster, still taking care not to make a sound. She was past the second-story garage and on the main floor when she heard the scream. A high-pitched wail of pure grief. She knew that sound. She'd made it as a child when Porcelli's men had killed her family. She closed her eyes briefly, but kept moving fast.

Roving bodyguard and the one by the car have been called upstairs, Casimir reported.

Again he sounded matter-of-fact, not in the least anxious. He didn't ask where she was, or how long she was going to be, but, like her, he was on the move, she could tell by his voice. She had only a short distance to go and she kept up her slow, steady pace, making certain not to make even the smallest noise. The wailing continued and it was loud enough to draw out other residents.

Lissa made it to the grate and found Casimir had already

removed it. She slid out, turned and lifted the cover, turning the small screws with her little tool almost in one motion. Casimir had the car right next to her, running, door open when she looked up. She dove in and removed her cap, allowing the black hair to fall around her face. She had drawn up a long, lacy black flowing skirt, scattered with bright flowers and removed her crepe shoes before they hit the street. The little ballet slippers went into her small purse and she put on boots. They were knee-high, black and had false laces up the front and a ruffle down the back. The zippers were on the side.

"Seat belt," Casimir clipped.

She glared at him. "The stop is right up the street."

"Seat belt," he snapped again.

She looked up at his face. Grim. Holding it together by a thread. That didn't bode well for their job in St. Petersburg. She had to be the one exposing herself to danger there as well. She hadn't sought the Sorbacovs out—although she'd made certain she was written up in their papers repeatedly. They'd taken the bait and contacted her. She'd taken their bait and replied. She sighed, snapped the belt in place and allowed herself a deep breath.

"You check his pulse?"

She nodded. "He's dead. He hit perfectly. The shards from the broken fountain probably killed him. I didn't take chances. He hit the back of his skull hard as well. I didn't want to leave bruises on his chest for a doctor to question, but I had to hit him pretty hard." She shrugged. "Hopefully I'll be long gone before any questions are raised."

"No one is going to question it," he assured, and pulled the car to the side of the street to allow her to get out. "I've got to return this rental to the agency, go into the airport and change into another role. I won't be back at the house for a while, Giacinta, so you watch yourself."

"Luigi needed an alibi. He knows where I am today and he had no idea when the deed will be done," she said, pouring confidence into her voice. "He's with Aldo's sister. You can bet he wants *her* to be his alibi."

He nodded. "Even so, *malyshka*, you watch your back."

He leaned across the seat and cupped her face in his hands, thumbs sliding along her skin, causing shivers. "I don't like you out of my sight."

He took her mouth, gentle. Tender. Almost reverent. The kind of kiss that always shook her. Always melted her. Her heart stuttered hard in her chest. Her arms went around his neck and she kissed him back, falling into him. Mesmerized by him. Loving him with everything she had.

Casimir pulled away just enough to rest his forehead against hers. "Promise me you'll be careful, *golubushka*, and don't call him until I'm back with you. He could already have contracted with one of his men at home."

She nodded because she still couldn't find her voice. She brushed her mouth over his, caught up her purse and exited the car. Slinging her camera around her neck, she hurried to the bus stop. She only had a minute or two before the bus showed up. It was all about timing.

Lissa stood with two other women, both locals, laughing and taking pictures when police cars and an ambulance screamed by, heading in the direction of the apartments. She paused for a moment, just like the women, staring after the emergency vehicles, and then the three of them began an animated conversation that continued even after the bus arrived and all three got on.

16

LISSA paced back and forth in the library. She had spent a lot of time in the library growing up. It had been her place to go when she was upset. Luigi rarely, if ever, came into the room and no one else did either, so over the years, it had become her sanctuary. She liked the connection of the old books with the new. She liked the peace. It was always quiet, allowing the chaos in her mind to calm.

Waiting for Casimir's safe return was nerve-wracking. She was certain he was safe, he had only to take the vehicle back and return as Tomasso, but until he was back with her, she couldn't quite get the feeling of impending disaster out of her stomach. She glanced at the clock. He shouldn't be much longer. She resisted the urge to text him. Phones were a hazard. Still . . .

She sighed and went to the large window that looked out toward the gardens. The estate wasn't huge, but it was beautifully kept. Luigi seemed fond of his flowers and trees. He had a large gardening crew. They were gone for the day, but she was certain old Alberto, the head gardener, would be making one last sweep of his domain before he left for the night. He always did a walk-through before he left.

The sun set with a fiery glow, the large ball seeming to drop from the sky into the sea, spreading orange and red across the surface of the water, turning the deep blue into a strange blanket of colors. She liked this time of day, between day and night, when the sun was setting and the moon was rising. Sky and sea seemed to come together, forming a beautiful, colorful illusion of fire pouring into the waves.

"Miss Piner?"

She turned toward the door. One of her uncle's newer recruits had his head only inside the room. He looked a little shy and very uncomfortable. Luigi had hired him right after she left the last time and he didn't know her at all.

"Yes? It's Raimondo, isn't it?" She smiled encouragingly. He was a little younger than the others and still had a bit of a baby face.

"I'm sorry to disturb you, but we have a situation and I can't get Signor Abbracciabene to respond and I'm not certain what to do. Old man Alberto is in the back gardens and he's very upset. I'm afraid he's going to have a heart attack. He's making me crazy. I can't understand a word he's saying. Arturo told us that if Signor Abbracciabene wasn't here then we're supposed to come to you."

"Do you know what set him off?" Alberto was known for his hysterics. He crooned to his flowers, swore at his workers, and occasionally had complete meltdowns that required pulling him back from the edge. Luigi had told many stories of taking knives and other sharp objects away from Alberto when he was having one of his fits. He had been with Luigi for as long as she remembered, always working in the gardens and only caring about his precious plants.

"I have no idea, but he's got long shears and he's threatening to stab himself through the heart with them. I don't want to get near him. He came at me once and I nearly took out a gun and shot him."

Lissa laughed. That was Alberto. Some things never changed. "Don't worry, Raimondo, I'll handle it. Where is he?"

"All the way in the back, Miss Piner. In the plot where those really tall bushes with the pink flowers are. The ones that grow over the arches."

She knew where it was. Alberto didn't allow his young gardeners to ever work that particular piece of the property. He did it himself. The plants growing there were very rare and difficult to grow, but under Alberto's care, they grew thick and wild and very tall. There was a small jungle of pure beauty, and the head gardener was extremely proud of it. She couldn't imagine if one of the others had touched his precious plants just what he'd do.

"That's not good," she murmured aloud. "I'll go."

"You don't need me, do you?" He sounded more nervous than ever.

She burst out laughing again. Seriously, he was one of Luigi's soldiers and he was afraid of an older gardener. "I can handle it," she assured him.

He waved and his head disappeared again. Lissa followed him out of the library, making certain the man had ascended the stairs. She couldn't imagine if her uncle was going to send an assassin after her that it would be Raimondo. He was too green, but she wasn't going to take chances. She heard the door to his quarters close and she found her vest and jacket, shrugging into them, fitting weapons into the specially concealed pockets.

Being cautious had kept her alive throughout her childhood, her teenage years and now into adulthood. She hadn't informed Luigi of Aldo's death, so she doubted if he'd put a hit out on her that soon. Still, Angeline was Aldo's sister. It stood to reason if his wife was informed of his death, she would call his sister. They were good friends. Luigi might know. Again, he always liked to hear details, and it would be awfully fast for him to set someone after her, but there was no sense in not taking precautions.

She wrote a note to Casimir, explaining where she was and that Alberto often had these little meltdowns. She'd join him the minute she managed to get the gardener calm again. Having dealt with Alberto on more than one occasion, Lissa took her time walking through the labyrinth of plants, exotic grasses, bushes and trees, hoping he'd calm down a little on his own.

The grounds were beautiful, thanks mostly to the head gardener. He was a master when it came to getting things to grow. She wound her way through the many plants and flowers until she heard the old man muttering to himself in Italian, threatening to cut the heart out of someone named Tito. She rounded a particularly spectacular flowering bush that was taller than she was and found the head gardener with his head in his hands.

"Alberto? What is it?" She spoke softly. Gently. His plants were like his beloved children, and she could see the hack job someone, presumably the absent Tito, had done to a rather exotic-looking plant. Three others lay on the ground, drooping, roots exposed. There was a gaping hole in the ground where the plants had been. The dirt was wet and a hose still spouted water, so that the ground was nothing but mud.

Her breath caught in her throat, one hand went up to cover the sound of distress at the sight. Someone had made a terrible mess of things. Alberto gestured wildly, flinging his arms around and pointing to the bare roots, mud and hole. He lifted one of the plants on the ground and threw it, his Italian so fast it sounded like automatic gunfire. He told her Tito had tried to transplant some flowers overgrown in another area to this sacred patch of the garden and in doing so had destroyed a rare plant that Alberto had been coaxing along for *years*.

Lissa had to admit, the mess was terrible. She couldn't

imagine that Tito would be keeping his job after making such a horrible mistake. Not only did Alberto look like he was angry, he looked close to tears. She had no idea what she could say to make this better. She stepped closer to the dying plants in an effort to buy some time to figure out the best way of handling the matter. Crouching down to inspect the ones strewn around, roots showing, she caught sight of the hole. Standing, she'd only seen a small corner of it. The rest was covered by the tall bushes around it. The hole was very deep and wide, like a grave . . .

Lissa tried to turn and stand at the same time, one hand still covering her throat. She felt the thin wire as it cut into the back of her hand and the side of her neck. He yanked her backward, toward him, so that she lost balance and fell against his chest.

"I'm sorry, girl," he whispered. "Have no choice." Alberto spoke in Italian to her, his head close to hers as he tightened the wire, twisting fast.

In that moment, when she was certain she was going to die, she still found time to note he sounded sad, remorseful even, but determined. She dug her heels into the ground and shoved backward, slamming her back against his chest, putting inches between them, allowing her to straighten.

"Damn it, quit fighting. He didn't want you to suffer," his voice hissed in her ear. "He said to tell you, 'sorry.'"

She slammed her foot down on his instep, her hand slipping into the inside pocket of her vest. Her fingers closed around the prize even as blood trickled in a semicircle around her throat. She drew the knife and slammed it, first into his thigh and then yanking it out, and back into his ribs. She didn't get a good angle on the ribs, but it went in.

He screamed, and for a moment his hands loosened their grip on the garrote. Before she could fling herself forward, he had control again, his hands tightening viciously, ignoring the knife in his ribs. Just as suddenly he was gone. She dropped to her knees, reaching to loosen the wire with one hand. Blood poured from the long slice on the back of her other hand and ran freely down her neck where the wire had sliced her skin.

She scrambled away from Alberto and turned to see Casimir, looking like Tomasso, his face a mask of pure fury. She could feel the heat coming off him in waves. His skin glowed, exposing the fire element burning inside his belly.

She tried to speak, to tell him she was okay, but no sound emerged. She flung the garrote onto the ground beside what would have been her grave and watched with a horrified fascination as Casimir nearly pulverized the head gardener with his glove-covered fists.

She made two attempts to get to her feet again, but failed both times. *Casimir. Stop. You're going to kill him.*

That's the fucking idea, he spat back, but after one last, very vicious punch to the face, he yanked the assassin to his feet. "Tell me who hired you? Who put the hit out on Lissa?"

His face contorted with pain, Alberto choked once and then shook his head. His gaze avoided Lissa's.

"You're going to die. How that happens is what we're discussing right now and it's entirely up to you, although I'm so fucking pissed at you I'd rather you choose the hard way. You want to go quick and painless, you tell me what I want to know. You don't talk to me, it's going to take you a long, long time and you're going to know what the word *agony* means." There was no mercy in Casimir's voice.

Casimir. Honey. I know you're upset but . . . Lissa trailed off. He didn't turn his head or look at her. His jaw was set, his face an expressionless mask. His eyes were flat. Cold. Dead. She was looking at the monster, the one shaped in that school from so long ago.

"Take a walk, Lissa," he ordered, snapping the command at her.

She tried again, her heart beating fast, her voice no more than a hoarse whisper. "Honey." She killed, yes, but she didn't torture, she didn't prolong a death. She tried her best to make it quick and painless, no matter what she felt about the target. Casimir didn't have the same scruples, that was very evident.

"Walk away *now*," he snapped.

Clamping a hand to her neck, she took a deep breath and moved away from the two men, but refused to leave. Casimir had saved her life. She knew that. She also knew there was no stopping what he was doing. He would extract the information he wanted in the way he chose, whether she approved or not. He was his own man, and he took her protection very seriously. She sank down to the ground, pulling her legs to her, keeping pressure on the wound at her neck. Alberto hadn't managed to open her artery but it was close.

Alberto screamed in pain. There was a sickening crack. She closed her eyes, listening to the gardener's breath come in horrible ragged gasps. "Luigi. He didn't want to do it. He told me he had no choice. He wanted it done quick. Without pain if possible. If she hadn't fought me . . ."

"And then what were you supposed to do?"

"Send him proof. Show her dead. Put her in the ground, cover her and replant."

"One picture? Two? Text saying it's done?" Casimir demanded.

Alberto hesitated and there was another mind-numbing scream. Casimir hadn't given him a chance to think about it. Lissa's stomach lurched. First Cosmos had sat at the table with her family and then he'd betrayed them. Arturo had held her when she was a little girl and wiped away tears. He'd betrayed her. Luigi, her own uncle, her father's brother, had set the entire mess into play by the ultimate betrayal, and now Alberto, another man she'd known since she was a child, had been willing to kill her as well.

She didn't want to sit there and watch this. She didn't want to hear any more. She wanted to cry her eyes out, somewhere safe.

"He wanted three pictures. One showing she was dead.

One in the grave. One with the grave covered and the plants back in place," Alberto confessed.

Look away, Giacinta, Casimir said. *I mean it, malyshka, look away now.*

She obeyed him immediately. She knew the moment she did, Alberto was dead. Casimir broke his neck. He lowered the gardener to the ground, dug his cell phone out of the man's back pocket and gestured for her to lie down next to the hole in the ground. He arranged the garrote around her neck, took a picture and then lowered her into the grave. It was muddy. Disgusting. Still, she lay down as if flung there. Casimir took another photograph and then helped her out of the grave.

Lissa staggered back to where she'd been sitting and watched as her husband rolled Alberto's body into the deep hole. He found the shovel and pushed mounds of dirt over the body. It took a while to completely cover the evidence and replant, so it looked as if the gardener had recently transplanted more flowers to the area. It was dark by the time Casimir took the last photograph and sent them off to Luigi.

"You can't stay here, *golubushka,*" he said. "It isn't safe. He has to believe you're dead. I doubt if he'll come back tonight, but we can't take that chance."

"I can't check into a hotel looking like this," she pointed out. She couldn't look at him. She didn't know what she was feeling, but she was close to tears and she didn't dare start crying. If she did, she would never be able to stop.

"Is there a shower in the gardener's shed?"

It wasn't exactly a shed, but a place for the crew working to use the bathroom and take breaks. Lissa had played in it as a child, but it had been years since she'd been there. She'd forgotten all about it. She nodded. "Yes, but I don't have any clean clothes."

"I'll get the things you'll need, Giacinta."

His voice was so gentle her heart turned over and a lump formed in her throat, threatening to choke her. She didn't answer him because she couldn't. She just nodded and turned away from him, stumbling toward the building back in the trees. No one would be there this time of day and she could cry all she wanted in the shower where no one could see or hear her.

The door was secured, but she had no trouble picking the ridiculously easy lock. The building was old and needed care, but the water was hot. She stripped out of her muddy clothes, turned the water on as hot as she could stand it and stepped into the stall. It wasn't in the least bit fancy, not like the showers in the main house, but the water felt good until it hit the lacerations on her hand and neck. That stung. And that started the tears. She put one hand on the tiled wall, stood under the cascading water and wept.

She had no idea how long she stood there, but then Casimir was there, naked, in the shower with her, turning her unresisting body into his arms and holding her tight against him. One hand went to the back of her head, palm against her wet hair, holding her face to his chest, while his other arm locked around her back. She stood stiffly for a moment, and then there was no resisting his comfort. His strength.

"I'm here, *lyubov moya*. I'm not going anywhere."

He knew. He knew *exactly* how she felt. The terrible feeling of betrayal, as if everything and everyone she knew, almost from the time of her birth, had conspired against her. This man holding her knew betrayal. He knew treachery at its worst. He knew what it felt like to live a role, to get so mixed up you forgot yourself, who and what you were. He knew all of that intimately.

She let her arms drift up his chest, that solid, hard chest, warm now, comforting, heart beating beneath her ear, strong and steady. She couldn't imagine him any other way but strong and steady. Of course he would be there. At her back. At her front, wherever she needed him.

Lissa let herself melt into his heat, holding him, weeping a storm of tears for both of them, for lost childhoods, for murdered parents and for his long-lost brothers, especially the oldest, who might be—and probably was—a total psycho thanks to a man in St. Petersburg who had murdered the parents of children, dragged them to schools and shaped them into killing machines, only to decide, after years of service, to have them all killed.

Casimir rocked her back and forth, his hands smoothing caresses down her back, fingers massaging her nape and scalp, whispering kisses and love at her temples and down the side of her face to the corner of her mouth. All the while, the water rained down on them, cocooning them in steam and love.

She *felt* his love surrounding her. Holding her up. Casimir Prakenskii. "All right. All right. I'm all right. I just have to let him go, don't I?"

"*Golubushka*. My beautiful wife. I love you with all my heart. With everything I am. This man you love, he is an illusion. Luigi Abbracciabene is an illusion. You loved your uncle. There is nothing wrong with that . . ."

She thumped her fist against his chest. "There is. He's a monster. He killed my parents. Wiped out so many people who were good to us. The gardener's *entire* family. He had children. They didn't even spare the children. He raised me to be a killer. He's involved in human trafficking. You can't tell me those women want to be doing what he forces them to do. I lived with him all those years, was loyal to him. *Loved* him. And he wanted me dead as well."

She couldn't keep the sorrow from her voice. Or the pain. She didn't want to feel pain. She wanted anger.

Casimir wrapped her up tight in his arms, just holding her, not arguing. Giving. That was all. Just giving. After a while the hot water ran out, and then her tears. She could only cry so long before there was nothing left.

He dried her body gently, wrapped her hair in a towel and pointed her toward her clothes. He'd packed a small suitcase for her. "The house is mostly empty. Two soldiers left behind.

I told them I was going to take the night off, but if Luigi called and needed me, he could reach me by cell."

Lissa's head was pounding, a clear reason why it was just plain dumb to spend half an hour sobbing. Wild weeping got you nothing but headaches. She sighed. "I'm not certain what to do." She sank into a chair watching the play of muscles rippling in his back as he pulled on a tight tee.

"We're going to drive twenty minutes to a little resort right on the sea and we're spending the night there. Clearly Luigi's aware Aldo is dead. The authorities or his widow called Angeline. Luigi will be very caught up with his wife's grief over the next few days. He'll probably even make the funeral arrangements, stepping into the breach for the two grieving women."

"Three," Lissa corrected. "Lydia is grieving as well. I hope Luigi isn't planning on taking her into his prostitution ring."

Casimir completed dressing and caught her hand. "He won't have the time. He's lost Arturo, and his other body-guards are not that intelligent or trusted. They spent way too much time beefing up. Taking steroids. I don't know if that's true of all of them, but they're definitely lacking in the brain department. I suspect that was a prerequisite to work for Luigi in this home. Word couldn't get back to Angeline. But now, without Arturo he's stuck with a crew that's fairly use-less to him."

He opened the car door for her—he'd brought Tomasso's vehicle around to the front of the building so she could leave the gardener's shed, take five steps and slide into the pas-senger side of the car. "Stay low as I pull out," Casimir cau-tioned. "I don't think anyone's paying attention, but if so, I don't want them remembering seeing you."

Lissa kept her head and body down as Casimir drove out of the estate and onto the road. She settled into the seat be-side him.

"*Golubushka*, put on your seat belt."

His voice was gentle. Low. Loving. So tender she felt a fresh flood of tears burning behind her eyes. "He thinks I'm dead."

"And he's going to continue to think it. He'll call Tomasso. He'll want to cultivate another man into Arturo's position. My resume's very impressive."

"He was going to kill you as well," Lissa pointed out. "You know he was. You were new. No family. No one you had sworn loyalty to. You were the perfect man to get the jobs done for him that he didn't want anyone knowing about, and then he could make you disappear, just like he does everyone in his way."

"Circumstances changed when Arturo died," Casimir pointed out. "He needs me now. He'll call me. We've got to work out the details and get set immediately."

She let her breath out and leaned toward him. She needed him. She'd never considered that she needed anyone. That was all she had to do, that little involuntary lean, as if he drew her like a magnet. He reached out instantly and took her hand, bringing the tips of her fingers to his mouth briefly before pressing her hand to his thigh in the way he often did.

Need, in a relationship, wasn't good. Need meant weakness to her, but she had to acknowledge, right then, she needed this man in her life. She wanted him there. She chose him and would choose him every day for the rest of her life. "I didn't want you," she blurted out. "When all my sisters were falling in love with Prakenskiis, I ran from the idea. I didn't want a man I knew would be dominant—at least I thought that was the reason."

"You didn't want to love someone that much because you were afraid," he said gently. "You'd already lost so much."

She nodded. "But I'm really glad you're in my life."

"We'll get through this, Giacinta."

"Are you always going to call me Giacinta? Because if you are, I'm going to have to confess who I am to everyone at home."

"That's who you are, *malyshka*. When we go home to our family, we're going home as us. As Casimir Prakenskii and Giacinta Abbracciabene-Prakenskii, so the people we love know who we are. So they see you and they see me."

She liked that. She had always detested that she couldn't tell the five women who had formed a family with her who her parents were. What her real name was. What her life was before she met them. She pressed her hand deeper into the hard muscle of his thigh. Just being with him comforted her. He didn't have to talk a lot. What he did say mattered.

He took his eyes off the road long enough to glance at her. "I was shaped in a hard school, Giacinta. I'm a man. I can't be anything else."

"I don't want you to be." She didn't either. She loved him just the way he was. Even overprotective—or what she thought might be overprotective. She found she loved that he cared enough to worry about her safety. She hadn't had that, not even from Luigi or Arturo. When she went on a job, no matter how dangerous, they didn't take her back—but Casimir had.

"We're going to butt heads occasionally," he said softly. "That's all right. We're both fire elements. We'll both flash hot and burn up in flames. The makeup sex will be phenomenal."

"I'm not sure it's safe to get any more phenomenal than it already has been," she admitted. "You get any better, Casimir, and I might not survive." For the first time, there was a small smile in her voice. In her mind. In her heart. Because of him. Because of man a named Casimir Prakenskii.

He brought her hand to his mouth again, teeth teasing the pads of her fingers. "I have all kinds of better to show you. You'll survive. I'll always make sure of that."

Her heart skipped a beat. She knew what he meant, and he wasn't talking about sex. He was going to make certain nothing happened to her. She took a deep breath and let go of the hard knot of betrayal that had formed in her stomach.

"I'll always make certain the same of you, Casimir. Nothing's going to take you away from me."

They drove the rest of the way to the small resort in silence. He got the key to their cabin while she stayed in the car where no one could see her. The resort had several private little cabins, each with a view of the sea. It was small and exclusive, a tiny little jewel run by a single family consisting of parents, a grown son and teenage daughter. They rented boats and bicycles to their cliental, but few other services were offered.

The cabins were clean and snug, with small porches that held two chairs and a two-person hot tub. The cabins were situated so each had a view of the sea, but complete privacy from one another. There were no phones and no television. It was a place for two people to enjoy each other rather than what was playing on TV.

The moment Casimir had the door closed and locked he turned to her, his face a mask, his eyes dark with hunger. "Strip. Right now. Clothes off."

Instantly her body reacted, melting. Going hot. Going damp. Nipples peaking. She hadn't thought it would be possible to go from a storm of weeping to one of need. Of hunger and lust. He could do that to her with his voice. With that look in his eyes. He stood just inside the door, making no move to undress, his eyes on her, his jaw hard.

Excitement pounded through her. Casimir was making a point. That chapter in her life was gone. Over. *He* was her life. She was in his world now. He was in hers. Both hands went to the hem of her tee and she pulled it over her head. She stood in front of him in her lacy bra and jeans, looking around for somewhere to put the shirt.

He jerked his head toward a chair as he removed his hair and the thin, realistic mask that covered his face. "Your bra next."

She loved the quiet in his voice. The command. It unleashed something wild in her. Stoked the embers that always seemed to be burning inside her into actual flames. She reached behind her and obediently unhooked the bra, never taking her eyes off of him. While she tossed it to the chair, he expertly removed his contacts and put them in a case. He tossed that aside and leaned lazily against the door.

"Jeans, *malyshka*. Get rid of them and your panties." Very casually he shrugged out of his jacket and then removed his own shirt. He didn't move fast or slow. Just did it with ease, with his muscles rippling, suggestive of hidden power beneath his skin.

He was making the fire burn so hot she thought she might just have a mini-orgasm from the way his eyes had gone liquid silver. Her hands dropped to the zipper in her jeans and she managed to shimmy them off her hips and down her legs. She stepped out of her sandals and tossed the jeans to the chair. Not once did she take her eyes from him. He hadn't taken his eyes from her. He had barely blinked.

Her heart went a little crazy, pounding like mad in anticipation. Her breath had already gone ragged and he hadn't touched her yet. She was damp between her legs. Her breasts ached. She wanted him with every breath she drew into her lungs. *He hadn't even touched her yet.* Her mind was filled with him. Only him. There was no room for anything or anyone else.

He moved then. Straightening off the wall. That was all, but her sex clenched and she felt more liquid fire rushing through her in welcome. He held out his hand to her and she immediately crossed the distance to take his. Wordlessly he tugged her to the thick rug in front of the window overlooking the sea.

"On all fours, facing the window," he ordered. His voice was soft. Mesmerizing.

She didn't hesitate. Giving him what he wanted. Going down to her hands and knees. He didn't make a sound. She knelt there, heart pounding. Waiting. When nothing happened, she started to turn her head to see what he was doing.

"Don't."

It was a clear order. She sucked in her breath and kept her eyes on the glass. On the sea. Waiting. Wondering. The pressure inside her coiling tighter and tighter. The burn growing hotter. Her entire focus was on him. Only him. Every sense she possessed straining for movement. For sound. For anything.

Her nerves were at a screaming point, every one on fire, so sensitive that just the air had her close to a climax. She wasn't certain she could keep staring out the window when she wanted to know where he was. What he was doing.

"Put your head on the rug, Giacinta."

His voice came from her left. Her body jerked at the soft command, but she obeyed instantly, grateful for the opportunity to move. To do something when her body threatened to go up in flames. She pressed her forehead to the soft thick wool.

"Turn your head to your left, cheek to the floor."

She did and she saw him. Sitting in a chair, his silver eyes on her. His legs sprawled out in front of him. His cock was hard and thick, enclosed in his fist. His hand moved lazily, pumping while he watched her. While his gaze burned his brand into her.

"Push that sweet ass of yours higher," he instructed.

The sight of his fist sliding up and down the length of his hard shaft was one of the hottest things she'd ever seen. She was certain the sight would be burned in her mind for all time. More liquid spilled.

"Widen your knees for me, *malyshka*. When I finally get over the sight of you kneeling there, waiting for me, I want to see how wet you are for me. How excited. How much honey you're going to give me before I fuck you so hard you won't be able to get up off the floor."

A low moan slipped out. She couldn't help it. She obeyed him again, widening her knees, but keeping her bottom up in the air. His thumb moved over the flared head of his cock, smearing drops of liquid all over it. She licked her lips, but she didn't say anything. Didn't beg for him in her mouth. His face was etched with lines of pure lust. His hooded eyes had grown more liquid, purely sensual. His fist mesmerized her with that slow, languid slide.

He kept her there for what seemed forever. All the while, her body grew tighter. Felt emptier. Needed more. Waited. She was aware of everything about him. The muscles in his chest and arms. In his thighs. His breath moving in and out of his body. The stillness in the room. The tick of a clock somewhere. Eventually even all that was gone and there were only his eyes and his cock and fist. She couldn't get anything else in her mind. There was no room because he'd driven out everything else and filled her mind with him.

When she was certain she was going to have to plead with him, when she was close to sobbing his name, he stood up with that same casual laziness and walked around her, out of her sight. She desperately wanted to turn her head to see what he was doing, but she didn't dare. She knew, absolutely knew, that he would start all over again.

His fingers brushed the inside of her thigh and her entire sex clenched greedily. Her thighs jumped, fingers of desire dancing up them. She was drenched with liquid heat, with lust. Panting. *Desperate* for him. His fingers moved away and she wanted to sob. She knew he could keep up this torment for hours. She also knew what he was doing—keeping her mind fully occupied with him so nothing else could get in.

Something velvet soft slid up her thigh. Oh God. Her body wanted to melt into a small puddle of need. His tongue. Touching the insides of her thighs. Barely there, but leaving a long trail of fire burning up her leg straight to the scorching-hot channel that clutched emptily. So in need. She felt the rasp of his jaw, a sharp contrast to the whisper of his fingers and the velvet fire of his tongue.

His fingers dug into her hips and dragged her back almost

savagely against his mouth. His tongue stabbed deep at the same time. That was all it took to have her tumbling over the edge, chanting his name, her body going wild. Over and over the waves came, swamping her, a strong quake there was no stopping or controlling. It went on and on. At the very height, the strongest of the contractions, he slammed into her, his body slightly above hers, giving him the best possible angle to go deep. He drove through tight folds, forcing his invasion, while her body clamped down on him like a vise.

He gasped. She screamed. Then he was pounding into her while flames seemed to consume her. There was no getting away from that rhythmic piston. She was helpless to do anything but take it as he gave it to her. There was no way to think, only feel. Only let the scorching fire take her, burn her clean, make her wholly his. She had no idea how many times her body convulsed around his before he finally emptied himself into her.

She would have collapsed, but his arms held her up, held her safe. It was Casimir who somehow found the strength to carry her into the bedroom, sheltering her against his body, holding her so tenderly she could barely believe he was the same man who had taken her body so savagely only a few minutes earlier.

He placed her in bed and came down nearly over top of her, his body to the side, but leaning over her as if he could protect her from everything. As if he would always keep his body between hers and any harm. Her body still rocked with after-shocks, and the more his mouth whispered gently over her face, took her mouth in tender kisses, the more of herself she simply surrendered to him. Giving him everything she was.

Her body sated, completely exhausted, her mind filled only with him, she drifted off, surrounded by his warmth, hearing the soft declaration of love whispered in her ear as she succumbed to sleep.

17

LUIGI smoldered with anger. He hadn't been able to grieve. All around him were wailing women, each determined to be more dramatic than the other. Louder. More annoying. Clinging to him until he wanted to pound them into the ground. When he wanted to knock them away from him. His stupid cow of a wife. Aldo's beautiful but idiotic widow who knew all along he had a mistress, but clung to him anyway because she didn't have a backbone. His own sons, weeping like children, following in their mother's footsteps, although he'd tried to teach them to be men.

He needed to be alone. Away from them all. He had surrounded himself with incompetent bodyguards and idiotic soldiers. Men who cared more to beef up their bodies than their brains. It was necessary at the time. Now, he needed intelligence. More than intelligence, he needed cunning. An ally. Someone to take Arturo's place. Giacinta could have been that person. She wasn't male, but she was smart. So damned smart and loyal.

He called the one soldier he decided would make the best bodyguard, since he couldn't have his niece. He called Tomasso and issued orders. He wanted Tomasso to come to his home and pick him up. He wanted to see for himself the man's reaction to the fact that he had two homes, a wife. Sons. If Tomasso wasn't the man he thought him, he'd kill the bodyguard and replace him.

Luigi prided himself on being a good judge of character. He had bested his all-powerful big brother. The chosen one. The one who had gotten the most beautiful woman Luigi had ever laid eyes on. Never once had Elizabeta looked at him. She had eyes only for Marcello. Luigi had been the one to tell Marcello about the beautiful woman he'd seen. Marcello had known Luigi wanted her, but he still went after her. He'd married her, and then his father left Marcello the family business. As always, Luigi had to protect Marcello simply because there was a birth order, not because Marcello was smarter. Hell no. He wasn't and he never had been.

The best thing his brother and his bitch of a wife had done was to have Giacinta. Even then, Luigi had been smart, making a fuss over the baby, coming around often to take her places and make both Marcello and Elizabeta think he adored their child. It was easy enough to talk them into getting dogs and a dog handler. Of course Luigi would handpick the man. Now that he'd been diagnosed with multiple sclerosis, a brilliant, masterful move on his part, he was put in a position of consultant and could slowly ease his way to buying a much needed restful retreat at the edge of the sea, a good distance away.

"Luigi!" Angeline's whiny voice set his teeth on edge. "Are you even listening to me? For God's sake, I just lost my brother. I can't understand why you're not paying attention to the boys or me. They've lost a beloved uncle."

The vision of his hands around her throat rose up. He'd been having that a lot lately. He couldn't get rid of her, not this soon. The only way to keep from strangling her with his bare hands was to put distance between them. He was even dreaming of killing her, not a good thing when he was sleeping in her bed. Still, she provided him with the best of alibis. He'd lavished attention on her from the moment he went to their house until he couldn't take another moment with her. Even with him putting himself out, the greedy bitch wasn't satisfied. She wanted every second of his time. *Every* second.

"Luigi!" Angeline shrieked his name.

Luigi winced at the tone. That was the tone he knew would one day set him off. Just. Not. Now. He couldn't afford a mistake, not when he was so close to his goal. From the moment he met Angeline Porcelli and conceived his plan, she'd been clingy. She would spend hours whining about how her daddy loved Aldo so much but she was just a woman and he would dismiss her as if she wasn't worth anything. Luigi poured his attention into her, but she would cry for hours and tell him how Aldo didn't have time for her anymore, now that he was married, working so hard and had a mistress. When Luigi was home, it was his sons who took his time, once more leaving her alone. Hell, if he strangled her, he'd be doing her a service, putting her out of her misery.

"I heard you, Angeline," he said quietly, keeping his head down, texting fast as he did. "I did everything you asked. The boys know they shouldn't have been making such a fuss with so many people around. They're just upset about Aldo's death, just like you, but I had a word with them. I spent time with them and reassured them nothing would happen to you or them."

"It will!" Angeline wailed and threw herself into his arms. Clinging.

Luigi held her, holding his cell behind her back and finishing his order to Tomasso to come and get him. He needed to get the hell out of there fast or he wasn't going to be responsible for what he did.

"Everyone is already looking to you, Luigi, to take Aldo's place in the family business. He was so busy. You're twice as busy. If you take his place, not only will you be gone all the time, but you'll be in danger. You know you will. And you'll put all of us in danger. I went out with you all those years ago because your family was small and no one was going to be jealous of your territory and come after you."

He winced. That was Angeline's way of belittling him. She was a passive-aggressive fighter, slinging little arrows at him when she wasn't getting her way. But she knew better than to use his family's name for her poison. He dropped his arms abruptly and stepped back, eyeing her with anger and a cold mask.

"You seem to forget that my brother, sister-in-law and niece were all killed, *slaughtered*, by someone. It was *your* family who stood to gain the most, and if I wasn't already dating you, I would never have believed your father when he assured me he wasn't involved in any way. Don't you ever say something like that again. Now get the *fuck* out of my sight." He ground out the last order from between his teeth.

Angeline stepped back, shaking her head, tears welling in her eyes. "I'm sorry. I didn't mean anything. I'm just so scared for you. For all of us."

"Go, Angeline. I have business to attend to. *My* family business. One of my men will be picking me up soon. In the meantime, I want you out of my sight so I can forget the things you just said to me." He kept his voice ice-cold.

Angeline had heard that tone before and she whirled and ran, sobbing. Luigi gave a sigh of relief and went to his study and firmly closed the door. She had clung to him constantly, not leaving him alone for a moment, so he'd taken to hiding in the bathrooms and outside on the grounds where she couldn't find him. Hiding in his own damned house. He despised her. She was weak. Useless. Angeline still believed he loved her because she *wanted* to believe it.

She hated sex and she'd made it clear to him that she was sacrificing to have sex with him because it was her duty, and because she loved him. Once he'd known that she didn't like it—not because she didn't feel anything when she was with him, but because she thought herself saintly and to her sex was dirty—he took a perverse pleasure in showing her dirty. Making her like it. She spent a great deal of time on her knees praying for her soul after nights with him.

Luigi rubbed at his pounding temples. Ironically, the one person who had been loyal to him, other than Arturo, he'd had killed. That bothered him. He hadn't considered that it would be so difficult, but he had almost convinced himself not to go through with it. He had known all along that Giacinta had to die. He wasn't a caring man, and he had no idea when emotion had begun to take hold of him. When he began to look forward to their talks. Their chess games. Her laughter. Just having her back in his house after long months in the States.

Giacinta was intelligent and she was loyal to one person— Luigi. He sighed and poured himself a drink, staring sightlessly out the window. Giacinta. She was gone. The one person who brought a little joy into his relentlessly dark world. His own sons couldn't match her intelligence or her drive. She was a secret weapon he could have used against his enemies. He'd never have another like her. He hadn't wanted her dead. It was necessary.

"Necessary," he murmured aloud, and tossed back the rest of his Scotch.

The car arrived in record time, a good mark for Tomasso. He greeted Luigi soberly, aware of the loss of his brother-in-law. The world knew of Aldo's loss and the scandal of his wife and mistress fighting while the body lay still warm.

"Are you all right, sir?" Tomasso asked, opening the car door for him to the back passenger seat. There was genuine concern in his voice.

Luigi nodded curtly. For some reason the question caused his chest to ache. A great stone pressed down on him. *Giacinta.* There was no bringing her back. He'd have to live with his decision. Luigi settled into the backseat, prepared for the long drive back to his estate, his sanctuary by the sea. He was grateful Angeline knew nothing of it because he needed peace. Quiet. He needed to come to terms with what he'd done.

"Are you all right, Signor Luigi?" Tomasso asked again softly, glancing at him in the rearview mirror.

Luigi lifted his hand up dismissively. "Just drive. Raise the glass between us."

He didn't feel like talking. He liked that the man hadn't asked a single question about his home, or why he had never mentioned being married. Tomasso would be a good soldier. He was strong. Intelligent. He knew when to keep his mouth shut. Luigi knew ruthless when he saw it. He knew dangerous. Tomasso was all of those things. He was also hungry for a home. Luigi would give that to him. But not now. Now he needed to grieve for his lost niece in peace.

He had contacted Alberto the moment Aldo's widow had called Angeline hysterically. She needed them desperately and Luigi had rushed Angeline to her side. Luigi was able to see Aldo's body and the blood at the mistress's apartment. He got to witness the widow making all kinds of accusations to the mistress, casting suspicion there, but he knew Aldo's death would be ruled an accident. There was a catfight, with Aldo's widow trying to claw scars into Lydia's face. The police had seemed more concerned with that than protecting the crime scene.

The coroner pointed out that little black spot on Aldo's finger where he'd pressed the doorbell. Around the doorbell the surface was blackened—all from an obvious short. The police told the widow what happened, that Aldo had jumped back from the electrical shock and hit his head on the fountain—the fountain Aldo had given to Lydia. It was priceless. Perfection. While chaos, screaming and weeping took place all around him, he'd stood there in silence, admiring Giacinta's work. She'd exceeded the master. Using that fountain to kill Aldo was a stroke of genius.

She was invaluable, and he'd been forced to kill her while his useless wife was still alive, an albatross hung around his neck. It hurt. It was so unexpected that he wanted to weep. He *had* wept. Angeline had seen him and thought he wept for her brother. He had wept for Giacinta. He hadn't even done that for Arturo and he'd known how much he cared for his friend and bodyguard. Giacinta. He had called Alberto and told him to do it immediately because he knew he would rescind the order if it wasn't already done. He would have stopped it.

In the week that had passed since Aldo's and then Giacinta's death, he had attended Aldo's funeral. The long procession honoring him had been a joke. What hypocrisy, the man had gone to church every Sunday and had killed men the next day without so much as flinching—but he still got a church funeral with the congregation weeping over him and the priest blessing his casket and saying prayers over his body. That night, Luigi had returned and spit on Aldo's grave, only by that time, he wished it were Angeline's grave. Because he had to play his part of loving husband and heir apparent to the Porcelli throne, he hadn't been able to pay tribute to his niece. To stand by her grave and whisper he was sorry and that he'd always keep her close.

Giacinta. He shook his head and wished for another drink. This wasn't a limousine. He'd had the interior of the car changed to suit him. He liked having a glass panel to separate him from the driver. He'd also had the car fitted with bulletproof glass. The doors had been reinforced as well. He knew when he took over the Porcelli family there would be many who wouldn't like him bringing both territories together, so he'd prepared, but he should have added in a bar. He needed a drink . . . badly.

He looked through the glass partition to the back of Tomasso's head. He was in his car, driving to the place he thought of as home. Not the house he shared with Angeline and their sons, but the home he'd made for Giacinta. How was it that he'd brought three boys into the world, male children, and none of them had his traits, but Giacinta, a product of his brother and his wife, was everything she should be?

He pressed his fingertips to his temples. He had to quit thinking about her. She *had* to die. He had no choice. She was too intelligent. He'd sent her to the United States when she was eighteen because he knew she was too smart to stay at home by the sea while he disappeared for weeks at a time—necessary to maintain his life with Angeline and the boys. Once she knew he had a wife, and who his wife was, she would start putting the pieces of the puzzle together and figure it out. She would know what he'd done.

Luigi nearly groaned aloud. That would almost be worse than killing her. He never wanted her to know the truth. He'd made the right decision, but damn, it hurt. Now he had to rebuild, find good soldiers, men who could be loyal and smart, men he could count on. He looked at Tomasso again. He needed more like him. Men who wouldn't hesitate to pull a trigger. Men who were hungry to have a family.

He'd told Alberto to make it fast. To make certain she didn't suffer. To bury her on the property where Luigi would care for her. Alberto had disappeared like he would after he took care of business, but when he returned, Luigi was going to ask a lot of questions, make certain he had carried out his orders to the letter. He didn't want to think Giacinta had suffered.

The car jerked hard, pulling to the right. He gripped the door handle and glared through the glass at Tomasso. Tomasso overcorrected, fighting the car. Obviously something was wrong. Something seemed to have gone wrong with the steering. The car jerked again toward the right. Luigi's heart accelerated as Tomasso fought that pull. Fought to keep them on the narrow, winding road above the cliff.

The jerk came again, this one much more pronounced, and Luigi's seat belt tightened almost to the point of pain, cutting into his flesh. Then there was the sound of squealing brakes, the car fishtailed and then slid. More sliding . . . The sensation was terrible. Slow motion. Off the road. Into the air. Soaring.

Luigi saw the sea rushing at them and had time enough to grip the door. His mind had gone momentarily numb. He couldn't think what to do, but he knew they were going to impact with the wide extensive turquoise blue surface.

The car hit the water hard, jarring him. It began to slowly sink beneath the surface. He gasped, his mind finally kicking into gear, realizing he was going to drown if he didn't get out of the car. The accident had happened so fast. One moment he was thinking of her—his beautiful niece—and the next he was fighting for his life.

He couldn't get the seat belt to loosen. He fought it, but there was no give. The woven strip was so tight he couldn't get to his knife, just inside his jacket. He looked through the pane of glass to Tomasso. The man was alive, and already on the move. He'd rolled down his window and was making his way out. Luigi could see his legs as they slipped through the car to the water outside.

Relief swept through him. Tomasso would get him out. He tried the seat belt again, but it refused to loosen. The car was filling with water as it sank. Already, the roof was underwater, the car sinking to the bottom as the sea tried to claim them. He *had* to get out. Soon the interior would be completely filled. Where was Tomasso?

He looked out his window when he caught a glimpse of movement. He froze. Shocked. Tomasso was there. Treading water. Holding on to the side of the car with his gloved hands. *Gloved hands.* Even as he watched the man, Tomasso reached up and tore off his hair and face. He stuffed both inside a bag he held.

Luigi's heart nearly stopped. He could hardly believe the evidence of his own eyes. Tomasso had been in his home a month. Over a month. Nearly two. And this? An assassin. There were rumors of course. There always were in his line of business. Even among hit men there were some considered the elite. Luigi knew he was looking at one of those men. Tomasso—or whoever he was—made no move to rise to the surface or swim away. He just stayed there, suspended outside of the car, watching dispassionately as it filled. Making certain of the kill.

Luigi cursed him, pounded on the glass, but he knew no matter what he said or did, there would be no mercy from this man. No amount of pleading. No bribery. There was no way to stop one of the elite. Luigi spat at him. Furious. Terrified. He'd never considered this could happen to him so fast. He tried for his knife again. Then his gun. The gun was tucked into his waistband at his back. There was no hope of getting to it.

There was movement in the water behind the assassin and for one moment, hope burst through Luigi. A woman swam up next to Tomasso, dressed in a bathing suit and tank. She carried a second tank with her. Tomasso took it and shrugged into the webbing, shoving the regulator into his mouth and then strapped the weight belt around his waist. There was no hurry in the movements, and Tomasso never looked away from Luigi. Just waiting.

Only then did the woman turn toward him. Stared right at him. His heart stuttered in his chest. Giacinta. Staring at him. Right. Through. The window.

Alive. She was real, not a figment of his imagination. Giacinta was alive. She knew what he'd done. All of it. He could see the knowledge on her face in spite of the mask she wore over her eyes. There was pain there. Regret. Sorrow. She had loved him—genuinely loved him, and that was more than he felt from any other living soul. He'd ordered the death of her parents. He'd ordered her death.

Involuntarily, he reached out to her. Pressed his hand to the window as the water closed over his head. She reached out to him but before her hand could touch the window, Tomasso circled her waist with his arm and caught her wrist in his other hand, preventing her from touching the car.

Panic hit first, panic so intense and overwhelming that he began to fight. To thrash. Kick his legs. He was frantic to get out of the tight seat belt that held him pinned to the seat. He tipped his head up, trying to get to the surface even though he knew it was impossible.

His lungs burned. He knew he couldn't hold his breath long. He'd never been able to swim and he certainly couldn't stay underwater long. His gaze went back to hers. His niece. His Giacinta. Pleading. Trying to tell her he was sorry. Trying to beg. Ordering her. Swearing at her. He didn't dare open his mouth, so he did it all with his eyes.

Then it happened. He couldn't stop it from happening. He inhaled. The water burned in his nose, down his throat to his lungs. He saw Tomasso's hand grip Giacinta hard, yanking her back and away. She resisted for a moment and then they were swimming away, while the water poured into him. He closed his eyes not wanting to watch his last hope swim away.

Lissa tried to keep her mind blank as Casimir kept her swimming away from the car. Twice she tried to turn back. For what, she didn't know. Her uncle had wiped out her family, turned her into a killer and then put out a hit on her. Seeing the desperation in his eyes, the mixture of pain, sorrow, even, maybe love . . . That had been so difficult. She tried to think of him as a monster, an illusion, not a real man. Not her uncle, the man who had raised her all those years . . .

She choked and realized she was crying, her tears filling her mask. She wasn't breathing properly for being underwater. Casimir swam close to her, his hand occasionally touching her, brushing along her shoulder or arm, just to let her know he was there. He knew how difficult this task had been. He probably didn't know it would haunt her for years. They all did. Every single one of the lives she'd taken.

Intellectually she knew they deserved to die. Her family wasn't the only family to be killed by the men she'd brought to justice. She even knew she'd saved more lives. That didn't matter when she went to bed at night.

They swam for a long distance, Lissa trying hard to keep her mind from straying back to the car. Casimir had packed her things and her suitcases were in the car waiting. Lissa Piner had to be on a train, on her way to Germany, to her next appointment, before word got out that Luigi Abbracciabene had died in a tragic accident right on the heels of his brother-in-law Aldo's accident. The driver, Tomasso, would never be found. His body either carried away by the sea, or perhaps he was a coward and fled when his boss had been trapped. Either way, the tire marks on the road would attest to the fact that he'd tried hard to keep the vehicle on the road. Once the car was examined, the faulty steering mechanism would be blamed.

Casimir touched her shoulder, indicating to start moving upward. She had left their boat far from where the car would go off the road and into the sea. They were two tourists, a couple, exploring the sea. She obeyed his directive, staying close to him, afraid she would be silly enough to swim back. By now Luigi was dead, drowned in the terrible accident and people had to be aware a car had gone off the road on the winding cliff above. They would be putting together a dive team. She couldn't be anywhere near the car and Luigi.

The moment her head broke the surface, she ripped off the mask and threw it into the boat. Casimir's hands spanned her waist and he nearly tossed her in after her mask. She crawled across the seat, removing the rented tank, and shoved her fist into her mouth, looking at Casimir with stricken eyes.

He took off his tank with slow, deliberate movements she had come to recognize in him. His gaze never left her face. "It's done, *malyshka*. These are the last tears I want you to shed for a man who doesn't deserve them. I know you're crying for him, not for you. We'll take the boat back, so you have the time it takes to do that to mourn him. After that, never again."

She nodded, although she wasn't certain she could follow

his dictate. She understood it. Luigi Abbracciabene, her uncle, was a monster. The man she thought she knew didn't exist. Casimir wanted her to understand the difference. She could cry for a childhood dream. For herself. For her loss. But he didn't want her crying for the man, because that man—the one she thought was good—the one she'd loved—didn't really exist.

She studied Casimir's set jaw as he guided the boat back toward the resort where she'd spent the last few days. He looked invincible, with wide shoulders and a muscular body. He wore his expressionless mask, something he did often out in public, but rarely did when they were alone.

Casimir despised Luigi, and she knew it wasn't just because he'd hurt her. Or even put a hit out on her. It had to do with the things he'd found in the warehouse where Cosmos's wife, Carlotta, had died. He didn't give her details, he hadn't wanted her to know. She knew Luigi was involved in prostitution, but it was far worse than that. She didn't want Casimir to give her specifics. It was hard enough to come to terms with Luigi's betrayal of her family.

Strangely, Casimir's wanting to protect her from that about her uncle, when he could easily have used those details any number of times when she'd burst into tears over Luigi's betrayal of her, made her love Casimir even more. Even now, when the tears ran down her face, he didn't reprimand her.

Looking at her husband, she realized there was no excuse for what Luigi was. What he'd become. His brother had loved him. *She* had loved him. His parents loved him. He'd had a good childhood. He hadn't seen his parents murdered. He hadn't been ripped apart from his brother. Taken to schools where he and his fellow students were tortured and brutalized to shape them into killing machines. Even Viktor, Casimir's oldest brother, had a code. He was loyal to his family and that included the others he'd gathered around him from his school.

Luigi had become a monster through jealousy and the

need to be able to live his perverted lifestyle, the need for power. He was hungry for others to admire and envy him. He needed the constant subjugation of others to make him feel powerful. She suddenly understood the truth. Even had Luigi ascended to the throne of both families, he wouldn't have been satisfied. He would still need more.

Casimir sat quietly, guiding the boat toward the resort, keeping a watchful eye on her. Caring for her. That care was genuine. Every word. Every action. He was a man who had suffered and could easily have become a monster, yet he hadn't.

His eyebrow went up. "What? *Golubushka*, you cannot look at me like that and not expect a reaction."

She realized the tears had dried up. Luigi Abbracciabene no longer held any sway over her. The man in that car wasn't anyone she knew or cared to know. Her uncle had died years ago, far before her father and mother. She had a life, and that life was the man sitting there looking at her as if she was his entire world.

"How am I looking at you?" she challenged.

"With love." His voice softened along with the hard lines etched deep into his face. "You're looking at me with love. Stark. Raw. For the world to see."

"Maybe that's because I love you like that. Stark. Raw. I don't care if the world sees it or not as long as you do."

"We've got a train to catch, *malyshka*," he said. "We're going to miss it, you keep looking at me that way."

"You don't like it?" she asked.

He flashed her a small grin. "You know better. You're tempting me on purpose."

She shook her head. "No, not this time. The truth, my amazing husband, is that I was thinking to myself how extraordinary you are and how lucky I am to have you."

His features stilled, went to stone. His eyes went liquid, a beautiful molten silver that held everything she'd ever wanted—or needed. Her heart stuttered. Her stomach did a slow somersault. She rubbed her thumb along the center of her palm, watching his face while she did it.

"We do have a private car, right? On that train? Because you wouldn't guess what I'm thinking right now." She centered her thoughts on his cock. On her mouth. On the delicious things she wanted to do with him.

"You're going to get yourself into trouble," he warned. Shifting his legs restlessly. "I can take us out away from shore and will if you don't stop. We'll be scrambling for another way to Germany."

She laughed, the wind whipping the sound back to them. "Such a missed opportunity."

"I'm not going to miss out," he corrected. "Just delay it until we're on that train."

Lissa stepped off the boat, tied it up and then hurried to her little cottage while Casimir took care of returning the scuba tanks and boat back to the resort's rental place. She'd already showered and dressed by the time he returned and was scrubbing down the cabin out of habit. After a lifetime of being careful, she wore thin synthetic gloves that had the fingerprints matching Patrice Lungren's identification. She wore her black wig and, unless she was inside, bound her breasts. The only time she didn't was when she was swimming, and then she used a long, shapeless cover-up.

"You have everything?" Casimir asked as he emerged from the bathroom, his jeans carelessly buttoned. He'd left the top button undone and was still barefoot.

"Now who's the tease?" she countered. "Seriously, honey, we've got to get out of here. The cottage is small, so it was easy enough to get things clean. I double-checked the drawers and under the bed, but I lived out of my suitcase. What about your things?"

Casimir had spent every night with her. He'd made appearances as Tomasso at Luigi's house just to see if anyone was talking about Luigi's disappearance. Early that morning he'd gone back and packed up Lissa's room, letting it be known he was taking her to the train station so she could make her next appointment. No one questioned him. They wouldn't. Without direction and figuring they had time off, the other bodyguards had scattered, finding women, drinking and playing hard while they had the chance. They never noticed they didn't actually see Lissa in the house.

"I'm good," he replied. "Let's go."

She paused in the doorway. "I liked this place. Not quite as much as the villa we had, but that's only because we had such complete privacy there and you're very creative when we have complete privacy."

"Lyubov moya." He shook his head, standing close, crowding her body into the doorjamb. "You aren't quiet when I push you past a certain point. I couldn't have the neighbors three cabins over calling the police. As it was, I had to bribe those next to us not to call."

She burst out laughing and pushed at the wall of his chest. "You did not. I'm quiet."

He raised his eyebrow. "Now you're just lying."

"Well," she hedged. "Maybe I get a *teensy* loud, when you won't let me come for like an hour."

He laughed at her, shaking his head. "An hour? Babe, I don't want to make you into a liar, so next time we're in a private place, I'll set my watch when I torment you."

He would. She knew he would. The thought of what he would do to her in that hour left her breathless. Instantly damp. Wildly excited. Casimir was very inventive and he always insisted on giving her multiple orgasms.

"You like watching me," she said softly as he took her arm and led her to the car.

He opened the door and handed her inside. "I *love* watching you, Giacinta," he corrected. "Put your seat belt on." He closed the door and then put their cases in the trunk before sliding behind the wheel. "I also love my mouth between your legs. Your taste is addicting. I go too long without it, and that's all I can think about."

He drove like he did everything else. Easily. Casually. Superbly. He didn't get upset with slow traffic, although they had a train to catch. He wasn't the type of driver to cut people off or give them the finger. He was an expert driver, another by-product of his training, so they made good time. He didn't take chances, but he never hesitated when an opportunity presented itself to get around other vehicles.

"Thank you, Casimir. For everything. You saved my life with Alberto. I wouldn't have made it out of that one alive. At least I don't think I would have. In any case, without you, I would have had a very difficult time these past few days."

"You don't have to thank me."

There was an edge to his voice that warned her to stop, but she needed him to know. "You helped me to see what Luigi was. Not what I wanted him to be."

"Giacinta," he reprimanded.

"No, honey. This needs to be said. *I* need to say it. I persisted in seeing Luigi as the uncle I wanted him to be. I did. Even after he ordered Alberto to kill me. I still had this tiny little hope in the back of my mind that a miracle would happen and he somehow was being framed."

She sighed. Ducked her head. The black wig fell around her face, reminding her that she needed to remove it. Lissa Piner had to get on the train, not Patrice. She pulled the wig off and tucked it into her bag.

"Today would have been impossible without you. I still hadn't come to terms with the truth. Seeing him like that, in the car. Even if I'd pulled that off without you, I wouldn't have left him there."

"I know. You don't have to tell me that."

His voice. She loved his voice. The way he could touch her physically when he wasn't touching her at all. Just his voice. Soft. Velvet. Brushing along her skin. Over nerve endings. The way he could use his voice like a caress was sinful.

"I do. I do have to tell you, Casimir. You have to know that you helped me see that the man I thought was family, was my uncle, never truly was. He didn't exist. *You're* real. You saw me when no one else could and you let me into your life. You loved me and married me. You're real. My sisters are real. We built a family together, the six of us. We don't share blood, but that doesn't make us any less of a family. They accepted me without condition. I believe that even knowing all of this, knowing what I've done, they'll still accept me because they have accepted their men without reservation. Your brothers are real. They call me family and it means something to them. Even Viktor, as much as he worries me because of Blythe, I believe he would put his life on the line for any one of us. I know your other brothers would. I have all that. Every one of us suffered something traumatic outside of our control. Luigi didn't. He simply wanted things he couldn't have and it twisted him into something malevolent. He wasn't anything like the child I was made him out to be. You gave me that insight."

"How did I do that, *malyshka*?" he asked gently.

"Just by being the man you are," she answered truthfully.

18

LISSA opened her eyes and found it was still night. A very bright night. There were no coverings over the window and the moon was a big round ball in the sky, so bright stars seemed faded into the background around it. Casimir lay sprawled out next to her, on his back, one arm under her, locking her to him even in sleep, the other over his eyes as if the light bothered him even in his sleep.

Casimir liked it dark. Very dark. In his room at Luigi's he always had the heavy drapes pulled over the windows. She lay partially over him, her head on his shoulder, one leg slung over his thighs. He preferred her sleeping on him. If not on him, then certainly so close she was tucked almost beneath him. He didn't like any distance between them at all.

The castle was still being renovated into a hotel. They had the entire floor to themselves, as it wasn't open yet to the public. Lissa really liked the owners. They had good business sense and everything they chose to do was done well, without breaking them financially. They wanted a chandelier for the very large great room they were using as a lobby.

Eventually they would purchase a second one for the dining room, but they were concentrating on first impressions at the moment. That and the rooms they would be renting to guests. Each room was actually a suite. They wanted the rooms to be exclusive, with full amenities, rooms everyone would want to return to. Lissa could attest to the fact that they had done a good job. The bed in their suite was amazing.

She studied Casimir while he slept. The moonlight played over his body with a loving hand. It was warm, so they had only slept with a sheet, and that had been kicked off some-time earlier. She had the chance to really look at him, to memorize every inch of him. He was beautiful. He really was. He might be masculine, but that didn't take away from his beauty. His muscles looked sculpted. He was perfectly proportioned. Her gaze moved down his chest to the sinful twelve-pack on his belly she wanted to just punch him for. He probably had been born with that. She had to work for that kind of core strength.

Her gaze moved lower, and her breath hitched in her lungs. She'd never given much thought to how men's penises looked in rest or fully erect. She had no inhibitions. It wasn't like sex embarrassed her in the least. To her, it was as natural as breath-ing. If one was going to engage in sexual activities, she believed they should strive to be the best they could for their partner.

She also believed that between consenting adults, particu-larly a committed couple, trust was vital and whatever they chose to do was between the two of them. Casimir was very creative and she was very receptive to his imagination. He liked to play and she always got the benefit of that play—eventually.

Her hand moved very gently over his stomach and then she slid over top of him, straddling him, her head on his chest. His arm moved with her, sliding around her back, locking her there for a moment. She kept very still until his arm lost the tension in it and he drifted back to sleep. Smil-ing, she turned her head and kissed his chest. Very, very slowly, she began to inch her way down his body. Trailing little kisses. Using her tongue to taste his skin.

She moved over his groin to straddle his thighs. Finally. She'd enjoyed every moment of kissing him, but she feared he'd wake too soon. She didn't often get this chance, not like this, and she was going to take it. She laid her head on his hip, curled her fingers around his cock and lifted it to her mouth. She wrapped her other arm around him and immediately drew him into the heat of her mouth. Deep. No preliminary, just took him deep.

He was awake instantly. That didn't surprise her in the least. Her man was a light sleeper and a part of him had to have felt her crawling down his body. His hand fisted in her hair, pulled at her scalp for a moment and then eased up. She didn't lift her head, but stayed relaxed, sucking. Pulling her head up to drag her lips and tongue up his shaft until he was almost out of her mouth and then diving down over it again. Fast. Deep. Wet. Tongue lashing. She used her free hand to caress his sac, to roll the velvet balls with gentle fingers while her mouth fed ravenously at his cock.

In her mouth he grew hard. Full. The girth and length increased and seemed to continue to increase until it was more of a struggle each time she took him deep. He was hot. Pulsing. His taste addicting. She wanted all of it. She didn't want him to interrupt her in the middle of what she was doing because she was enjoying herself.

Sometimes she thought she could bring herself to orgasm, not with her hands, but just with her mouth on his cock. She loved feeling his pleasure. Knowing she was giving that to him. She loved going down on him, but once she did, once she started that play, he usually took over, flipping her onto her back and reciprocating. The hand in her hair bunched tighter in a silent command and she knew from experience he was going to do just that—stop her so he could have his fun. She sucked him deeper in protest, shaking her head.

"*Malyshka*, I see you are going to be stubborn and insistent. At least turn around so I can have the same fun."

She knew him now. Knew he would insist, and if she

didn't cooperate he would stop her and take what he wanted anyway. Moaning her protest, keeping him in her mouth, she turned her body so that she straddled his shoulders. It was a stretch. Uncomfortable. His hands caught her hips and he yanked her down over his face. His tongue stabbed deep and she opened her mouth to gasp at the pleasure bursting through her from just that initial touch.

"You love my cock," he stated. "You're dripping honey all over me."

"Mmm." That was all she could get out. He was large, and moving her mouth up and down him, using her tongue and lips, drawing him deeper and deeper, took all of her concentration.

Lissa immersed herself in her work. She had to pull off of him a couple of times to pant when Casimir's mouth and fingers drove her crazy. She was close, so close. She wanted him to take her over so she could concentrate wholly again.

"No. You're going to come when I do. I'm not there yet. I'm enjoying your mouth too much to let that happen."

He had a huge control over his releases. She knew he could hold out a long time, which meant Casimir planned to devour her for a long time. Already her entire body shuddered with pleasure, and deep inside the need coiled tighter and tighter. She didn't care. She had what she wanted in her mouth and she worshiped him. She wanted to show that to him, make him feel it. Covering her teeth with her lips, she used her tongue to get him wetter, suckled hard as she moved up and down, strangling him with suction, lapping at his most sensitive spots, working him and enjoying every single second.

Each time she got too close to release, Casimir stopped what he was doing, giving her a breather, enjoying the heat of her mouth. She knew she had him though, because his hips were picking up the rhythm she'd set and he was thrusting into her mouth now where before he'd been content to allow her to be in complete control.

He brought her close for the fifth time, adding his fingers. Sometimes his thumb slid over her clit, teasing her with how very close he could bring her. She ground down, setting her own rhythm, hoping to catch him before he could stop her climax, but he just laughed as he yanked her hips away from him.

"Don't cheat, *golubushka*, we made a deal."

She was gasping for breath and had to pull her mouth off of him in order to breathe through the terrible need for release. "*You* made the deal. I didn't agree."

"You're going to have to agree because I'm the one in control here."

Her breath hissed out of her. His taste was there in her mouth. His cock was beautiful, there in her hand, the velvet crown broad, so wet and inviting. She knew what he felt like in her mouth and temptation drew her. She licked at him, drew him into her mouth and then let go in order to protest.

"You're not in control. This is a partnership."

He blew warm air over her slick, tight folds. "No, *lyubov moya*. Not here. Not now. Now, we do things my way."

She drew him deep into her mouth. Sucked hard. Heard his swift intake of air. She hummed just to prove a point. The sensation vibrated right through his cock so his entire body shuddered. She'd found that little trick accidentally, but he'd reacted so beautifully to it. She'd used it often ever since.

"This is my morning. I woke you up." She took him deep again. Felt his stomach muscles go rigid, dance with the heat and fire sliding into his belly and centering in his groin. She did a wicked little tongue dance and felt his hips buck, driving him deeper.

He groaned softly. "We'll see, Giacinta." He dragged her down to his mouth. His very talented mouth. He knew how to use it. Every. Single. Wicked. Trick.

She gasped. There was absolutely no way she was going to win this silly battle with him. She didn't have his discipline and right now she didn't care. She lavished attention on him, determined to bring him at least to the very edge of his control. Mostly, she just wanted him to feel the most pleasure possible.

In the end, she had no choice holding out. He insisted they share the same climax and he continued to torment her for a long, long time, bringing her right to the edge until she was nearly screaming for release.

"Now, baby," he said, his voice hoarse, his cock swelling.

Finally, *finally*, she felt him let go. Erupt. With his eruption came hers. Huge. Fireworks. The best. She lay on him, wrapped her arms around his hips while her body shuddered with pleasure. The taste of him would be forever in her mouth. In her mind. She *loved* him. She loved everything about him, even his impressive control.

He rubbed the right cheek of her bottom. Gently. Soothingly. Her body contracted. Rippled. Wouldn't stop for the longest time. It was . . . extraordinary. Like him. Like Casimir.

"*Malyshka.* Come here, *moya lyubov.* I want to hold you."

"I'm sleepy. Can't move. I like it right here," she murmured, nuzzling him.

He didn't argue with her. He reached down and shifted her body, turning her around until he had her in his arms, her body sprawled over top of his. He drew up the sheet. "Then go to sleep. Right where you are, Giacinta."

"I'm upset with you." She kissed his chest, her lashes drifting down.

His hand speared deep into her hair, fingers massaging her scalp. It felt wonderful. She was drifting on a wave of satisfaction and love.

"Why would that be? Are you going to tell me you didn't enjoy that?"

Lissa turned her head and nipped at his skin in reprimand. "I was telling you how much I love you. Showing you. You one-upped me. That's *so* not cool."

"I heard you, *golubushka*, and I answered you."

He had a point. In any case, she was too sleepy to care. His body was always warm. There were so many intriguing muscles to trace as she let herself just float on that sea of absolute beauty. She felt thoroughly loved, and he'd only used his mouth on her.

"You feel loved?" she murmured.

"Very much."

He woke her an hour later and made love to her. Slow. Lazy. Sensual. Beautiful. He watched her the entire time, his eyes never leaving hers. She saw love there. She felt it. She watched his face as the beauty of their joining came over him. That exquisite moment when she couldn't breathe. When she couldn't focus. When his body threw hers into a phenomenal climax that lasted forever and her body took his with it, surrounding him with fire.

Casimir stayed locked in her, his full weight on her, his arms tight around her. She couldn't breathe, but it didn't matter in the least. She wanted him there. She held him tight while he buried his face in her neck.

"You're my world, you know that, don't you, Giacinta? You brought me back to life. You. My beautiful wife."

She loved that he thought that. She was fairly certain it was the other way around, but she couldn't help but love his declaration.

"It's important to me that you know that, *moya lyubov*, very important. When we're in Russia . . ." He trailed off and lifted up just enough to lean on his hand, taking his weight from her, but keeping their bodies locked together. "I don't want you taking any chances."

She cupped the side of his face with her hand. Could a woman love a man any more? She doubted it. Sometimes, like now, when she just looked at him, love was overwhelming. She heard the honesty in his voice. He gave her that. Stark and raw. His feelings. To the rest of the world, he would wear a mask, but not to her, with her, he put himself out there, right on the line, without hesitation.

"Casimir, do you think I'd deliberately risk what I have with you? I didn't expect to have you. Not ever. You're a miracle to me. I'm not giving up what we have together easily. I swear to you, I'll be very careful."

He rolled over and took her with him, so once again her body was sprawled over top of his. "You have to understand what you're dealing with. Who they are. What they're like."

"My childhood monsters were Cosmos, Aldo, and Luigi, although I didn't realize Luigi was a part of the conspiracy against my father. The point I'm trying to make is that your childhood monster was Kostya Sorbacov. He's just a man. One that we can take down. We've got a plan, Casimir. It's a good one. I'm not going to put myself in harm's way unless I know I've got a better than average shot at making it out alive. We'll do this together, and that more than doubles the odds in our favor."

He sighed. Heavily. "I can't go back to living like that. Behind a mask. No one seeing me. There's only you for me." He took her hand and opened her fingers one by one, exposing her palm. His fingers closed around hers and he brought her palm to his mouth. His tongue touched the center, stroked a caress right over her heart. "No one else, Giacinta. There never will be. I'm a man who believes his woman should do the things that make her happy. That fulfill her. But . . ."

Her heart fluttered. Ached. She hadn't thought it was possible to love him any more, but she did.

"Honey, there is no way I'd throw my life away. You're important to me too. *This*, what we have together, is too important. I swear to you, I'll be careful."

He pressed his lips into her palm. She felt his kiss somewhere deep. Her heart. Her soul. He just nodded, not saying anything else.

* * *

ABOVE the Neckar River Valley, the castle was nestled snugly between the Black Forest and Swabian Hills. There was no doubt in her mind that the family would make a huge success of their business. The castle had been in their family for well over two hundred years, and they'd taken amazing care of it, modernizing when needed.

They already had private stables, a golf course and an indoor swimming pool. The walking areas were gorgeous and the riding terrain even more so. The castle had a wedding chapel as well as rooms set up for conferences. Lissa felt lucky that the owners had seen and admired her work. She'd been there four days with Casimir and every day had felt like a honeymoon.

Once their business had been completed, the owners had graciously offered her to complete her stay with access to anything they wanted to use. Casimir wanted to ride horses. Lissa knew Lexi eventually wanted to have horses on their farm. She'd been pushing for a barn and stable, especially now that they had four children on the property. Everyone thought it was a great idea.

Gavriil had brought two Black Russian Terriers with him, huge dogs that were extremely loyal and protective of their owner and household. Those two had turned into six more. There was no doubt Lexi would get her way over the horses, because, of course, there was no reason not to have them. Lissa didn't ride. Not. Ever.

She didn't mind exploring the countryside. The views from the terrace were breathtaking. On horseback, she was positive the surrounding land would be gorgeous. But horses were huge. Even bigger than Gavriil's dogs. A *lot* bigger. This was their last day and she wanted a picnic somewhere on the vast grounds. To tell Casimir that had been a huge mistake. For some unknown reason, the moment she'd uttered the preference, Mr. Romantic decided to make her dream come true. But his idea of romance somehow included horses.

"Mmm." She licked her lips when he turned his gaze on

her. He had those eyes, those quicksilver eyes that went from glittering to molten in one second flat. That look robbed her of her ability to speak. She was certain he needed to be outlawed. His eyes were an unfair advantage and he knew exactly how to use them.

He curled his fingers around the nape of her neck and drew her close to the heat of his body. "Let me take care of everything. I've gotten directions to a very secluded section of their grounds. We'll have a private ride and picnic. I also secured their gentlest horse for you to ride."

"But . . ." She tried to protest but the words wouldn't come. His look was purely sensual, and excitement skittered down her spine in spite of the fact that she was a little scared of an animal so much taller and weighing a ton, or whatever they weighed.

"Give me this, *moya lyubov*. I want our last day to be a memory you'll never forget. Say yes. Just trust me, Giacinta."

There was no way she could deny him. She nodded, her heart thundering in her ears. The horse not only had better be gentle, but it had better have impeccable manners as well.

"I've laid out the clothes I'd like you to wear for me. *Only* what you see on the bed. *Everything* you see eventually will be on you when we ride."

She glanced at the bed. Her heart jumped. She raised her gaze to his. "Casimir . . ."

"Trust me."

"I can't possibly ride a horse in a skirt." She chose the easiest thing to protest first, but she wasn't looking at the skirt. She was looking at the fine golden chain with the clips on either end.

"You can. It's long and will cover anything important. We'll be alone."

She moistened her lips and let his hand at her back guide her to the bed. The skirt he chose was very long, down to her ankles and if she didn't wear heels would sweep the floor. With boots, it just touched the floor. The material flowed around her loosely, giving plenty of room to stretch her legs over a horse.

"These panties are . . ."

He shook his head, and she trailed off. She picked them up. A webbing of lace. The lace was stretchy and the crotch was nearly nonexistent. Where did he get them? Where did he get the chain? She snuck a peek at it. The ends, looking like tiny screws, were tipped with rubber. She let her breath out and her sex spasmed. Went damp. Her breasts actually ached.

She picked up the matching bra. This was lace, a demi bra, but one that was extremely low-cut. Her breasts would be pushed up and the nipples would show above the lace. She couldn't help thinking the black panties and bra were very sexy. Spending the afternoon alone with him, riding beside him, knowing she would be wearing these clothes would make her crazy with need.

"I've got everything ready," he explained, casually scooping up the chain and pocketing it. "Get dressed and we'll go down to the stable."

She nodded, and he walked out. Her heart went wild as she stripped. She had never been more excited. In a short period of time, she'd gotten married and now her husband was showing her a wild, erotic, amazing and very romantic honeymoon. She *loved* every second of it. The anticipation and secret thrill of wearing the clothes he'd chosen for her as well as wondering where and when he'd ask her to wear that gold chain nearly gave her a mini-orgasm.

Even with riding boots, she felt sexy as she braided her hair and left the room to find him. Casimir waited by the stairs. His eyes went molten and a dark look of lust mixed with love and approval gave her another violent spasm. He reached out to her and without hesitation she put her hand in his.

"Beautiful, *malyshka*. Totally beautiful. Thank you for giving me this."

"I'd give you anything you asked for, Casimir," she admitted, stripping herself bare for him. Making herself even more vulnerable. It didn't matter. It was the truth and she wanted him to know. Especially now. They were facing the Sorbacovs, his family's greatest enemies. Two powerful men who were ruthless and had powerful friends. One misstep and they'd both die. Lissa was determined Casimir would have everything and anything she could give him before they left for Russia. This was her chance.

Her reward was the look on his face. He kissed her knuckles and slid one hand down her cheek before leading her down the stairs and outside to the stables. The horses were saddled and waiting for them. She saw immediately that Casimir was an experienced horseman. He caught her around the waist, directed her on how to bunch her skirt up to her thighs and set her on the back of the animal. He kept possession of the reins, patting the horse's head and speaking soothingly to it.

He had put some sort of soft padding with small, sweeping fibers sticking up over the saddle so when she settled onto the seat, the material brushed against the vee at the junction of her legs and every nerve ending came alive with need. They hadn't even gotten out of the stable and she was already hot, slick, needy. So ready for him.

He handed her the reins and swung up easily on the much larger horse, saluted the groom and led the way to the secluded trail. The motion of the horse, rocking her back and forth, stimulated her more. It felt as if a thousand fingers pushed through the lace to continually caress and stroke her. She was too stimulated to be scared of her horse anymore. She couldn't think about anything but the beauty of their surroundings and the fire building and building between her legs.

They'd ridden for about forty-five minutes, neither speaking because . . . well . . . she couldn't speak. She could only breathe away the hunger that had become so ravenous she thought she would have to beg him to stop and give her some release. She breathed a sigh of relief when Casimir stopped abruptly and dismounted.

Lissa looked around her. They were in a grove of trees. The sound of water trickled somewhere nearby. It was very secluded and she sent up a little prayer of thanks. When he lifted his arms to her, she went into them immediately. He held her close while she got her legs back under her.

"Take off your blouse, *golubushka*," he said softly. "But leave your bra on."

She didn't hesitate. She was *so* ready. She unbuttoned her blouse. He took it from her, folded it carefully and put it in the bag attached to his saddle.

"I noticed you like me to play with your breasts. That really turns you on. And you especially like me to be a little rough with your nipples." He drew the chain out of his pocket. "These will feel like fingers applying pressure, keeping your breasts stimulated. But, *malyshka*, if it doesn't feel good, we won't do it."

She *wanted* the chain. It was beautiful, and she could see in his eyes that the very idea brought him pleasure. She nodded, her breath caught in her lungs.

He drew her toward him, hooking her around the waist. "You'll like this, Giacinta. This is fun for both of us, preparing you for your clamps."

That brought another spasm deep in her sex. If he didn't get on with it, she wasn't going to need his cock inside her, she'd be having a wild orgasm all by herself.

He bent his head to her breasts. He had a talented mouth and he used it. Licking. Sucking. Biting. His hands kneaded the soft mounds while his mouth and tongue worked her nipples. She found herself nearly sobbing, cradling his head to her, pressing on him, wanting more. Needing more. Her nipples were so hard, standing straight up, and she could barely speak.

"Honey, I can't stand it. I need more. Let me have your . . ." She reached down for the front of his jeans.

He stepped back and held up the chain. "I think you're ready now. I'll be gentle." He opened the clamp to the fullest and, watching her face carefully, began to screw it on.

Her breath left her lungs in a long rush at the pressure. Fire raced from her nipple straight to her clit. He stopped just before it went from pleasure/pain to sheer pain. He bent and brushed a kiss over her nipple and turned his attention to the other breast. When she was fully clamped and the chain was suspended between her breasts, he stepped back, his hand skimming down her bare midriff before he just stood there studying her.

"You look so beautiful. I knew that black skirt and bra would look so fucking hot with that gold chain. Come on, *malyshka*." He beckoned to her.

She walked toward him. Slow. Each step deliberate. Watching his face, loving the look. When she reached him, her spanned her waist with his hands.

"Pick up your skirt like you did before," he whispered, his hands stroking over her body. Touching her. He tipped her face back with fingers under her chin and took her mouth. There was possession in his kiss. Command. He took complete control. "Do it," he murmured against her mouth. "Lift your skirt like I showed you." He kissed her again. And again. Over and over.

Lissa could barely think with wanting him. Her blood roared in her ears, rushed through her veins like a fireball, settling low until the pressure and the burn were so strong she tried moving into him to wrap one leg around him.

"Your skirt." There was iron in his voice.

She obeyed without thinking. Instantly he lifted her and set her on the back of the horse. She clutched the animal with her thighs automatically, squeezing hard. The fibers in the thin pad he'd strapped over the saddle seat rubbed into her sex. Her horse side-stepped, sending her breasts and the chain swaying, adding tension and pressure to her nipples. She gasped at the dual sensations.

"Honey," she breathed. She looked down at his upturned face. He stared at her with a look she'd never seen before, one that made her slick with desire. Her channel spasmed. She wanted to see that look a million more times. Sitting in the saddle, dripping with need, lust rising, desire so intense she barely knew her own name, was worth it just for that look.

He adjusted his jeans, opened them in the front to give the thick girth more room and swung on his horse.

"Casimir, someone might come along . . ."

"They won't." He didn't say anything else, but he rode beside her, watching her face more than the trail.

With every step the horse took, her breasts swayed. The fibers caressed and stroked her hungry sex. She tried subtly rubbing her body along the pad in the hopes it would relieve some of the tension coiled so tight in her, but the action, along with the rocking motion of the horse, only increased her need. Every so often, without a word, Casimir leaned over and hooked his finger in the chain, lifting it gently. The action lifted her breasts and increased the pressure on her nipples until she cried out, nearly sobbing for relief. She arched her back and rubbed her thighs frantically.

"Honey, I need you." She whispered the admission, unable to stand the scorching fire between her legs one more minute. Her entire body felt on fire.

"I'm sorry, Giacinta." He kept riding, smiling down at her. "I didn't hear you. What did you say?"

She sighed. He was in the mood to play. "I said I need you. I really do."

"What do you need from me?" he asked.

"You know very well."

He put his boot heels into the side of his horse and instantly it began a slow trot. Her horse automatically followed suit. With every bounce, lightning sizzled from nipples to clit. She swore it flashed through her body, strike after strike.

"I need your cock," she called. "Please, honey. Right now. I need it inside me, right now."

He immediately turned his horse around, back to hers. His hands went to the front of his jeans. Standing in the stirrups, he freed his cock completely, so it jutted out in front of him, an intimidating steel spike. She wanted to weep with joy at the sight. She needed him so much she was nearly incoherent.

He took the reins of her horse from her hands and hooked a lead rope onto the animal's bridle. "Hold your skirt up," he ordered, and reached for her.

Her breasts swayed as he transferred her from her saddle to his horse. He set her on the larger animal, one hand sliding under her skirt, the other steadying her. He ripped the lace away from her body, wadded it up and shoved it in the pocket of his jeans. Her breath came in frantic, ragged gasps. She couldn't stop her hands from stroking his cock, that magnificent part of him she needed so desperately. In truth, she barely was aware of her panties being gone, she couldn't take her hands or her mind from his heavy erection. Other than his exposed cock, he was fully clothed. For some reason, that made her feel all the more erotic sitting there in her bra, the gold chain and her skirt hiked up nearly to her waist with no panties.

He stood in the stirrups again. "Take out my balls, Giacinta."

Nearly sobbing for him, licking her lips, she did so immediately, widening the gap in his jeans so she could bring his heavy sac into the open air. His hands spanned her waist again. Casimir lifted her, her breasts brushing his chest.

"Keep your skirt up," he commanded again. She did so, feeling the crown of his cock pushing against her slick entrance. "Is this what you want, *malyshka*?"

She gripped the base of his cock, holding him still, but he continually moved her body, holding her suspended over him, all the while controlling the horse with his thighs.

"Yes." She could see that wasn't enough for him. He teased her, smearing her slick heat all around the head of his cock without letting her impale herself. "*Please*, honey, I can't stand it."

She was going to go insane. Her entire attention was focused on the junction between her legs, the fire roaring there, and his beautiful, long, thick cock.

"So desperate. Since you ask so sweetly . . ."

He slammed her down hard, his shaft driving through her scorching-hot folds, the fit so excruciating tight he threw back his head and roared. The breath left her lungs. She screamed, forgetting for a moment that they were on his horse. The animal moved restlessly and Casimir controlled it with his legs. He reached behind her and caught up the reins of her horse as well.

Bending his head, he sucked the chain into his mouth and lifted his head. She cried out again as the movement lifted her breasts higher. He urged the horse forward, into a trot, using the stirrups to control their movement. The action sent his body moving in hers. Filling her. Stretching her. Burning her from the inside out. Her fingers clutched his shoulders, nails digging into his flesh right through the material of his shirt. This was almost as bad as the fabric rubbing against her. It was more stimulation, but she needed *much* more. She tried to hold on to his shoulders and lift herself, to give her the rougher, harder strokes she needed.

He lifted his chin more and turned it to one side, controlling her body with the chain in his mouth. She cried out again as fire flashed through her. She closed her eyes and surrendered herself to him. She couldn't force him to do what she wanted, and she knew, in the end, he would take care of her. She had to trust him to do that for her. She trusted him always to have her back in a dangerous situation, and she knew exactly what he was doing now. He wanted *complete* trust. Complete surrender to him. She was his and he would care for her in every way. Always.

The moment she relaxed into his body, melting around his cock, he increased the speed of the horse so that every jolt was felt through her entire body. He rose and fell with the gait of the horse, giving her long, hard strokes until she was sobbing, so close, her breasts aching, her nipples feeling as if a thousand fingers held them tight, pinching and rolling with every step.

"Give me that gift, *malyshka*. Give it to me."

At the sound of his voice, that soft, sexy command, she exploded. The orgasm roared through her like a fireball, going from her center to her belly and then engulfing her breasts. She wailed, chanted his name. She had never felt anything that intense, and it went on forever. Her body grasped at his. Milked and insisted.

He drove up again, over and over. All the while his mouth worked the chain, and the next wave of flames roared through her, this one far hotter and stronger than the last, a towering inferno that swept him along with her, so that his hoarse shout mingled with her frantic cries. He let the chain slip from his mouth and she fell forward, her forehead pressed tight against his chest.

Casimir slowed the horse, finally bringing it to a halt. His arms swept around her. "Giacinta," he said softly.

She lifted her face and he captured her mouth, kissing her over and over, all the while still buried inside of her. Very gently, he caught her around the waist to lift her off of him. "Step into the stirrup."

She did so and then she was thankfully on the ground. She had to clutch the stirrup to steady herself and then he was beside her. He wrapped his arm around her waist and led her, with the horses, to a small clearing in the center of a grove of trees.

"How did you know this was here?"

He flashed a smile as he tied the horses to low branches, giving them plenty of room to graze on the grass. "It's a wonder what a few bribes will get you."

Casimir spread a blanket on the ground and gestured for her to sit. She watched as he pulled out the picnic basket and set it down before kneeling in front of her. "I need to take off the clamps and this can get intense."

Her hands went to her tender nipples. He shook his head and gently pushed her hands away. "Let me. I'll be gentle."

She let her hands slide down to his thigh. All the while she kept her gaze glued to his face. He looked happy. *Happy.* That was her making him happy. She'd never realized until that moment that the look on his face was rare.

His fingers brushed the swell of her breast. "Okay, *golubushka*, I'm going to have you take a deep breath and I'll take the clamp off. While I do, release your breath very, very slowly. It's going to hurt for just a moment, but I'll make it feel better." He waited for her nod.

She took the breath and let it out slowly as he removed the clamp. Blood rushed back and she nearly cried out at the bite of pain. His mouth covered her nipple and he gently licked and stroked with his tongue, soothing the ache. He sucked gently and almost at once the pain subsided.

He lifted his head. "Better?" She nodded. "Now the other one. Don't tense up. Take a breath. I'm right here."

His mouth was a miracle, his touch so gentle she wanted to cry. After making certain there was no pain, he caught the hem of her skirt, tugged it up and then took two cloths from his bag. One was wet, in a plastic bag, and he used it to clean her between her legs and then dried her with the second one.

"If you like the clamps," he said, as he cleaned her off, "we can use them occasionally but for no more than ten minutes or so."

"Casimir, they had to have been on for an hour."

He grinned at her. Shook his head. "Ten minutes. We were quick once we got going. I was so hard I was afraid I'd shatter. And you were scorching hot." He finished cleaning himself off and then leaned over and took her breast into his mouth again, still gentle, his tongue soothing her nipple. "Are you sore?"

"Sensitive more than sore. You didn't have them on that tight."

He opened the picnic basket, handed her a sandwich and took one himself. "I've never seen anything hotter or more beautiful than you were with your skirt up around your bare thighs, that bra and the clamps with the chain. I didn't think I was going to last. You held out a long time."

She took the bottled water he handed her, the cap off, and sipped it. "You wanted me to trust you with everything, didn't you?"

He nodded, his silver eyes moving over her face. "I need that from you. To know whatever I ask, inside the bedroom or out, you trust in me enough to give it to me. After all the betrayals in your life, I wouldn't blame you if you couldn't, but having your trust is important to me."

"I'm inside your head, Casimir. It's hard to lie to someone who can see inside your head sometimes."

He nodded his agreement. "I know it is, but it's more than that. You gave me something much more than seeing inside my head, Giacinta. You surrendered to me. That's something I don't take lightly. Your surrender is something I'll always treasure, so that you'll always know you're safe with me."

They shared their picnic lunch, enjoying each other and the beauty of their surroundings. Casimir led the horses to the small stream so they could drink before tying them up again. She had his cock for dessert and then fell asleep in the afternoon sun, sprawled as usual over top of him. He woke her an hour later and made love to her, starting slow and gentle, giving her a sweet, satisfying orgasm, and then flipping her over, yanking her up on her hands and knees and slamming into her hard and fast, her very favorite. They finished together and collapsed again.

Lissa slipped her hand into his. "Best honeymoon ever, Casimir. Thank you."

19

WITH the golden domes soaring into the sky, the hotel was considered one of the treasures of St. Petersburg. It was built in the time of masters of architecture, the building a work of art, carefully preserved and modernized. It was clearly undergoing another renovation, but Lissa was surprised it was being done with the utmost care. She had expected the Sorbacovs—both father and son—to be wrecking balls, crude, rude men who stepped on others to get what they wanted.

Neither man appeared to be in the least like that. Both were charming, elegant and very charismatic. She could see how Uri could easily finesse his way to the presidency. Both were dressed in suits and came immediately to meet her, not making her wait even five minutes. Both bowed over her hand. Uri looked her over, his gaze as surprised as hers.

"Your pictures don't do you justice, my dear," he said in perfect English. "I thought you attractive, but you're stunning."

She smiled up at him and allowed him to tuck her hand into the crook of his arm. "Thank you."

"Have you eaten? We thought it would be good to take a tour of the hotel first and while we talk business, we have a little something prepared if you're hungry."

"I will confess I took a nap and skipped eating, so that would be lovely, thank you." She flashed a smile toward the older Sorbacov, studying him under her lashes. He was handsome, not quite as good-looking as his son, but certainly handsome. No scars. Not a single one. Every single Prakenskii brother had scars. Sorbacov had been instrumental in putting those scars on them when they were just boys. He didn't look like a monster. In fact, he looked like the furthest thing from a monster she could imagine—but then, to her, Luigi hadn't looked like a monster either.

The two men walked her around the lobby, a huge room with very high ceilings and astonishing details along the walls. Little alcoves were carved into the walls where old-fashioned sconces were nestled, adding to the ambiance of the room.

She indicated them. "Those are beautiful. Whatever you get for overhead lighting, or dramatic effect, you will definitely want your chandeliers to incorporate those colors and the designs of the wall sconces. No one has anything like that anymore." She didn't have to pretend enthusiasm or admiration. She *loved* the sconces. They were from another era and yet fit perfectly into the modern world.

Uri and Kostya both studied the sconces as if seeing them for the first time. "I hadn't thought of that," Kostya said. "But now that you mention it, they really do stand out."

"It's more than that," Lissa said, excitement entering her voice. "Look at the colors. The outside domes are gold. The domes on the sconces match perfectly. They have that thin stripe of orange . . ." She broke off. "I'm sorry. I get carried away when I see beautiful glass pieces like that. You have no idea how difficult it is to replicate something that gorgeous." She looked around the huge room. "They're worth a fortune."

Uri patted her hand. "It's a pleasure viewing our hotel through your eyes. What would you suggest for a chandelier? You must have ideas now that you've seen the room."

She nodded. "I can't help having ideas when I see a place I would love to work with. This hotel is really extraordinary. The outside as well as the inside. I'd want to incorporate the colors of the sconces for certain. Make that your signature brand. Blend old-world elegance—and Russia has beautiful examples of that—with modern times. In other words, the rooms where guests stay have all the modern amenities, but your décor gives your guests a taste of the beauty of your country, its architecture and artistry."

The two men looked at each other and smiled, as if delighted by her opinions. "I couldn't have put it better myself," Kostya said. "We've had a few arguments about modern versus old-fashioned, and I think you settled it and we both won."

"Not old-fashioned," Lissa corrected, frowning at Uri, guessing he was all for modernizing every aspect of the hotel. "Old-world elegance is never old-fashioned. Russia is famous for its crystal chandeliers. If I were going to incorporate both the modern and the old world, I'd do it with my lighting as well. You don't have to sacrifice one for the other."

Uri threw back his head and laughed. The sound was pleasing. Again she was struck by how different the men appeared from what they actually were. "We should have invited you months ago. We've paid the designers a fortune and haven't liked a single idea they've come up with to brand this place and you do it in five minutes."

"I'm a redhead, Mr. Sorbacov, that means I'm opinionated and don't hesitate, even when I should, to give it."

"I'm Uri, not Mr. Sorbacov," he corrected. "My father is Mr. Sorbacov."

"Not to Lissa. I will call you Lissa, my dear, and you must call me Kostya," Kostya said. "I'm an old man and should be able to do as I like."

"I don't think you can be very old, Kostya," Lissa said.

"Don't encourage him," Uri scolded, tugging on her hand to lead her across the lobby toward a door. "He's a terrible flirt. Tell us about yourself. Are you married? Do you have children? Where do you live?"

She was very grateful for all the years of training. She kept her smile in place and didn't so much as blink. The cat-and-mouse game had officially begun. "Not married. I guess I didn't have time. I was too busy trying to establish myself as a serious artist to date, so no children either. I live in a very small village called Sea Haven on the northern California coast. It's beautiful there and very inspiring. Quite a few artists make it home, so the town has kind of an artsy feel to it." She tipped her head back to look directly into Uri's eyes. "What about you? Same questions."

The two men walked her through the main lobby and down a wide hall. She was immediately conscious of the fact that the sound of the workmen's voices faded away and there weren't any people around. She was alone with the Sorbacovs, and of course they had known she was from Sea Haven. Not only had it said so in the magazine article she'd been written up in, but it was on her business card and website as well. They might not know about the other Prakenskii brothers residing there, but they would know Ilya made his home in Sea Haven and so had Gavriil.

Lissa reminded herself she was prepared for this. She knew they contacted her because of the article they'd read. The Sorbacovs had contacted her, not the other way around. She'd sent them designs, just as she did every other potential client. When they had arranged for her to come out to discuss chandeliers for their hotel, she had been very forthcoming about her itinerary, the fact that she had several appointments in various countries. She had given them a list of dates and they had chosen this one.

"Not married, no children," Uri said. He threw his father a quick smile. "My father is not happy that I haven't done right by him. Like you, I've been busy establishing my career, although he has reminded me enough that time is slipping by."

"You're lucky your father is alive to remind you," she pointed out softly, including Kostya in her gentle smile. "I lost both my parents some years ago. It's nice to have family." She glanced up toward the ceiling. "This hotel is extraordinary. I especially love the high, cathedral ceilings. I'm always looking at them in order to see what kind of lighting would work best."

There was a construction crew working on the hotel, but the hotel itself had been closed while the renovations were taking place—unusual in that a hotel of that size couldn't lose money every day. Casimir suspected the shutdown was due to the fact that the Sorbacovs didn't want anyone to stumble onto the fact that they were building secret tunnels they could use for complete privacy, coming and going at will.

"Sea Haven," Uri murmured aloud. "An unusual name, and yet I feel as if I've heard of this place before." He frowned as he held the door open for her to another room. Over her head he looked to his father as if the silent communication would yield him the reason why he remembered the name.

"It's very small," Lissa volunteered, preceding father and son into the room. That meant turning her back on them and she felt a shiver of fear skitter down her spine. She continued into the center of the room, shoulders straight, walking with confidence.

This was clearly a conference room, designed to make anyone feel as if they had the world at their fingertips. A long table at one end of the room held several dishes with various foods. Bottles of champagne were in ice buckets. Clearly the room was set for celebration. They hadn't struck a deal yet, but they counted on her being eager to make a sale, so they probably hoped she would be distracted.

She walked straight across the room to the window, checking out the view, keeping her back to them, although there was a distinct itch between her shoulder blades.

"Isn't Sea Haven where our dear friend resides?" Kostya asked, sounding as if he'd just thought of it. Casual. Almost bored even, as if the conversation was taking a turn he wasn't in the least interested in.

They were good. Smooth. Both of them. She hadn't expected them to be so charming or charismatic. She turned toward Kostya, her back to the window. "A friend lives there? The town is very small, and I do a lot of business there."

"Ilya Prakenskii moved there, Uri," Kostya said. "Some time ago. A good man. He was an Interpol agent and he retired from that business and went into private security. I hear from him from time to time, although not often."

"Of course," Uri said. "Ilya." He quirked an eyebrow at Lissa as he pulled one of the champagne bottles from the bucket. "Do you know him?"

The champagne was the real deal. The bottle was iced and Uri expertly wrapped the neck with a cloth and popped the cork.

"I think everyone knows of Ilya Prakenskii, not just in Sea Haven, but everywhere. He married one of the Drake sisters, Jolie. She's a very famous musician and performs all over the world. In our town, the Drakes are considered royalty of sorts."

"Have you met him?" Uri asked as he poured the champagne into three flutes.

Lissa didn't take her eyes from the man. She didn't want him slipping anything into her drink. She was very aware the two men had cleverly orchestrated their charming interrogation of her. There were few witnesses to her entry into the hotel. Only a few of the construction crew had actually seen her. The Sorbacovs could make her disappear with very few questions asked.

"Yes, I have. He's very good friends with the local sheriff,

Jonas Harrington. Jolie, his wife, is related to a friend of mine, Blythe Daniels, so I've been introduced a time or two. We don't run in the same circles. His wife is on tour a lot, but he seemed . . ." Deliberately she hesitated as if searching for the right word. "Protective, I think is the best way to describe him. He doesn't take his eyes off his wife."

Kostya let out a hoot of laughter. "Scary," he corrected. "The big son of a bitch is scary. Even to me, and I'm his friend."

Good manners dictated she turn toward him when he was speaking, but that meant taking her eyes off of Uri. She had no choice but to take the chance, looking at Uri's father, the monster who had ordered the murder of so many people simply because they opposed his politics. He'd taken their children and forced them into becoming weapons for him, or he killed them. After they had served him and their country for years, he ordered their deaths as if they weren't human beings, but trash he could dispose of.

"I am far too polite to ever say such a thing," Lissa said primly, smiling at him.

He laughed and took the flute of champagne Uri handed him. Then Uri was in front of her. Close. She'd taken time to study every aspect of his personality before she'd ever left the States on this mission. He was photographed often with various women. He liked beautiful women with figures. He wasn't into thin models. He'd dated an actress a time or two, but it wasn't at all about fame. He just liked women with figures. She played up her curves when she dressed. She'd worn a skirt that clung to her hips and emphasized her small waist. The blouse was almost see-through, but wasn't, just hinting at the generous breasts beneath the thin material. Her jacket was short and fitted, tight over her breasts, narrow along her rib cage, tucked into her waist and then flaring over her hips. The outfit was very feminine, a beautiful shade of dark, forest green. Her legs were shown off by the very sexy heels she wore, designer, with lots of straps going up her ankles.

She could see the appreciation in Uri's eyes. The speculation. The interest. She also knew he could be a very violent
man, attracted or not. She took the flute of champagne with
a soft murmur of thanks.

"What a coincidence that Ilya would move to that same
small town," Kostya continued. "How long have you lived
there?"

"About five years. I set up my studio about four years ago,
but before that, I worked in the basement of my house. It was
close quarters when glassblowing. And hot." She wanted the
subject to go back to her work.

"Such an intriguing profession for such a beautiful
woman," Uri said. "So unusual. I appreciate the unusual." He
stared directly into her eyes.

Definitely flirting. She smiled at him and brushed back
her hair, a purely feminine gesture, a small sign that she
found him attractive as well. "There's something very satisfying about making a piece of art that will hopefully be
around a long time."

She took a small sip of the ice-cold champagne. It was
awesome. The best she'd ever tasted. Kostya stood close to
the window overlooking the street. She raised her glass at
him. "The hotel has beautiful views. The river. The amazing
architecture of the buildings across from you. This is a perfect location for a hotel."

Kostya took the bait and stepped right up to the window
and looked out. "I haven't seen my city through someone
else's eyes in a long time."

She started toward him and Uri moved with her, one hand
at the small of her back. The window shattered and Kostya's
head exploded, the sight shocking and obscene. Blood
sprayed everywhere. She froze, screaming. The exquisite
crystal flute fell from nerveless fingers to the floor.

Uri swore, hitting the floor, dragging her down with him.
She jammed her fist in her mouth. "Oh, my God. Oh, my
God." She chanted it over and over. Men poured into the

room, guns drawn. Some were pointed at her head. "What just happened? Uri? Your father. What just happened?"

The men positioned themselves around Uri in a protective circle. Only then did he rise, yanking her to her feet. "You're coming with us until I figure out if you're a part of this or not."

"I don't understand." Her gaze strayed to the body on the floor, the blood pooling around it. "Part of what?" She looked around at all the guns, looking dazed, terrified, very confused.

Uri didn't answer. He snapped an order out and the men began moving, Uri and Lissa inside their closed ranks, as they hurried from the room and down the hall toward the huge mirror at the end of it. Lissa had to practically run to keep up with them. Uri's grip on her wrist was a vise. She knew she'd have bruises. In a way she couldn't blame him. He'd just witnessed his father's head blown off by some unknown sniper.

"Uri, why would someone do that?" she whispered.

"Shut up." The command was terse. Clipped. His grip didn't loosen in the slightest.

Lissa complied, stumbling a little, slowing them down, but Uri didn't let go of her. His grip didn't loosen for even one second, forcing her to go with him. The group abruptly stopped moving, and a panel slid open in the wall just to the right of the mirror. She was shoved through the door by the guard behind her even as Uri jerked at her arm. She stumbled, teetered in her high heels and then fell, her body crashing into Uri's.

His fingers gripped her arms hard, digging in, shaking her. She knew instantly he barely was aware of her. He was caught between fury and grief. She would have felt sorry for him but she knew he was the reason the orders had been given to kill those men and woman originally attending the schools his father had set up. Because he was ambitious. Because he couldn't afford a scandal if he wanted his political aspirations to be met.

She cried out, a lost, terrified cry. She clutched at him for support. "I'm so sorry, Uri. That was . . . *horrible*." It was. Shocking and horrible. Casimir was clearly an expert marksman. From what she understood, no one left the schools without being an expert in all ways to kill.

Uri maintained his hold on her but didn't answer. Instead he turned to his men. "Find out where that shot came from."

"Sir, the building across the street. On the roof. Right after the shot, there was an explosion on the roof. Our men are headed there now."

"I don't want him killed. Do you understand? Bring the shooter to me alive. Make that clear. I want him alive."

He turned on his heel after snapping the order, and began hurrying down the tunnel fast, once again taking Lissa with him. She dragged air into her lungs and looked around her. The tunnel was narrow, necessitating they go in single file or two abreast at the most. Uri kept her right next to him. There was no real way to drop behind him, not yet.

LED track lights at the seams of the ceiling lit the way. More were strung along the floor. She was very aware that Uri's fury was growing with every step they took because his fingers clamped down harder and harder on her until, midway down the seemingly endless tunnel, he abruptly stopped, turned to her and shook her hard.

"You *bitch*. I'm going to hurt you like you've never been hurt before. You're going to live a very long time and you'll beg me for death and I won't *ever* give it to you. You did this. Don't lie to me. You did this."

She was very aware of the men surrounding them. All had weapons. All were looking at her as if she were their greatest enemy. She shook her head. "Uri. I don't know what you're talking about . . ."

He slapped her. The blow was delivered open-handed but it was so hard it felt like her entire cheek exploded. The pain radiated up to her eye and down to her jaw. Her ears rang, a peculiar buzzing noise that drowned out her gasping cry. She staggered back, but he yanked her forward, driving his fist into her stomach. She doubled over and choked on bile.

Uri snatched the gun from the nearest soldier and shoved the barrel against her skull, hard. "Talk to me right now. Is it Ilya out there? Are you working with him?"

She gasped for air, still choking, trying to straighten, but the blow to her stomach held her immobile. She could only try to shake her head.

"Where's your rendezvous point? Where are you going to meet him?" he barked.

She opened her mouth and nothing came out but a thin wail.

"Lock the city down," Uri snapped to his men. "I want that bastard found. Now. He has to go somewhere. Someone has to know how he got into the country and how he plans to get out. Find that someone, and do it now." He shoved the gun back at the soldier and forced Lissa into an upright position.

His hands settled around her throat. "You're going to tell me what I want to know and you'll do it now."

Her breath hitched. Her eyes welled with tears. "I can't tell you what I don't know. I couldn't possibly . . ."

His hands cut off her air supply, fingers squeezing hard. She struggled violently as her lungs fought for air, but he held her helpless. She saw black around the edges of her vision, her hands batting at his and then finally falling to her sides. He let go and she slumped forward, gasping for breath.

"Talk, you bitch. I don't believe in coincidences. You come here from Sea Haven where you just happen to know a Prakenskii, and then someone blows my father's head off." His hands settled around her throat again. "Where is he? How's he going to get out of the country?"

"I don't know," she wailed. "I swear . . ."

He cut her off a second time, fingers viciously digging into her neck, applying pressure so that she felt almost giddy. Then she was light-headed and dizzy. Her air was gone and she fought him again. Tears ran down her face and her fingernails ripped at his arms and the backs of his hands. Once again she began to lose her ability to fight, her arms like lead. Instantly he let her go again.

"There's no sign of anyone on the roof. No shells, no scrap of paper. No disturbance in the dust or dirt," the lead guard told Uri, clearly getting the information over his cell. "There was a suitcase containing a weapon, but it was blown to bits."

Lissa fought for breath, one hand going to her throat. Already it felt bruised and swollen. There was no talking to him, so she didn't bother to try. She just kept her head down, fighting to draw as much air into her lungs as possible.

Uri swore over and over, savagely, his anger raw and wild. "These men are ghosts. You aren't going to see any signs of them. But there are cameras everywhere. In the building. On the stairs. In the elevator. Out on the street. There's no way to miss all of them."

He began to walk fast again, dragging Lissa with him through the tunnel. She counted the steps to herself, still struggling to breathe properly. Her high heels clicked loudly on the paved flooring, much louder than the boots of the soldiers. From the blueprints she'd studied, she knew they were more than halfway through and just up ahead was a small room, they had been certain, for prisoners.

The tunnel was the perfect place for interrogating prisoners. No one knew of its existence. It was soundproof and they could torture their prisoner for days or even months if they desired. No one would ever find the missing person. No one would ever know. The small room had been designed solely with interrogation in mind. Electricity ran to the room. There were manacles and chains actually incorporated into the wall. She knew because Casimir had entered the tunnels and explored them, knowing she would be taken into them. She dreaded, but knew, she would end up in that terrible room.

Uri yanked the door open and thrust her inside, the hand

on her back hitting her so hard she flew forward and fell to her knees. The rough pavers scraped, ripping her nylons and lacerating her skin. She didn't try to rise, frozen to the spot, afraid to move. Her body trembled and she wept continuously, the picture of abject despair and misery. She was going for both, and hoped to throw dazed and confused in there as well.

Uri didn't appear to buy into her innocence. He caught her by her hair and dragged her so that she had to crawl on her hands and knees to the chair bolted to the floor. One shoe came off just inside the door where he'd first pushed her, and the second was ripped off as she crawled. He hauled her up by her hair, slapping her viciously across the face repeatedly.

Lissa raised both hands to try to protect herself, but there was no getting away from his attack. She had to fight her every instinct to attack him, trying desperately to act like an innocent woman caught up in something she had no idea of. She had no weapons on her and that was just as well. She wouldn't have been able to stop herself from retaliating. She hadn't expected it to be so difficult to be passive, pleading and sobbing when she wanted to defend herself with every bit of training she had.

He slammed her down into the chair and pointed a finger at her. "You stay there or I swear I'll cut your throat and be done with it."

She nodded vigorously, trying to swallow a sob, cowering in the chair, staring at him with frightened eyes. Her face was swelling. She could actually see the bruise rising under her eye. Her cheek throbbed and burned. Her lip was cut and she could feel it swelling. Her fingernails were broken from clawing at his arms, and there was some satisfaction in knowing the scores on his arms and hands were deep.

There were no clocks in the room. She knew Uri would want his prisoner to have no idea of the passing of time, hours or minutes, days or weeks. They would suffer, and time would seem to stretch out endlessly.

Staring like a terrified rabbit, she studied her enemy as he gave out orders to his men. They rushed to do his bidding, leaving behind two men to guard him. When the room was empty, he turned and looked at her. Defensively, she drew her knees up, and put her hands up on top of them as if she could ward him off.

He stared at her for a long while, the cat playing with the cornered mouse, deliberately prolonging the moment, letting her nerves scream in terrified anticipation. "So, Lissa." His voice had gone gentle. His cold demeanor was far worse than his fury. He walked toward her. "You really need to talk to me. This is your one chance to come clean. I don't care about your part in this. I just want the shooter. His name. I'm not asking you for anything else. Just his name. This man killed my father."

She gave a broken sob, staring at him, mesmerized, a canary trapped by a large, hungry cat. She jammed her fist in her mouth to still the sound of her weeping. Her eyes grew bigger as he stalked across the room toward her. When he got close, she threw her hand out as if that flimsy defense could possibly stop him. As she did so, she glanced at her watch. She just had to stay alive a little longer.

Shaking her head, she hunched in on herself. "Don't hurt me. I swear to you, I came here because *you* invited me. Before coming here, I was in Germany, at a hotel there, and before that, one of the hotels in Italy. I didn't do anything. How could I have?" Her trembling voice rose a few notes higher as he closed in on her like a predatory animal.

"Shh." He put a finger to his lips, his voice pitched low. Very soft.

Lissa covered her mouth with her hand as if that was the only way she could be assured she obeyed his orders exactly. She didn't take her eyes from him as he stepped very, very close to her.

Bending, Uri put a hand on either armrest, leaning into her. "Take a breath, Lissa. I want you to think about this for a moment. Can you do that? Think about what I tell you before you answer me?"

So reasonable. So quiet. Keeping her hand pressed to her mouth, she nodded her head vigorously up and down. Her hair, already coming out of the loose weave, spilled down around her face in long red sheets.

"The Prakenskiis are killers. Every last one of them. It seems strange that you come from a very small town all the way to my country and you know one of these killers. You just happen to be from the same little town."

She kept nodding her head, never taking her gaze from his, as if hypnotized by him. More tears fell, but they were silent, as if she didn't dare weep aloud. She didn't lift a hand to wipe them away. Her face was a mask of terror. Dark mascara trickled down her face along with her tears.

"Can you understand how I might think that you helped to set my father up?"

She nodded and then shook her head violently. Vehemently. Denying his charge. Mixed up in how to answer him.

"This man. Ilya Prakenskii. When he found out you were coming here, that we invited you, he forced you to help him, didn't he? These men, these killers, they do things like that. I understand. I know when you're coerced into something, you're really not to blame. He probably threatened you. Did he do that? Did he threaten you?"

Lissa shook her head. "I've never really talked to him," she managed to get out in a small, scared voice. "I was only introduced once. He didn't know I was going to Europe. How would he? Only my family knew."

Uri straightened, and she flinched back, ducking. He shook his head at her, reached deliberately to tuck strands of her bright red hair behind her ear. "That's not the answer I want. You know that, don't you? It isn't a good idea to lie to me."

He struck then, coming at her so fast she didn't see it coming and had no way to deflect. He caught her arm, yanked her from the chair, spun her around so her back was to him, but her arm was locked very high behind her back. He wrenched it up even farther very, very fast. Hard. Twisting viciously as he did so. There was an audible crack. Lissa screamed as pain radiated up her arm to her shoulder, down through her body to the pit of her heaving stomach. She fell to her knees, catching herself with her good arm.

She tried to breathe away the pain, looking around her to get her bearings, the long sheets of hair protecting her face as she did so. She heard the beep of her watch as her alarm went off and she scrambled forward on her knees. He kicked her with his impeccable dress shoes, the ones he wore so elegantly with his three-piece suit. She sprawled out on the pavers, glanced over her shoulder to see him coming at her again and then dove for the only cover in the room. He had a desk, a very heavy desk set up facing the chair bolted to the floor, so he could work right there while his prisoner watched him. She scuttled beneath the desk, using her left hand to depress the little tiny button built into her watch. The one that looked like it belonged on the watch to wind it.

The explosion was loud in the tunnel, rock and dirt falling with a terrible roar. She heard rocks pelting the desk and she ducked lower still, making herself as small as possible. She heard the yells and grunts of the two guards. Uri's startled yell. The sound of human voices cut off abruptly, and then someone screamed. That sound too was cut off.

She lay beneath the desk, her legs curled tight under her, cradling her arm, straining to hear anything. When no sound was forthcoming, and all the dirt and debris seemed to have settled, she crawled out from under the desk. The top was cracked nearly in two, and sagging in the middle where the split was, a large rock was resting on it. It was impossible to see the surface, covered as it was in dirt and dust.

The room was nearly filled with various-sized rocks, far more dirt, and steel bars that had been in the concrete used to hold the tunnel in place. Dust swirled in the air, forcing her to cover her nose and mouth.

She picked her way to where Uri lay, half buried under a pile of rocks. His gaze jumped to her face. Bright red blood bubbled around his lips and nose. She could see that his injuries were too severe for him to live. She sat down beside him, careful of her arm.

"All those young children your father took from their parents, the parents he *murdered*, those children served their country. They took orders and gave up their own lives to carry out your father's orders. You rewarded them by sending killers after them. You had to have known that sooner or later one or more of them would retaliate."

She looked around her, taking in the fallen rocks and destroyed tunnel. "You're so predictable. Kostya always preferred underground for his dirty work. He liked to have escape tunnels and little places to interrogate his prisoners so there was no chance he could be discovered. Every single one of those very skilled assassins your father had trained knew that about him."

She turned back to him with a little smile. "They study their targets. I study mine. That's all you ever were, Uri, a target. They'll work frantically to dig us out of here. You'll be dead. Your men will be dead. They'll pull me free, battered and bruised with a broken arm, but alive. I'll be a heroine for their newspapers. Of course I'll say what a wonderful man you were and how we were drinking champagne one moment and the next someone was shooting at us. I look quite convincing weeping, don't I?"

He coughed and blood poured out of his mouth.

"That doesn't look good. Your lungs are filling up with blood. Nasty way to die, although it seems fairly fitting, since you intended to bring your prisoners here to die." She smoothed back his hair. "I'm married to one of those men." She smiled at him. "I make him very, very happy. I intend to continue to make him happy. He'll be having a great life, and believe me, we won't think about you ever again."

He tried to spit at her, but he couldn't. He only succeeded

in making more blood dribble down his chin. She made no move to wipe it away. Instead she stared at him just as dispassionately as he had her.

"It was so easy. You thought you were so clever inviting me here, telling me all that nonsense about how you read about me in a magazine. The truth was, Gavriil came to Sea Haven. He led you right there. You knew he settled on the farm with my sister and you figured you'd get me here, introduce me to this room and get the information you wanted about the Prakenskii brothers. I knew that's what happened the moment you sent me the invite. Still, I figured killing you would be a good thing, so here I am."

His eyes clouded over and more blood bubbled around his lips. He coughed, spewing blood, and then his head turned slightly and his staring eyes went glassy. She waited a heartbeat before checking his pulse. He was gone. She checked the other two soldiers, found them dead and settled back to wait for her rescuers.

Her arm hurt like crazy. It was difficult to breathe the air in the small room. There was also the terrible feeling of claustrophobia, knowing more rocks could fall at any time, but that didn't matter. Her family was safe. Her sisters. Casimir's brothers. She was still alive, and somewhere out there, her husband waited for her.

20

CASIMIR pushed open the hospital door, his heart thudding so hard, his chest hurt. Two days of hell. Pure, fucking hell. He was done. Finished. He didn't give a damn what Giacinta thought. He'd give her the moon if that's what she wanted, but not this. Not ever again. She had done her last job and she was going to be glued to his side where he could see her twenty-four hours a day and ensure she was alive and well.

The hospital room was small, the bed dominating the interior. Instantly his gaze was caught and held by the small figure lying there asleep. He drew in his breath, feeling the raw, *hideous* terror that had gripped him for those endless hours when she was trapped in the collapsed tunnel with Uri Sorbacov.

Killing Uri Sorbacov with the tunnel collapsing seemed a good idea. They both knew Uri would take Lissa to the interrogation room. He might not know Gavriil Prakenskii was residing in Sea Haven, but it was known worldwide that Ilya was. Every tabloid and gossip magazine happily reported his every move. The moment Casimir had pulled the trigger and taken out Kostya Sorbacov, the man who had ordered his parents murdered, they knew Uri would turn on Lissa.

Casimir pressed his fingertips to his temple, still frozen, his feet refusing to move to cross the space to her side. Stupid. *Stupid* idea. When they conceived of it, both thought it brilliant. A perfect plan. And then the tunnel collapsed and Giacinta was caught in it and Casimir had no idea if she was dead or alive. For hours. Long, terrible hours of absolute terror. The seconds took hours. The minutes did. He was sick with the need to know if she was alive.

He'd tried to use their connection, pressing his thumb time after time into the center of his palm, but that had failed him as well. And that's when the terror rose to such a level he nearly lost every vestige of control and discipline he'd acquired with his years of training and practice.

He saw them pull her out of the wreckage of the hotel, her body limp, on a stretcher, rushed to the hospital. He couldn't get near her. She was under heavy guard, an American caught in the collapse of one of their hotels.

Casimir forced his body to move. He knew he didn't have much time. There were guards outside her door. His credentials had been put together fast. The American Embassy had sent him to check on one of their citizens. He took a breath, forced it through his burning lungs and stepped up to the bed.

She was asleep, her long lashes covering her eyes. One eye was swollen, her face covered in bruises. There was a cast on her arm. Each breath she drew in seemed labored, as if her body hurt. His eyes burned. His throat clogged. He took her hand and stroked the back of it, bending down to brush his mouth over her temple.

Immediately the lashes fluttered. "Casimir." She whispered his name, her voice drowsy. "I knew you'd come."

"Shh, *moya lyubov*, you need to sleep."

She tried to smile, and then winced when the movement pulled at the cut on her lip. He felt the wince like a punch in his gut. Hard. Painful. Taking his air. "You got these injuries from Uri, not the cave-in."

"I'm all right now." Her voice was low. She tried again to open her eyes, the lashes fluttering again, but she didn't succeed. "You're free. That's all that matters."

It wasn't all that mattered to him. He pressed her fingertips to his mouth. "You have to know something, *malyshka*. I would give you the moon, anything you ask me for, I'll do my best to make it yours, but not this. Never again. I won't let you do this again. You have to know something about me, Giacinta. You have to learn this right now. My woman doesn't take this kind of risk again. It's not going to happen."

This time her eyes did manage to open. The sight of her one eye so swollen and black and blue made his stomach lurch. He kissed her fingers while her gaze drifted over his face. She was looking at a very distinguished gentleman with graying hair, wearing a suit. His identification hung from a clip off the pocket of his vest.

"I'm not trying to be a dictator, *malyshka*. It's in my nature to be one, I won't lie about that, but I will never go through this again. You're going to be glued to my side twenty-four hours a day where I can make certain you're alive."

"I love you, Casimir," she whispered, and her lashes drifted down over her eyes.

She was alive. That was all that mattered. But he was dead serious. It didn't matter if she took him that way or not, his woman would be safe. Hell. She wasn't going outside her home to rake the leaves off the ground without him.

Casimir hadn't known it was possible to be terrified. Emotions like fear had been beaten out of him years ago. He always believed that his instructors had done the worst to all of them so anything that happened after that was nothing to them. There was no way to prepare for having someone you loved with every breath you took be in danger. He just knew he couldn't go through that again. Those minutes and hours where he didn't know if she was alive or dead. That time when she was out of his sight, in danger, with men who had no respect for life.

He kissed her fingertips again, looking down at her. The woman who held his heart in her hands. He couldn't stay. But he'd be back. "Not ever again, Giacinta," he whispered. Meaning it.

LISSA had been prepared for the questions from the police. Someone from the embassy was always close, but truthfully, she wasn't concerned. No one questioned her story. She really was Lissa Piner from the United States. She really did come to St. Petersburg at the request of Uri and Kostya Sorbacov to talk about chandeliers for their hotel.

They were celebrating their deal with champagne when a bullet came through the window and ended Kostya's life. Uri and his men had rushed them down into a tunnel and into a room where they were going to stay to be safe while Uri's men had scattered to get information on the shooter. The tunnel had collapsed with no warning.

Lissa had been fully prepared to answer the questions from the police. She was careful not to repeat her story over and over without changing or adding little details so it didn't sound rehearsed. She hadn't been prepared for the reporters. They'd been a nightmare. She told herself it was good for her business to get so much publicity, but the reporters made it difficult to be with Casimir. All she wanted was to be with him.

He'd come to the hospital three times during her stay there. That scared her. He was placing himself in terrible danger, but nothing she said dissuaded him. She had one more night in the hotel the Russian government had put her in before the doctors would sign off on her going home. One more night and she was back with Casimir and they could go home.

The knock came and her heart nearly stopped. He *wouldn't* dare. This was a government hotel. Cameras were everywhere. They only had one more night to get through and then they were home free. She hurried across the room to the door, putting her eye to the little peephole. She couldn't see a thing. She knew, though. Shc knew by the way her body reacted. The way her heart had gone crazy. It would always go crazy when he was near. Her husband. Casimir Prakenskii. She *loved* that. Loved that once they left this place, he would be able to reclaim his true birthright. All of his brothers would be able to without fear of consequences.

Lissa flung open the door. Casimir stepped inside, kicked the door closed and swept her into his arms. Lifting her, holding her to his body so close, so tight, she couldn't breathe, but she didn't care. She circled his neck with her one good arm, closing her eyes, feeling safe for the first time in more than a week.

Casimir carried her to the bed, sank down onto the mattress and cradled her on his lap. His hands framed her face. He didn't speak, his eyes staring down into hers. He was wearing contacts. Hazel eyes this time, but she would know him anywhere. It didn't matter what role he played, to her, he would always be Casimir.

His mouth came down on hers. Gently. So gently it brought tears to her eyes. His tongue flicked along the cut on her mouth. It was nearly completely gone now. The swelling was gone from her face, but she did have a lot of color here and there. His mouth wandered over the bruises, brushing little kisses over every single one of them. She didn't have to tell him what happened in that room. He knew just by looking at her. She knew if she gave him details it would just make him crazy.

"I should never have let you go into that situation," he whispered against her lips. His tongue dipped again, ran along the seam of her mouth.

He kissed her again and this time she opened her mouth to him. An invitation. He took her up on it and swept them both away. She could taste passion. There was always that explosive chemistry leaping between them, but this time, there was something so profound, so beautiful, she wanted to weep.

His arms were strong, almost steel surrounding her, yet he was gentle. His mouth was hot, commanding, yet tender. Loving. She felt that in his kiss and the way he held her, treating her like she was made of the most fragile glass in the world. She felt fragile. Sitting in that terrible room with three dead bodies, the air impossible to breathe, her arm excruciatingly painful, especially if she moved it, had been the thing of horror movies.

She had crawled back under the desk, listening to the creaking and groaning of the debris overhead. She thought she smelled gas at one point and feared that might kill her before the hotel collapsed in on itself right over top of her. She had had nightmares every single night since they had pulled her out of the rubble. Still, she held on to the fact that the Prakenskii brothers were free for the first time in their lives since Sorbacov had murdered their parents.

"You shouldn't be here, Casimir," she reprimanded. Holding him. Grateful he'd come. Knowing it was a terrible risk and yet so happy he was there.

"Did you think I could stay away when I finally have the chance to be alone with you? I know how to slip past a camera. We practiced in these very hotels. I'm very familiar with them." He tipped her face up to him. "That bastard managed to do a lot of damage in the short time he had you." Very gently he set her on her feet. "Take your clothes off, Giacinta. I want to look at you."

She shook her head. Backed away from him. "I don't think that's such a good idea. Let's just be grateful we're both alive, we got the job done and we're going home tomorrow."

He reached out and curled his long fingers around her leg, preventing her from moving. He stood up and closed the distance between them in one long stride, standing in front of her. Close. Both hands went to the buttons of her blouse.

"It's late. You need to be in bed. We've got a long plane

ride ahead of us. Before I tuck you in, I want to see what that bastard did to you."

"Honey, really, I don't want you to." Both hands went up to stop his.

He didn't stop. Lissa sighed. Casimir was always sweet to her, but there was a side to him that was ruthless and dangerous. A side that she usually didn't see because he never directed it toward her. He was right on the edge of that. Implacable. Letting her know without words she wasn't getting her way on this, but she had to try.

"You're already blaming yourself for something we both agreed to. It was our plan together, Casimir. I could tell at the hospital you were upset."

He frowned, his jaw hard, stony. His eyes glittering with a smoldering fury. "Upset? Is that what you think I was? It was *hours*, Giacinta, *hours* before they pulled you out of there. I couldn't get to you. I didn't know if you were dead or alive."

His voice was low, but it made her wince. It was a lash, a whip of sheer anger. She knew his anger was directed at himself. He had her blouse open and he peeled the soft material off one arm and then very gently pulled the other side down over her cast.

"You didn't see yourself lying so still in that bed, *malyshka*. Your face so pale you looked like a ghost. Bruises and swelling. Your lip." He touched the small, already healing cut. His gaze dropped to her chest, her breasts encased in the lacy bra. He closed his eyes and stepped away from her, swearing in his native language over and over.

Lissa watched him pace across the room. The temperature rose alarmingly. The room took on a reddish glow. She felt his anger, a tangible thing, a force of destruction, filling every bit of space around her. She knew what he saw. Uri had gotten in a few punches, as well as a kick or two. She still bore those bruises.

"It's over," she reminded.

He swung around, fingers curled into two tight fists. Then he was on her, his hands yanking at her jeans, dragging them down her hips. She was grateful she was barefoot because he all but picked her up, tossed her on the bed and pulled them off her legs. He would have taken her shoes right off had she been wearing any. Lissa tried to curl in on herself but his hand caught at her hip, stilling her.

"Don't you fucking move, Giacinta," he snapped, harsh this time.

She took a deep breath and tried to relax under his furious glare. There were more bruises on her body. Suffice to say, the beast wasn't tamed. Scrapes on her knees and legs from being dragged across the rough pavers. A large bruise where Uri had kicked her hard.

"Turn over."

"Casimir." He would *detest* what he saw.

"Turn the fuck over."

She winced. He rarely swore in English. It was almost always in Russian, but he was so close to tipping over the edge into a place she didn't want to ever see him go. Reluctantly she turned onto her stomach, careful of her arm. She put her head down on the pillow and closed her eyes.

Lissa heard his sharply indrawn breath. He sank onto the bed beside her. His hand moved down her back, settled into the curve of her spine. He hesitated a moment and then his fingertips brushed along the terrible bruise on her hip and left cheek of her buttocks where Uri's shoe had landed, driving her forward.

"Giacinta." He breathed her name.

Oh God. He sounded like he was weeping. Her heart thudded. Wept with him. She tried to turn, but he kept one hand pressed between her shoulder blades, preventing her from turning over or really lifting her head high enough to see him. She felt his breath, warm and soothing over the bruise. His lips touched her. So gently, like a whisper against her skin.

He stayed like that for a long time, his head resting in the small of her back, one hand between her shoulder blades, one arm wrapped around her rib cage, palm cupping her breast. She didn't talk. What was there to say? She loved him.

She would have given anything to take away those terrible hours when he didn't know if she was dead or alive. She would have protected and spared him anything she could, because she loved him more than life itself. She couldn't be sorry for their choice. She had known the risks going into it, and those risks were well worth the outcome. Her husband, the love of her life, was free.

"I don't want you to sleep with clothes tonight. I know I can't make love to you, but I don't want anything between us."

"Honey," she murmured, "I'm not so battered that we can't make love."

He stood up and she was able to turn over. She watched as he took off his shirt. He shook his head. "No, I'm selfish, *malyshka*, but not that selfish."

His hands dropped to the zipper of his slacks and her mouth watered. He might not be that selfish, but she wasn't so certain she could say the same. Naked, all those wonderful muscles flowing enticingly, he slid next to her and drew up the covers. Turning, he circled her waist and pulled her in close to him, the way he always did. He liked close. Very close. Lissa was happy to oblige.

She had missed him. Missed the feel of his warmth. His hot skin. The way his body was so hard and solid, making her feel safe. She needed safe after enduring all those hours in that horrible room, praying the rescuers would find her soon. She'd never tell him. He was already angry, blaming himself. But she still needed him real and solid wrapped around her.

Lissa didn't think she'd drift off to sleep so fast, but truthfully, she was still exhausted physically from the beating and the pain in her arm. With Casimir's body tight against hers, his heat melding with hers, she felt cocooned in warmth.

She jerked awake two hours later, her heart pounding, his name on her lips, in her mouth. She'd used him as her talisman a hundred times under the desk while the rocks creaked and dirt kept falling. She lifted her head and looked at him.

She'd left the lamp across the room on low because she didn't want to be in the dark, not after spending so many hours in the dark of that sadistic interrogation room. She could see Casimir's face. He was on his back again, like usual. He always started on his side, but then, once fully asleep, he turned on his back, taking her with him. The way he slept was very familiar to her now. She liked that he was sprawled out on the bed, taking up space. A *lot* of space. He liked to pull her body over his so she was on top of him, her head pillowed on his chest. One arm was slung across her back. His other hand was on her butt.

He was beautiful. Masculine. She studied his face a long time. Watching him breathe. His lashes were far too long for a man's but didn't detract in the least from his hard, male features. She liked the little bit of shadow on his jaw, shivering a little when she remembered how it felt rasping against her inner thighs.

They were supposed to meet on the plane. Not even in the airport, but the plane itself. Their seats together. Two strangers meeting. She should have known he would come to her. She missed him every moment they were apart, and he certainly didn't love her any less. She loved him all the more for being there, even though he was a little crazy for taking the risk.

She ran her hand over his chest, letting the pads of her fingers absorb the feel of his muscles. She loved that she lay over top of him sleeping and he'd put her there. She especially loved waking up with his body under hers. She shifted just a few inches and she was straddling him, her legs on either side of his hips. That felt—amazing. Wanton. Definitely erotic.

He had said he couldn't make love to her. Nothing had been said about her making love to him. She would just have to be careful that she didn't bonk him with her klutzy cast. She took her time, moving slowly, lazily, savoring every moment she had, committing his body to memory, burning it into her mind through her fingertips and lips. Tasting his skin with her mouth. With her tongue. Tracing her name into his muscles. His rib cage. His impressive six-pack that was more like an eighteen-pack. She scooted down his body, one slow inch at a time. Every inch of him was worshiped, because that's what she did—she worshiped him, and he needed to know that. She wanted him to feel the overwhelming *intense* love she had for him.

She had woken three times to him in her hospital room. Casimir. Risking everything. His very life. Just to check on her. Just to make certain she was safe and unharmed. Love welled up, so strong, an almost painful, *terrible* love, one she knew would always last. He would always be her first thought. He would be her last thought.

"Malyshka."

She loved that he called her baby in his language. Well, not baby exactly, more like little girl, but all the same, she loved the endearment, especially when he said it in a velvet soft voice that seemed to slide over her skin in a long caress.

She licked along his hip bone, sliding her tongue along the edge, wondering at the fact that she could be so lucky. So happy. She was alive when she hadn't expected to be. She was with her husband. *Husband.* The best man in the world.

"Casimir." She breathed his name against his belly. Her hand caressed his inner thighs. She loved how strong they were. She especially loved the way his muscles tightened under her brushstrokes. She kissed him, right along the sweet line of dark hair rising around his amazing erection.

"You're hurt, Giacinta. You need care right now."

"I do." She murmured her agreement and licked along his long, beautiful shaft. So thick. She loved how hard he was, just like steel. Her body reacted, going damp at the thought of him inside her. She loved how that steel seemed to be encased in velvet, soft and silky, sliding inside her body, giving her such pleasure.

He groaned softly in reaction to her tongue, his body shuddering.

"I do need care." She murmured her soft agreement, pleased with his reaction. Her sex contracted, a powerful reaction to his.

Her fingers moved up the inside of his right thigh until she found his heavy sac, already tight. She stroked more caresses there while her tongue ensured his shaft was wet and slick. Her fingers moved lower, brushing that soft spot that had him groaning and shifting his legs restlessly. She chose that moment to take him in her mouth, engulfing him, sliding her lips tight around him.

His hips bucked. She tightened her suction, determined she had the control. Her fingers never stopped their worship of him. Her mouth settled in for enjoyment of her task. She was merciless, driving him higher and higher, wanting him to feel the intensity of the love she had for him.

"I'm close, *golubushka*." He groaned the admission. The warning.

She immediately slid up his body, straddling him. "Sit up, Casimir." She kept her fist wrapped firmly around his heavy erection.

He complied instantly, his back toward the headboard, Lissa on his lap. She kept her fingers curled around the base of his shaft and slowly lowered her body so she could impale herself. She kept control, going slow, her tight muscles protesting the invasion, giving away reluctantly.

His arms went around her body, holding her close to him so that her nipples brushed his chest. Her breath exploded when she was fully seated on him. Instantly his arms tightened even more until her body seemed to melt into his and there was no separation between them. It seemed as if they shared the same skin. She felt his every heartbeat. His every breath.

She wrapped her cast around his back and leaned into him as she rode him. Slow. Easy. Her muscles tight. Her body hot. A lazy, sexy ride that she hoped made him feel as loved as she was trying to convey with her body. He nuzzled her shoulder, his mouth on the side of her neck. She'd have a strawberry there.

She rode him for a long while, holding him close, savoring their bond. "I love you," she whispered into his ear. "I love you more than life, Casimir. I'll always love you." She spiraled down his shaft, a slow, tight fist gloving him. Stroking him with scorching-hot caresses. Slowly milking him. An exquisite torture.

He bit her gently, right where he'd sucked and licked. The spot that drove her wild. The little bite of pain sent sparks radiating through her body. She cried out. Dug her nails into his shoulder.

"Not yet, *malyshka.*"

She took a breath. She was so close. So very close. She hadn't thought it was possible, not going so slow. Not with her doing all the work. She hadn't even recognized that she was coiling so tight, the pressure building, the fire burning so hot. She was so busy working him, wanting this moment for him, that she hadn't even seen that she was so close.

"I don't want it over. Not yet."

She breathed deeply. For him. Stopping herself. For him. She didn't want to end this moment either. She was in his arms—safe. She'd always be safe with him.

"I love you, Giacinta Prakenskii. So much. You're my life. My everything. There's no more danger for you. No more putting yourself in harm's way. I can't ever do that again. Those hours without knowing . . ." His body shuddered against hers. His hand slid down to her bottom, fingers digging deep as he urged her body into a deeper, faster rhythm.

Fire streaked through her. She actually felt the stark terror unfolding in him for her. She thought it was the worst, those hours under the desk while overhead the roof creaked and spread more debris. On the floor were the dead men, crushed beneath the heavy fall of cement, rock and dirt. His terror was worse. She knew that. He'd been safe. He hadn't known what happened to her.

"Say it," he demanded, his other hand sliding down the curve of her back to her hip. "Say you're finished."

"Anything for you, honey," she whispered.

"Anything?" His hips bucked up hard into her.

The fire turned scorching. Her breath left her lungs in a rush. "The world."

"Babies?"

"Anything. All of it."

"Now, *malyshka*, with me now."

She fragmented. Shattered into a million pieces. He was there. Casimir. To catch her. To keep her safe. To put all those pieces back together. He was there. She laid her head against him, gasping for breath while her body rocked around his, gripped his like a vise, a velvet, silken glove, squeezing and milking so that he was right there with her. She would have collapsed, but his arms held her tight against him. They held each other for a long time.

"I wanted you to feel loved," she whispered.

"I feel loved," he answered. "I want to go home. I've never had a home, and that farm of yours feels like the real thing."

"It is the real thing. And it's ours. We're married." She lifted her head and frowned up at him, suspicion in her eyes. "You don't have a really weird chair or something ugly you're going to want to put in our front room, do you?"

He laughed and she felt his laughter vibrate right through his body to hers. She wanted to hear his laughter until the day she died. "I love you," she whispered again. Meaning it. She had that now. Her own family. Her sisters. His brothers. Casimir Prakenskii. Her husband.

Keep reading for an excerpt from the first book
in the new Shadow series by Christine Feehan

SHADOW RIDER

Coming in 2016 from Piatkus

STEFANO Ferraro pulled on soft leather driving gloves, his dark blue eyes taking a long, slow scan around the neighborhood. *His* neighborhood. His family knew everything that happened there. It was a good place to live, the people loyal. A close-knit community. It was safe because his family kept it safe. Women could walk the streets alone at night. Children could play outside without their parents fearing for them.

He knew every shop owner, every homeowner by name. The Ferraro family territory started just on the edge of Little Italy. He knew every inch of Little Italy as well, and those residing and working there knew him and his family. Crime stopped at the edge of the Ferraro territory. That invisible line was known by even the most hardened of criminals, and no one dared to cross it because retaliation was always swift and brutal.

He glanced at his watch, knowing he didn't have a lot of time. The jet was fueled and waiting for his arrival. He needed to get into his car and get the hell to the airport, but something held him there. Whatever it was, the feeling he had was disturbing. The compulsion to stay was strong, and anytime that happened, every Ferraro knew there was trouble coming. He carefully and very quietly shut the door to his Maserati, rounding the hood and then retreating to the sidewalk.

Urgency was always about work, and nothing ever interfered with the Ferraro family business. Nothing. He played hard when he played, but work was important and dangerous, and he kept his head in the game when it was time to get down to business. He needed to get his ass moving, but he still couldn't force himself, in spite of all the years of discipline, to get into his car and get to the airport. The compulsion in him was strong, not to be ignored, and he had no choice but to give in to it.

A voice drifted to him above the normal sounds of the street. Elusive. Mysterious. Musical. He turned his head as two women rounded the corner just at the very edge of his territory and began walking deeper into it. He recognized Joanna Masci immediately. Her uncle, Pietro Masci, was a longtime resident in Ferraro territory, born and raised there. He owned the local deli shop, a very popular place for residents to buy their produce and meats. Pietro had taken Joanna in when his brother died years earlier. A good man, everyone in the neighborhood liked Pietro and respected him.

It wasn't Joanna who caught his interest. The woman walking beside her was dressed totally inappropriately for the weather. No coat. No sweater. There were rips in her blue jeans, although the jeans clung lovingly to her body. And she had a figure. She wasn't thin like most girls preferred; she actually had curves. Her hair was wild. Thick. Very shiny. She wore part of it pulled back from her face in an intricate, thick braid, but the rest tumbled down her back in waves. The color was rich. Vibrant. A true black. He couldn't see her eyes from that distance, but she was shivering in the cold Chicago weather, and for some reason he had an entirely primal reaction to her constant shivering. His gut knotted and a slow burn of rage began in his belly.

It wasn't her looks that caught his interest or made him stand utterly still. It was her shadow. The sun was throwing light perfectly to create tall, full shadows. Hers leaked long tentacles. Thin. Like streaks reaching out toward the shadows around her. Everywhere there was a shadow, hers connected to it with the long feelers—with long tubes. His breath hitched. His lungs seized.

She was the last thing he ever expected to happen because, frankly, a woman like her was so rare. He didn't know how to feel about it, but suddenly there was nothing else more important, not even Ferraro family business.

He had his cell phone out and punched in numbers without taking his gaze off of her. "Franco, I'm going to need to take the helicopter this morning. I have business to attend to before I can leave. Half an hour. Yeah. I'll meet you." He ended the call, still watching the two women and the strange shadow the stranger cast as he punched in another number. "Henry, I'm not going to use the car after all. Please return it to the garage for me." The Ferraro family had a temperature-controlled garage with a fleet of various cars and motorcycles. They all liked them fast. Henry took care of all vehicles and kept them in top running order.

Stefano snapped the phone shut and stepped off the sidewalk to cross the street. He held up his hand imperiously and of course the cars stopped for him. Everything stopped for him when he demanded it.

FRANCESCA Capello prayed she wouldn't pass out as she walked with Joanna toward the deli. She'd never felt so weak in her life. She was hungry. She'd made tomato soup using ketchup and water, but that was all she'd had to eat for the last two days. If she didn't get this job, she was going to have to do something desperate, like ask the homeless woman she'd given her coat to where the nearest soup kitchen was.

Maybe it hadn't been such a great idea to give the woman

her coat. Her clothes weren't the best for a job interview, but they were all she had. She needed the job and she definitely wasn't looking very professional in her faded but very soft vintage blue jeans—a perfect fit, which was rare for her to find in the thrift stores. There were holes in the knees and one small one on her upper thigh, but some of the designer jeans featured rips. The tears in her jeans just happened to be from real wear.

"Wow, the deli's packed," Joanna observed as they stopped in front of a glass door. She yanked it open and ushered Francesca inside.

Francesca thought she might faint from all the smells of food. Her stomach growled and she pushed on it with one hand, hoping to quiet it. People were three deep at the counter and every small table throughout the room was filled.

"Popular place," she observed, because she *had* to say something. She'd let Joanna do most of the talking because, well, she *couldn't* talk. She wasn't bursting into tears in front of her friend. Not after all Joanna had done for her.

"I told you." Joanna flashed a grin, caught her arm and tugged her through the crowd to the window on the far side opposite the door. "We can wait here until Tio Pietro has a couple of minutes."

Francesca didn't think he was going to be free anytime soon. Now all the smells blended together, making her feel nauseous. She didn't want to throw up right there in his deli. She was fairly certain that wouldn't get her the job, but her stomach was so empty.

Her lungs burned from holding her breath, waiting for Joanna's uncle to get free enough to come interview her. Joanna had promised her the job. Francesca had spent nearly every cent she had—the money she'd borrowed from Joanna—getting to Chicago and into the tiny apartment right on the very edge of Little Italy. She had nothing left for food or clothing. She *had* to get this job. She could survive another week if she was very, very careful, but not much longer. She'd be living on the street with Dina, the homeless woman. She'd done that once already and it wasn't fun. Truthfully, she wasn't altogether certain that her apartment was better than the street. Still, it had a roof.

Francesca couldn't stop shivering, no matter how hard she tried. The cold was biting and penetrated right to the bone. It didn't help that after the wild storm there were puddles everywhere, impossible to avoid, and her shoes and socks were soaking wet. The soles were thin and the water had easily gotten inside her shoes. Not only were her feet wet, but her toes were numb.

Still, if she got the job, this was the perfect place for her. The neighborhood was small. Everything was in walking distance. She didn't own a car, or anything else for that matter. She was starting over, determined to rise from the ashes like a phoenix. But seriously, if Pietro didn't hurry up, she'd be on the floor soon.

If she didn't need food and to warm up so bad, she would have been happy with the evidence that the store was popular as a small specialty grocery store and sandwich shop. Clearly Pietro needed help. She could handle a cash register, no problem. She could make sandwiches. She'd held a job in a deli while putting herself through school and she was certain this would be a piece of cake.

The door opened and a blast of cold air swept into the shop, chilling her further. She turned her head and froze. She had never in her life seen a man more gorgeous or more dangerous. He was tall, broad-shouldered, tough as nails and totally ripped. His hair was jet black and seemed messy, but artfully so, as if even his hair refused to disobey him.

He wore a three-piece dark charcoal pinstriped suit that had to have been tailor-made in Italy or France and looked to be worth a fortune. His tie was a darker gray to match the thin stripes in his suit and was worn over a lighter shade of charcoal shirt. He wore butter-soft gloves and a long, dark cashmere overcoat. Even the shoes on his feet looked like he'd paid a fortune for them. He made her acutely aware of her shabby clothes.

She wasn't the only one who noticed him. The moment he entered, all chatter in the shop ceased. Completely. No one so much as whispered. No one moved, as if they were all frozen in place. Pietro came to attention. Beside her, Joanna took a deep breath. The atmosphere in the store went from friendly chatter and light-hearted gossip to one of danger.

His face was carved in masculine lines and set in stone. He had a strong jaw covered by a dark shadow. He was easily the most gorgeous man she'd ever seen. His eyes were such an intense blue she almost didn't believe they were natural. The blue eyes swept the room, taking in everything and everyone. She knew he did. So did everyone in the room. Just like her, they were all staring at him. The eyes came back to her. Settled. Narrowed.

The impact was physical. Her breath rushed from her lungs. He could see right through her. She had far too many secrets for him to be looking at her and seeing so much. Worse, his gaze drifted over her, taking in the cropped sweater that molded to her breasts and just barely reached her waist. Her jeans rode a little lower than her waist, so she had to resist pulling at the hem of the sweater, although her fingers automatically curled around the hem to do just that. The sweater was one of the few things she owned that was warm.

His gaze traveled down her holey jeans to her wet shoes and back up to her face. She wished the earth would open up and swallow her. The tension in the deli went up several more notches. Francesca knew why. Not only was this man gorgeous and dangerous, he was angry. A black wall of intense heat filled the room until no one seemed able to breathe. She could actually *feel* his anger shimmering in the air. The room vibrated with his fury.

She found herself trembling and shrinking back under that brilliant blue stare. She didn't understand why he'd singled her out, but he had. His diamond-hard gaze was fixed on her, not on any of the other customers—just her. She took a deep breath and let it out, tugging self-consciously on the hem of her sweater. When she did, his scowl deepened.

"Mr. Ferraro." Pietro stepped around the counter.

Pietro's shoulders were square, his face a mask of concern, his tone respectful. He looked as if he might faint any moment. Everyone did. Francesca didn't understand what was happening, but clearly Joanna was very aware. Her friend trembled and put one hand on Francesca's arm as if to steady herself.

They were all afraid of him. Francesca could see why— he looked and felt dangerous. But every single person in the store? Afraid? Of. This. Man. That was a little terrifying. She wished fervently he would stop looking at her.

The man, Mr. Ferraro, stepped in her direction. He looked—predatory. His gaze didn't waver. Not for one moment. If she wasn't mistaken, he didn't blink either. The crowd instantly parted, just like the Red Sea, leaving a straight path open to her. She felt more vulnerable and exposed than ever. She couldn't even ask Joanna who he was and why everyone was afraid of him or even how they all knew him. Or why his anger would be directed at her.

Everything in her stilled. Unless he knew. Oh, God. He couldn't know. She had nothing left, nowhere to go. If she didn't get this job, she'd be on the street again. Her face burned under his scrutiny. She knew he saw everything. Her thrift store clothes. Her wet shoes. Her lack of makeup. His suit easily cost thousands, as did his coat. His gloves probably cost more than her entire outfit when it had been brand-new. What he spent on his watch could probably buy a car.

She felt her color rise and she couldn't stop it. Her gaze lowered, although she felt defiant. Just because he was wealthy—and he was more than wealthy, anyone with eyes could see that—he had no right to judge her.

God, but he was good-looking. Italian-American. Olive skin. Gorgeous blue eyes and thick black hair that made a woman want to run her fingers through it. No man should be able to look like he did. She tried to look away from him, but something in his steady gaze warned her not to and she didn't dare defy him. She couldn't imagine anyone crossing him. He didn't exactly walk up to her. He stalked, like a great jungle cat emerging from the shadows. Silent. Fluid. Breathtaking.

"Poetry in motion," she murmured under her breath. She'd heard the expression, but now she knew what it meant, how the words could come alive with a man moving.

He stopped abruptly. Right in front of her. Had he heard? She felt more color creeping into her face. A deep red. She was mortified to be singled out of the crowd. That was bad enough, but if he'd heard her . . .

"I'm Stefano Ferraro. You are?" It was a demand, nothing less.

She opened her mouth. Nothing came out. She actually felt paralyzed with fear. Of what, she wasn't certain. Joanna's fingers dug into her arm, hard enough to get her to blurt out her name. "Francesca. Francesca Capello."

"Where the fuck is your coat?" His voice was pitched low. Soft. It sounded menacing, as if all his anger was directed at her because she didn't have on a coat.

She winced at his language and the abruptness of his completely shocking question. She tipped her chin up and instantly his eyes were on her face, following that gesture of defiance. "It isn't your business," she said, keeping her voice as equally low.

A collective gasp went up in the store, reminding her they weren't alone. She *felt* alone, as if there were only the two of them.

"It is my business," he returned. "You're shivering so bad your teeth are chattering. Where the fuck is your coat?"

She opened her mouth to tell him to go to hell, but nothing came out. Not one single word.

"She gave her coat to the homeless woman," Joanna supplied hastily. "On our way here. We were walking along Franklin and there was a woman sitting under the eaves there and she was cold so Francesca gave her coat to her."

"Dina," Francesca muttered.

"Dina?" he repeated.

"She has a name. It's Dina," she repeated before she could stop herself. She knew she sounded snippy, but she didn't care.

"I'm well aware who she is," he said. "I'd like to know who you are."

Francesca was both horrified at his interest and mortified that she was in the spotlight. She sent up a little prayer for the floor to open up and swallow her right there.

This was met with silence, so Joanna jumped to fill the breach. "She's a friend of mine and I talked her into coming here to live from California. Uncle Pietro needed someone to help in the deli and she has tons of experience." The words tripped over one another in her haste to get the information out. "That's what we're doing now, applying for the job."

Francesca was well aware everyone in the store was staring at her, including Pietro. She was certain she looked homeless in her thrift store clothes, but really, the woman on the street had been freezing. Francesca, at least, had four walls to protect her—until the end of the month, and then she'd be sharing a cardboard box with Dina.

"I see." Stefano Ferraro said the words thoughtfully, his eyes still fixed on her. "You know her, Joanna? You vouch for her?"

Joanna nodded her head vigorously, her dark cap of hair flying around her face. Francesca could feel her trembling, which was unusual. Joanna had always had tons of confidence in herself. She'd been popular at school and always, always had an opinion to give. Everyone liked her, yet she was definitely shaking.

Stefano, still watching Francesca's face, pulled out his

wallet, shoved a handful of bills into his coat pocket and then removed the coat. He held it open in front of Francesca.

Her lungs seized. She shook her head and tried to step back but she ran into Joanna's trembling body. Who was this man that everyone was so afraid of? Francesca knew the blood drained from her face, she could feel it. She shook her head again, more vigorously so there could be no mistake that the answer was a resounding, emphatic *no*.

Impatience crossed his face. "I don't have time to fuck around, *bambina*. Get your arms in the coat and come outside with me for a moment. We'll talk." He glanced at his very expensive watch. "I have about two minutes and then I have to be somewhere."

She considered stalling for the two minutes so he'd have to leave, but both Joanna and Pietro looked desperate. He had to be a criminal. Mafia. One of the strong-arm men who came in and took all the money from the stores like on television. He looked far too elegant for that, but he also looked as if he could easily break bones and not break a sweat.

Joanna actually pushed her toward Stefano. Resigned, Francesca turned her back to him, slipping her arms in the sleeves. To her horror, he reached around her to button up the long coat. *Around her.* Caging her in. Her back was against his chest and his arms were long, enclosing her while he buttoned the coat. She felt his warmth. His strength. For the first time that morning, she stopped shivering.

His arms felt enormously strong, his chest an iron wall. More, with every single breath she took in, she breathed him in. His scent. Very masculine. Spicy. He turned her around to face him and then stepped in close to her—too close, because again, she couldn't breathe. The coat was warm. Heaven. Soft. It smelled like him. And he smelled good. He actually made her weak in the knees, unless really, he had nothing to do with it and she was just hungry.

His hand slipped down her arm and his fingers shackled her wrist in a firm grip. She looked up at him, bracing herself for the moment their eyes would meet, but he was looking at Joanna's uncle. He wasn't smiling, but he offered his other hand.

"Pietro. Good to see you. I trust you'll take good care of what's mine." His voice was low, sexy. She actually felt a strange answering vibration move through her body, like a song, a note tuned only to him.

He looked down at her again, and the impact of his eyes was enough to send her into a mini-orgasm. It was the truth whether she liked it or not. Joanna made a little sound in her throat, saving her, allowing her to turn her head toward her friend at Stefano's declaration. Pietro's head jerked up and his gaze shot to Francesca's face. Francesca frowned, trying to read the local language, but she had no idea what had passed as conversation between Pietro and Stefano Ferraro.

Gritting her teeth, she went with Stefano because it was time to give the man a piece of her mind and she couldn't do that in front of everyone. And also because he didn't really give her any other choice. Not only were Pietro and Joanna staring at her, but once again, everyone in the store was as well. She didn't like or need attention on her.

The blast of cold hit her as Stefano opened the door and allowed her to emerge first. She was too aware of him, of that hard, muscular body moving so close to hers. He kept her close with his grip, so that when she took a step, her body brushed against his continuously.

He stopped just outside the deli, to the right of the door, under the eaves. Her hands dropped to the buttons of his coat. Instantly his hand covered hers, preventing her from sliding the buttons open. His body blocked hers from the wind, crowding her. He put one hand to her belly and pushed gently until she took the three steps necessary for her back to be against the wall of the building, and then he easily caged her in.

"Use the money to eat something. Buy a decent pair of shoes. Do *not* give my coat away. I'm rather fond of it."

His voice was a little impatient, definitely authoritative, as if everyone in the world would obey his every command—and they probably did. She detested that she was standing in front of the world's hottest man and he could see she had nothing. Absolutely nothing. She wasn't taking anything from him either.

"I am *not* taking your money or your coat," she snapped.

His hands kept hers trapped. His thumb slid over the back of her hand and even through the soft, buttery leather of the glove, the gesture sent a tingle of awareness down her spine.

"The coat is a loan, and the money . . ." He shrugged.

"I'm *not* taking it," she reiterated.

"Is there a reason why you're allowed to be kind, but I'm condemned for the same gesture?" he asked softly.

Her eyes met his and that was a mistake. A huge mistake. She felt as if she were falling into those hard, piercing eyes. She knew instantly he hadn't given her the coat because he was being kind. She just didn't know why he'd given it to her. Or why he'd taken an interest in her at all.

"Francesca?" he prompted.

She tried not to scowl at him. "No, of course not. It's just difficult to accept charity." She took a breath.

"It isn't charity."

That's what she'd been afraid of. Her gaze slid away from his. "I can't accept . . . That is . . . From you . . . Because you're . . ." *God.* She couldn't even talk. He was too close. Surrounding her with heat. Too handsome. Too dangerous. Too everything she wasn't and would never be.

His jaw hardened even more, if that was possible. She had her eyes fixed on his very sexy five-o'clock shadow, so she saw very plainly his impatience. Her belly tightened into little hard, apprehensive knots. She couldn't help herself, she pressed her hand deep to try to stop the tension coiling there. His gaze dropped to her hand and then came back up to her face.

"It's because I have money." He made it a statement.

His accusation stung, mostly because it was the truth.

The color deepened in her face. He made her sound preju-
diced. She hated that he called her on it, but the truth was
she would have been much more able to accept the coat from
someone who had far less. She caught her lower lip between
her teeth. Of course that wasn't the only reason, but she
couldn't enumerate those reasons either. That he was gorgeous, super hot. Or that he was dangerous and she thought
he might be a member of organized crime.

"Francesca."

Her stomach somersaulted. He said her name low. Commanding. He was used to deference. Obedience. She took a
breath.

"Look at me."

She let her breath out slowly and forced her gaze up his
handsome face until her eyes collided with his. Then the
breath slammed out of her lungs, leaving her fighting for air.

"Keep. The. Fucking. Coat." He bit out each word.

He scared the crap out of her. He wasn't touching her or
threatening her, but she felt menace rolling off of him in
waves. There was no use fighting him on it. He was going to
get his way. Both of them knew it.

"Thank you." The words tasted a little bitter, but she managed to choke them out.

He nodded his head and glanced at his watch again. "Get
something to eat," he added, turning away from her. "I'll be
back for my coat."

She cleared her throat. "Mr. Ferraro?"

He spun back. Graceful. Impatient. "Got things to do,
Francesca."

She didn't care. She had to know the truth. "Why is everyone afraid of you?"

His blue eyes held hers captive for so long she heard her
heart pound. "Because I'm not a man you ever fuck with."

She blinked up at him, a little shocked at the honesty in
his answer. She was fairly certain he was right. He'd brought
an entire roomful of people to a standstill. No one had

moved. No one had spoken. He definitely looked like a man no one would dare fuck with. Least of all her.

She cleared her throat. "I don't like that sort of thing."

He pressed one hand to her belly again, pushing her back against the wall, stepping in close to her until his heat and the scent of him surrounded her. "What sort of thing?" His gaze dropped to her mouth. Held there.

Her lips trembled and a million butterflies took wing in her stomach. Her heart pounded. God. He was so close. Too close. He was taller than her by at least a head and a half. His shoulders blotted out the street behind him. He smelled— delicious. She didn't know a man could smell that good. It was freezing cold outside and he wasn't even shivering when she had his coat.

"The F-word sort of thing." She blurted it out, saying the first thing that came into her mind without thinking.

His eyebrow shot up. She hadn't thought that anyone really could do that. Shoot up one eyebrow. It was incredibly hot—at least on him.

"The F-word?" he repeated. "*Dolce cuore*, you can't even say *fuck* for fuck's sake."

She felt the color creeping into her face, although she didn't know why. She wasn't the one spouting off inappropriate language to a complete stranger. She wasn't staring at his mouth, although she wanted to. She resisted, because that was what was polite. She wasn't pressing him against a wall and holding him there with a hand in his belly and another by his head. She wouldn't dare touch him.

There was nothing to say to that, so she didn't say anything. She just stood there waiting for him to release her.

He glanced at his watch again. "I really have to go. Eat. I mean it, Francesca. Don't give the money or the coat to anyone else. I'll know, and I won't like it."

She made a face. "Should I be afraid of you?"

For the first time amusement softened his features. "Only if it keeps you from giving away my coat and ensures you eat today." He reached out and bunched her hair in his hand and then allowed the strands to slip out of his fist. "Don't forget to buy a decent pair of shoes."

"I'll use your coat, but the money . . . I don't know when I can pay you back."

"Pietro pays a decent wage." He turned away from her.

"I don't have the job yet."

"You have the job." He lifted a hand and started down the street, moving easily, quietly. Looking more gorgeous than ever.

"Wait. How do I return the coat?" she asked a little desperately. He'd made it clear he wanted his coat back.

"I'll find you."

She watched him stride away. Watched how people on the sidewalk moved out of his way. He seemed to flow across the sidewalk, a force to be reckoned with. She felt a little bit battered, as if she'd been in the middle of the sea during a terrible storm. She didn't move, not for a long time. She huddled there in his long coat and forced herself to breathe deep, trying not to feel faint.

Joanna caught her by the arm. "Oh. My. God. Did that just happen? Tell me that didn't just happen." She practically shook Francesca in her shock.

Francesca glanced through the window of the deli. No one had moved. The attention of every individual in the store remained completely riveted on Stefano Ferraro. She ducked deeper into the warmth of the coat. The cashmere smelled like him. Was warm like him. Elegant like he was.

"What did just happen?" Francesca asked Joanna. "Because I have no idea."

"He just told Tio Pietro to hire you. *Ordered* him."

"He can't do that." Francesca frowned, alarmed.

"Yes, he can, and he did. No one goes against a Ferraro. No one, Francesca."

"Great. Your uncle is going to blame me for having someone step in and tell him what to do in his own store."

"No, he won't. He's excited that he gets to do a favor for Stefano. That's rare and it means something. You do a favor for one and they *all* feel they owe you. The entire family. That's huge, to have a Ferraro owe you. Tio Pietro was practically dancing around the shop."

"Why would that man get so angry because I didn't have a coat?"

Joanna looked confused. "I have no idea. I just know it's super-cool that you attracted his attention. I've been around for years, since I was a little girl, and they all know my name and they know me, but they've never taken that kind of interest in me."

Francesca clenched her teeth. "Why would that be?" she asked, already knowing the answer and not liking it.

"We don't exactly run in the same social circles. That family is total celebrity. Everyone knows them."

That didn't make Francesca in the least bit predisposed to feeling better about Stefano Ferraro's interest in her. "I don't know them. I don't want to know them." Which wasn't altogether true. She'd heard the name. She knew the name was associated with an international bank and a very prestigious hotel as well as a racing team.

Joanna caught her arm and tugged in the direction of the deli's door. "Come on, it's cold out here. Tio Pietro wants to meet you."

"You said *them*. There's more than one of him?" She knew a Ferraro drove a race car, but surely the name wasn't that uncommon.

Joanna nodded solemnly. "And they're all that gorgeous. I kid you not. Stefano's the oldest. He has four brothers, equally hot. One sister, totally beautiful. When they walk around together, people just stare at them. That's how hot they are. Each one of them is super-cool as well, which makes them all *scorching* hot. I'm a little in love with them, including their sister. That's how totally gorgeous they are."

Francesca couldn't help it. She started to laugh. She hadn't laughed in months. It was good to see Joanna again. She was not in the least complicated, nor did she want to be. She always found humor in everything and she loved to party, go to clubs and dance the night away.

"I can't believe Stefano Ferraro claimed you."

The statement tumbled out, leaving Francesca feeling weak and more confused than ever. As they entered the store, all eyes turned to her. The deli was eerily silent. Color infused her face. She wanted to turn and run.

"Joanna, come behind the counter and help out while I talk to your friend," Pietro ordered, beckoning to his niece.

Joanna squeezed Francesca's hand. "Tio Pietro, this is my best friend, Francesca Capello."

"Yes, yes, you talk about her all the time," Pietro said, beaming. He waved toward the customers. "Hurry, before they take their business somewhere else. I'll look after Francesca for you."

He indicated for Francesca to follow him and she did, winding her way through the throng of people, back behind the counter. Once behind the counter, she was up close to the smells of the food and her stomach growled again. She found herself pulling the coat closer around her like a shield, trying to hide from all the eyes staring at her. Trying to hide the fact that she was *starving*. She followed Pietro through a narrow hallway to the rather messy office.

Pietro waved her toward a chair. "Sit. I'll get you an application, but that's just because I need your information. A mere formality."

She winced, wishing it were easy for the average person to get a new identity. She'd actually made inquiries only to find out it would be impossible when she didn't have money and didn't know anyone in the criminal world—well, only one someone—so she'd remained Francesca Capello. Her fingers gripped the outside of the coat, gathering the material into her fists, holding so tight her knuckles turned white.

"Tell me how you know Stefano Ferraro. It sounded as if

you just met, yet he said . . ." He trailed off, clearly looking for more information.

She looked across the desk at Pietro, her heart beginning to pound. She *needed* this job. She wasn't good at lying, but . . . She didn't know what to do, how to answer him. "I'm sorry, Mr. Masci, I never laid eyes on him before today." There. She told the truth. She found she was trembling from head to foot. She had to get the job. She leaned toward him. "Please. I'm a really hard worker. I've had tons of experience. Really." She just couldn't put down any references. Not a single one.

Pietro sat back in his chair, frowning at her. "You've never laid eyes on him before today?" He repeated her denial softly. Thoughtfully. "He *claimed* you. He asked me to take care of you for him. Do you have any idea what that means for us? How can you not know him?"

She was getting desperate. Food had been scarce for the last few weeks. Hiding in old buildings trying to stay alive when you were being hunted could make food not a first priority. The bus trip had been long. She had to save her money to try to get a place to stay. That didn't leave a lot for food.

"I met Joanna in school—in college. When . . . things happened to me . . . to my family, she was kind enough to help me out. I took a bus out here from California because she thought I could work in your store and build a new life here."

He put both hands on the desk. Flat. Leaning toward her. Eyes piercing. Her heart sank.

"Are you running from the law?"

Relief was so strong she wanted to cry. She shook her head. "No, sir. I'm not. I did get into some trouble back home, but I'm not in trouble with the law. I really need this job. I don't have much money left . . ." That reminded her of the folded bills Stefano Ferraro had stuffed into the pocket of his very warm coat.

"Why would Stefano Ferraro ask a favor of me for you? Does he know your family?"

She shook her head, feeling dizzy. "I swear to you, I don't know him. I don't know why he gave me his coat, or acted the way he did."

"He took you outside and had a conversation with you. What did he say?"

"Nothing. He didn't want me to give away his coat. He said I had to buy some shoes with the money. He was being kind."

Something in his eyes shifted. "The Ferraros are a lot of things, but they are not kind. He wants you taken care of. My niece has asked as well. I'll hire you. You can start tomorrow. Fill out the papers and I'll go get you food. You look as if you haven't eaten in a while."

Francesca had to admit she didn't think Stefano had helped her out of kindness, but certainly Pietro's expression was kindly, and she sagged with relief. She was going to put down the entire incident with Stefano as weird, treat it like he meant the gesture kindly. She wouldn't spend his money, but she'd wear his coat and then hang it carefully in her apartment until she figured out how to get it back to him.

She filled out the application, leaving just about everything blank. Her name. Her social security number. That was it. There was nothing else she could safely tell him.

Do you love fiction with a supernatural twist?

Want the chance to hear news about your favourite
authors (and the chance to win free books)?

Keri Arthur
Kristen Callihan
P.C. Cast
Christine Feehan
Jacquelyn Frank
Larissa Ione
Darynda Jones
Sherrilyn Kenyon
Jayne Ann Krentz and Jayne Castle
Lucy March
Martin Millar
Tim O'Rourke
Lindsey Piper
Christopher Rice
J.R. Ward
Laura Wright

Then visit the Piatkus website and blog
www.piatkus.co.uk | www.piatkusbooks.net

And follow us on Facebook and Twitter
www.facebook.com/piatkusfiction | www.twitter.com/piatkusbooks

piatkus